D1590125

Praise fc •

"Ann Charles has p
unforgettable story. C
put down."
~**P. J. Alderman**, New York Times Bestselling Author

"A must read! Ann Charles possesses the rarest of rare talents—she combines laugh-out-loud funny with suspense so intense you forget to breathe. Dead Case in Deadwood is absolutely superb."
~**Robin Weaver**, Author of Blue Ridge Fear

"Dead Case in Deadwood delivers one of the most relatable heroines of today in this blockbuster paranormal mystery series."
~**Kriss Morton-Weekley**, The Cabin Goddess Reviews

"This series has it all, mystery, thrills, romance and corpses."
~**Lindsey Anderson** of Reads, Reviews of a Tortured Select-Soccer Hostage

"If you haven't already been whipped by Deadwood, this is the book that will knock your socks off."
~**Natasha Jennex**, A Great Book Is The Cheapest Vacation Reviews

"Full of non-stop suspense, Charles takes her Deadwood series to a hilarious and thrilling new level."
~**Wendy Delaney**, Award-winning Author

"Book three is funny and eerie at the same time. The question isn't IF you should read Dead Case in Deadwood, but rather what time in the wee hours of the morning will you finish it."
~**April Rickard**, Author

OPTICAL DELUSIONS
IN DEADWOOD

Also by Ann Charles

Deadwood Mystery Series
Nearly Departed in Deadwood (Book 1)
Optical Delusions in Deadwood (Book 2)
Dead Case in Deadwood (Book 3)
Better Off Dead in Deadwood (Book 4)
An Ex to Grind in Deadwood (Book 5)

Short Stories from the Deadwood Mystery Series
Deadwood Shorts: Seeing Trouble
Deadwood Shorts: Boot Points

Jackrabbit Junction Mystery Series
Dance of the Winnebagos (Book 1)
Jackrabbit Junction Jitters (Book 2)
The Great Jackalope Stampede (Book 3)

Goldwash Mystery Series (a future series)
The Old Man's Back in Town (Short Story)

Coming Next from Ann Charles

Dig Site Mystery Series
Look What the Wind Blew In (Book 1)
(Starring Quint Parker, the brother of Violet Parker from the Deadwood
Mystery Series)

Deadwood Mystery Series
Meanwhile Back in Deadwood (Book 6)

Jackrabbit Junction Mystery Series
The Rowdy Coyote Rumble (Book 4)

Dear Reader,

I had a blast writing this third book in the series, especially after experiencing one of Deadwood's haunted hotels first-hand while participating in the South Dakota Festival of Books. Did I see a ghost while staying in the hotel? No, but the bathroom door kept swinging open in the night. That alone was enough to make me sleep with the covers over my head. Unlike Violet in this series, I'm a big chicken when it comes to ghost-filled rumors.

Instead of telling you more about the background for this third book in the Deadwood Mystery series, I want to talk about the kind and welcoming people of the Black Hills—the real characters, not the fictitious ones I've created within the pages of this book.

From the start, a goal of mine with this series was to promote one of my favorite spots on earth—the Black Hills. I have always loved visiting the area, and I wanted to give readers a reason to go there, to see the beautiful vistas, to learn more about the colorful history, and to have fun in one of America's marvelous playgrounds.

When we published the first book in the series (*Nearly Departed in Deadwood*) and started promoting it in the Deadwood-Lead area, I breathed into paper bags for days while waiting to see what kind of response the book would receive from the locals. This was the big test. If the book tanked in the Black Hills, I'd have no local support and I'd have to dress in disguise the next time I visited my mom (who lives there). Worse, I would have let the locals down.

Then the positive reviews began to pour in. Support began to build. Several wonderful area businesses allowed me to place promotional materials next to their cash registers, on their walls, in their windows. Word began to spread about a new series set in the hills from an author who had spent part of her childhood in the area. Best yet, my mom could still go shopping at the grocery store in Lead without wearing a veil of shame.

We released the second book in the series (*Optical Delusions in Deadwood*) to the public. Again I waited, breath held and fingers crossed. More emails and phone calls came from the locals, full of kind words that made my smile spread from ear to ear. The series was taking flight with the help of many. It was an author's dream come true—my dream.

Now, as you hold this third book of the series in your hands, here I am again, crossing everything I can cross, waiting. Will the locals like it? Will you like it? Will I faint from holding my breath?

Many of you are back for the third time. I can't thank you enough for your continued support.

For those of you who wonder how many more books there are to come in my Deadwood Mystery series, buckle up, we're just getting rolling. It's going to be a wild ride.

Have fun back in Deadwood!

Ann Charles

www.anncharles.com

DHEAD CASE
IN DEADWOOD

ANN CHARLES

ILLUSTRATED BY C.S. KUNKLE

Cover Art by C.S. Kunkle
Cover Design and Graphic Art by Mona Weiss
Editing by Mimi the "Grammar Chick"
(www.grammarchick.com)

Printed in the United States of America
First Printing, 2012

ISBN: 978-1-940364-18-6
Published by: Ann Charles

This one is for all of the kind and wonderful fans of Violet, Harvey, Doc, and the rest of the Deadwood cast.

Without your reviews, emails, call-outs, online posts, and cheers, I'd have no legitimate excuse to continue having these crazy conversations with invisible characters in the bathroom mirror, the grocery store checkout line, and the car on the way to work.

You make the late writing nights worth the foggy-brained, red-eyed mornings.

Thank you for your support!

Acknowledgments

Some of the wonderful benefits of writing and publishing have been the friendship and support that have come along the way. With every book I finish and prepare to share with the world, I am humbled by all those who are willing to give their time and share their knowledge in exchange for a simple smile and a "thank you." Following are just a few of those people who have offered their help with this third book in the Deadwood Mystery series.

I always start with thanking my husband because without him I'd eat nothing but tomato paste and corn chips while writing. Not only does he listen to me talk about my books 24/7, he helps me with brainstorming and critiquing, he tells me it will be okay when I insist the sky is falling, and he encourages me when I wonder if I can write yet another book.

Thanks to my brother, Charles Kunkle, for being so easy to work with to create cover art and illustrations.

Thank you to Mona Weiss for your help creating one of my best covers yet.

Thanks again to my mom, Margo Taylor, for all of your help talking up my books in the Black Hills, and to my brother, Dave Taylor, for making sure mom stays out of trouble—ha! Thanks to my aunt, Judy Routt, and her family for spreading word about my books in Northwest Ohio. And thanks to Marilyn Smith for joining the publicity crew and helping me make headway in Arizona.

Thank you to all of my advance readers, editors, and critiquers: Beth Harris, Wendy Delaney, Marcia Britton, Mary Ida Kunkle, Paul Franklin, Jacquie Rogers, Jody Sherin, Renelle Wilson, Sue Stone-Douglas, Bill Stone, Robin Weaver, Marguerite Phipps, Denise Garlington, Stephanie Kunkle, Devon Chadderton, Joby Gildersleeve, Sharon Benton, Margo

Taylor, Carol Cabrian, Gigi Murfitt, Cheryl Foutz, and Cammie Hall.

Thanks to Mimi "The Grammar Chick" for your editing and all of the crazy laughs. You're wild!

Thanks to the super-kind reviewers who offered your time to read and comment about this book; and to the awesome authors who gave me killer quotes.

Thanks to the Deranged crew: Jacquie Rogers, Wendy Delaney, and Sherry Walker for years of help with my writing. Thanks to Gerri Russell and Joleen James for your weekly page-goals encouragement and thumbs up.

Thanks to Amber Scott for your friendship and career help. Think BIG!

Thank you to my coworkers for always cheering me onward through the pages. You make coming to work fun.

Thanks to Vickie Haskell for all of your help with shipping ARCs and figuring out which actor to cast as Doc.

Thanks to Neil McNeill for your help with paranormal investigating information.

Thanks to my family for all of your love and teasing.

Thank you to the awesome people of the Black Hills of South Dakota for your wonderful support and promotional help as you waited for this installment of the series.

Thanks to Dr. Steven Fox in Lead. You know why.

And finally, thanks to my brother, Clint Taylor, for talking up my books, and for running headlong right next to me into the jellyfish-filled ocean off the Georgia coast when we were kids. Man, did we learn a lesson that day.

DHEAD CASE
IN DEADWOOD

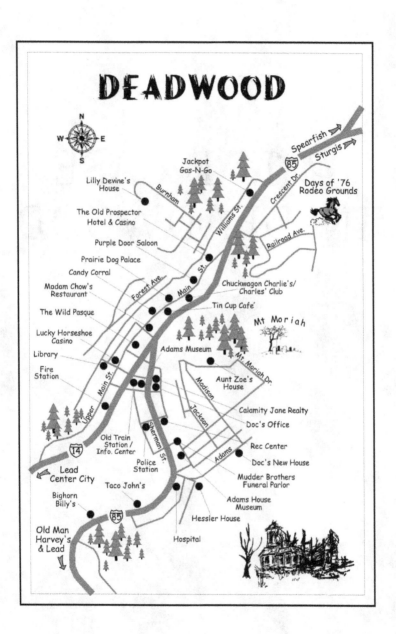

DEADWOOD

N W E S

Spearfish

Sturgis

85

Jackpot Gas-N-Go

Days of '76 Rodeo Grounds

Lilly Devine's House

Burnham

Williams St.

Crescent Dr.

The Old Prospector Hotel & Casino

Railroad Ave.

Purple Door Saloon

Prairie Dog Palace

Candy Corral

Forest Ave.

Main St.

Chuckwagon Charlie's/ Charles' Club

Madam Chow's Restaurant

Tin Cup Cafe

Mt Moriah

The Wild Pasque

Lucky Horseshoe Casino

Adams Museum

Mt. Moriah Dr.

Library

Madison

Aunt Zoe's House

Fire Station

Jackson

Calamity Jane Realty

Upper Main St.

Doc's Office

Sherman St.

Rec Center

Adams

Old Train Station / Info. Center

Doc's New House

14

Police Station

Mudder Brothers Funeral Parlor

Lead Center City

Taco John's

Adams House Museum

Bighorn Billy's

85

Hessler House

Old Man Harvey's & Lead

Hospital

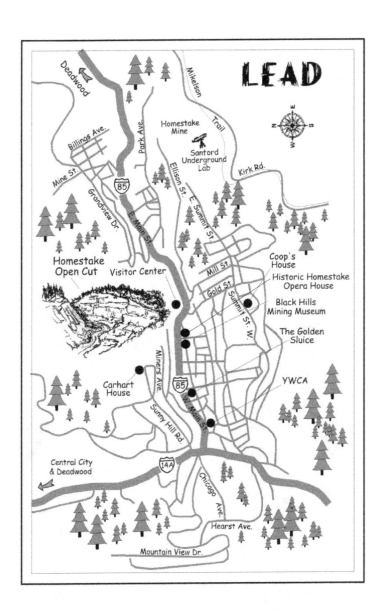

Chapter One

Deadwood, South Dakota
Friday, August 17th

Nothing good ever happens at the butt-crack of dawn. No doubt, the headless corpse on the autopsy table in front of me would agree.

Detective "Coop" Cooper scowled at me from the other side of the body. A Daniel Craig look-alike right down to his granite cheekbones, Cooper had called a half-hour earlier and ordered me to meet him in the basement of the Mudder Brothers Funeral Parlor before I headed in to work at Calamity Jane Realty.

His lack of patience with my wakeup routine prompted my current caffeine deficiency, which explained this morning's forecast: bristly with a chance of a black eye.

"As I told you the other day, Detective," I enunciated all three syllables of his title, "when you so kindly dragged me into your office and forced me to look at pictures of this." I pointed at the body, not really wanting to think of it once being a whole human. "I have no idea who this was. Standing here next to the actual body changes nothing."

Cooper squinted at me with his stainless-steel-colored eyes, not missing a single one of my blinks. I wondered if he practiced his gunslinger stare-down in the mirror every night while he brushed his teeth.

I glared back. While facing off with Cooper often spurred stomach cramps, I'd be damned if I'd let him intimidate me over a dead guy, who just happened to be palming my business card post mortem.

"Ms. Parker," Cooper spoke through a clenched jaw,

something I often did when dealing with my nearly ten-year-old fraternal twins. "You have to at least look at the body before stating for the record that you don't recognize the victim."

"What's there to look at? His head is gone."

Cooper's nostrils flared. Surly bulls had nothing on him. "Do you recognize any other parts of him?"

"Like what parts in particular?"

"The remaining ones."

"Nope."

Cooper growled loudly enough for me to hear. "Look before you answer."

"Fine." I took a deep breath, thankful for the overwhelming scent of bleach-based cleaner in the air, and willed the troop of monkeys bouncing around in my gut to sit still. I could do this. No problem. It was just a dummy. A mannequin. One of those CPR dolls.

I had to do it, for my own safety's sake, as well as my kids'. As much as I hoped it was just a coincidence that the dead guy had been holding my business card, I had to make sure this wasn't a sadistic warning message of some sort.

I knew that kind of thinking was paranoid, but after the wacky crap that had happened to me over the last couple of months, these days I'd be suspicious of a jolly white-bearded man in a red suit carrying a bag over his shoulder.

Focusing on the dead guy's furry chest, I tried to keep my eyes from glancing up at the void where the head should be … and failed. It was such a clean slice through the neck. What—and who—could have done such a seamless job?

I remembered what I was inspecting and turned away.

"You know, if you can't handle this …" Cooper started to say, the rigid tone in his voice softening.

"I can handle it," I interrupted and swallowed the acidic taste of nausea that climbed up my esophagus and onto the back of my tongue.

For some stupid reason, I had this irrational need to prove

to Cooper that I could inspect dead bodies over black coffee and maple bars just like him and the other guys on the police force.

I looked over my shoulder at Eddie Mudder, who leaned against a group of floor-to-ceiling cupboards with his arms crossed over his black vinyl apron while we admired his handiwork. Looking and sounding like Lurch from the *Adams Family*, Eddie was the younger of the two brothers who owned and operated Mudder Brothers Funeral Parlor. His oddities went beyond his physical appearance to his love of eccentric organ music, such as the pipe-organ version of the Bee Gees' "Stayin' Alive" that was currently playing through the overhead speakers. Did psychiatrists have a label for someone who danced with dead bodies?

"Eddie, will you please cover this"—I hovered my hand over the missing head area—"with something?"

He lumbered over in two long strides and draped one square of paper towel over the space where the head should be. "Better?"

I'd have preferred two. Was there a paper towel shortage in the Black Hills? "Sure. Thanks."

I glanced in Cooper's direction and noticed his lips twitching. Oh, how I longed to jam a paper towel up his nose.

Another deep breath. Okay, back to the dead guy.

His milky ash-colored flesh had a marbled look to it. A thick coat of black chest hair covered his ribs and pectorals. I leaned closer, sniffing, picking up the smell of stale, raw hamburger meat—or maybe that was just my imagination.

I searched for a tattoo, a scar, a pierced nipple, something unique, but I couldn't see anything through the hair, not without a weed whacker, anyway.

Shrugging, I stepped back. "Nope, I don't know him."

Cooper crossed his arms over his chest. "Keep looking. Unless it's too much for you."

I curled my lip at him, and then returned to scan the corpse's less-furry stomach. "He has some lint in his belly button," I observed aloud.

"That's not lint," Eddie said from his spot back by the cupboards. "It's a black wart."

Eww! I grimaced across at Cooper.

A flicker of a grin rippled across his granite features. I had an inkling that torturing me rated high on his fun-things-to-do list, right after cleaning his handgun. He schooled his features and pointed down at the body, indicating that I wasn't finished.

Cursing him six ways from Sunday under my breath, I scooted down the table, past where the paper sheet covered the corpse's private bits and pieces, and looked at the toes. Small tufts of hair popped out from the knuckle of each toe.

"This guy must be part Yeti."

"I'll be sure to make a note of that in the report," Cooper said.

I moved up to the corpse's knees. They looked like a regular set of kneecaps to me. Nothing remarkable.

I hesitated at the paper covering the man's junk, my determination wavering. I avoided glancing at Cooper, knowing any eye contact at this point would make me chicken out.

Would looking at a dead man's penis scar me for life? Would I ever be able to look at another live version of one without recoiling? This could seriously cripple my love life, which had barely limped along since the twins had arrived.

But Cooper was watching, waiting for my white flag. I gulped and pinched the corner of the little sheet.

"Wait, Violet." Cooper reached toward my hand.

The autopsy room's double-doors opened. Old Man Harvey crashed into the room, loud and grinning, as usual. His two gold teeth gleamed under the florescent lights.

He stopped short of me, eyeing me up and down. "Woo-wee! You look finer than frog hair. Did you wear that pretty dress to impress Coop, Eddie, or the dead guy?"

I smoothed down my new coral-colored knit dress, feeling

my cheeks heat up. "You're late," I told him, avoiding an answer.

"Sorry 'bout that. I had trouble gettin' out of bed."

"Your trick hip keeping you up again?" I asked.

"More like Viagra and an old flame." His grin hung from his earlobes. "You should see the tricks that girl can still do with her hips. The way she wiggles you'd never guess she has an AARP card."

Criminy. I'd waltzed right into that one.

Willis "Old Man" Harvey was my partner in crime and self-appointed bodyguard, whether I liked it or not.

He also owned the ranch I was trying to sell in spite of the dead body parts that kept showing up there—parts such as an ear still connected to half a scalp that was found in one of Harvey's somewhat illegal traps. And the very corpse under my nose, which the old bugger's lazy yellow dog had partially dug up from the cemetery out behind his barn.

I stepped back to give Harvey room to inspect the corpse. His arrival had saved my future sex life, and my knees wobbled with relief.

"You figure out who it is?" Harvey asked, joining us at the table and looking from me to Cooper.

"Not yet," Cooper answered.

"Jesus H. Christ, boy." Harvey said to the detective, who also happened to be his nephew. Pretty much everyone in Deadwood was related by blood or marriage, which was something I'd grasped since moving from the prairie to the Black Hills six months ago. "Do I have to do everything around here?"

Harvey leaned over the corpse and sniffed. "Hmmm. Smells like that homemade goop I rub on my bunions." He poked the corpse in the ribs hard enough to slide the body over an inch or two.

"Harvey!" I said, poking him in the ribs in turn.

"What? He's dead. He didn't feel it." He nudged me aside and danced toward the feet, singing along in a high voice, doing a spin as the disco-playing organ hit the final chorus. The Bee Gees would never be the same for me again.

"Any tattoos?" Harvey asked.

Cooper shook his head.

"His legs remind me of your Aunt Gertrude's."

Cooper kept shaking his head, a small grin surfacing.

Harvey had reached the paper towel covering the man's family jewels. Without hesitation, he yanked off the towel.

"No! God!" I covered my eyes—a half-second too late.

"Hmph. Reminds me of the last time I skinny-dipped in Pactola Dam."

"Ahhh!" I cringed. No amount of soap was going to scrub that image from my eyes.

Something rustled, and then Cooper said, "You can uncover your eyes now, Violet."

I peeked out between my fingers first just to be safe. Harvey had returned to my side, his thumbs wrapped around his suspenders.

"So, neither of you two recognize this man?" Cooper's eyes bounced between Harvey and me.

"No," I said.

Harvey scratched his head. "Hold up. Did he have just one testicle?"

"Yep," Eddie confirmed.

Harvey reached for the paper towel covering the corpse's jewels again.

I squawked and turned toward the door. Another glimpse of the dead guy's package and I'd never be able to have sex again. "If we're done here, Detective, I need to go to work."

"You're free to leave." He came around the corpse and walked me to the double doors, holding one open for me. "You aren't planning any trips out of state, are you?"

I stopped on the threshold and frowned up at him. "Are you asking me that as my client?"

Cooper had hired me to sell his house a couple of weeks ago. The plan was to put it on the market this week.

"No, I'm asking on behalf of the Lawrence County Sheriff's Department."

"Are you working for the Sheriff on this?" I pointed in the general direction of the body. Detective Cooper worked for the City of Deadwood and was hired out to Lead, but last I'd heard he only played poker with the local sheriff, not cops and robbers.

"Not officially. But until we figure out who this guy is and how he lost his head, you and Uncle Willis both need to stay close."

The sound of that made the hairs on my neck bristle, just as I'd forecasted. "Are you saying we're suspects in his murder?"

"Not suspects, just persons of interest. So stick around." His gunslinger squint returned. "And keep your big nose out of this case."

Chapter Two

The town of Deadwood was suffering from a hangover. A week had passed since the Sturgis Biker Rally officially ended, and while many of the thousands of motorcyclists had headed home, numerous Harley Davidsons still stacked up domino-style in parking lots around town—chromed-out horses lined up along an invisible hitching post.

Thanks to the Kool Deadwood Nites party revving up, the Black Hills continued to rumble like an empty belly throughout the day as strings of souped-up classic cars began to roll into town, mufflers growling.

Harvey's ancient green Ford pickup, which I was currently borrowing, growled back. Fondly named the Picklemobile by its grizzled owner, the old gal spat and sputtered along. It also backfired every time I shut the damned thing off.

If only that red-taloned bitch hadn't torched my Bronco last week. That's what I got for mixing it up with a sadistic, demented, demon lover. The next time I agreed to sell a house, I was going to include a *No Demons* clause in the contract. Seriously.

I chitty-chitty bang-banged through the parking lot behind Calamity Jane Realty, searching for one classic car in particular—a late '60s black Camaro SS with white rally stripes belonging to the only guy around who could make my lingerie melt with a single glance: Doc Nyce.

The sight of Doc's slick car parked two stalls down from my usual spot spurred invisible bluebirds to tweet and flap around my head, whistling Disney style. If there was one thing I needed this morning to calm my nerves after sniffing around that decapitated body, it was a touch of Doc. Or ten touches. Maybe a squeeze or two, as well.

I parked in my spot and then lifted my sunglasses to look in the rearview mirror for a makeup check. My insomnia-induced red-rimmed eyes stared back at me. Ugh.

Shutting off the engine, I counted under my breath, "One, two, three," and then winced as a loud boom reverberated from the Picklemobile's tail pipe.

Lowering my sunglasses as a shield from the way-too-bright sun, I shouldered my tote and grabbed the drink holder full of lattes from the floor of the passenger side. With a solid butt bump, I shoved the heavy door closed and weaved through the parking lot to Calamity Jane's back door.

Jane Grimes, the owner and my boss, wasn't in yet; her office was dark. I placed her latte on the desk, anyway.

Our usual Friday morning staff meeting at Bighorn Billy's diner had been cancelled this week due to Jane's messy divorce currently screwing up her life and all of her left-brained, ultra-anal routines.

I could smell the sweet jasmine perfume of my favorite coworker and mentor, Mona Hollister, several steps before I found her sitting at her desk, her long pink fingernails clacking away on her laptop keyboard as she talked on the phone.

She smiled at the latte I set in front of her and blew me a silent kiss.

Ray Underhill, the jackass who brayed and kicked at me hourly from the desk next to mine, wasn't in yet, thank God. We'd have to save our daily glare-down for later.

I dropped my tote on my desk after digging out my cell phone, left my sunglasses in place, and carried the remaining two lattes out through the front glass door.

Doc's office shared a wall with Calamity Jane Realty, a wall that I had pressed my ear to more times than I'd like to admit. Jealousy wasn't a pretty sight, and on me it looked like Medusa with bed head.

After a glance up and down the street, making sure my best friend, Natalie Beals, wasn't around to see me, I pushed through the door into Doc's office. The subtle scent of his woodsy cologne reached in through my sinuses and tickled my libido. Doc looked up from the book he was reading, his dark chocolate eyes unreadable as I placed a coffee on the desk in front of him.

I pretty much fell into the seat opposite him. Spending the morning disco-ing with Cooper's dead guy in the Mudder boys' basement had taken a toll on me, making everything south of my neck a little wobbly. Being around Doc had a similar unsteadying effect on my limbs. The guy had my number. Hell, he had my whole roll of numbers, including the queue-generating machine that spat them out. It was no wonder that Natalie had it in her head that Doc had her number, too—and that she stood at the front of the line.

"I have a problem," I said, jumping right into the fire.

Doc's eyelids narrowed. "You hung up on me last night."

"Sorry about that."

"Right in the middle of detailing the slinky satin nightgown you were barely wearing."

Which had really been an old pair of boxer shorts and an Elvis T-shirt, but Doc didn't need to know the finer details of my nightly ensembles. "Right."

"And you never called back."

"There's an explanation for that."

He sat back and crossed his arms over his chest. "I'm all ears."

"You mean about last night?"

"To start with."

"Natalie needed to use the bathroom."

"You were in the bathroom?" At my nod, he asked, "In the tub?"

More like on the floor next to it. "Sure."

"Why do you lie to me when I can clearly see your nose twitching?"

Damned tell-tale appendage. I frowned and covered it.

"What's with the sunglasses, Marilyn Monroe?"

"It's bright in here," I lied from behind my hand.

He leaned forward, resting his forearms on his desk, his gaze traveling down the v-neck of my dress and settling on the big twisted knot at my sternum. "Great dress." He stared as if I were lying naked on a bear skin rug. "You didn't answer my question last night."

Lowering my hand, I frowned at him. "I did—you asked if I was wearing any underwear."

"Not that question. The one about when I could see you next."

Oh, that one. That was part of my bigger problem, the one that had brought me here. I tried to ease into my answer. "You're seeing me now."

"I want to see more of you." The heat sizzling in his gaze when it crawled back up to mine made my upper lip sweat. "Preferably in my bed, but I'll settle for wherever I can get you alone."

I had to change the subject before I hurdled his desk, tackled him, and tore off his navy blue dress shirt with my teeth. "Detective Cooper told me this morning that I'm a person of interest in the headless corpse murder case."

To Doc's credit, he adjusted to this conversation shift with merely a tightening of his lips. "You were at the police station already today? That must be a record for you."

"No, Cooper had me meet him at Mudder Brothers."

His forehead furrowed. "Why there?"

"To try to identify the victim."

"You were looking at a decapitated body this morning?"

I nodded. And dead guy's family jewels, minus one precious stone, according to Harvey.

Doc's jaw grew rigid. "Why in the hell did Cooper make you do that?"

"Because the victim had my business card in his hand."

"I know. I was there when you got the call, remember?"

I grinned. Of course I remembered. We'd been half-naked at the time.

Doc continued, "I'm referring to your current mental state."

"There is nothing wrong with my current mental state."

"Still having those nightmares every night?"

Yes, in spite of Natalie playing slumber party with me ever since the Carhart mess almost a week ago when my client and her Bronco-burning girlfriend tried to subject me to demon copulation. When that plan failed, they'd settled with trying to gut me like a pumpkin. Such experiences tended to have a lasting effect on one's nerves.

I opened my mouth to deny the nightmares, but Doc cut me off. "The truth, Violet. You promised me."

Oh, *fahrvergnügen*! He was right. While we hadn't locked pinkies over it, if I wanted Doc to come clean with me about everything under the sun on a regular basis, I needed to do the same.

"Okay, so I'm having a few not-so-good dreams at night." When I actually slept, anyway.

"Admitting that was like pulling teeth for you, wasn't it?"

Speaking of choppers, "Cooper also took the teeth."

"You mean that box you found in the Carhart attic?"

At my request for some ancient history on the house for a ghost-loving potential buyer, I'd been allowed to take a box from the Carhart's supposedly haunted attic that contained several historical artifacts, including a box of 187 human canine teeth. Who would have collected all of those teeth and why they stockpiled them was still a mystery, but now it was Cooper's problem to solve, not mine.

"Yeah, that one. Cooper heard about it from Wanda," I said, referring to the Carhart widow and only member of the family not dead or locked up in prison for murder.

"How did Wanda know about them?" Doc asked.

"Prudence told her."

"Prudence, the Carhart ghost?"

I nodded.

"But I thought you didn't believe in ghosts."

Until lately, that had been true, unlike Doc, who claimed to have some sixth sense that allowed him to sniff out Casper from across a room. I'd played skeptic when Doc first fessed up to this after an encounter that knocked him on his ass, but after witnessing multiple confrontations and similar reactions from a feet-firmly-on-the-ground type of guy, the jury was now locked away in deliberations.

"I don't know what to believe anymore, Doc. But I did believe Cooper when he threatened to lock me up if I didn't hand those teeth over."

"He's not cutting you any slack is he?"

"Cutting slack is against his religion." I crossed one of my legs over the other, smoothing my dress on my thighs, remembering Cooper's parting shot earlier. "He also said I have a big nose."

Doc looked up from my legs. "He's right."

"Gee, thanks."

"Metaphorically speaking, that is. But that doesn't mean he has to be so rough on you."

"I think Cooper enjoys roughing me up."

"That's what concerns me."

"Because of my current mental state?"

"No, Violet, because I like you." Rising from his chair, Doc walked to the glass windows that faced the street. "What I don't like is the detective making you look at decapitated bodies in the basement of a funeral parlor first thing in the morning when your hand shakes just holding your latte."

"I'm not shaking." I placed the plastic cup and my cell phone on his desk.

"Okay, when your hand trembles." He lowered the blinds on both big windows, shading the room. "Better?"

I nodded, but didn't remove my sunglasses. "It was no big deal. Harvey was there with me."

"Having your self-appointed bodyguard on site doesn't change the fact that for most people examining a dead body is a bit stressful." Doc moved to the door, dead-bolting it. "And most people haven't witnessed death up close and personal like you have twice now within a month's time." He flipped his Open sign to Closed. "What else did Cooper have to say?"

"He wants me to keep my nose out of his case."

"Great idea. You're going to listen to the detective, right?"

"Sure." No lie there. I had other things to figure out, such as what my coworker, Ray the asshole, and the Mudder brothers were up to on the sly. Playing Nancy Drew regarding a decapitated body was low on my list of to-dos.

"Why do I feel like you're just feeding me a line of bullshit?" he asked, holding out his hand, which I took without thinking.

"I'm serious."

He pulled me to my feet, then released my hand and stepped back, sitting on the edge of his desk.

"I don't know why the dead guy had my card, nor do I care."

Well, I cared a little since the corpse had ended up on Harvey's ranch, which I was trying to sell, but not enough to get involved. I was happy to stand back and let Cooper do his job on this one.

"Doc, what are you doing?" I asked when he made a circle motion with his index finger.

"Turn around, Boots."

The nickname he used for me whenever he wanted more than just conversation shot shivers up my legs and down my back. Doc had a thing for my purple cowboy boots ever since the first time I'd dug my boot heels into his bared flesh and held on tight while he rocked my world.

I lowered my eyelids a little, trying to look all sexy, then remembered that I had my sunglasses on. "Why?"

"Just humor me."

I did as told, adding a little sashay with my hips as I obeyed his command.

He whistled under his breath. "Damn, those sandal straps wrapping around like that make me want to lick your ankles. Turn all the way around."

I faced him again.

He shook his head. "That is one hell of a dress."

I'd hoped he'd like it when I picked it out the other night at the mall down in Rapid City. I'd lied and told Natalie the dress was to snare clients, avoiding her eyes in the dressing room mirror. But my Aunt Zoe had taken one look at the flirty dress and the way it hugged my chest and smiled at me. She knew which "client" I was trying to snare.

"You like it?" I adjusted the form-fitting bodice, using the twisted knot to shift the thin cloth over my breasts.

Doc watched without blinking. "I've been wanting to tear it off of you since you waltzed through my front door."

The images his words conjured stole the breath I needed for a response, so I just grinned like a big idiot.

"Take off your sunglasses."

I hesitated, not wanting him to see the interstate map lining my eyeballs.

He reached out and pulled them off for me, setting them on his desk next to my drink and cell phone. His forehead furrowed when he looked at my eyes. "Another Visine morning, I see."

"You know how it is, too much partying every night."

His gaze inched toward my bellybutton, leaving a scorched trail all the way down. "I want to touch you, Boots."

What a coincidence. "I want you to touch me, Doc."

He rubbed his palms together slowly. "If I start, I don't think I'll be able to stop."

I gulped, my body trembling now for a whole different reason. "If you start, I'll definitely want you to finish."

My need for Doc overshadowed all logical reasons why we should not be having sex at eight a.m. on a Friday morning in downtown Deadwood. My worries about getting caught by Natalie faded. My up-in-the-night anxiety about this wildfire of a crush I had for Doc suddenly seemed trivial. I stood there, waiting, wanting, willing him to touch me.

My cell phone rang.

Of course it did.

"That's Mona," I said, able to tell by the Bach ringtone I'd programmed in for her.

"You should probably get that," he said.

"Yeah."

He groaned and handed me my phone.

"Hello?"

"Vi," Mona said. "Where are you?"

"Next door at Doc's, why?"

"Natalie is here looking for you. Want me to send her over?"

"No!" That came out too sharp. I mellowed my tone. "Um, just tell her to stay put. I'm on my way back over."

"Okay. Say 'hello' to Doc for me."

I'd rather have wild and freaky sex with him on his desk. "Will do," I said and hit the end button.

Doc was staring at my dress as if it were see-through.

"I have to go, Doc."

"I know."

"I have a problem."

"I do, too, thanks to that dress. It's going to ache like hell when you leave."

I clasped my hands together to keep from touching him, just in case Natalie decided to step outside and peek in at us. "Natalie has appointed herself my guardian angel."

His gaze met mine. "What does that mean?"

"She's staying over at Aunt Zoe's with me 24/7."

"Which means you haven't told her about us?"

I avoided the accusation in his eyes. "Pretty much, yeah."

"Which also means I can only touch you behind closed doors and drawn shades."

"Exactly. Whenever I can shake her from my tail, that is." Which hadn't been easy over the last few days.

"What about after she goes to sleep?"

"She's occupying the other half of my bed."

"Damn it, Violet."

"I know."

"Would you just tell her the truth already?"

"I'm working up to it."

He pushed off the desk and strode over to the door, unlocking and holding it open. "You'd better get over there."

Shoving my sunglasses onto my face, I grabbed my drink and made my exit. "I'll call you later."

He caught my arm as I passed in front of him, halting me. "Violet."

I lifted my brows.

"Tell her."

"I will. I promise." As soon as the time was right.

His grip on my arm turned into a caress before he released it. "And keep your *little* nose out of trouble."

"Always."

His "Right" followed me out into the sunshine.

Inside Calamity Jane Realty, Natalie sat in the chair opposite my desk with her long tanned legs stretched out in front of her. The cast encasing her lower right leg was covered with graffiti drawn by my children—hearts, ice cream cones, and stick chickens from Addy; a diagrammed horse's skull thanks to Layne. Mona was nowhere to be seen, her usual jasmine calling card overrun by the scent of Natalie's coconut suntan lotion.

"How's Doc looking this morning?" Natalie asked as I set my latte down next to my keyboard.

The question sounded casual enough, but my cheeks heated, anyway, being that I'd been next door attempting to seduce the man of her dreams. "Same as usual."

"Hot and drool-inducing then," she said, making a gurgling, purr-like noise in her throat.

"Is that supposed to sound sexy?" I forced a crooked grin, trying to joke my way off the subject of Doc. "You sound like you're choking a cat."

She grinned back. "Better a cat than 'the chicken.'"

"Oh, tacky. Kiss your momma with that mouth?"

"Said the kettle. You taught me everything I know."

"Where's Mona?" I asked.

"Gone. She said to tell you she has an appointment with a client up in Lead. You can reach her on her cell phone." Just when I thought I'd sidestepped the Doc-noose, Natalie said, "So, you're still taking Doc coffee each morning?"

"Yeah." Which was a nice, seemingly platonic way to spend time with him right under her nose. As piece-of-shit best friends went, I drew the most flies in all of the land. "I feel like I owe him a month's worth as thanks for taking a chance on a new Realtor."

"Did he say anything about your outfit?"

I lowered my eyes, unable to hold her gaze even through my sunglasses while guilt chewed a hole in my gut. "Not really, why?"

Natalie shrugged. "I'm just wondering if his lack of interest in females extends to blondes, as well as brunettes." She patted her brown locks. "Maybe if I dyed my hair red like his ex-girlfriend, he'd start treating me like more than just a paying client."

I didn't want to think about Doc and his Jessica Rabbit-like ex, Tiffany, who also happened to be a real estate agent in Spearfish—talk about small freaking world. Just thinking about Miss Redhead made me want to do very bad things to innocent bunnies. "Doc and I maintain a professional relationship." *In public.*

"It's cool that you two are still friends now that the house deal is done."

"He's easy to be around." And I was embarrassingly "easy" when he was around. Crack whores probably played harder to get than I did.

Natalie's chair creaked as she leaned forward and took a sip of my caramel latte. "I didn't think Doc was there this morning. His blinds were closed when I drove by."

Whew! That was close. Had Natalie been able to see inside, she'd have caught him holding my hand. "I asked him to keep it shaded because of my eyes."

"Still burning?"

"Big time."

"Nightmares or more insomnia?"

No use trying to hide anything from her, not with her sleeping a couple of feet away from me every night. "A little bit of both."

"Let me see."

I flashed her a peek at my red-lined peepers.

"Why don't you wake me up?"

"What good would that do? You'd have a matching set."

"Vi, I'm supposed to be helping you get through this. I can't do that if you won't tell me what's going on in your head."

As much as I loved Natalie, I hadn't exactly asked for her help. The unending slumber party was her idea, not mine. And the constant poking, prodding, and concern about my feelings by one and all was starting to make me grind my teeth. I appreciated that Natalie's interest was born out of love and caring, but her sitting on me like a mother hen day in and out was beginning to make me feel smothered. Pretty soon, feathers would fly from my mouth when I coughed.

"What's there to tell?" I said. "I have bad dreams and trouble falling back to sleep afterward. This too shall pass; I just need more time for my brain to cram this in a drawer and be done with it."

"Well, your aunt wants me to stay as long as you need me, so until you kick me out, I'll be by your side day and night."

Swell. Wonderful. Terrific. I was so hosed.

The front door whooshed open, letting in a rush of traffic noise and hot August air. I looked up and my jaw unhinged at the sight of a tall, gangly version of Abraham Lincoln standing just inside the threshold—top hat, cane, and black suit jacket included.

"Who in the hell …" Natalie's whispered words echoed the voice in my head. Was I seeing one of Doc's ghosts?

"I'm looking for Violet Parker," Abe said, striding toward us, his cane banging on the wood floor, his bare, boney wrists sticking out from his too-short jacket sleeves. He removed his top hat when he stopped next to Natalie; his jet black hair matched his pointed goatee.

"I'm Violet," I said after I'd dug my voice out of the back of my throat where it had lodged itself.

Was the circus in town?

He slid his round sunglasses down his long, narrow nose. Cornflower blue eyes peered out at me, their intensity startling me back a step.

"I'm Cornelius Curion."

No way was that his real name.

Somehow, I managed to paste a smile on my lips. A glance at Natalie's bug-eyed, mouth-gaping stare confirmed that I wasn't the only one flamboozled by the pale-skinned oddity of a man.

"Hello, Mr. Curion. How can I help you?"

"I need to hire your services."

No. Absolutely not. I'd never live it down if the locals saw me cruising around in the Picklemobile with this guy.

I skirted the issue by asking, "Are you looking to buy or sell in the area?"

"Buy." He reached in his pocket and pulled out a wad of hundred dollar bills thick enough to choke a rattlesnake. "And I plan to pay cash for it."

On the other hand, there was my utter lack-of-money situation. Plus, Deadwood residents already had me labeled as a ghost-loving freak, so a cruise through town with a top-hat wearing, dead president body double couldn't really hurt. Abe Lincoln was carved into Mt. Rushmore, after all, so Cornelius was practically a celebrity already around these parts.

"I'd be happy to help," I told him.

Natalie let out yet another gurgling sound, drawing Cornelius' and my gazes.

"Sorry," she said, faking some coughs into her closed fist. "Something in my throat."

"You should get that checked out," I told her with a zip-it glare.

She turned away from us, her shoulders shaking from more than a coughing fit.

"Excellent," Cornelius said, focusing those cornflower eyes back on me.

"Did you have a particular house in mind?"

"Not a house," he said, smiling—well, half-smiling. Only one side of his mouth seemed to be participating. The other side twitched twice, but stayed flat. "A hotel."

Hotel? Okay, I could make that happen. Probably.

"One of the hotels in Deadwood?" I asked, trying to remember if there were any for sale on Main Street. Hotel owners sometimes tried to keep that sort of information hidden from the public in order to keep business flowing without any hiccups.

"Yes," Cornelius said, stroking his pointed goatee. "The haunted one."

Chapter Three

It really should have been no surprise that an Abe Lincoln lookalike waltzed into Calamity Jane's and asked me to help him buy a haunted hotel. After all, I had started the day looking at a dead guy's deflated penis, a surefire omen of how my day was going to go. It was foolish of me to think things couldn't get any worse.

Natalie had totally bailed on me in the midst of Cornelius' visit, which was not very guardian-angel-like of her at all. Luckily, after she left, Cornelius had only stayed long enough to secure an appointment with me at Calamity Jane's at two o'clock.

An hour after Honest Abe exited stage left, Ray Underhill burst through the front door.

Sweat stained the pits of his lemon yellow shirt. His usual good ole boy sneer was replaced by a pinched brow; his tie crooked, his fake-tanned cheeks extra ruddy. A waft of air riding on his coattails hit me, making my throat burn. He must have flea-dipped in Stetson cologne this morning.

"What are you gawking at, Blondie?" he asked, a snarl on his lips as he shot me a glare bloated with contempt. "Did I yank on your chain?"

I shrugged and focused on my computer screen again. "You remind me of something the cat puked up."

Ever since I'd landed the Associate Broker position instead of his nephew, Ray and I had shared a love-hate relationship, as in we loved to hate each other—loudly and often. But a week ago, we'd both had our hands slapped by Jane for not playing nicely together. Now we kept our "kiss-my-ass" and "go-blow-a-goat" jabs to a minimum, except when Jane was out of the office, such as this very moment.

"Slept with any new clients lately?" Ray asked, tossing his keys on his desk. "Is that why you're wearing the shades? Too many late nights spent boinking our neighbor boy?"

Ray knew Doc and I were playing hanky-panky behind closed doors. Not long ago, he'd used a pair of women's underwear to trick me into lowering my mask and showing my crazed-jealousy face.

Fortunately, he thought I was just a slut who slept with all of my clients, and he had no idea how big of a secret my Doc business was. But that didn't keep the back of my knees from sweating every time Natalie came within ten feet of the spray-tanned asshole.

Before I could trade any more insults with Ray, my cell phone rang. My parents' number appeared on the phone's screen. "Hello?"

"Hey, Mom," Layne said, breathing hard. I heard Addy squeal and slip into a fit of giggles in the background. "Are you going to come pick us up tonight?"

My kids had been hanging out at my parents' place down in Rapid all week. At first, I'd sent them there to protect them. But after the Carhart mess blew over, I'd let them stay longer to enjoy the pool and last throes of summer before the school year kicked into gear.

A little quiet time for me to recuperate hadn't hurt, either. I just wished I could get some damned sleep. Or sex with Doc. Or both.

"Not until tomorrow, sweetie. Are you guys having fun with Grammy and Grandpa?"

"Sure. But I miss you."

Ah, Layne, my darling son. I needed to buy him something for that long-distance heart squeeze.

Layne dug archaeology almost as much as Indiana Jones did. Maybe I'd get him a book on the Maya culture in the Yucatan, where my brother, Quint, had written he'd be heading next spring, after he finished up a couple of photo jobs in Canada.

"Is Addy keeping her cast dry like I told her to?"

Addy had broken her arm chasing Elvis into an old mine weeks ago. She needed that cast on a bit longer, and the only way I'd allowed her to go in the pool at all was with a promise from her and my mom that the cast would not get wet.

"Yes. But mom," Layne added in a quiet voice, which was almost drowned out by the sound of Ray's cell phone ringing. "Aunt Susan is here,"

Susan!

Just hearing my younger sister's name made me feel like I'd chugged a bottle of Jack Daniels. Fire flared up my esophagus, trying to blast from my mouth and fry everything in my path with a force that would make Godzilla proud.

I swallowed the flames as Ray stood, his cell phone pressed to his ear, and walked toward the rear door.

"What is she doing there?" I asked. Susan was supposed to be in Florida ruining someone else's life.

"I don't know. Grammy said she's going to stay here for a while."

What!?

"Something about Aunt Susan needing to get back on her feet."

That would be a change. In my experience, she spent most of her time on her back.

"Layne, you and Addy need to stay away from her."

"Mom, why don't we like Aunt Susan again?"

Besides the fact that she had a bad habit of sleeping with whichever man I happened to be dating, including the kids' father, she was taller, thinner, her hair silkier and straighter, and she could tie cherry stems with her tongue. But I was talking to Layne, so I kept it simple. "She has cooties. Really big, gross ones."

"Ick."

"Yeah, so stay back."

"She bought us bubblegum ice cream cones. Double

scoops."

"She did?" What angle was Susan playing? Why was she bribing my kids?

"And she took us to the movies and let us pick out two kinds of candy. I let Addy have my extra bag of M&Ms."

The back of my neck prickled.

"And she bought Elvis a little rain coat."

Elvis was Addy's pet chicken. She loved to roost on my bed when nobody was looking, even though she wasn't allowed upstairs. The damned bird was the other reason, besides Nat's smothering ways, that feathers might fly from my mouth when I coughed these days.

I'd heard enough about Susan's suspicious generosity. "Let me talk to Mo—I mean Grammy."

"Okay. I love you, Mom."

"I love—"

There were several loud clinks, as if Layne had dropped the phone in the sink, and then I heard my mother's voice. "How are you feeling, Violet? Getting some rest?"

"I'm great, Mom," I lied. I wasted no time on pleasantries. "What's Susan doing there?"

"She's visiting her parents like a *good* daughter." My mother was toying with me. She knew how much I'd like to tie my sister to a satellite and salute her goodbye as she blasted into outer space.

"How much money does she need this time?" I asked.

"Really, Violet? You're going to start with this already? Your sister is a changed woman."

Right, she'd probably just grown another horn. "I've heard that story before, Mom."

"She really means it this time."

"And you believe her?"

"Yes."

"Is she slipping drugs into your coffee?"

Mom chuckled, as if I were joking. "No, dear."

"Don't leave my kids alone with her."

"You're overreacting."

"Have you forgotten about bailing me out of jail because of her?"

A sigh came through the line. "No, I haven't."

"Both times?"

"I'm familiar with our family history, Violet."

"Do you still think I'm overreacting?"

"A little."

"Fine. But this time, you're going to have to spring for bail and three month's rent while I look for a new job."

"Nothing is going to happen. I'm telling you, things are different now."

"Unless Susan has been bitten by a werewolf and grows a fur coat on her back every full moon, I doubt it."

"If you're done being a big, fat downer, I'm going to get back in the pool with the kids and finish our game of Marco Polo."

Downer? My mother, the flower child. "Fine. Make me out to be the bad guy."

"I love you, too, dear," Mom said and hung up on me.

I glared at my cell phone for several seconds, debating whether to drive down to Rapid this very moment and snatch up my kids.

I didn't like Susan being back in the state, let alone staying with my parents. And I definitely didn't like her buying stuff for my kids. Something was going on there, and I needed to keep it as far from me and mine as possible.

"I know." Ray's hushed voice interrupted my internal rant. "You already said that." He was still on his phone, apparently not realizing the long, wood-floored hallway acted as an excellent conduit for his voice.

He should have shut himself in the bathroom or Jane's office if he wanted privacy.

I faced my computer and typed my password into the MLS site.

"I know what I saw, George."

George? I froze, fingers hovering over my keyboard. As in George Mudder of the Mudder Brothers Funeral Parlor? My ears perked.

"They followed me," Ray said.

A pause followed.

"Yes, I'm positive."

Another pause.

"No, I made sure they didn't see it. I did exactly as you told me. It's like they knew where I was going the whole time."

Pause.

"No. You couldn't pay me enough to do that."

To do what? Was Ray just saying that, or was George really paying him to do something?

"Shit, Jane just pulled in." Ray must have been looking out the back door, his voice bouncing off the glass. "I have to go."

I shed my sunglasses before Jane came in, praying that last dose of eye drops made me look a little less zombie-ish.

"I'll see you tonight after the viewing," Ray said.

What was happening after the viewing? Maybe I could convince my so-called guardian angel to join me tonight at the funeral parlor and distract her old friend, George Mudder, while I found out.

A month ago, I'd seen Ray and George Mudder lug a big crate out the back doors of the funeral parlor and load it into Ray's SUV. Later, when I'd asked Ray what he and George were up to, his face had turned blood red. I'd swear steam hissed from his ears and nostrils, followed by an unveiled threat to mind my own beeswax, "or else."

It was threats like this, and his numerous attempts to get my ass canned, that made me feel a bit ornery at times.

Like now.

Ray's boot heels thudded across the wood floor, nearing. I looked up at him. "How's our buddy, George? You two still moving big crates around town?"

Ray's face scrunched up tight, his eyes mere slits. "Don't you have some client to fuck, Blondie?"

He wasn't pulling punches today. Fine. "What's happening tonight after the viewing, Ray?"

His fists tight, he leaned down in my face. His breath reeked of stale coffee. "Listen you little troublemaking bitch—"

"No!" I shoved him backward, out of my face. "I'm done listening to your goddamned mouth, Ray. And I'm done putting up with your—"

The back door opened.

Ray shot me a parting squint. He dropped into his chair, slamming his cell phone on his desk so hard that the battery casing popped off.

Jane stopped by her office long enough to put her purse down. She came out front with the latte I'd bought her earlier this morning.

With her fuchsia-colored scarf, matching short-sleeve striped sweater, touched-up blonde highlights, and pert smile, she looked just like the mom from those old Partridge Family reruns. Only Jane had a core of titanium instead of psychedelic love, and she liked to recite To-Do lists for us instead of singing songs.

"Thank you for the coffee, Violet." She put it in the microwave, looking from me to Ray and back again, her gaze assessing.

I smiled, all bright sunshine and rainbows, as if I hadn't been on the verge of flattening Ray's nose with my knuckles a few seconds ago.

"Did you get my message?" she asked.

Earlier this morning, I'd called to see if there would be any problem with my representing a client in a commercial real estate deal and got Jane's voice mail. In her message back, she'd said that legally I could represent clients for both residential and commercial properties, but I'd need her help.

"I got it," I said. "I already contacted the seller's Realtor and set up a meeting this afternoon for a walkthrough with my client."

"What about financial info on the place?" Jane asked. Buttons beeped, then the microwave hummed.

"The Realtor will bring it with him."

"Perfect."

"Who's your new client?" Ray asked, kicking back, resting his Tony Lama boots on his desktop. His smile looked as fake as his orange-tinged tan. He was obviously playing bosom-buddies for Jane's benefit.

I joined his game, smiling back. "You wouldn't know him. He's from out of town."

Possibly even from another planet.

"Try me."

"I'll introduce you some other time."

His smile curled into a sneer for a heartbeat. "You sure he's not a figment of your imagination?"

I glanced sideways at Jane. She stood with her arms crossed, lips pursed, watching us.

"He's definitely real. Natalie was in here when he came in." Until she left in a coughing fit of laughter.

The microwave beeped.

"I'm curious," Jane said, pulling out her latte. "What's his name?"

I was on the spot. Damn Ray. I winged him with a fleeting glare. "Cornelius Curion."

Ray snorted. "You're making that up."

"Nope." It was even on his Nevada driver's license.

"Which property is he interested in?" Jane asked.

I'd much rather discuss this in the privacy of her office. "One of the hotels in Deadwood."

"Which one?" Ray had his fangs sunk into my ass and refused to pull out.

I looked at Jane, hesitating.

"Spill it, Violet," she ordered.

Damn it! "The Old Prospector Hotel."

Jane closed her eyes and shook her head.

"Another nut job," Ray said, laughing in my face. "I love it! Spooky Parker strikes out again."

If I only had a baseball bat. "I'm not going to strike out. He's paying with cash."

Jane's eyes flashed open. "He told you that?"

Ray's Tony Lamas hit the floor. "You're full of shit."

"I'm not." I sent a silent prayer to the realty gods that Cornelius had more bundles of cash in a bank somewhere. I'd happily sacrifice a chicken named Elvis as a bribe.

"This sounds promising, Violet." Jane's little smile was back. *Whew.* "Does he know that the Old Prospector Hotel is rumored to be haunted?"

I opted for another truth. "Yes."

Ray stood all of a sudden. "Jane, Mona or I should represent this client. If he's really paying cash, we need a homerun here, and Violet doesn't have the experience or the best batting record."

"What!" I leapt out of my seat, my mouth gaping. The lousy rat-faced fink! Where was that bat? I'd show him how well I could hit.

"Landing this deal might help us expand further south, gain more ground down in Rapid, bring us more customers," he continued as if I weren't standing next to him huffing like the little engine that could.

Jane sipped on her coffee, nodding her head, apparently considering Ray's line of bull crap.

"I can do this, Jane," I said, imploring her with my eyes to agree with me. "Cornelius came in looking for me. Not Ray. Not Mona. You can ask Natalie; he wants me."

Ray shot me a snide look, his gaze creeping down to my chest. "I'm sure he does, Violet. That's a real purty dress."

His ogling made me want to take a shower with a wire brush and lye soap.

Asshole! "Shut up, Ray."

He shrugged and turned back to Jane. "Like I said, you

need someone with a lot more experience than—"

"Jane—" I started, but stopped when she held up her hand.

"Enough! Violet gets to keep the client. Mona will mentor her through it, which will take care of the lack of experience issue you brought up, Ray."

Ray swore under his breath and shot me a look of love, as in he'd love to bury his fist in my kisser.

I smiled back with tons of warmth, looking forward to finding out what he and George Mudder were up to so I could roast Ray's balls over the fire until they crackled.

"However, Violet," Jane said, breaking up our eye-dagger duel, "You'd better not lose this deal for us."

"Or what?" Ray prodded.

"Well," Jane took a sip of her latte, and then focused on me, a frown pinching her brow. "As much as I like you, my soon-to-be ex-husband is draining me dry. If you lose this sale, I won't be able to afford to keep you on."

When she put it that way—*oh, shit!*

I nodded once, as if it were already a done deal. "I won't let you down, Jane."

* * *

Fifteen minutes before Cornelius' appointment time, I stood in the parking lot behind Calamity Jane's, frowning at the Picklemobile as the afternoon sunshine cooked my roots.

The old truck wasn't going to cut the mustard today, not for a cash-paying customer, not when my job was on the line … again.

I fished my cell phone from my purse, coughing on the oil-rich exhaust fumes spewing from a nearby flame-covered 1950s Ford Thunderbird. It sputtered and struggled to idle, just like the Picklemobile did until it was good and warmed up—yet another reason I needed a different set of wheels to impress Cornelius.

Doc answered his phone after the third ring. "Hello, Trouble."

"I need a favor," I said, walking along behind several parked cars and trucks.

"Hmmm. What can I expect in return?"

"I don't know. Maybe you should hear the request first."

"A savvy poker player would win the hand before showing her cards."

"I never claimed to be savvy."

"Fine. You can show me your legs, then, instead of your cards."

I chuckled. "Deal. You grant me this favor, I'll flash you some skin."

"I require more than a flash. What's the favor?"

"I need to borrow something." I stopped behind a familiar black Camaro with white racing stripes.

"What?"

"Your car." A pause on his end pushed me to explain, "I have a cash-paying client I need to show a property to shortly, and I need to impress him."

"Is that why you wore that dress today?"

I hesitated, and then admitted, "The dress is for you."

"Good. Where's the property?"

"Main Street in Deadwood."

"A house?"

"No, a hotel."

"Which one?"

"The Old Prospector Hotel."

This time, he hesitated. "You realize that place is supposedly haunted."

"So I've been told. Have you been in it?"

"Just once."

"Is it really haunted?"

"You don't believe in ghosts."

I sighed. "Are we going to do this dance again?"

"I'd rather just watch you dance."

"I've always wanted to learn how to belly dance," I said. "So, is it haunted?"

"Maybe. When you say belly dancing, are you talking finger cymbals and one of those coin-covered bras?"

"I'm more partial to velvet covered with sequins and a tambourine—something I can hit. What happened when you went inside the Old Prospector Hotel?"

"Nothing. I wasn't in there long enough to get a feel for the place. What is it with you and haunted sites?" he asked.

"It's my new marketing angle."

"Ghost busting?"

More like trying to save my job. But Doc didn't need to know that. "Who you gonna call?"

"You'll need new business cards. Does your client know about its haunted reputation?"

"He's the one who told me."

He let out a single sarcastic laugh. "Right. I should have guessed that."

"So, can I use your car?"

"Of course. What's this new client of yours look like?"

"Why?" Was he jealous? Doc usually didn't suffer from the green-eyed monster's wrath. It must be the dress.

"Because I just saw Abe Lincoln's twin pass in front of my windows and head for your front door. I'm guessing he belongs to you."

"Ack! That's Cornelius." I rushed toward Calamity Jane's back entrance.

"Cornelius?" Doc chuckled. "Did he escape from the set of *Planet of the Apes*?"

"Cute," I said hauling open the door. "I gotta go."

"I'll bring my keys over in a minute."

"No," I whispered, not wanting anyone to see Doc hand me his car keys. "I'll grab them on my way out."

"As you wish, Trouble."

I hung up, stuffing my phone in my purse.

Cornelius stood next to my desk, waiting alone, his half-smile in place.

Ray must have been using the bathroom.

"Hello, Cornelius," I greeted him with a full show of teeth.

"You remind me of someone in those glasses."

"Marilyn Monroe?" I threw out Doc's usual reference.

"No, it was this poster I saw last year on the side of a bus in San Jose while on my way to the Winchester Mansion. It had a blonde poodle wearing sunglasses and a bikini top.

Nice. I fought off the urge to give Cornelius a Three Stooges two-finger poke in the eyes and grabbed a hair clip from my desk drawer. With a quick twist, I secured my poodle-like hair in a French knot.

The sound of the toilet flushing down the hall spurred me to usher Honest Abe's twin toward the front door. I didn't want Ray to see him if I could help it for reasons I'd analyze later. "If you're ready, let's go."

"Sure." He stepped through the door I held open for him, his cane clicking on the sidewalk as I led him about twenty feet beyond Calamity Jane's and Doc's windows.

"If you'll wait here for just a second," I said at the corner of the building. "I need to run back and grab something."

Doc's front room was empty when I crossed the threshold. "Doc?"

He stepped out from the back room, a folder in his hand. "The keys are on my desk."

"Thank you." I scooped them up.

"Violet."

I paused at the door and glanced back at him.

"Be careful."

"I won't leave a single scratch." I hoped not to, anyway. How hard was it to buff out scuff marks?

"I'm not talking about the car."

Oh, that. "What could possibly go wrong?" I was going to be at a busy hotel in the middle of the day.

"Something that I haven't thought of yet."

"The story of my life." I gave him a two-fingered peace sign and stepped back into the harsh sunshine.

Cornelius waited for me with a dew of sweat coating his upper lip. His little round sunglasses covered his bright blue eyes. His long-sleeve black suit jacket must have been hot as hell. With a nudge of my head, I led him to the back parking lot.

He whistled as we approached Doc's Camaro. "Sweet ride."

Yes, it was. So was its owner, but those kinds of thoughts needed to be tucked away in my lingerie drawer for later when Doc was in attendance.

"Reminds me of a few months ago when I was down near Baton Rouge visiting the Myrtles Plantation. One of my associates has a fetish for classic muscle cars. He has a tattoo of a red convertible '68 Stingray across his back."

The Myrtles Plantation? How did I know that place?

I slid behind the wheel, inhaling the mixed scent of warmed leather and Doc's woodsy cologne, shooting a quick glance at Cornelius to see if he noticed the lack of a sugar-and-spice-and-everything-nice girlie scent.

He appeared to be too busy ogling the customized dash with its dials and lights to have noticed.

Starting the car, I rolled down the windows to replace the tell-tale scent of Doc with some of Deadwood's own *Eau-de-pine tree parfum*.

"So, Cornelius, did you recently move here from Las Vegas," which was listed on his driver's license as his home town, "or are you just visiting?"

He tapped one of the fancy dials on Doc's dash. "Just visiting. For now."

Slow and easy, I steered the Camaro out of the parking lot and headed for Main Street. "How did you hear about the Old Prospector Hotel?" Was the other realty office advertising nationally? Jane might be interested in hearing about it, if so.

"On the Internet. I was reading about the Adam's House

on a site and an ad for the hotel popped up in the sidebar."

"The Adam's House, huh?" Which was also rumored to be haunted. Suddenly, I remembered where I'd heard of the Myrtles Plantation—on a documentary about haunted houses in the United States. "It sounds like you're into ghost stories."

"You could say that."

Lovely, a ghoul groupie, my specialty.

So long as his money was green and the bank took it without alerting the Feds, I could deal with some hints of kookiness in a client. Besides, I doubted he could match straightjackets with my previous customers, Wolfgang and Millie.

Maybe he was a famous author incognito. That might explain his eccentric outfit and gobs of money. "Are you writing a book about ghosts or something?"

"No. But that's an idea I've considered."

I pulled into the hotel's packed side parking lot, taking a stall with a *Reserved* sign, and killed the engine. "Okay, let's go inside and take a look at the place. The hotel manager is expecting us."

So was the other Realtor.

Cornelius seemed to hesitate, tugging on his goatee as he stared at me through his little round sunglasses.

"What's wrong?" I asked, anxiety tickling my chest.

Please don't tell me you lied about the cash.

"There is something I should probably tell you before we go inside."

Crud!

I hoped Jane wouldn't hold Cornelius' lack of funds against me. I took a deep breath, steeling myself for what was to come. "What?"

"I have a condition."

"I'm sure the hotel's owner would be willing to consider whatever condition you offer."

If Cornelius really had the money to buy the hotel, his cash would do the talking for us. If not, maybe we could wheel and deal a little.

"Not that kind of condition. A physical condition."

I cocked my head to the side, frowning. "Are you ill?"

"Some people would say so, but I think I'm perfectly fine, just genetically advanced."

Genetically advanced, huh? Did he have wings under that black coat? "What are you talking about, Cornelius?"

"I have this extra ability."

Great. Here we go again. It all made sense now, the references to the haunted places, his quirks.

"Let me guess," I said. "You can see ghosts." Him and everyone else but me in this town.

"No, I can't see them."

Oh. Okay. "So, what's the problem then? Is it about the money? Do we need to look into financing?"

I'd help him fill out the paperwork if I had to in order to sell him the damned place. Another vehicle to replace my dead Bronco wasn't going to be cheap, neither were Addy's new glasses, the two pairs of shoes I had to buy for Layne, plus school supplies—ugh! The commission I made off of Doc's house would only stretch so far.

"No," he waved me off. "I have plenty of cash to pay for this place."

Thank God. "What then?"

"I'm a ghost whisperer."

I stared at him for a couple of blinks. "Come again?"

"I can summon and talk to ghosts."

Chapter Four

Cornelius and I struck the mother lode in the Old
Prospector Hotel.
Gold-colored carpet softened our footfalls, gold faux-silk
wallpaper coated the walls, gold-painted tiles shimmered on
the ceiling. If Deadwood had a hidden rainbow, we'd found
the leprechaun's stash.

With a fake smile etched on my face, I led Cornelius
through several banks of jangling slot machines. Heads turned
as we walked through the casino's cooled air, mumbles and
sniggers following in our wake. All of the attention made me
miss the smoke that used to fill the air before Deadwood
enacted the no smoking in casinos law. We could use a cloud
of exhaled nicotine to hide behind.

A full-sized stuffed mule weighed down with prospecting
gear stood next to the front desk. A plaque at its hooves
claimed "Socrates" had belonged to the hotel's original owner.
Decades of petting had rubbed bare the top of poor Socrates'
nose.

I'd have to bring Addy and Layne here someday to see the
old mule. Then again, Addy might get the idea in her head of
rescuing Socrates. Thank God he was too big to fit in her
bicycle basket and too dead to be a pet. Although, Layne
might be interested in Socrates' skeleton.

Cornelius pocketed his glasses and pointed at the mule.
"Is that for real?"

I could ask good old Honest Abe the same question, but
since he was a client and the sale of this hotel would ensure I
kept my job, I just pinched my lips together and nodded.

We sidled up to the front desk where a young receptionist

stood, her gaze glued to her computer screen. With her gold lamé shirt and sun-kissed long blonde locks, she reminded me of Addy's Safari Skipper Barbie.

"Welcome to the Old Prosp—" Her jaw gaped at the sight of Cornelius, who tipped his top hat at her.

I waited a few seconds to see if she'd snap back to life on her own. When she didn't, I waved my hand in front of her face. "Hi. I'm Violet Parker from Calamity Jane Realty. We're here to see the manager."

"The manager?" she repeated and dragged her focus back to me, frowning as if I'd spoken Portuguese.

"Yes. The manager." I spoke with a dose of enunciation. "I'm with Calamity Jane Realty. We have an appointment."

"Uhhh, okay. Hold on." She stole one last peek at Cornelius, and then scurried through a door behind her marked *Office*.

"That went well," I said under my breath.

Cornelius stroked his goatee, a smug look on his face. "I tend to have that effect on people."

I wished he'd save his special effects for some other time, preferably without me in the same town. I'd been building enough of a tarnished reputation in Deadwood without his help.

"There are definitely ghosts in this place," Cornelius said loudly enough for any passersby to hear. "I sensed at least one over near that group of Triple-Seven slot machines. Maybe three."

Before I had a chance to recover from my flush of mortification and shush him, the office door opened and Tiffany walked out.

Tiffany.

As in Doc's gorgeous ex-girlfriend.

The Jessica Rabbit look-alike.

My flame-haired rival.

It was my turn to gape. *What in the hell was she doing here?*

Tiffany's eyes moved from me to Cornelius and back, her

smile smooth and wide, as if she was selling tooth whitener on a pop-up Internet ad.

Jeez, she was good. Not even an extra blink at the sight of Cornelius leaning on the counter beside me.

Her white knit shirt and matching skirt hugged her in all the curvy places. I sucked in my baby-stretched stomach. With that perky figure, there was no way she'd ever pushed out a kid—let alone two within minutes of each other.

"Hello." She held her hand out to Cornelius, who had removed his top hat at the sight of her. "I'm Tiffany Sugarbell from Canyon Realty."

Sugarbell. I grinned, remembering Harvey's crack about Tiffany being Tinker Bell's porn-star cousin.

"Ms. Sugarbell." Cornelius took her hand, bowing his head a bit. "What a pleasure to meet you."

Her Stepford wife smile landed on me.

I tried to mimic her expression, stretching my cheeks toward my ears, and held out my hand. "Violet Parker from Calamity Jane Realty."

"Yes," she said, her eyelids narrowing a fraction as she took my hand. "We've met before."

We had. Twice. First with Harvey, then with Doc. Only the last time, her hand had been slapping Doc's face instead of squeezing my hand in a silent challenge. Dang, the wench was strong. I pulled free, my knuckles throbbing from being crushed in her Kung-Fu grip.

Cornelius' cell phone rang from somewhere within his black suit coat. He dug it out. "Excuse me a moment, ladies." He walked away from us. "I told you not to call me until tonight," he said as he walked away.

I turned to Tiffany, who was staring at me point blank, her smile now set on dim. I decided not to waste time with talk about the clouds or lack of them.

"I'm surprised to see you here, Tiffany. I thought you were with Roughlock Realty."

She snorted. "Not anymore. They were too mom-and-pop

for my taste, dealing mainly with locals." She eyed Cornelius as if he was marbled with fat and delivered fresh from the butcher. "I prefer to play ball with the big boys, especially if they're from out of town. That's where the money is."

Ah, realty as a sport. She would enjoy sparring with Ray, then.

"Where is Leroy?" I asked. Leroy was the guy I'd talked to when I'd called Canyon Realty this morning to set up the walk-through.

"He ate his last greasy hamburger at lunch and keeled over."

Holy crap! "He's dead?" I could still hear his wheezy voice in my head.

"Nah, it was just a little heart attack."

"Just a little one?" A heart stopped for any length of time seemed like a *big* problem to me.

She waved off my concern. "It's his third. The doctor told Leroy's wife that if the greasy food didn't stop, Leroy's heart would, and the next time it would be for good."

That meant I'd be trying to help my ghost-whispering client buy a haunted hotel from a guy who had a ticking time bomb in his chest. Just my luck.

"Should I contact Leroy then, if Mr. Curion decides to put an offer on the property? Or you?" Or could I hear what was behind Door Number Three, please?

"I'm taking it over. Leroy and I will split the commission."

Splendid. I couldn't wait to be reminded on a regular basis that Doc had had sex with Tiffany. Maybe I should find out what her favorite positions were so that the images in my head were accurate during my spasms of jealousy.

She pursed her lips. "How long have you been with Calamity Jane's? I don't remember seeing you around before that open house I had up on Terry Peak last month."

"I started working for Jane this spring."

"Doc Nyce is a client of yours."

It wasn't a question, but I nodded, anyway.

"He says you're good."

At what? The realty business? Keeping secrets? Knocking boots?

Why was he talking about me to Tiffany? More importantly, *when* was he talking about me to her?

"Oh, yeah?" I tried my damnedest to feign indifference.

"He said you got him a nice deal on his new place."

Had she been in there? How many times? Naked?

Criminy! This insanity had to stop. What was it about Doc that turned me into such a green-eyed, untrusting, paranoid nutcase?

"We were in the right place at the right time," I said, and changed the subject before we started comparing notes on Doc's kisses. "Have there been any previous offers on this hotel?"

"Just one, but the buyer backed out early after learning it had a reputation." She looked at Cornelius. "How'd you find this guy?"

"He just walked in the front door and I was available." She didn't need to know he'd come looking for me in particular. That would open a nest of questions I'd rather avoid.

"Like he fell out of the sky, isn't that crazy? How'd he hear about the hotel?'

"The Internet."

She checked her cell phone, and then asked, "How do you like working with Ray Underhill?"

I'd rather eat a bowlful of hissing cockroaches soaked in rat piss. "It has its ups and downs."

She leaned in close. "Has he tried to get you into the sack yet?"

Her bluntness caught me off guard. As much as I wanted to confide to a peer about the crap I'd dealt with from Ray, I thought of Jane's policy about badmouthing coworkers. For all I knew, Ray could be using Tiffany to set me up for a fall.

"Ray's been a perfect gentleman for the most part." That lie even tasted bad.

Tiffany's sculpted eyebrows raised. "We are talking about the same Ray Underhill, right? Fake tan, fake smile, fake charm, fast hands?"

Yep, that was the same dickhead. Although, I'd only witnessed Ray's charm when he'd used it on his clients. "I think so."

"Hmmm. Maybe I have him pegged wrong." She frowned at my hair. "Or he's not into blondes."

"That's probably it."

He would never be into me, mind or body, not as long as I continued to stand upright and breathe oxygen.

Wait! Maybe that's what Ray was doing with the Mudder Brothers crates—necrophilia. I cringed at the morbid nosedive I'd taken and tried to pull out of it.

"I think he prefers redheads." Like Mona. And Tiffany.

"They all do," she said with a smirk, "at first."

And we were back to the "Tiffany Does Doc" show in my head, damn it. How much did lobotomies cost these days? Maybe I could sign up for a payment plan.

I tried to steer my head away from the images of tangled legs and focus on learning more about Ray, the lesser of two evils. "Have you worked with Ray a lot?"

"A little bit here and there over the years."

"He's a good salesman," I baited.

She shrugged. "He knows a lot of people with money to burn."

"I wish I knew what tree he was finding them in," I muttered. "I could use a few more hanging around my desk at work."

Tiffany looked me up and down, her alabaster forehead wrinkling. "Violet, can I be honest with you?"

Oh, crudmeister. This couldn't be good. Where'd I leave my Kevlar vest? "Sure."

"I don't understand your hair."

My hair? I hadn't seen that coming. I tucked some loose curls behind my ear. "What's to understand?"

"You're not using it to its potential."

My hair had potential? For what besides ensnaring small flying animals?

"You should put some volumizer in it, fluff it up a bit more, work the Dolly Parton angle."

Make it bigger? Was she serious? I wouldn't be able to fit through doorways.

Tiffany looked down over my hips. "You definitely have the curves for it."

I looked down over my so-called curves, trying to suck in the extra speed bumps. "I don't know. I'm a little light up top to pull off Dolly." Make that a lot light.

"Nah. You just need a push-up bra."

In addition to the one I already had on? My chin would be resting on my boobs. A blush raced down my neck, bee-lining toward my substandard cleavage.

"Or you need a better one." Tiffany added. She must have smelled the embarrassment smoking out of my pores. "In the meantime, try this."

She adjusted the knot of fabric at my sternum, tugging it and refitting, and then pulling on some of the fabric near my armpits, exposing cleavage I didn't realize I had. She stepped back and eyed me again. "That's better."

I frowned down at the tops of my boobs puffing out of the dress, looking a cup size bigger. How'd she do that? I had a hell of a time just making them point in the same direction most days.

"Now shake your hair out, like this." She did a shake and fluff with her red locks and motioned for me to try it.

Glancing around to make sure nobody was watching, I took out my hairclip and followed her directions, curls flying everywhere.

"That's it." She scrutinized me like a sculptor eyeing a big pile of clay. "Now you look like a woman who knows how to get what she wants."

Right. I shoved some curls out of my face. Just like that, buyers would start lapping at my feet. I wished.

"Trust me," she said. "I know what I'm talking about. I haven't won all of my awards for my brains alone. I know how to flip a property—any property. And dressing the part is half of the secret."

"Thanks." *I think.*

I felt like I'd just gone through a makeover to increase my curb appeal, and I couldn't quite figure out why she'd offered her services. Would she be so willing to give advice if she knew that I was sleeping with the guy who got away?

According to Doc, Tiffany had moved on to new prey. I hoped he was right, because ten bucks said going head-to-head with this she-wolf would leave me scratched, bitten, and crazy from a nasty case of rabies.

I didn't doubt for a moment that Tiffany fought for keeps. Hell, I'd witnessed her outright hostility when she'd attacked Doc in front of clients. Her head had almost spun clear around. If Tiffany was going to be the seller's Realtor, I didn't need her to find out about me and Doc until Cornelius had this hotel in his back pocket.

"Sorry about that," Cornelius returned to my side, his gaze on Tiffany.

"No problem." Tiffany pointed at my chest. "Violet lost her necklace. You haven't seen it, have you?"

Cornelius' gaze followed her finger, his eyes widening slightly. The big lug-head grinned at me as if he just now realized I came with breasts attached. "No, but I'll keep looking." His focus dipped back down to my chest before returning to Tiffany.

Yeah, I bet he would.

Tiffany winked at me. "Like I said, half the secret." She nudged her head toward the casino. "You two ready to take a look at the place?"

"Lead the way," Cornelius answered, making no attempt

to hide his admiration of her butt as she walked in front of him.

I shook my head and followed. It's no wonder Doc had slept with her. He was a mere mortal male, after all.

Her tour started with the main floor. Casino space took up two-thirds of the square footage. The remaining space held a dining room and a few windowed offices for the management, custodial, and maid services.

I was standing in the laundry room next to Cornelius, the smell of bleach heavy in the humid air, when he started making a low burbling noise in his throat. It took me a moment to realize the noise wasn't coming from the sloshing washers on my right.

Tiffany must not have heard him, because she continued reading staffing figures from the financial report.

The burbling morphed into a high-pitched whine, like a fan belt getting ready to snap.

Tiffany flipped the page and listed off several more percentages.

I nudged him.

The whine stopped. He opened his eyes.

"You okay?" I asked.

"Do you hear that?"

"Hear what?"

His eyes scanned my face. "The whispers."

Crap. He was talking about ghosts again.

I glanced at Tiffany, who had stopped reading.

Her gaze rested squarely on me. "Do you need a moment alone with your client?"

I looked up at Cornelius. "Do I?"

He cocked his head to the side, listening for the count of three. "No, they're gone."

"Maybe we should check out the second floor now," I suggested, wanting to escape from the laundry room before Cornelius got squeaky again.

Besides a set of handicap-equipped guest rooms on the

first floor, the other fifty-two rooms were located on the second and third floors, including the two grand suites.

Unfortunately, the Midas touch didn't extend beyond the first floor. Dingy stained maroon carpet lined the long narrow hallways on both levels; a deer trail was worn along the center. Scuffed and patched yellow walls bracketed the way. Even the light coming from the ceiling fixtures seemed aged, fading.

A bulb flickered overhead as we walked down the hall.

Cornelius tapped my shoulder, and then pointed at the problematic fixture. "Someone is trying to get our attention."

It's called loose wires, you buffoon. I smiled, keeping my skepticism firmly locked behind my closed lips.

A hint of stale cigarette smoke lingered inside the two grand suites on the third floor, the flowery-scented air fresheners not cutting it. The bathroom fixtures needed an upgrade, as did the faded bed covers, dinged-up furniture, and outdated curtains. The carpet looked tired, worn out—that made two of us.

Catching the guest rooms up to the present day would take a chunk of capital. The reduced price on the place now made sense, as did the sad state of the financials.

We were standing next to the window in one of the suites when Cornelius asked, "Do you guys hear that?"

Don't ask what.

"Hear what?" Tiffany asked.

Crap.

"That whispering," he said, moving over to the wall near the laminated headboard.

"What whispering?" Tiffany cocked her head to the side.

Cornelius pressed his ear to the wall and closed his eyes. "They're in here."

"According to the paperwork," Tiffany said, flipping through the papers in her hands, "an exterminator recently visited the premises. If you're hearing movement, I can arrange for a second exterminator to inspect the building."

He held up two fingers. "I hear two of them."

"Two mice?" Tiffany frowned at me. "He can count how many by sound alone?"

I need to pull on the hand brake before this train jumped off the tracks. "Tiffany, could I have a moment alone with my client?"

She shrugged. "Sure. I'll wait in the hall."

No, that was still within hearing distance. "We'll catch up with you at the elevator."

I counted to five after the door shut behind her before whirling on Cornelius. "Okay, explain."

He pointed at the wall behind him. "There are two entities in the wall. I can hear them whispering."

I'd heard a similar ghostly tune before from Doc, so my eyes didn't bug out even slightly. I decided to play along, let him get this out of his system.

"Why are they inside of the wall?"

"Sometimes they get caught."

Really? I thought they were ghosts—all wispy and ethereal. I let that one go. "Why are they whispering?"

"Usually, it's because they don't like to be heard." He tapped his cane on the wall. "But to be positive, I'd have to ask them."

"And how do you do that? How do you speak to them? Through a Ouija board?" My second guess involved lighting candles, holding hands, and chanting. If he'd buy the hotel, I'd bring the matches.

"Those things don't work. You have to have the ability to communicate, plain and simple." He tapped his cane lower down on the wall, near the baseboard.

"Communicate with the dead?"

"Exactly."

We needed to get out of here before he put a hole in the drywall. I pointed at the door. "What do you say we wrap up here, get a copy of those financials, and talk about this more over a cup of coffee?" I certainly didn't want to take him back to Calamity Jane's, not with him telling ghost stories.

He hesitated. "I don't drink coffee. Caffeine makes me sleepy. I stick with protein shakes."

That confirmed it. He was an alien hiding inside a clone of Abe Lincoln. "Some ice water?"

"Okay, but absolutely no ice."

My last client had had ice tray hang-ups. Cornelius would have gotten along well with her.

"And I want to come back again," he added.

Fine. Whatever. "I'll arrange that with Tiffany."

"At night."

Nope. Nay. No way. "I'm sure that'll be no problem."

He followed me out into the hall. Tiffany waited at the other end, her toothy smile a beacon.

"All set?" Tiffany asked as we approached.

When I nodded, she pushed the down button. The doors dinged open.

On the main level, we followed Tiffany back to the front desk.

"Is there anything else you'd like to see today?"

Cornelius shook his head. "Not in the daylight. The ghosts are more active in the evening."

I shot Cornelius a warning look.

"Especially at dusk and dawn," he continued, seemingly oblivious to my telepathic shout to shut the hell up.

"Did you say 'ghosts' or 'guests'?" Tiffany asked, her eyes narrowed.

"Gho—"

"Guests," I interrupted. "He said, 'guests.'"

Tiffany's cell phone rang, saving my day. "I'm sorry, but I've been waiting for this call. It will take just a second. Do you mind?"

"Not at all." It would give me time to duct tape Cornelius' mouth closed.

She walked to the other side of Socrates, the mule, and stood with her back to us. "Hello?"

I poked Cornelius. "Ixnay ethay ostghay alktay," I said in

Pig Latin.

He cocked his head. "I don't speak French."

"I said nix the—"

"Of course, Doc," Tiffany's voice cut through my thoughts. "I've been waiting for your call all afternoon."

"—ghost ..."

Cornelius asked something again, but I didn't hear a single word. My ears were tuned into the sound of Tiffany's voice. She'd been waiting for Doc's call this whole time?

"Yes, of course." She practically cooed.

Cornelius said something about a room. I nodded without looking at him.

"I'll just come by your office later," Tiffany said. "Maybe I can entice you to go to dinner with me."

What! I took a couple of steps closer.

She giggled, all flirty.

I wanted to strap her to the dead mule and rub her nose raw with my elbow.

"Great. It's a date. I'll see you then."

I was practically standing in her shoes by the time she hung up. She turned, her smile opening into a surprised "O." She stumbled back a step at the sight of me.

"God, Violet. You scared me. What are you doing?"

"Cornelius has a question for you," I lied without a hitch.

Her eyes narrowed. "I said I'd just be a second."

"Sorry, but he's in a hurry to leave."

She looked over my shoulder. "You sure about that?"

I turned to find Cornelius leaning on the front counter, his wallet open, credit card in his fingers. Safari Skipper was saying something to him while typing on the computer keyboard.

I joined him. "What are you doing?"

"Renting the haunted suite."

"Why?"

"So we can hold a séance in there. Do you know where I can get some raven feathers?"

Chapter Five

When life handed me lemons, I preferred to slam back Lemon Drops, extra heavy on the vodka. However, drinking in the afternoon was not a good habit for a mother of two young kids, so I would have to settle for the next best thing—my Aunt Zoe's famous homemade lemonade.

I pulled into the drive in front of Aunt Zoe's fixed-up, but not too fancy, century-old Victorian, which she was sharing with me and my kids until I managed to make enough money to fly solo. Well, make that solo with two fledglings clinging to me.

The Picklemobile shuddered, sputtered, and then backfired, announcing my arrival to the neighborhood crime watch group. A dog barked at me from the porch three houses down, probably pissed at me for interrupting its afternoon nap.

I growled back, then rested my forehead on the steering wheel.

What had I done in one of my past lives to deserve a client like Cornelius? I must have sat accidentally on the last Dodo bird and its eggs.

Cornelius had rented one of the suites at the Old Prospector Hotel for a whole week. He'd passed up my offer to spend some time this afternoon talking more about the hotel property and opted to go shopping for all of the items he'd need to perform a séance later this evening.

When invited to join in and hold hands, I'd claimed another engagement. But Safari Skipper had been more than willing to participate, her eyes wide after hearing he planned to chit chat with the hotel's ghosts. I just hoped the so-called ghosts would tell Cornelius to buy the damned hotel so I could keep my job. Just thinking about Jane's threat to make the sale or say *adios* to my job made my eye twitch.

It was time to drown my sorrows in sweetened lemon juice.

I grabbed my purse and slammed the pickup door behind me extra hard. I had to, or the dang thing wouldn't latch, which I'd learned earlier this week when it flew open in the midst of a hard right onto Main Street.

The yard and front porch seemed empty without my kids around to litter both with their toys. I opened the screen door and ran smack dab into a solid, broad chest covered in a dark green T-shirt.

"Whoa there, Sparky, where's the fire?" a familiar deep, gravelly voice asked.

"Reid?" I stepped back, blinking in surprise at the salt-and-pepper-haired Sam Elliot look-alike, who also happened to be the captain of Deadwood's fire department. The spicy, musky scent of his cologne seemed stronger than usual, like he'd been hanging out at the cologne counter in the mall down in Rapid.

My surprise at seeing him was many-sided. Lately, I'd had a bit of bad luck with fires—neither of which were my fault. I'd grown accustomed to seeing Reid in the aftermath of flames and smoke. As far as I could see and smell, Aunt Zoe's house sported neither at the moment.

"What are you doing here?" I asked

"Risking my life," Reid answered, the usual sparkle in his blue-blue eyes noticeably absent. "Your aunt is unstable."

Which hit on the other reason I was surprised to see him on Aunt Zoe's threshold. The last time Reid had exited Aunt Zoe's front door, she'd told me she didn't want the fire captain in her house ever again. From the steel in her tone when she'd said it, I hadn't expected to see Reid on the inside of her screen door anytime this century. Yet here he was just a week later.

I decided to ignore his comment about Aunt Zoe and keep to neutral subjects. "Where's your truck?"

He pointed across the street at Miss Geary's house. A big red dually pickup truck sat in her drive, the Deadwood Fire Department emblem clearly visible on the passenger side door. I'd been too busy pouting about my new client to notice the red beast when I'd driven up.

"I gotta get back to the station. Nice dress, Sparky. Your hair looks flammable when it's poofed out like that. Stay away from matches." He left with a wink.

Patting down my curls, I watched him walk away, noticing his tense shoulders and stiff strides. He usually sauntered through life. What had happened?

The screen door *whapped* shut behind me. I tip-toed across the living room's hardwood floor, wondering if I'd find my aunt ready to throw plates after Reid's visit. I peeked around the kitchen archway and locked eyes with old man Harvey.

His thick caterpillar eyebrows scrunched up at the sight of me. "What are you sneaking around for, girl?" He kicked out the chair opposite him at the table. "Have a seat. I have a bone to pick with you."

Now what? I skirted the chair and headed for the fridge, which smelled like fresh lemons when I pulled it open. "Where's Aunt Zoe?"

"In the basement sufferin' from a case of ruffled feathers."

I grabbed the pitcher of lemonade from the top shelf. "Did Elvis get stuck behind the washer again?"

Addy's pet chicken shared several quirks with its King of Rock-n-Roll namesake—a cowlick (or in the chicken's case, a comb that flipped to the side in front), a love for peanut butter and bananas, and an ability to drive some women crazy—namely me.

"No. She's looking for shotgun shells."

That made me pause midway to the counter, pitcher in hand. "Shotgun shells?" At his nod, I asked, "Is Bessie low on ammo?".

Harvey had named his favorite shotgun Bessie. I'd had the pleasure of meeting the pee-my-pants end of Bessie's double barrels up close and personal the first time I'd visited Harvey's ranch. Lucky for me I worked for a realty office wanting to help him sell his ranch and not a bank trying to take it away.

"Bessie is fine. The shells are for your aunt's shotgun."

"Does this have anything to do with a certain captain of the Fire Department?"

"Yep. He's knocking on the back door again … well, make that the front door this time."

I lowered the pitcher onto the counter. "What are you doing here?"

"Beatrice wasn't home." He said it as if Miss Geary, Aunt Zoe's hot-pants-wearing neighbor, being gone explained everything.

"Was Reid here when you got here?"

"No, he dropped me off."

"Where's your other pickup?" I reached for a glass from the cupboard and palmed a weighty, blue-tinted drinking glass, one of Aunt Zoe's original pieces she'd blown in her glass workshop out behind the house.

"Coop is using it to move some of his stuff into storage while you try to sell his place. Which reminds me, Coop wants you to visit him tomorrow at the station."

That made it sound like Detective Cooper and I were going to have a nice little picnic together. I was getting tired of hanging out in the Deadwood Police Station. If we kept this up, the detective might as well make me an honorary deputy so I wouldn't have to sign in, anymore. "Did Cooper say why he wants to see me?"

"Coop never explains why, he just barks orders and expects everyone to follow them. It probably has to do with that damned corpse of yours."

"It's not mine." I cursed under my breath.

Cooper's drill sergeant style brought out the ornery mule

in me. The fact that he kept wanting to talk to me about a dead body had my heartburn trying to melt my esophagus. What part of "I don't know, dammit!" did he not understand?

Rather than burn through any more stomach lining about why Cooper undoubtedly wanted to prod me again about the dead guy, I returned to the subject of shotgun shells.

"So, what happened between Aunt Zoe and Reid?"

"How should I know?"

"Weren't you sitting right here with them?"

"I was in the john. My damned prostate has me dripping like a leaky pipe today."

I made a note to have that visual memory removed during my upcoming lobotomy.

"When I came out, she was already spittin' fire and threatenin' to fill him full of buckshot if he didn't get the hell out of her kitchen."

"Then what happened?"

"The fool laughed."

I grimaced.

"Exactly. That man has been around long enough to know better than to even twitch a lip at a pissed off woman who owns a shotgun."

"I wonder what happened between them in the past that has her so mad."

"Why don't you ask her?"

"I did. She wouldn't spill."

Well, that wasn't entirely true. Aunt Zoe had told me that until I came clean on what was going on between me and Doc, she refused to explain what her problem was with Reid. It was basic Spaghetti Western Mexican Standoff 101 stuff.

"Hmph. You get your big ole stubborn ass from her."

"Leave my big ole ass out of this."

His gold teeth gleamed through his wide grin. "Anyway, I told Reid to get the hell out of here before she came back upstairs and filled him full of daylight."

"Good thing he listened."

Harvey snickered and pulled a chocolate chip cookie from Aunt Zoe's Betty Boop cookie jar. "I ain't ever seen your aunt so fired up before. Reid really steams her buns."

In more ways than one, I'd bet, judging by the man's charm and good looks.

"Speaking of steamed buns," Harvey said, "did you pay a visit to Doc today?"

"Yeah, why?" Did Harvey know something about Tiffany's phone call?

"I figured." He pointed a cookie at me. "Just wondering how much he appreciated that there dress you're about to fall out of."

"Oh, shut up." I yanked up the knot at my sternum, tucking my boobs in behind the fabric as best I could.

Harvey was the only soul in town who officially knew about my rolls in the hay with Doc. The old buzzard might be a blow hard, but his beady eyes didn't miss a thing when it came to the soap opera that was my life.

After one last tug, I wrinkled my nose at him. "And quit looking at my chest."

"When you leave them hanging out like that, anyone with half a testicle can't miss 'em. Doc still has both of his jelly beans, right?"

My neck warmed. "None of your business, old man."

He wheezed out a few laughs. "That's what I figured."

I finished pouring my glass of lemonade, shoved the pitcher back in the fridge, and stole half a soft cookie from Harvey's grasp. No sooner had I dropped into the other chair when the basement door banged open.

Aunt Zoe strode into the kitchen, her jaw rigid, her long silver-streaked hair pulled back in a ponytail. Cobwebs stuck to her red knit shirt and faded blue jeans.

She slammed a dust-covered box of shotgun shells on the table. "Where is that bastard?"

"He had to go see a man about a fire." Harvey grabbed two more cookies.

"Wise choice." Aunt Zoe stomped over to the sink and cranked on the faucet.

Behind her back, Harvey and I exchanged raised brows and shoulder shrugs, and then played tug-o-war with the cookie jar. I won.

I hugged Betty Boop to my chest to hide my exposed cleavage before sneaking a peek at my aunt.

The obvious question about her and Reid bounced on the tip of my tongue like an Olympic high diver. But in the end I valued my hide too much, so I crammed another cookie between my lips instead.

"What are you doing home so early, Violet?" Aunt Zoe asked, drying her hands on a plaid kitchen towel.

"Finding my happy place." I said through a mouthful of crumbs and chocolate. I was fairly certain chocolate chip therapy would help me in my search, especially while sitting in Aunt Zoe's sunny, yellow kitchen.

Harvey wiped cookie bits from his beard. "Who popped your balloon, little girl?"

Where to start? I decided to skip all of the gut-twinging parts involving Doc and Tiffany sitting in a tree, K-I-S-S-I-N-G, for obvious reasons.

Aunt Zoe tossed the towel on the counter. "Is this about your sister moving back in with your folks?"

I paused mid-chew, my vision coated in red for several seconds.

No. Huh-uh. I wasn't going to focus on that problem, either. Instead, I announced, "I have a new client. He's going to pay with cash."

"I have just the ranch for him. How does he feel about headless corpses?"

Knowing Cornelius, he'd probably kick up his heels at the chance to talk to one. Could a decapitated ghost talk? Maybe it could mime to Cornelius about how it ended up clutching my damned business card and save me from earning any more of Cooper's squinty-eyed glares.

I swallowed and sat back, shoving Betty Boop Harvey's way. "He wants to buy a hotel."

"That's good news, isn't it?" Aunt Zoe dropped into the seat between Harvey and me. "Jane must be thrilled to have a cash buyer interested in such a big property."

"He wants to buy the Old Prospector Hotel."

"Oh," Aunt Zoe winced. "That's too bad."

Harvey grunted. "I used to date one of the housecleaners who worked there. She swore on her mama's grave those ghost rumors were true."

"My new client would agree with her. He claims he can hear ghosts *and* communicate with them."

"No shit," Harvey said, squinting. "I could use somebody like that."

"You could use a ghost whisperer? Why?"

"Well, he'd need to speak a lot louder than a whisper. My grandpappy never could hear well after that dynamite accident when he was a pup."

"Are you saying what I think you're saying?"

"Probably not. You like to use a lot fancier words than I do most of the time."

"You believe this guy can actually talk to ghosts?"

"I don't know. Let's take him out to my place and see."

"You truly believe you have ghosts?"

Doc and I had had a conversation several weeks ago on this very subject. During a visit to Harvey's, Doc's so-called smell radar had rung his bell so hard upon stepping through Harvey's front door that he'd been knocked down. Literally. Falling right onto me.

Later, when I'd questioned Doc about the whole incident, he'd mentioned smelling a ghost at Harvey's—one that had been there for a long time. But whether I believed Doc or not, I couldn't tell Harvey anything about Doc and his admission, due to my promise to keep my lips zipped regarding Doc's sixth sense.

"Yes, I told you that before when you asked if I believed

in them, remember?"

Oh, yeah. That was right after Harvey had figured out Doc and I were fooling around. It's no wonder I'd blocked out the ghost bit. I could only handle one closeted secret at a time.

"And you think it's your grandpa?"

At his nod, I glanced at Aunt Zoe to see if she was buying any of this. She stared down at the cookie in her hand, her brow pinched. I had a feeling her mind was elsewhere, probably at the lynching of a certain fire captain.

Back to Harvey. "What makes you think it's your grandpa?"

"The ghost hits the liquor cabinet every night at nine, just like my grandpappy used to do."

"Define 'hits.'"

"Opens the liquor cabinet door, sometimes both of them."

I waited to see if he was going to deliver a punch line, but apparently there wasn't one. "Maybe your cabinet is just off-balance."

"Really, Miss Smarty Pants? And gravity works its magic at the same time every night?" He shook his head. "It's got to be Grandpappy. My pa always reminisced about his daddy's drinking habit, said you could set your clock by him. In the end, the damned firewater killed Grandpappy's liver, taking him along with it."

"So, you want my client to confirm it's your grandpa?"

"No, I want your client to ask Grandpappy where he buried those damned jars of money. I've dug up the whole yard and can't find 'em anywhere."

"I have a metal detector down in the basement you can use," Aunt Zoe said, rejoining us. "Maybe it would detect the lids if there are no coins in the jars."

"I've tried metal detectors. There's somethin' in the dirt out there that makes the radars go all scatterwonky." He scratched behind his ear. "No, I need Violet's ghost talker.

He'd go right to the source."

I groaned and shook my head at Aunt Zoe. "I can't believe we're having this conversation."

"Stranger things have happened around these parts," she explained with a shrug.

"I've always wanted to ask my grandpappy if that old story about the two miners trapped in the mine up behind my barn is true or just a tall tale."

"This is crazy, Harvey."

He continued as if I hadn't tried to inject some rationale into the conversation. "According to the old timers, the miners had three bags full of gold that they'd stolen from the mine superintendent's safe in Slagton. They were stashing the gold when the mine caved in, trappin' them."

Harvey's words went in one ear and out the other. I was busy trying to envision Cornelius talking to ghosts in Harvey's living room. "Even if ghosts do exist, how could they talk without a larynx?"

"The old timers swore that for decades after the cave-in, if you went up in the mine, hiked back to the rock-fall, and stood really still and quiet-like, you could hear someone tap-tap-tapping on the other side of the timbers."

Chills spread across my shoulders and down my arms. "Ghost or no ghost, that's just creepy."

"I remember hearing that story years ago in the Golden Sluice up in Lead." Aunt Zoe said, referring to the gritty local bar where I'd met one of Lead's high-ranking, tail-chasing, council members weeks ago to talk about a potential sale. Unfortunately, that buying client of mine now sat in jail awaiting trial. Such was my luck in the realty business.

Zoe continued. "The miner who told us the tale used to live back in Slagton before the government evacuated most of the town. He refused to go back to Slagton, swearing there was something in the water that turned everyone sour in the head. How did he say it? 'Made 'em just not right, anymore.'"

Harvey nodded. "That's why my pa called them

Whangdoodles. One step short of plum-shit crazy."

I tried to rub away my goose bumps. After the last story I heard about Slagton, which involved a milky-eyed demon who supposedly dug up the graves in a local cemetery and chewed on the bones, there was no way I'd go to Slagton. Not even with a six-pack of fully-armed Navy Seals leading the way.

"Anyway," Harvey said, "if I can find that cash my pa swore my grandpappy buried, I wouldn't have to wait for my ranch to sell to buy a house in town."

I sat up straight, my chain yanked. Did someone say *buy* a house?

Harvey grinned. "I'd be your second cash-paying customer this month."

Okay, so I wasn't sold yet on the whole concept of ghosts existing, and maybe the idea of Cornelius talking to them was a tad bit loony, but what if—*just what if*—there really were jars of money hidden on Harvey's ranch and Cornelius had some way of figuring out the general vicinity where Harvey should dig? Wasn't that worth baiting Cornelius a little with the promise of another ghost and taking him on a mini-road trip out to Harvey's ranch?

No, that was just too desperate.

True, but could it really hurt to give it a try?

I chewed on my lower lip, torn between my sensibilities and my need for food and shelter for me and mine.

My cell phone rang. *Doc?* I wondered what he'd think about Harvey's request.

I grabbed my cell phone. Nope. The screen displayed Natalie's name. "Hello?"

"Hey, girlfriend, I'm tied up down here in Rapid."

"Were you abducted this time or is it voluntary again?"

Natalie chuckled. "It's voluntary, but not as fun as last time. I'm still dressed."

"Oh, well, maybe next time. Do you need my help?" It would be a good excuse to swing in down at my parents and grab my kids without being obvious about getting them away from my sister.

"No, I'm good. I didn't want you guys to wait for me for supper tonight. I probably won't be home until after eight."

Two things bugged me about that.

First, I didn't like how she was beginning to think of Aunt Zoe's place as home. While I loved Nat, I loved her better when she didn't share my bedroom.

Second, I needed her tonight. There was a viewing at the Mudder Brothers, and she was my ticket in.

I'd just have to figure out some other way to sneak into Mudder Brothers without George thinking I was some kind of nutty funeral-home junkie. "Leftovers will be in the fridge."

"Save me a beer. I'm gonna need it after this shitty day."

She and I both.

I hung up and smiled wide at Aunt Zoe. "You feel like paying your respects to a recently deceased member of the community tonight?"

Her eyes narrowed. "I can't. I have to finish that order for the Denver gallery tonight."

Well, crap.

"Whose funeral?" Aunt Zoe asked, still eagle-eyeing me.

Squirming a little, I tried to remember the name of the guest of honor.

"Are you talking about Elsa Haskell's viewing?" Harvey asked.

That was it. "Yes!" I said with too much excitement. I tried to frown a little and do my best sad-faced impression, but going by the pinch of Aunt Zoe's lips, she wasn't buying my act.

"How did you know Elsa Haskell?" Aunt Zoe was digging her claws in; I could feel them. Shit.

Aunt Zoe didn't know anything about my obsession with George Mudder and Ray. If she did, she would chew my ass up one cheek and down the other like it was an ear of corn.

I pushed away from the table and carried my empty lemonade glass to the sink so I could hide my tell-tale, twitchy nose. "Elsa was a friend of Jane's. I'm going out of support for my boss."

"You're attending a viewing in order to further your career?" she asked.

If my catching Ray in the act of a crime could get his chauvinistic ass fired, then yes, I was. "Maybe."

Harvey snorted. "Elsa would have liked your spunk. She was into burning her bras and wearing short skirts long before it was the hip thing to do."

"You knew her?" I asked.

"Sure. She was a ways ahead of me in school, but I used to try to peek up her skirt when she was shaking her pompons at the high school football games. Her sweaters were like a second layer of skin."

Aunt Zoe chuckled. "That never changed. I ran into her last month in the Piggly Wiggly. She'd left the price tag on her bra, and I could see the shape of it through her way-too-tight shirt."

I crossed my arms over my own too-snug dress and stared at the president of the peanut gallery. Harvey by my side at a viewing? That just might work. He was well-known around town, so there'd be no question as to why I was there. And if I needed a distraction, a dirty old man with a trick hip who still liked to look up women's skirts would fit the bill.

"Harvey, how do you feel about going to Elsa's viewing with me tonight?"

He hesitated, then slapped the table. "What the hell? Elsa's daughter owns that little bakery in Central City. Maybe she'll bring some of her mama's favorite doughnuts to share."

I pointed at his faded jeans. "You don't happen to have a nice shirt and pair of pants stashed somewhere around town, do you? Like at Cooper's?"

"Or next door at Miss Geary's," Aunt Zoe said.

Her neighbor was one of Harvey's on- and off-again girlfriends. At least once a week, his Ford pickup sat in her drive overnight.

"It's your lucky day, girly-girl. One of my old flames keeps her dead husband's suits hanging in her spare closet, and wouldn't you know, I'm his exact size."

No shit. "What are the chances?"

That his old flame still mourned her husband so much made my throat burn a little in sympathy.

Harvey's eyes twinkled. "Pretty damned good. She's a picky woman."

"You mean she likes her boyfriends to be built the same as her husband?"

"Yep. Saves her from adjusting the inseam."

My heart twanged. Blue stories like this made me determined not to fall in love. There was too much to lose. I already had my hands and heart full with my two kids. "That's so sad."

"Sad? What are you talking about?" His eyebrows were all scrunched up again.

"Your old flame's undying love for her dead husband."

He snorted. "You have the story all wrong. He was a cheatin' asshole. She likes me to dress up like him so she can spank me for being a bad boy."

"Blahhh!" I plugged my ears too late.

Aunt Zoe covered her eyes and shook her head.

Maybe going to the viewing with Harvey tonight wasn't such a great idea after all.

Chapter Six

My day had begun with a visit to Mudder Brothers Funeral Parlor to view a dead body, so ending it with a return to the century-old, two-story renovated house and its massive front gable seemed fitting.

Same place, different dead body.

I really needed to get a life.

It was Friday night, for crap-sake. I should be spending my time staring into Doc's eyes, a bottle of Merlot and a thick T-bone steak separating us, clothing optional.

Instead, here I was leaning against one of Mudder Brothers huge neoclassical front-porch columns, watching the sun set behind the hills while I waited for Old Man Harvey to show up in his Sunday best … or rather some fancy duds belonging to an S&M-loving widow's dead hubby.

Jeesh. With friends like Harvey, who needed television?

I'd insisted Harvey take the Picklemobile without me to go get his suit. Knowing what I did about the widow's extra-curricular activities, there was no way I'd be able to look her in the eye without my cheeks flaming.

After Aunt Zoe had dropped me off at Mudder Brothers, I'd tried to scope out the parking lot behind Doc's office from my porch viewpoint, searching for a certain red-headed Realtor's black Jeep parked in the vicinity of Doc's Camaro. But there were too many pickups and RVs in the lot to see much in the twilight. I squelched the temptation to race over there and search the lot one vehicle at a time. My jealousy hadn't reached the temporarily insane level … yet.

Once again, I reminded the silly, needy teenage girl in my head that there was more to life than Doc Nyce. Things such as dead bodies and their missing parts.

I picked at some loose paint on the column. Dang it, where was Harvey? The clock was ticking and I wanted to get in and out of Mudder Brothers while the place was filled with other people who'd distract George from my presence.

I pulled out my cell phone and checked the time again. Frowning at the screen, I debated about calling Doc, going so far as to pull up his number. Was he with Tiffany? Were they out to dinner as she'd mentioned in their earlier call?

A knot of jealousy coiled in my stomach, taking my breath away. Damn it.

Life was so much easier without men and sex. But lonelier. Not as colorful. I thought of Doc's mouth and a thrill raced over my skin. Or as exciting.

I typed a text message: *Hi.*

Before I could chicken out, I hit the Send button.

Then I waited, tapping my phone against my hip. Would he reply? Could he? Or were his hands full at the moment … full of Tiffany's perky breasts?

"Stop it!" I chided my inner green ogre, growling under my breath in frustration.

An ancient, ocean-liner-sized Lincoln pulled into the empty handicap spot in front of me. Two gray-haired heads bobbed just above the dash's surface. Who was captaining the Titanic? Would they recognize me from my realty signs or business cards stapled to corkboards around town?

I moved to the other side of the column, hiding from view. I didn't need any questions about how I had known Mrs. Haskell, not without Harvey at my side to back me up.

My phone vibrated. With my heart halfway up my esophagus, I looked at the screen. *Hi back.*

What's new? I typed.

You texting me. You usually call. What's up?

Nothing. Thinking about U—with Tiffany, I didn't type.— *Where R U?*

Was he alone?

In my office. Where are you?

I looked around, trying to come up with an answer other than the truth. While I'd promised to start telling Doc more about my comings and goings, sharing the fact that I was standing outside of Mudder Brothers about to go snooping in George's home-away-from-home, shouldn't be done in a text message.

The little old ladies disembarked. Their whole knitting club would fit in the Lincoln.

I'm w/Harvey, I texted back. That was kind of true, since I'd be with him shortly. *U R working late.*

I added *R U alone?* on another line, and then deleted it.

Have a lot to do. Where are you and Harvey?

Harvey's doing fine. I skirted his question.

Violet, what's going on?

Nothing. Can't I just say Hi?

You never just say Hi. Where are you two?

I blew out a breath. If I told him, he might walk over here. As much as I wanted to see him right then, I had a mission, and Doc would get in the way.

I typed, *Hanging out.*

I could hear the Picklemobile's exhaust pipe coming closer from a couple of blocks away.

Your nose is twitching, Doc wrote.

U can't see me from there.

Come closer. Within reach. Bring your boots.

My shiver had nothing to do with the cool evening air. He must be alone. He wouldn't be texting this much if Tiffany was sitting there, would he? I sighed. *Can't tonight. Got company.*

Tell her.

My gut twisted in a whole new knot just thinking about hurting Natalie with the truth about Doc and me.

But he was right. This game had gone on long enough. I wanted to stop worrying about who was watching when I tackled Doc and slobbered all over him.

The Picklemobile pulled into Mudder Brothers parking

lot.

Gotta go, I texted, listening to Harvey drive around the side of the building.

Stay out of trouble, Violet.

Always.

Right.

My flares of jealousy doused, I shoved my phone back in my purse and peeked around the column at the two older ladies, who had made it to the top of the porch ramp. The backfiring boom of Harvey's exhaust surprised a *yip* out of the older, more rotund of the two, her walker jerking in her hands.

The younger one leaned over and said in a loud voice, "Did you hear that gunshot, Norma Jean?"

Norma Jean nodded with a grunt. "I hope the sheriff got the bastard."

I blinked, scratching my head. Had I heard her right?

Norma Jean's walker creaked past me. "We'd better stop by the powder room, Lucille. That shot just about scared the piss out of me."

Cackles of laughter followed the two women into the funeral parlor.

The door had no sooner shut behind them when Harvey rounded the corner of the building, a walking cane in hand.

At the site of him, I nearly fell off the porch. "What in the hell is that?"

"What? Is this damned thing crooked again?" Harvey straightened his black bow tie. "Or are you talkin' about my fancy walking stick?"

I pointed at his yellow plaid leisure suit jacket, my jaw still hanging down to my belly button. "You look like a canary wrapped in a wire fence."

He tugged on the too-short sleeves. "It's a little short in the arms and the crotch. I'm built a bit long for this suit, if you know what I mean." He waggled his bushy eyebrows.

I'd need a plunger to remove that visual from my brain.

"Harvey, I said you needed to blend in. The only place you'd fit in wearing that suit is at a clown convention."

I caught a whiff of strawberries in the air. Lucille or Norma Jean must have left a trail of perfume in their wake.

"You're one to talk about blendin' in with that hair of yours," Harvey said, pointing at my head.

I patted my coiffed and tucked-in curls. "What's wrong with my hair?"

"Besides, all of the other suits were at the cleaners," he said, obviously ignoring my question. His gold teeth appeared behind his wide smile. "We've been experimenting with some homemade edible love goops lately and things got a bit messier than usual."

"Oh, dear God."

"They taste purty good, but the Lovin' Lava jelly really burns my—"

"Gahhh!" I shouted, holding my hand out for him to stop.

"Burns my *fingers*," Harvey finished, his grin now smug. "Coop was right, you have a gutter mind."

Coop? "I have the gutter mind? Why were you two talking about my mind?"

Harvey shrugged, looking at the parking lot, avoiding my squint. "No reason. Just shootin' the breeze."

"Your pants are on fire."

"I know. This polyester doesn't allow my twig and berries to get much air. Now, are we going to this viewing or what, girl?" He lifted his cane and tapped me on the calf. "At this rate, I'll be the one in the coffin."

"What's with the cane?" I asked, leading the way across the porch.

"It makes me look more debonair."

The big canary needed more than a cane to pull that off, I thought. But I held my tongue … and the door.

A blast of cold air greeted us in the front foyer. One thing I'd learned after attending multiple viewings over the last few weeks was that George Mudder liked to keep his visitors chilled, whether they were alive or dead. I pulled my black shawl around my bare shoulders.

The scent of lilies perfumed the room, thanks to two huge bouquets of the fragrant flowers standing guard in front of the open French doors leading into the parlor. I hesitated outside the parlor, listening to the organ music piping through a speaker in the ceiling.

"Is that *Mammas Don't Let Your Babies Grow Up to Be Cowboys*?" I whispered to Harvey. I hadn't heard a funeral-ized version of the song before now, only jazzed up elevator stuff. This had organ riffs in place of a saxophone. Another Eddie Mudder special.

He nodded. "Elsa Haskell was a big Willie Nelson fan."

I stepped aside to allow Harvey to lead the way. He grabbed a seat at the back of the room. He'd read my mind. I dropped into a chair next to him, staring into the mirrored one-way glass lining the wall on my right, trying to see through it.

A couple of weeks ago, I'd been in the room on the other

side of that glass, sniffing around, searching for evidence of body-part trafficking, hiding from Eddie Mudder in a crate. All of the usual stuff a person would do in a funeral home.

Tonight, I wanted to sneak back in there to make sure nothing had changed, as in no body parts were chilling on ice, awaiting transportation to some black market set up in a back alley down in Rapid.

"I still have a bone to pick with you," Harvey's volume blended in with the low murmur of conversation that rippled throughout the room.

I picked up a whiff of strawberries again and searched the room for Norma Jean and Lucille, not seeing their curl-covered gray heads.

At the front of the parlor, a tripod holding a heart-shaped wreath of orchids, roses, and some purple flower tipped over and fell onto the end of the casket. A wave of gasps rippled through the parlor. A moment of silence held for a count of three, and then a child began to wail.

George Mudder stepped out of the doorway from the hidden room and picked up the tripod and flowers. A young, platinum blonde mother snatched up her child, scolding the bawling boy all of the way up the aisle and out the French doors. I empathized, having dragged my kids out of many a room and restaurant while dodging stares.

George righted everything and smiled at the handful of people sitting in the front row. I could see his tiny yellow teeth and grimaced at the memory of the close-up I'd had upon our first meeting. He walked over and closed the door to the room behind the glass, then sat down next to a petite woman, who was wrapped in black from head to toe.

Had George seen me trying to stare through the glass? What was he doing back there?

Harvey leaned toward me and said, "Why are we here?"

My eyes still on George, I answered with the obvious. "For Elsa Haskell's viewing."

"Don't try to sell me any cow patties. I own the ranch."

I focused on him. "What?"

"You didn't even know Elsa."

"Jane did." At least I assumed that was true since Jane had had a business in town for well over a decade.

"That may be so, but if you're here only on your boss's behalf, then I'm as green as a shavetail in the sack."

Again, "What?"

"You're up to something and knowin' you, it starts with 'no good' and ends with 'trouble'."

I hesitated. To tell or not to tell, that was the question. Natalie was the only one who knew about my Ray-and-the-Mudder-Brothers conspiracy theory. If I told Harvey, would he laugh at me? Well, besides for the reasons he usually did. Would he believe me or think I needed an examination from the neck up, like Natalie did.

"Cough it up, girl. Don't make me hang you up by your ankles and whack it out of you."

Here went nothing. I looked around to make sure George and Eddie, or anyone else for that matter, wouldn't hear me. "Okay, but you need to swear that you won't say anything about this to Aunt Zoe."

"I swear every damned day."

"You know what I mean. Swear you won't tell her."

"Fine, I swear."

"Or Doc." There were no ghosts involved, and he'd made it clear earlier that he agreed with Cooper about my "big" nose, so the less he knew at the moment, the better.

"Or Doc. Shit-criminy, girl. What now? Should we cut our thumbs and share blood over it?"

"Back in July, I saw George Mudder and Ray carry a crate out the back doors of the funeral parlor and load it into Ray's SUV. Whatever was in it weighed down the back springs."

I paused to read Harvey's expression. His eyebrows were still smooth, his eyes only slightly narrowed. No scoffs yet.

"Later, when I asked Ray what was in the crate, he got all snarly and surly and told me to mind my own business. Only he didn't say it quite so nicely, and he threw in a threat for emphasis."

I sat back and let that settle in with Harvey.

His head cocked to the side. "So, just to be clear, I'm sitting here as hot as a whorehouse on nickel night in this damned canary suit because you saw an asshole carrying a crate around in his truck?"

"It's an SUV. And there's a little more to it than that." I leaned in closer, picking up the scent of strawberries again. "Why do I keep smelling strawberries?"

"I think we got a couple of drops of strawberry love goop on this jacket last time I was over."

Eww! I pulled back, my nose wrinkled. "Oh, my God."

He rolled his eyes. "Don't get yourself in a snit. We were just taste testing. Now get a wiggle on and wrap this up. My skivvies are getting sweaty."

Grimacing, I lowered my voice and leaned in again, trying to ignore the strawberry odor and thoughts of Harvey's sweaty boxers. "Natalie and I came here two weeks ago for a viewing and I snuck in the room behind this wall of one-way glass."

He glanced at the glass, then back at me. "I've always wondered what's back there. Figured it was some kind of private mournin' room for immediate family."

"It is, but it's also a storage room. When I was in there, there were two crates that looked exactly like the one George and Ray had loaded into his SUV."

"What was inside of them?"

"Nothing. Both were empty—well, except one had a little cooler in it with a biohazard sticker on its side." At his raised brows, I added, "The cooler was empty."

"Is that all you got?"

"Not quite. Earlier today, Ray was talking to George on the phone and said something about somebody tailing him. Ray told George he hid the goods from the tail, but thought his follower seemed to know where he was going the whole time."

Harvey's forehead creased. "Why am I sitting here in this canary suit, Violet?"

"I just told you."

"No, you just gave me some cockamamie story about Ray, a couple of crates, and George, which was mostly full of hot air and guesswork. Lay it out in one sentence, girl. Why are we here?"

"I think George is paying Ray to haul crates of illegal stuff somewhere."

"Illegal stuff?"

I glanced around again, then whispered in Harvey's ear. "Body parts to sell on the black market."

Harvey stared at me for several seconds, his face scrunched. "Just what do you think you're going to find here tonight? A receipt for goods sold?"

That would be nice and easy, but my life didn't roll that way. "A clue. Something that tells me I'm on to something." Something that I could use to catch Ray red-handed and knock him off his high-and-mighty perch.

"What do you want me to do?"

"Distract George long enough for me to get into that room and see if both crates are still there." I nudged my head at the one-way glass. "I want to find out if Ray was talking about hauling one of those crates around in that conversation I overheard earlier."

He sniffed, straightening his bow tie again. "A distraction, huh?"

"Yes." I shot him an extra-wide smile, willing him through my teeth to say he'd help me.

"You could scare little kids with that face," Harvey said, echoing something Doc had said over a week ago about my attempt at a convincing smile.

I dropped the smile and scowled instead. "Are you going to help me or what?"

Harvey tapped the cane on his shoe. "You really think Ray

and George are up to something fishy, huh?"

"Yes."

"Feel it clear down in your belly?"

"To my toes."

"This isn't about some fight you and that horse's ass you work with are having?"

Yes. Sort of. "No."

He squinted at my nose. "Don't lie to me, missy."

"Fine! It has a little something to do with taking Ray down a notch, too. Now are you in or not?"

He grinned. "Just try to keep me out of it. Besides, as your bodyguard, it's my duty."

I patted his leg. "Thank you."

"But you need to give me a swearin' of your own."

"What do you mean?"

"Promise me that if things start to get a little kooky, you'll tell Coop about all of this."

Cooper? No way. He'd throw me in jail. Harvey was staring at my nose, so I couldn't outright lie. "I'll definitely consider going to the cops if things start getting hot."

"That didn't sound like the same thing I said."

"It was."

"If you don't, I'll tell your aunt."

"Okay, okay. I'll contact Cooper, I promise." Harvey couldn't see my fingers crossed behind my back.

"Good." Harvey looked at the front of the room where George stood with several mourners, obviously consoling. "You ready?"

He didn't wait for me to answer, just grunted as he stood. "One distraction coming up."

I grabbed my purse and waited, hovering at the back of the room as he hitched his way up front. I watched with bated breath as he bent over the casket, glanced to his left and right, then reached inside. In a flash, his hand was back out.

The old buzzard moved lightning fast, which explained his "mongoose" nickname over at the senior center.

Stepping back, Harvey pointed down at Elsa Haskell. "George," he spoke loud and clear across the low hum of conversation. "We got us a problem here."

While all heads swiveled in his direction, I slipped out to the foyer just as the bathroom door creaked open. I grabbed a brochure from the side table holding the lilies and buried my nose in the piece of paper. Slowly, I sidestepped behind the long green leaves, hiding as much as possible.

A steady squeak-squeak-squeak drew closer. I peeked through the bouquet and saw Norma Jean making her way toward the parlor entrance; Lucille followed in her wake.

Holy horny toads. Had they been in the bathroom all of this time? What were they doing in there? Painting it?

Neither seemed to have noticed my presence yet. I silently urged them to hurry it up before someone else joined us in the foyer and screwed up my chance at alone time with two big crates.

Both women paused on the threshold. I held my breath, waiting for one of them to peer through the flowers and see me.

"Lucille," Norma Jean whispered loud enough for me to hear from my foliage hideout. She leaned over her walker and adjusted her glasses. "Is that Willis Harvey up front by Elsa?"

"Well, pinch my pooch, I believe it is," Lucille said. "I barely recognize him with his clothes on."

What?! I did a double take. Was Lucille one of Harvey's women? She was about his age, which was about ten years older than he usually preferred his partners.

"What on God's green earth is he wearing?" Norma Jean asked.

"I don't know, but he looks sharp with his hair combed."

Norma Jean harrumphed. "You mean with the mud washed out of his hair."

"He's been looking younger lately. You think it's all of that mud he's been wrestling in?"

"More like something to do with all of those young girls

he's dallying with."

"I wouldn't mind doing a little leg wrestling with him again, but I hear he's been hanging out at Beatrice Geary's a lot lately."

Norma Jean gave another harrumph. "The girls at the center said something about him spending a lot of time with that curly-haired blonde who works at Calamity Jane Realty. The one they say can talk with ghosts."

My face warmed. Damn. Hanging around with Cornelius was going to cement this silly rumor even more firmly in everyone's heads.

"You think she's Willis' new girl?" Lucille asked.

"Or his nephew's. You know, the bossy cop. I'd like to take that boy by the ear some days."

Cooper and me? No way. I like my men rough and tough, but I draw the line at rabid grizzlies high on PCP.

Norma Jean continued, "Us girls have a bet going."

"What's the bet?"

I leaned into the plant more, a leaf tickling my earlobe.

"Come on, my feet are achin' standing here," Norma Jean said. "I'll tell you after we sit down."

The walker squeaked away with Norma Jean at the helm.

I almost followed them in to find out what exactly was being said about Harvey, Cooper, and me. But I was pretty sure it wasn't going to make me feel like sunshine and lollipops, so I returned to the task at hand—finding body parts, or the lack of them. Or something like that.

I glanced around again—not a soul in sight. Giddy up.

Dropping the brochure, I darted over to two nondescript doors on the far side of the room. I grabbed the door knob on the left door and turned it. It was unlocked.

Glancing at the door to my right, I hesitated. I knew from some past nosing around that behind door number two was a storage closet lined with shelves full of oversized leather-bound death records. Would George keep notes if he was shipping body parts? If so, slipping them in amongst a century or more of death records would be a great hiding place.

The sound of a toilet flushing nearby spurred me to action. I slipped inside the storage-viewing room, inching the door closed behind me, and locked it.

It took my eyes a few seconds to adjust to the semi-gloom. The room smelled unused, musty, tinged with a hint of cardboard. The one-way glass allowed a dull glow into the room, giving me just enough light to get into trouble.

The room held several rows of empty chairs facing the parlor in a silent, private vigil. The chairs had been there last time I was in here, too. Either Elsa's family wanted to sit in here away from community eyes during tomorrow's funeral, or George preferred to leave the chairs set up indefinitely.

I turned to the other side of the room—the storage half. Lining the wall were shelves, laden with Kleenex boxes, vases of all shapes, stacks of folded linens, wreath-supporting tripods, and anything else beloved family members might need in their hours of grief.

I found myself humming *On the Road Again* by Willie Nelson under my breath and realized Eddie's damned kooky organ music was the source of my inspiration. The chords were partially muted on this side of the glass.

The last time I was in here, two big wooden crates had been stacked end-to-end against the far wall, next to a fancy-looking rack of stereo equipment. I'd lifted the lids off with little force. Today, the stereo equipment was still there, the equalizer lights going up and down, but one of the crates was missing.

I walked over to the remaining crate, which sat in the spot of the one I'd hidden in last time when Eddie had come into the room to adjust the sound system. Today, the lid wasn't loose, though. It was padlocked shut. To add to my curiosity, it was nailed closed.

What was in that crate? I tried to lift one end of the crate, grunting in effort. It barely budged. I leaned into it and shoved, but it only gave a centimeter or two.

What was in the crate?

I squatted next to it and sniffed the wood. No rank of rotting flesh or formaldehyde, just the scent of sawdust.

I pressed my ear against the scratchy boards, my hair snagging on some of the splinters and listened. I wasn't sure what I expected to hear—breathing, sniffing, huffing and puffing? There was only silence.

Raising my fist, I used the old ripe-melon test to try to determine how full it was. I knocked three times, listening to the depth of the thuds.

Something knocked back.

I yelped and fell back on my butt, scrambling away from the crate. My heart pinged in my chest like a pinball caught between bunkers.

Clunk clunk. The knocking came again … from the door to the room, the one through which I'd entered.

Not from the crate.

I smacked my forehead, feeling like the biggest numskull this side of the Mississippi. Pushing to my feet, I tiptoed toward the door with my heart now thundering for a whole different reason.

Who was on the other side of the door?

Through the one-way glass, I could see George and Harvey still standing near the casket. Harvey talked with his hands in a chopping motion; George with calming, open palms spread wide.

There was no sign of Eddie, who was probably down in the basement wearing his rubber apron. Just the thought of the black-warted dead guy I'd seen this morning tickled my gag reflex.

Three knocks sounded, faster, more intense.

Easing up to the door, I listened, hearing nothing but my own quick, shallow breaths. A shift in the thin slice of light coming from underneath the door caught my eye.

I dropped to my hands and knees and peeked underneath the door. An eyeball stared back at me.

Chapter Seven

For the second time within minutes, I almost swallowed my tongue. I scurried backwards, gurgling in fear as a scream bubbled up.

"Vi, it's me," a voice I now heard morning, noon, and night whispered through the crack. "Let me in before somebody sees me."

Natalie!

Lunging upright, I unlocked the door and dragged her inside by the arm. After a peek behind her to make sure nobody was watching, I shut the door and locked it again. I leaned against the wood, needing a moment to convince my tongue to stop clinging to my tonsils for dear life.

"Whoa, take 'er easy there, pilgrim," Natalie said, impersonating John Wayne, her gray gauzy skirt swishing as she tried to imitate his swagger.

Taking a deep breath, I said, "Your tone is all off. You really need to stop such blasphemy of the Duke." I pushed away from the door. "What are you doing here?"

"Me?" She laughed too loud for my comfort.

I shushed her as I passed. She smelled like the underside of a car hood.

"Okay, I get it, the old top-secret agent game," she whispered, following me with a dull, rhythmic *thump* thanks to the medical boot encasing her lower right leg. "But I should be asking you what you're doing in here, not the other way around."

"How did you find me? And why do you smell like you've been bellying-up to a crank shaft."

I heard her sniff. "It's carburetor cleaner. My cousin

Ronnie is in town—you remember Claire's older sister, right?"

I remembered Veronica all too well. She always used to steal the tin can away during our neighborhood Kick-the-Can game as a show of older-sister dominance. "Mom mentioned she was back," I answered. "She also told me about Veronica's sleazy ex-husband."

"Yeah, I hope the jerk's dick falls off while he rots in that kid-gloves-version of a prison they put him in. Anyway, Ronnie had some engine troubles at the mall. I tinkered around under her hood for a bit."

"When did you learn how to fix engines?"

"I didn't. We had to call a tow truck. When I dropped Ronnie off at my aunt's place, I saw your sister sunbathing next to your parents' pool."

"The bitch is back."

"Yeah, that's what I thought, too. I took the liberty of rescuing your kids from her wickedness and dropped them off at your aunt's. Hope you're okay with that."

"Oh, hell yes. You saved me having to snarl and growl at Susan in person." I just hoped Aunt Zoe was okay with my two kids there while she worked in her workshop.

"Zoe told me Harvey and you were at Mrs. Haskell's viewing, so I changed clothes and zipped down here."

That explained her *eau de* carburetor.

"When I saw Harvey out there harassing George," Natalie continued, "and you weren't hiding in the john, I figured you were either in here or in the basement. Knowing what Eddie does in the basement, I decided to try my luck here first."

"Did you see Eddie anywhere?" I stopped short and peered through the wall of glass windows, my armpits sweaty at just the thought of him coming in this room again while I was sniffing in corners and crates.

"No, but his fancy new Silverado pickup is parked out back, so he's around." Natalie leaned her hip against the crate. "Is this one of the crates you told me about last time?"

"Yeah." I joined her.

She tugged on the lid. "It wasn't locked up like this before, right?"

"Right." I moved to one end and nodded toward the opposite. "See if you can help me move it."

"To where? We can't exactly sneak this out through the foyer under our skirts."

"I just want to see how heavy it is and if anything shifts when we lift it."

Natalie rounded the other end. "I can't put much weight on my bad leg, you know."

"So, lift with your good leg, silly." I wrapped my fingers around the top edge. "Ready? One, two, lift."

Natalie grunted. I strained. We were able to get just a fraction of ground clearance before we had to set it down again.

"Christ," Natalie wiped her hands on her skirt. "What in the hell is in this? A buffalo?"

"That's the million dollar question."

I tiptoed over to the door that opened into the parlor and ran my fingers along the jam, finding several indents midway down. Upon returning to where Natalie now sat on the crate, I told her, "They bring them in and out through the parlor door. It's a tight squeeze."

"Excellent deduction, Nancy Drew. Didn't you say there was a cooler in the crate you hid in last time?"

"Yes, it had a biohazard sticker."

She tapped on the lid. "Is this the same crate?"

"I'm not sure. It looks the same, but I was a little distracted when I was here last time." I inspected all three sides of the crate for any tell-tale markings. "You think there's a body in here?"

"I doubt it or we'd smell it."

"Not if they sealed it tightly in a plastic tub."

Natalie frowned at me. "That's twisted. You've seen that movie *Phantasm* too many times."

"Maybe the Mudders have, too."

"Next, you'll be telling me you saw the 'tall man' digging up graves on Mount Moriah."

I shivered just thinking about that creepy film.

"Short of coming back here with a crowbar or some x-ray glasses," Natalie hopped down from the crate, landing on her good foot, "there's no way to tell what's in this thing."

"Is your toolbox in your truck?"

She cocked her head. "Vi, we're not—" her eyes flicked behind me. "Cooper's here."

I spun around and watched, my breath locked up tight in my chest.

Detective Cooper strode toward the front of the parlor and sidled up next to his uncle. He leaned down and said something in Harvey's ear, then he turned and glared at me through the one-way glass.

I gasped. Blood roared in my ears like a jet engine. I took a step back and grabbed Nat's arm, lugging her toward the door. "Cooper knows we're in here."

"How? He can't see us," she said, thumping behind me.

"I don't know. Maybe he wears special police-force contacts. Or he's not human. We need to get out of here before he catches us spying."

At the door, I shot a glance back through the glass. Cooper was hemmed in, Norma Jean and Lucille had him blocked as they made their way side-by-side toward the casket. He stared into the glass again, squinting.

I opened the door a crack and peered out, almost expecting to see Cooper looming there. The foyer stood empty. "Let's go."

We slipped into the foyer and raced to the front door as fast as Natalie's boot would allow, not slowing until we'd crawled into her pickup, slammed the doors, and locked them for good measure.

Natalie checked the rearview mirror. "Here he comes." I yanked her down out of sight.

We ducked there in silence for a couple of seconds, then

she giggled and said, "Got ya."

I glared at her. "You big brat." I sat up, twisting in the seat to check on the front doors. Both were closed, no Cooper in sight.

"I'm sorry, Vi. But you should have seen the freaked out look on your face when your tractor beam locked onto Cooper back there. I thought your eyes were going to pop right out of your skull."

I pinched her upper arm. "Shut it, be-otch."

"Hey, ouch!" she rubbed her arm. "What's your deal with Cooper, anyway? He's just a cop, you know. He cleans his guns the same as the rest of us."

I fanned my dress at chest level. "He makes me sweaty."

"Really?" Natalie's gaze narrowed. "Do you think he's hot?"

I frowned. Only in a branding-my-ass sort of way. "I meant sweaty from nervousness."

She rolled her eyes. "I know you did. Let me rephrase my question—would you sleep with him given the right circumstances? If you were the last two people on Earth."

"Can I dress him up like Elvis and slather him in chocolate and caramel first?"

"Cute. Answer the question."

"No. He's not my type." Under her steady squint, I shrugged. "But I suppose many women would find him sexy." Mona, my coworker sure did. The woman practically steamed up the windows whenever Cooper walked into the office.

"You know," Natalie said, "I think he's exactly your type. You always go for the rugged, tough guys."

"Yeah, but when you ask Cooper if that's a gun in his pocket or if he's happy to see you, it's really a gun." Unlike Doc, who was just happy to see me.

Natalie laughed. "Come on, Cooper's not that bad."

"Then why haven't you ever dated him?"

"Who says I haven't?" She winked.

After thirty-five years of living in the same town, Natalie

had dated most of the single guys in Deadwood—twice. "You'd have told me by now if you had. So, what's the deal?"

She sniffed and looked away. "He's not interested."

"Right." A guy would have to be a eunuch not to find Natalie's hips and lips at least a little bit sexy.

"I'm serious. About five years ago, I was playing pool with him at the Purple Door Saloon, flirting here and there. When I asked him if he wanted to go somewhere a little quieter for another drink, he told me he didn't get involved with 'local citizens.'" She made the quote signs in the air at those last words. "Then he hung up his pool stick and left without a backwards glance. Ever since then, I've kept my distance, and he's been as cold as Terry Peak in January."

"Maybe he doesn't like women."

"Oh, he definitely does. A while after that night, I saw him in a bar down in Rapid getting hot and heavy with this curvy blonde. There was no way she was just reaching for his gun."

"Really?" I had trouble picturing Cooper doing anything with his mouth besides chewing glass.

"Yeah, but I haven't seen him get excited about a woman since then. Although, he certainly keeps his eye on you when you're in the room."

"You mean his stink eye."

"I'm serious." Her eyes narrowed. "You're blonde and curvy."

"Cut the chatter about my curves."

"I bet he likes you."

I leaned back against the door, my palms out to ward off her crazy talk. "Trust me, that man does not like me. In fact, he seems to maintain a steady pissed-off state whenever I'm around."

"That's because he wants you."

"Shut up."

"It makes total sense, all of that bristling and glaring. He's got it bad for you."

Cooper? The glares? The growls? "No, that isn't desire, it's irritation with a healthy dose of rage peppered into the mix."

"And you think he's sexy." Natalie appeared to have hearing problems tonight.

"I didn't say that."

"Yes, you did."

No, Doc was sexy as hell in a dark and dangerous way. Cooper was just dangerous. "I said some women may find him sexy, not me. He's way too bossy for my taste, and his constant scowl turns me off."

She pointed at something over my shoulder. "You mean that one."

I turned and jerked back at the sight of Cooper's scowling face in my window. Harvey's bearded mug leaned into view next to Cooper's shoulder.

Shit! Shit! Shit!

"Unlock this now," Cooper ordered through the glass.

As soon as I obeyed, he hauled open my door. His broad shoulders blocked my escape route. "Violet Parker, you're under arrest."

All of my internal organs froze as a cold blast of panic howled through me.

Had he found out I had withheld evidence in the Carhart case? Who had told him about the demon cult book? Doc and Wanda Carhart were the only two around who knew about it.

Or had someone linked me to the dead guy in Mudder Brothers basement?

"What for?" I croaked out through ice-coated vocal chords. Jail was not a good option for me. I had kids and a job and a reputation that was about to get a lot worse.

"Creating a public nuisance."

"What?"

"He means me," Harvey explained, and grinned wide enough to show both gold teeth.

"What did he do?" I asked. Okay, dumb question. "You

can't arrest me for that."

A muscle in Cooper's jaw ticked. He took a step back, holding the door wide. "Get out of the pickup right now."

I climbed down, straightened my dress, and faced Cooper.

In my peripheral vision, I noticed a familiar pair of blue-haired babes standing next to their Lincoln cruise ship, both gaping at the show. Norma Jean would have plenty to gab about with her poker buds at the senior center now. I could practically hear my reputation being ripped to shreds.

"Explain your presence here tonight," Cooper demanded, his hands on his hips, his shoulder holster and pistol butt visible.

"Why are you packing heat at a funeral?" I tried to steer Cooper off course.

"He always packs heat," Harvey said. "He even sleeps with it under his pillow. One of these days he's going to blow off the Tooth Fairy's fingers when she comes a callin.'"

Cooper's eyes stayed glued to me. "That's none of your business—just answer the question."

There was no budging him, so I fell back on my usual defenses and jutted my chin. "You didn't *ask* me anything. You demanded, as usual."

"She has a point," Natalie said, sidling up next to me, leaning against the bed of her pickup. "You need to be a little nicer to her if you want Vi to warm up to you."

I shot Natalie a squinty-eyed, don't-make-me-stuff-my-socks-in-your-mouth look.

She winked back. "Violet isn't one of those women who likes to be dominated. She's spent too many years being a single mom, reigning over her own empire."

Nat was spot on. My gut reaction to a dominant male was to shoot him in the ass with a tranquilizer dart, and then relocate him to another continent.

"Violet," Cooper warned through clenched molars.

"You'd better cough it up, girl," Harvey said. "Ol' Coop is a regular curly wolf, especially when it comes to taming shrews. He gets that from my side of the family."

Fine, but I was only giving in because of that damned police badge. "I am here for Elsa Haskell's viewing."

"Then why weren't you in there looking at her with everyone else?"

"I had to use the restroom." Did Cooper know about my twitchy nose telltale sign? Was it illegal to lie to a cop? Were different degrees of lying allowed? I wasn't under oath ... yet.

"You were in the bathroom for over fifteen minutes?"

Is that how long I was in that crate room? It seemed longer. "I had ... err ... complications."

Natalie chuckled.

"Really? That's funny. Norma Jean Russell and Lucille James said they didn't see you in the bathroom at all."

They hadn't seen me standing outside the front doors when they arrived either, nor hiding behind the bouquet of lilies, but I wasn't going to brag about my invisibility powers to the fuzz. "That's because I was standing on the toilet."

One blond eyebrow arched. "Do you do that often?"

I shrugged. "When the mood strikes."

"Why didn't you join my uncle when you finished standing on the toilet?"

"I ran into Natalie."

He raised the other eyebrow, but said nothing, apparently waiting for more.

I added. "She had something to show me."

Both eyebrows still waited.

"In her pickup."

He glanced behind me into the cab of the pickup, and then focused on Natalie. "And what was that?"

"Show him your tattoo, Natalie." I crossed my fingers behind my back, willing her to play along like she used to when we were kids and got busted.

"Which one?" she replied without hesitation.

Whew! "The latest."

"The one on my butt or my right boob? I got them on the

same night."

"Really?" Cooper's disbelief curled his upper lip. His gaze dropped below Natalie's chin for a split-second. If I had blinked twice, I'd have missed it.

"Show him both," Harvey chimed in. "Coop, you'd better double check them for authenticity."

"Are you into tattoos now?" Cooper asked Natalie.

"Sure. What can I say? It was one hell of a wild Tupperware party." I could practically hear her grinning. "Those tattoo parlor girls know how to shake, mix, and stack like nobody else."

"Show him the one on your left cheek," I told her, referring to the knife-stabbed heart she'd had tattooed there one very drunken night after walking in on her then boyfriend bare-back riding some floozy wearing tassels. Seriously, who walked around with nipple tassels on? Hiding them under a shirt would be a real trick.

"Just lift up the back of your skirt," I added.

"Raise that skirt an inch and I'll arrest you for indecent exposure," Cooper said, his face a mask of granite. The guys up on Mount Rushmore had nothing on him.

He stepped closer and pointed his finger in my face. "Violet, if I catch you here again, you'd better be sitting in that parlor when I walk in the door."

Yikes! He was dead serious.

Was knocking Ray off his mountain really worth having the town's detective breathing down my neck day and night? Waiting to lock me up? "Or what, you'll arrest me for improper loitering in a funeral parlor?"

Addy would try to sneak me a nail file, only she'd probably use the cardboard kind I kept in my makeup drawer. Layne would burn off his eyebrows again while trying to make me a small bomb to blow a hole in the cell wall.

"I'll have George file a restraining order against you."

My mouth fell open. "You can't do that."

"Yes, I can. It's for your own protection as much as

George's. I don't have enough manpower on the force to keep you out of trouble."

"I was just attending a viewing."

"I highly doubt that. If I dusted for prints, I wonder where I'd find evidence telling me otherwise. Besides the bathroom, of course."

Oh, crap. Fingerprints. I needed to start carrying gloves under the Picklemobile's seat if I was going to keep up this snooping business. Maybe I should just focus on passive aggressive attacks on Ray, like Mona and her spoonful of Benefiber in his orange juice.

Cooper plucked something from my shawl. Then he grabbed my hand and dropped a one-inch sliver of wood into my palm.

The crate.

"Stick to selling real estate, Ms. Parker. I don't want you to be the next one lying on that autopsy table in Eddie's basement." He took a step back. "Come to the station tomorrow afternoon. I need to talk to you in private."

"I have an appointment with another client." I wasn't bullshitting him this time. I had some open-house prepping plans to discuss.

His nostrils flared slightly. "Don't make me use my handcuffs."

Bully! "Fine, I'll stop by."

With a slight head nod at Natalie, he strode away. Norma Jean and Lucille waved at him as he marched by them.

Natalie whistled under her breath, "Damn, that was hot. I can still smell the sexual tension in the air."

I rolled my eyes. "That was not hot, it was irritating as hell." I turned to Harvey. "Has he always been that bossy and pushy?"

"Yup. Ever since he was knee-high to a prairie dog."

"What are you going to do?" Natalie asked. "Are you going to stop nosing into Ray and George's business?"

"Coop ain't bluffing," Harvey said. "He will throw you in

jail if he can figure out a good enough reason why."

I crossed my arms and glared at the detective as he drove off in his unmarked police sedan. "I don't know what to do."

"Well, keep me posted." Harvey squeezed my shoulder. "I need to get this canary suit back to its cage. I'll bring the Picklemobile back before dawn."

I knew better than to ask where he was going when he had that glint in his eye. He headed for the pickup, whistling something happy-go-lucky sounding while he went.

Must be nice to crawl into someone's bed without worrying about who was watching.

"Let's go home," I said to Natalie. I wanted to soak in a cool bath with a steamy romance and fantasize about Doc until all of this Cooper business was just a distant disturbance in my Force.

"Your wish is my command."

We climbed in her pickup and headed out of the parking lot, but she turned right instead of left.

"Home is that way." I pointed up the hill.

"I know, but I want to check on something first."

"What?"

She took another right and drove toward Calamity Jane Realty. "A suspicion I have."

"About what?"

As we neared the office, she slowed.

Doc's front blinds were closed, but the lights were on behind them. Calamity Jane's windows were blind-free and mostly dark, just a single florescent on over Mona's desk so the cops could see in during their nightly drive-bys—and tourists could see me making out with Doc on my desk. The former I'd been told back when Jane hired me, the latter I'd learned from a cheek-warming experience.

Natalie whipped into the parking lot behind the office and cruised along the line of parked cars, old and new. The orange glow of the street lights painted everything in bronze.

"What are we looking for?" Personally, I was searching

for Tiffany's Jeep.

"Hold on."

We passed Doc's Camaro. I tried not to even glance at it in case Natalie was looking my way. She pulled into a parking spot about ten cars down and cut the engine.

"Okay, Nat. What's going on?"

"You spying at Mudder Brothers tonight gave me an idea."

"I wasn't spying."

"Weren't you there hoping to catch a glimpse of Ray and George in the act?"

"Well, yes."

"How is that not spying?"

"Fine, I might have been spying a little. What's your idea?"

"I'm going to spy on Doc."

That didn't sit well in my gut for a multitude of reasons, most of which revolved around me. "I don't think that's a good idea."

Natalie stared out the rearview mirror at Doc's back door. "Why not? I'm not hurting anyone."

"It's an invasion of his privacy."

"You're doing it to Ray and George."

"Yes, but we like Doc." And *we* don't want to get caught by *our* best friend sneaking around Doc's back door. "And he's not committing any crimes."

"Ray might not be, either. Just because he's a huge jackass doesn't mean he's breaking the law with George."

"So, now you're taking Cooper's side?"

"No, I always stand by you, you know that."

Deep down I did, and yet I'd gone and slept with the man on whom she'd staked a claim. My guilt weighed heavy, like a Saint Bernard sitting on my chest.

"I'm just saying," she continued, "that maybe until you have something more solid than just suspicions you should back off from Ray and George. I don't want to be bailing you out of jail again. I will, but your name in the newspaper for trespassing or invasion of privacy won't sit well for your future in realty in this town."

I sighed. "Yeah, I know." The idea of my kids visiting me through a square of Plexiglas with holes in it didn't appeal much, either. "Okay, I'll back down a little."

"That's more like it."

"But only if you back off of Doc."

"Why do you care?"

I met her wrinkled brow head on. "For one thing, he's a friend of mine."

"Fine. Then set me up with him, help me out here. I'm flopping and flailing in front of him."

"You're supposed to be on sabbatical," I reminded her.

Last month, after Natalie's last boyfriend cheated on her and left her pissed and heartbroken—again—she'd sworn off men for a year. That so-called year hadn't even lasted a day before she saw Doc pass by Calamity Jane's front window. Her infatuation for him had grown like a wildfire—fast and uncontrollable. For that matter, so had mine.

"How am I supposed to stay away from men with someone like Doc in town?"

"He's not all that." I lied and turned away from her to stare out my window so she wouldn't see my nose twitching. Stupid tell.

Mudder Brothers Funeral Parlor glowed in the distance, the back doors lit by a nightlight installed over them. "I'm sure he has plenty of faults just like everyone else," I added for good measure.

"Name one."

He's having sex with me. I hesitated, the truth on the tip of my tongue, but dread holding me prisoner. "Sometimes he doesn't shave."

"Which makes him look killer sexy."

Hear, hear!

"Name another," she said.

"He acts really odd at times." Like each time he sniffed a ghost and keeled over in a faint.

"He's mysterious. Next."

"Ummmm." *Tell her. Tell her. Tell her.* "He's not always good about returning phone calls," I added, thinking of how I'd wanted to break every cell phone I could get my hands on when he kept dodging my calls after the first time we'd had sex.

"He's his own man. That's a turn-on. Anything else?"

Yes. "Well, there is something I kind of need to tell you."

The sight of Ray's SUV pulling behind Mudder Brothers and backing up to the double doors under the night light stopped me in my tracks.

"Nat, look," I whispered and slunk down in my seat, even though I doubted Ray could see me in the dark, not even with the orange parking lot light overhead. "It's Ray."

She leaned over my lap and stared out my window. "George is opening the back doors for him."

From our viewpoint, we could see the profile of Ray's vehicle. As we watched the snake glanced around, and then opened the tail end doors of his SUV.

"Ten bucks says there is a crate in the back," Natalie said.

"That's my bet. You can't take my bet."

"You snooze you lose, babe."

Ray climbed into the back of his SUV, the suspension bouncing under his weight. George waited at the tailgate. Together, they hauled out a crate. The missing twin.

"Holy freakin' moly," I said under my breath.

"I win."

"What's in that thing?"

We watched as they hefted it out and lowered it to the ground. George pulled a bar from behind him and leveraged the lid open. I held my breath.

"Can you see what's in it?" Natalie whispered.

"No, it's too dark. We need night vision goggles."

George lifted the lid, stared for a count of five, and then

dropped the lid with a thud that echoed across the grass and parking lot. He staggered over to the back quarter panel of Ray's SUV and buried his face in his hands, shaking his head.

Ray stepped close to George, leaning into his face. He reached behind him and pulled something from his waistband. Something small and pointed.

"Oh, my God! Is that a gun?" Natalie asked.

"It kind of looks like it." I squinted and leaned out the open window, white-knuckling the sill. "But it could also be a big stick of celery."

"Or a knife," Natalie grabbed my forearm. "If he's threatening to hurt George, we need to call Cooper."

"We are not calling Cooper. Not unless we are one hundred percent positive that is a gun or a knife. Not after the warning he just slapped me with."

"Does Ray always lean in like that when he talks?"

"In my experience, only when he's leering or threatening." I watched as Ray and George separated and each grabbed an end of the crate, carrying it through the back doors of the funeral parlor. Where was Eddie?

Natalie sat back as soon as the doors closed behind them. "What now?"

I kept my eyes glued to those back doors. "Let's wait a bit and see if they bring the other crate out."

Ten minutes later, several cars had rumbled past us through the parking lot, but Ray's SUV still sat there, the double doors still closed.

"Maybe we should drive over there," Natalie said. "We might be able to find some evidence in the back of his SUV."

"No way. That's too risky."

"*Bak bak bak,*" she clucked.

"Hey, if Ray catches me and calls Cooper, I'm dead meat. I'll have to be more careful when I snoop now."

"Does that mean your investigation of the Case of the Missing Crate is back on?"

While I pondered that question, Ray came around from

the front of the funeral parlor and climbed into his SUV. Nat and I slunk down in our seats again as his headlights flashed across Nat's pickup.

When we sat back up, she said, "Damn it."

"What?"

"We missed Doc leaving."

Sure enough, Doc's Camaro was gone. Good! "Oh, darn."

She started the engine. "So, what were you going to tell me about Doc before Ray came knockin' round George's back door?"

As much as I wanted to spill my guts about Doc and me, I couldn't say the words. My moment of courage had slipped away.

"Nothing important," I said.

She accepted my answer with a nod, which made my chest constrict with guilt.

"What are you going to do about that crate business?" she asked, shifting into gear.

I stared out the open window at Mudder Brothers Funeral Parlor. "I'm going back in that room."

Chapter Eight

Saturday, August 18th

The Picklemobile sat ticking in the drive the next morning when I stumbled out into the eye-watering sunshine. The keys dangled in the ignition.

The smell of bacon floated my way from Miss Geary's house, making me drool. The uber-healthy granola bars Natalie had brought for breakfast tasted like wood chips, undoubtedly similar to the ones we poured into the bottom of Addy's new gerbil cage last night.

Damn my sister and her so-called "gifts" for my kids. One chicken was already one too many pets for my family. Lucky for me, Aunt Zoe's tolerance for Addy's stray pets rivaled an Appalachian moonshiner's tolerance for hooch.

Shaking my head, I backed out onto the street and shifted into Drive. Sunlight hit the windshield, emphasizing all of the smudges and wiper streaks—and a bare footprint on the glass right under the mirror. *A footprint?* I recoiled.

"Oh, come on!" I yelled in the rearview mirror at Miss Geary's house.

I smacked my palm down on the dash, sending dust swirling. Harvey was getting nooky all over town, including inside his damned old belching truck, and I had to resort to phone sex each night from the bathroom while letting the water run. No freaking fair!

Squirming on the seat, I grimaced at the thought of Harvey's bare butt rubbing on the cracked vinyl bench seat. I tucked the extra folds of my green sundress between my legs and scooted up against the door, cursing the lucky old buzzard under my breath all the way to work.

I didn't even bother stopping in at Calamity Jane's first this morning. Doc's Camaro sitting in the parking lot was invitation enough for me to knock twice on his back door and let myself in before anyone saw me.

"Hello?" I said, peeking in the back room and finding it empty.

"In here," Doc's voice came from the open bathroom doorway.

I leaned against the doorjamb, admiring his reflection in the mirror. His right jaw and neck were covered in shaving cream; the minty scent of the foam filled the small room. His chest and back were bare, his khaki cotton slacks slung low on his hips. A dark green dress shirt hung from a hanger on the wall behind him.

I lowered my tote to the floor, and then clasped my hands together to keep from touching anything. Or rubbing. Or stroking.

When I finally raised my eyes to his, he shot me a lazy grin through the foam. "How's the phone?"

"Not so good. We're going to give it another day to dry out before declaring it officially dead."

"Were you actually in the tub last night?" He scraped the razor down his cheek, leaving a strip of bare skin.

"Yep. Covered in bubbles."

He paused, razor in midair, his dark eyes drifting down the front of my dress. "Completely covered?"

"All except the tips."

He groaned and banged the razor on the lip of the sink. "You know, I have a tub at my place." He made another swipe with the razor. "It's big and white and just waiting to be tried out."

"I require bubbles. Lots of 'em."

His eyes darkened. "So do my fantasies."

The stark hunger in his gaze lit me on fire everywhere south of my forehead. It took me a moment to douse the flames and unpeel my tongue from the roof of my mouth. "Hurry up and finish shaving."

He rinsed the razor and made another couple of swipes. "I have an appointment. He'll be here in fifteen minutes."

"I can be done in five."

His laughter rumbled from deep in his chest, sounding all sexy and inviting. "Once isn't going to cut it after what you teased me with last night." He drew a swath down his neck, leaving just a single thin trail of foam left over his Adam's apple.

I batted my eyelashes. "You liked that little teaser?"

"Liked it? I spent half of the night imagining it, the other half dreaming about it." He scraped away the last stripe and rinsed the blades under the faucet, then splashed his face, reaching for the hand towel to dry the drips from his jaw. "The next time you drop the phone in the water, make sure you finish what you started first."

I was happy to finish right here and now, to hell with best friends, gerbils, haunted hotels, and dirty old men. "You want me to whisper the ending in your ear?"

"Violet." He threw down the towel.

"What?"

"I can't do this."

"What?" I could have won an Oscar for how well I feigned innocence.

He pulled his shirt from the hanger. "I can't touch you for just a few minutes, and then try to converse rationally about retirement plans across my desk."

"Why not?"

"You mess up my ability to add numbers."

That made two of us. "So, wing it. It's only money."

He put on his shirt. "I want more than just your mouth."

"Yeah, but that's such a great place to start."

He stared at my mouth as he buttoned his shirt, then shook his head. "I meant what I said last night."

"About the spurs?"

His lips quirked, but when his eyes locked with mine, the flirting glint faded. "About you hiding things from me. We had a deal."

I leaned my head back against the door and sighed. "Didn't we talk about this enough last night?"

"No. We just got started. Then Natalie needed to use the bathroom, so you pretended I was your dad, and told me how much Layne is obsessed with the Maya since your brother sent him that book on ruins in the Yucatan."

"Oh, right." Lucky Quint and his photojournalism job. I often daydreamed of Quint's life, exploring all around the world with no offspring to tie him to one place, require a diaper change, or need new school clothes. But would that get lonely?

"I swear we talked about Harvey after Natalie left," I said.

I distinctly remembered cursing the dirty bird and his five-gallon bucket mouth—for telling Doc that Cornelius claimed he could talk to ghosts—before I had a chance to decide how much I wanted to share on that particular subject.

"We did."

"See. I knew it."

"But only because I brought up again what he'd told me about your new client."

Man, Doc's teeth were locked onto this Cornelius business with a bear trap grip. "Like I said last night, I was gonna tell you. I just hadn't gotten a chance to yet." I'd been too busy sneaking around Mudder Brothers, and then spying on Doc with Natalie. "It's really not a big deal."

"Your client claims to talk to ghosts in a supposedly haunted hotel. When word about this gets out, which we both know it will in Deadwood, your reputation will take another hit."

"Cornelius likes to grandstand." His Abe Lincoln outfit alone was evidence of that. "He just wants some attention."

"Then he should get a lap dog." Doc buttoned his shirt sleeves. "Tell me more about this guy."

"I told you most everything last night."

"No, you mentioned he was from Vegas and had money, but then Addy had some emergency with her cat and a gerbil, so you had to hang up for a few minutes."

"Right, the gerbil." I scrubbed my hand down my face. "Bogart had nosed into The Duke's cage and got his head stuck inside the exercise wheel. Unfortunately, The Duke was in the midst of exercising and got stuck between the wheel and Bogart's neck. So, all hell broke loose."

"The cat tried to eat the gerbil?"

"No, Bogart's a vegetarian."

One of Doc's eyebrows lifted. "A vegetarian cat?"

"Yeah. Go figure. I told Addy she should have called him Gandhi, but she likes to name her pets after my favorite actors. She thinks I won't make her get rid of them then."

Doc undid his pants. "That explains Elvis, the chicken."

"Bingo." I watched as he tucked his shirt in, resisting the urge to reach inside his pants and help. "Natalie says using the King's name like that is just wrong, but when Addy gets something fixed in her brain, nothing short of electroshock therapy can change her mind."

"That apple fell straight from the tree," he said, zipping up.

I dragged my focus back up to his face. "What's that supposed to mean?"

"You. The Hessler house. The Carhart place. The stubborn way you charge forth despite rational people warning you to stop."

Any notion I'd had about telling him of my adventures with Cooper, Ray, and the Mudder brothers last night evaporated under the weight of his grimace. My nose knew a fishy odor when it rose up, and Ray stunk like a bucket of chum. I didn't need Doc's rationality at this point.

"I'm not 'stubborn.'"

"Oh, really?"

Lifting my chin, I said, "I'm determined."

He grabbed his belt from the towel rack. "Spin it however you want, you and I both know the results of your past sleuthing."

"Yeah, the bad guys lost."

"At the cost of some of your sanity."

I waved him away. "Hell, I lost most of that when my kids popped out."

"Look at yourself, Violet." He pulled me in front of the mirror, standing behind me, his chin level with the top of my head. "You're a mess."

"Hey!" So my hair was spiraling here and there more than usual, and my eyes were a bit raccoon-ish and bloodshot around the edges. I knew many parents who looked like they'd been run over by a herd of buffalo on a daily basis.

"I was rushed in the bathroom thanks to Natalie's extra-long shower." I leaned closer, wiping at some eye shadow that had landed a little off the mark in the chaos that was my morning. "Cut a girl some slack."

"Let me rephrase that." His arms slid around me, pulling me back against him. The heat of his body soaked through my dress, toasting my backside like a marshmallow over a flame. "You're a beautiful, sexy mess and I can't stop thinking about you …" he pulled aside the neckline of my sheer white sweater, baring my shoulder except for a blue spaghetti strap, "naked." His lips caressed my bared skin, sending a barrage of quivers down to my fingertips. "Covered in bubbles."

"If you're trying to charm me out of my clothes after calling me a mess, it's working." I leaned my head back against his chest, watching him in the mirror as he worked his magic on me. "Don't stop."

His hands spanned my hips, pulling me even closer. "Have I told you how much I want you, Boots?"

"Every night." I groaned and moved his hands for him, one north, the other south. "On Aunt Zoe's freaking phone."

"Tell Natalie about us and we can toss the phones."

"I'm working on it."

Doc's mouth reached the crook of my neck and he glanced up in the mirror, catching me peeking as his fingers caressed. "What are you doing, Violet?"

My face flushed at being caught peeping at my own peep show, but I held his stare. "Watching you touch me."

He cupped my breast, stroking with his thumb. "Do you like watching?"

"Touch me some more," I pressed my hips back into him, the fabric a thin barrier between us. "See for yourself."

For a moment, he pushed back, exploring further. Then he sucked in a breath and stepped back, holding his hands up like a dealer about to leave the card table.

"Damn, woman. You make me want to tear your clothes off."

Gripping the edge of the sink, I scowled at him in the mirror. "Prove it."

His lips quirked. "Frustrated?"

I growled. "I'm practically throwing myself at you here."

"And it's incredibly sexy."

"It aches like hell."

"I ache every night after you hang up."

Him, too? Comments like that weren't cooling my jets any. "You could be a gentleman and help a girl out."

He shoved his hands in his front pockets, adjusting his pants. "Come back after lunch when I have more time and I'll see what I can do."

"I can't. I have to go see Cooper."

His eyes narrowed. "Why?"

"I don't know. He told me last night that he has something important he needs to talk to me about in private."

"Last night? Did you call him from the tub before you called me?"

"No, I ran into him after …" *the viewing* "work."

"Come by my office when you're done talking to him."

I shook my head. "I have to go to Jeff Wymonds' to prep for tomorrow's open house."

"Fine, call me on your way to Wymonds' place."

"Okay," then I thought about Cooper's threat and added, "that's if Cooper doesn't throw me in jail."

"I'll accept your collect call and come spring you."

I turned and blinked up at him. My chest warmed like I'd downed three shots of tequila without pausing to swoon. "You'd bail me out of jail?"

He tucked a curl behind my ear. "Of course, Trouble."

"That's sweet. Why?"

"Are you fishing?" His grin was playful.

I planted my hands on my hips. "I've been dangling bait in front of you since I walked in your back door."

"What exactly are you fishing for?"

Hmmm. Good question. I chewed on my lip. This thing with Doc was not supposed to be happily-forever-after, just fun-for-now. But the prudent part of my brain kept insisting that if I was going to break my best friend's heart, it should be for something a bit more substantial than just a good time under the covers.

The question was, did Doc want more? Or was casual sex plenty for him?

Now was not the time to dig into that conversation, partly because of his soon-to-arrive client, but mostly because the idea of talking about it aloud with him made my stomach contents want to bubble up my esophagus.

With a shrug, I skirted his question. "Only my mom and Natalie have ever bailed me out of the slammer."

"How many times have you been in jail, Violet?"

I laughed way too loudly. "Who counts that kind of stuff?"

His forehead crinkled. "This is beginning to feel like an episode of *Hee Haw*."

The front door of his office jingled.

I raised my eyebrows. "You installed bells."

"I didn't want to be caught off guard if I was busy in back."

Busy with whom? I almost asked, then bit down on my jealous ogre's tongue.

Doc leaned out into the hall. "I'll be right out."

I picked up my tote to leave, and then remembered the peace offering I'd brought. "I have something for you before you go," I whispered.

He glanced toward the front of the office as I pulled out the centuries-old book I'd snuck from the Carhart place after my showdown with the demon-raising bitch who'd torched my Bronco—also known as Lila to those who didn't get a stabbing headache at just the sound of her name.

Holding the book out to him, I continued under my breath, "To show you that I'm not hiding things from you,"— *well, only a couple of things*—"here."

He took the book and turned it over in his hands. "What is this?"

"The demon cult book I borrowed from Lila." My lip curled into a sneer just saying her name; I couldn't help it.

"*Borrowed?*"

"She doesn't need it, anymore."

"Does Cooper know you took it?"

"Of course not. You can't tell him, either. He'd lock me behind bars in a heartbeat for withholding that."

Doc flipped through the pages, his face growing more rigid with each creepy drawing of hideous demons committing vile acts. He closed the book, his jaw taut.

"Truce?" I offered my hand for a shake.

Taking it, he pulled me toward him. Then he leaned down and spoke quietly in my ear. "Thank you, Violet."

I breathed in the musky scent of his aftershave, letting it soak into my senses to savor later. "For giving you a freaky book on demons?"

"For not hiding it from me."

My gut twinged, my conscience reminding me about the things I was still hiding. The urge to bury my face in his chest and tell him everything about Ray rolled through me, but the creak and groan of a chair out front kept my lips locked shut.

I glanced toward the front room. "I'd better go."

"Call me," he emphasized his request with narrowed eyes.

"I will."

"And tell Wymonds to keep his hands to himself." Doc dropped a quick kiss on my lips, then winked at me. "When it comes to you, I don't like to share."

My cheeks heated at the memory of Jeff and the kiss he'd stolen a couple of weeks ago. "If you're worried about Jeff kissing me again, don't. It's not going to happen."

I'd sooner have my tonsils removed while I was wide awake, which is kind of what kissing Jeff had felt like.

"Good." He rubbed his thumb along my jaw. "You give me enough other things to worry about."

"What can I say? I live to torture you."

"More than you know." His lazy grin in place, he led me to the back door. "Now go sell something." After a nudge into the sunshine, he added for my ears only, "And try to stay out of jail."

* * *

I forced my feet to walk across the sizzling asphalt parking lot toward the front doors of the Deadwood Police Station. The afternoon sun rained heat down on my head, just like Cooper was doing.

I jutted my middle finger at the sky on the way up the steps.

When I grabbed the metal door handle, I got the static-electric shock of my life. It zapped me clear to my toes.

"Yabba dabba!" Jerking my hand back, I stepped back, twisted my ankle, stumbled sideways, and slammed my hip into the center handrail. "Damn it!"

This didn't bode well. I hadn't even made it through the front doors yet and I was already taking a beating.

Straightening my shoulders, I yanked the door open and

limped inside. The acrid stink of burnt popcorn in the cool air set me even more on edge.

Behind the front desk, a silver-haired cop with a red, bulbous nose, who knew my name all too well from my past visits, didn't even bother trying to hide his laughter.

With a huff, I pointed back at the doors. "You need to do something about that."

"Sure thing, Ms. Parker," he said between snickers. "How 'bout I arrest it for battery?"

Leveling a glare at him, I dropped my purse on the floor and leaned on the high counter. "Funny guy, eh? Here's one for you. How many cops does it take to screw in a light bulb?"

He glanced behind me. "I'll bite, how many?"

"Just one, but he's never around when you need him."

The cop grinned. "You hear that Detective Cooper? I think Ms. Parker has a bone to pick with you about our inability to make it to her crime scenes on time."

I groaned inwardly and turned to find Cooper standing behind me in jeans, a button up shirt, and loosely knotted tie covered with little dots.

Where had he come from? Thin air?

His glare drilled holes clear through my skull. "I'll have to be more diligent about trying to read her mind when she stumbles blindly into her next kidnapping."

Natalie was confused. Cooper didn't have a crush *on* me; he just wanted to crush me, period.

I lifted my chin, my back all rigid as usual when facing off with Cooper's stainless steel eyes. "Don't bother. I think at a college-reading level. You'll just get frustrated by all of the big words."

A low whistle came from the desk cop. "You going to let her get away with that, Detective?"

"Probably not. Keep your cuffs handy." Cooper nodded toward the long hallway that led to his office—a route I knew from first-hand experience, unfortunately. "Let's go."

He made me lead the way. My low heels clacked on the

scratched linoleum, the sound echoing off the scuffed white walls.

Dead Realtor walking.

His stealth had me glancing back to make sure he followed. He did, his expression unreadable.

Inside his four walls, I dropped into the chair opposite his desk and waited for him to start chewing me a new asshole.

He shut his office door and leaned against it. "My house is ready to show."

"Uh …" It took me a couple of heartbeats to grind gears and shift from playing cops-and-suspects to Realtors-and-clients. "Okay. I'll bring a yard sign over later this week."

He pulled two keys from his pocket and handed them to me.

The keys were warm in my palm. Cooper had body heat? No shit. There went my theory about him being a killer robot sent back in time to terminate me before I spawned the child who would save mankind's future.

"One is for my back door, the other for the garage."

I slipped the keys inside my purse. "Do you have an alarm?"

Shaking his head, he sat on the edge of his desk. "No need. Everyone around here knows I'm a cop."

"Right." Which led me to ask, "Do you have any guns in the house?"

He shook his head again.

"Did you take down the artwork over the mantel?" I was referring to his oil painting of dogs sitting around a poker table cleaning their guns—handguns, shotguns, and semi-automatics. As intriguing as the dogs with guns were, the Georgia O'Keefe "Black Iris" print I'd found at a thrift store would add more buyer appeal and looked great with Cooper's black leather furniture and the dark maroon curtains we'd hung.

"Yeah, I switched to that flower print."

"Great."

"Uncle Willis won't stop staring at it, though," he said, a shadow of a grin hovering on his lips.

I looked to the heavens and sighed.

Harvey had fallen in love with the print at first sight. But his fascination had little to do with O'Keefe's talent, which became clear after he declared the print reminded him of some good times he'd spent dallying with a dark-skinned *señorita* in a brothel just over the Nevada state line.

"Thanks to him," Cooper added, "I'm having trouble seeing the damned thing for the flower it is."

I changed the subject to something less squirmy for me than talking about female nether regions with Cooper. "Why am I here, Detective?"

He picked up the grip-strengthening thingamajobbie he kept on his desk. Some people squeezed stress balls for relief. Cooper worked on improving his choke-hold.

He squeezed the grip a couple of times without answering me, lines criss-crossing his forehead.

I listened to it *squeak squeak* with dread crowding the oxygen from my lungs. I was about to wheeze when he finally spoke.

"We found a cell phone on the body."

Where? The only thing I'd seen was tons of hair and that icky black mole. Then I thought of a certain hiding place and recoiled. "You mean stuffed up his … uh," what was the CSI word for it? "Anal cavity?"

Who'd mined out that nugget of evidence? Eddie?

Cooper grimaced. "You watch too much T.V." *Squeak squeak.* "It was in his pants pocket."

"You mean he was dressed when you found him?"

"Yes."

"Then why did I have to look at him naked?"

"We had to remove the clothing for the autopsy."

"Couldn't you have clothed him again before I came?"

"He's not a Barbie doll, Violet. We don't play dress up with bodies held in the morgue."

Hold the phone! I sat up. "Deadwood has a morgue?"

His eyes narrowed, giving Dirty Harry a run for his money. "Sort of."

I snorted. "How does one 'sort of' have a morgue?"

"It's a modified garage."

Of course! The small building out behind Mudder Brothers Funeral Parlor. "It's the Mudder brothers' garage, isn't it?"

Squeak squeak. "That's not important."

I envisioned big chest freezers lined up around the walls, the hearse parked in between. Now I knew where they stored the fresh bodies.

I needed to get into that garage.

"Stay away from the Mudder brothers, Violet."

"Sure." Dang it. I said it too fast.

He pointed at me. "I meant what I said last night about the restraining order."

"I know." I held his stare for as long as humanly possible. Then I lowered my gaze to his loosely knotted tie, noticing that what I'd thought were polka dots were actually little skulls.

"So, what's this cell phone have to do with me?" I asked

Squeak squeak squeak. "Your name was in it."

Fear tickled the back of my throat. I tried to gulp it down. "So, I make a lot of phone calls every day. It's part of my job."

"It was a text message not a call."

"I could have texted the number by mistake."

"It's not from you."

"Oh."

"Your full name was written inside the text of the message."

"That's weird." The tickle in my throat became a burning itch.

"The *only* text message on the phone."

That was uncomfortably weird. I cleared my throat,

fighting the urge to claw at it. "What did it say?" My voice sounded croaky.

He pulled out a little notebook from his shirt pocket and flipped it open. "I quote, 'Violet Parker from Rapid City. Mid-thirties. Curly blonde hair.'"

My windpipe felt like it had been dipped in hot sauce. I coughed into my fist, trying to cool the burning. "There has to be some …" I paused to cough again, "some rational explanation."

Rational? Really? A crazy-sounding cackle erupted inside my skull. I squashed my lips together to keep it from spewing out. What were the chances of there being two curly-haired blonde Violet Parkers in Rapid City around my age?

Cooper grimaced at me. "There's one more thing in the text."

"What?" I wheezed, suddenly wishing I'd waited to cram that chicken and peppers burrito down my gullet until *after* I'd left the police station.

He held the notebook out in front of my watering eyes.

I blinked and read his scrawl—three times just to be sure my eyes weren't fucking with me.

The burning in my throat raced down to my stomach. I gulped. "I think I'm going to throw up."

"Disturbing, I'm sure." Cooper slapped the notebook closed. "So, what we need you to do is—"

Coughing on a bubble of stomach acid, I scrambled to my feet. "Where's your wastebasket?"

"Violet." He reached toward my shoulder. "Are you okay?"

"No! Get back!"

He should have listened better.

Chapter Nine

One hour, one trip home for a midday shower and teeth brushing, and one change of clothes later, I sat in the warm afternoon sunshine on the Picklemobile's tailgate in Jeff Wymonds' drive with my cell phone in hand.

I pulled up Doc's number, hit the call button, and then pressed the phone against my ear.

Squeals of laughter drifted my way from Jeff's backyard where my two kids were playing with Jeff's daughter, Kelly, who was also Addy's best friend. I'd tried to get the three of them to help Jeff and me prep the house for tomorrow's Open House—my first—but cleaning the inside of a monkey cage with the monkeys still in it would have been less frazzling.

Doc wasn't answering his phone. After four rings, I hung up, not wanting to leave another message on his voicemail. Three were plenty. A fourth would push me over into the desperate girlfriend zone that might be the start of a downhill slide into love-'em-and-leave-'em valley.

I weighed the idea of going back inside with Jeff. He could use my help re-painting the laundry room. But my feet dragged at the thought of bumping paintbrushes and elbows in a room much too small to share with an ex-football player who was determined to make me the other half of his Brady Bunch family.

Jeff was a good dad, and even though he cleaned up nicely and had an impressive set of biceps, his repeated comments about wanting to share a kitchen with me and leave some little "buns" in my oven conjured crazed visions of me laughing hysterically as I slammed my stove door on his rolling pin.

More than once.

While I was still physically able to pop out a little gingerbread girl or boy, Violet's Baby-Making Bakery had closed its doors for good ten years ago. Another pregnancy would go over like a cast-iron stork.

With a glance at the thick clouds stacking up on the horizon, I dialed Natalie.

"Dick's Hotdogs," Natalie answered on the second ring. "If you like hotdogs, you'll like Dicks!"

I chuckled, swinging my legs while inspecting my paint-spattered arms. "Nice. You hear that one during your last conjugal visit to the Pennington County Jail? "

"Nah, I got it from your mom. What's up?"

I didn't dally. "The Mudder brothers have a morgue in their garage."

"I know. They cremate bodies there, too."

"What?" My legs stopped swinging. "Why didn't you tell me this before?"

"Ummm, because you used to be sane."

"I want to sneak inside of that morgue."

"Whatever happened to the good ol' days when our sneaking involved the boys' locker room after basketball games?"

"Ugh. I'd forgotten about all of those jockstraps." I hopped to the ground, pacing.

A top-heavy cumulus cloud slipped in front of the sun, giving me a break from the heat.

"How are we going to get into that garage?" I asked, running a few scenarios through my head involving Natalie and me in black ski-masks and cat suits.

"We?" Natalie chuckled. "Oh, no, sister. I'm not going in there with you. That's too damned creepy."

"Natalie, what could happen? They're all dead."

"Dead bodies make weird sounds."

"So did your ex, and you slept with his sorry ass."

"They smell funny."

"Your ex ate *chili con carne* by the can."

"They're freaky looking."

"One word for you—tattoos," I said, referring to her ex's obsession with ink on his skin. "I can do this all day, Nat. You're going in with me."

Thunder boomed to the west. Wyoming was sending some loud, wet love our way.

"No," she said, and then growled in my ear. "Why me?"

"Because I'm too chicken to go alone."

"What! You just said—"

My phone beeped.

I pulled it away from my ear. Natalie's ranting sounded tiny and far off, like it was being piped in from Dr. Seuss's Whoville. A peek at the screen made my silly heart skip a beat. Doc was calling back.

"Nat," I interrupted her mid-rant, "I gotta go. I'll talk to you tonight."

She was still grumbling when I hung up and picked up the incoming call.

"Hi, Doc." I leaned against the tailgate, trying to sound all cool and sexy.

"Hey, Trouble. You okay?" His deep voice caressed my eardrum, making me shiver a little. It was pathetic how warm I was for the guy's form.

"Yeah. Why?"

"You sounded a little upset in your messages. Especially those first two."

A little upset? He was being kind. I was pretty sure I'd hit a Level 5 on the Nuclear Event Scale.

I'd made those first two calls to him on my way home from the police station, the acrid taste of my own lunch remains still burning the back of my throat. My heart hadn't stopped jackhammering yet from what Cooper had shown me. "That's because I was still freaking out."

His chair creaked through the line. I envisioned him leaning back at his desk. "Why? What happened?"

"I threw up on Cooper's skull tie."

His pause lasted for a rumble of thunder. "You what?"

"Threw up on—"

"Why?"

"Well, I think it was partly because that chicken and green peppers burrito I had for lunch had been well past its expiration date—it tasted funny from the start and didn't get any better by the last bite. But mostly it was because of what Cooper showed me."

He cursed under his breath. "Did he make you look at the dead guy again?"

"No. He showed me a text message."

"And you accuse me of being cryptic."

"Sorry." I took a calming breath and started in again. "The cops found a cell phone on the headless dead guy and it had a text message in it with my name."

Thunder rumbled again, louder, closer. Good timing, I thought and wrinkled my nose at the gang of dark clouds looming. I could smell the coming rain.

"The dead guy sent you a text message?"

"No, someone else sent him a text message about me."

"Who?"

"They don't know. It was listed only as a number, no name. And the number no longer works."

"How old was the text?"

"Over a month."

"What did it say?"

"It read like a singles ad. Listed my name, my hair color, and that I'm from Rapid."

Doc's chair creaked again. "Shit."

I nodded into the now-cool breeze leading the storm. "There's more."

"Of course there is. What else did Cooper find?"

"I meant there was more in the message. It mentioned Aunt Zoe."

"What about her?"

"The text described her, too, including where she lives."

As in where I now lived—with my kids.

A flash of lightning split the sky to the south, a curtain of rain falling below the looming tower of dark clouds. I frowned at the storm, wishing Jeff had been mowing the lawn earlier this afternoon instead of helping me paint two layers of white over the pea-soup green his soon-to-be-ex had chosen for their master bathroom walls.

"What did Cooper have to say about this text message?" Doc asked.

"That I should mind my own business, focus on selling his house, and let him figure out who's behind it all."

"Are you going to listen to him?"

"I will do my damnedest to sell his house."

"Violet," he warned.

"Doc, this isn't just about me. Aunt Zoe could be in danger. So could my kids."

"Christ, woman. You're too much some days."

"What's that supposed to mean?" Too much for him to handle? Or too much of a pain to keep around?

"It means that I'm going to lose more sleep."

Oh, that's all he meant? Sleep was for babies and old men. "Welcome to the Insomnia Club. We have matching pillow cases."

He chuckled. "I have a fix for your nightmares."

"What? Pills? Hypnotism? Ben Stein reading poetry?"

"A new bed."

"I doubt my mattress is part of the problem."

"Probably not, but my new mattress is definitely part of the solution."

Sex with Doc on a flat surface? Hmmm, definitely worth a shot—if I could shake Natalie.

"You have a new bed?" I hopped up onto the tailgate, kicking my legs again.

"The delivery guys were at my place when you called—the first time, anyway."

"I like the bean bag," I said, smiling at the memory of him working his magic on me in that bag of beans.

"It's still here in the back room. Come over and see for yourself."

"I can't. Jeff and I have more painting to do."

"How's Wymonds?"

"Eager to sell."

"Keeping his hands to himself?"

It wasn't his hands I was worried about touching me. "Yep."

Harvey's old Ford pulled into the drive next to the Picklemobile, a cloud of dust making me cough.

"I have to go, Harvey's here."

"Perfect. You need a bodyguard today."

"I can handle Jeff."

"It's not Wymonds who has me worried. Have you talked to your newest client? Mr. Planet of the Apes?"

"His name is Cornelius." Although, I preferred *Honest Abe.* "And I have not talked to him yet today. Why?"

I'd planned to touch base with him later this afternoon. That would give him a solid twenty-four hours in that hotel before I began pestering him to buy it.

"I'll let Harvey fill you in." His tone vibrated with suppressed laughter.

Harvey crawled out of his pickup and limped toward me, grimacing while rubbing his hip.

"About what?"

"Call me tonight after your kids go to bed."

"What is there to tell me about Cornelius?"

"Oh, and Violet."

"What?"

"Don't drop the phone in the water this time," he said and hung up.

Damn him.

"Was that Doc?" Harvey asked.

I put the cell phone on the tailgate next to me. "You

know, he's not the only one I talk to on the phone."

"Right. Did he tell you about your ghost-talking friend with the corny name?"

"His name is Cornelius."

"That's right. The chimp played by Roddy McDowell." Harvey stroked his beard. "I always thought his chimp wife, Dr. Zira, was kind of sexy. Nothin' like Nova, though. That woman knew how to wear a pelt."

I sighed. We were regressing.

"Harvey, what's going on with Cornelius?"

Please, please, please don't say he's skipping town.

"Doc told me that crazy Corny riled up some ghosts at the Old Prospector Hotel last night. Some mirrors were shattered in the guest suite. And a window broken. Or was it two? I can't remember."

Son of a bitch.

"How did Doc know about this?" And why didn't I?

"Tiffany told him."

I blinked. Come again. "Tiffany?"

"Yeah, you know, that hot little redhead number with the tight—"

"When did she tell him this?"

If Harvey said "last night," I was going to sneak over to Doc's house after Nat and the kids went to sleep tonight, strap him to that new bed of his, and pour hot wax on his tender parts.

Harvey shrugged. "Around lunchtime, I think. She was leaving his office when I showed up for my weekly appointment with him."

I gritted my teeth. Which explained why my second and third calls went unanswered.

Thunder boomed over our heads, impending doom knocking.

I flipped it off with both hands, and then squinted at Harvey. "Do you have any tequila?"

He scoffed. "Tequila is for pussies. If you want something

to take the edge off, I've got just what you need."

I hopped to the ground. "Bring it on, old man."

Fifteen minutes later, I stood up from leaning over Jeff's toilet. I wiped off my lips, flushed the toilet, and then rinsed out my mouth with sink water.

Old man Harvey's reflection grinned at me in the mirror from his post against the doorjamb. "And that's why you don't chug firewater."

"Firewater?" I dried my face on a hand towel and threw it on the sink vanity. "More like paint thinner."

I'd just stripped the lining from my guts and flushed it down the john. Criminy. I'd thrown up two times already today and the sun was still up. I was on a real bender.

"Is she done puking?" Jeff hollered from the other room.

Harvey's brows raised. "You done airin' your paunch now, girlie?"

"Yes, she's done," I answered loud enough for Jeff's ears and poked Harvey in the chest as I passed him, receiving a satisfactory grunt in return.

Jeff waited for us in the kitchen, leaning against the counter. Speckles of white paint added a sugar-like coating to his sandy blond hair, black biker rally T-shirt, and faded jeans. He held a glass of water out toward me.

"Thanks." The water turned out to be the sparkling kind. Even better.

I leaned against the counter next to him and his broad shoulders, glaring at Harvey's gold-toothed grin over the rim of my glass. The fizz tickled my nose.

"I don't know why you got your bloomers all cinched up over Crazy Corny," Harvey said.

"His name is Cornelius." I didn't need Harvey's new nickname for my cash-buying client to catch fire and spread throughout town. I tried to shush Harvey with a squinty-eyed glare. "And we can discuss this more later."

"Cornelius who?" Jeff asked.

"Everyone in town knows that hotel is haunted," Harvey

said, obviously ignoring me. "What's a few pieces of broken glass?"

"It's not the glass that's bothering me. It's what happened that caused the glass to break and who else was involved."

Was Safari Skipper, a.k.a. front desk clerk there? Any other employees or locals or tourists? Had there been any newspaper reporters nearby? Anyone taking pictures or videos that would show up on the Internet? I had a not-so-good reputation to protect, damn it.

"Which hotel are you talking about?" Jeff asked.

"Never m—" I started.

"The Old Prospector," Harvey blared.

Jeff nodded. "One of the painted ladies hangouts."

"Painted ladies?" My stomach bucked a little. Harvey's firewater still boiling in my tank. "You mean prostitutes?"

"Yes, indeedy." Harvey's grin split even wider. "One of Deadwood's finest traditions."

The place had been a bit seedy looking, but, "Really? I thought the FBI cleared out the last of the brothels back in the early eighties."

"They did." Jeff grumbled. "The damned Feds just couldn't leave well enough alone."

Harvey dropped into one of the kitchen chairs. "The Old Prospector used to house a bunch of the 'girls' on its third floor up until the late sixties. Then there was some big fight between the hotel owner and several of the girls and they were kicked out. The owner remodeled the rooms, tore out some walls, and turned the third floor into fancy suites."

Maybe they used to be fancy, but they weren't so shiny, anymore. That explained the faded look to the rooms.

"So, let me guess," I said, "the hotel is supposed to be haunted by some poor prostitute killed by one of her johns."

Jeff scooted closer to me, nudging my shoulder with his. "For a blonde, you're a smart cookie, Violet Parker. Our kids would be cute and clever."

He said that like I should now sigh loudly while little

hearts floated around my head.

Harvey snickered.

I scooted away from Jeff. "Has anyone ever actually seen this ghost?" I asked Harvey. "Or is it all glowing orbs and shadows in pictures?"

"I told you yesterday that one of the housecleaners swore the ghost existed," he answered. "She talked about cleanin' the rooms on the third floor and feelin' warm breath on the back of her neck. Of course, nobody would be there when she turned around."

I tried to remember if there were any vents in the ceiling in those rooms. Maybe it was just a weird air current. "Was that it? Hot breath on her neck?"

Harvey tugged on his beard. "No, there was another story about spooky messages left on one of the mirrors in the room at the far end of the hall."

"You mean with lipstick?"

"No, if you steamed it up, there were weird things written there."

"Like what?"

"I don't remember. Seems like the gal I heard that from said it was some kind of foreign language. The hotel owner took that particular mirror out of there and it stopped."

A haunted mirror? Maybe the ghost was Snow White's evil queen.

Jeff crossed his arms. "I remember hearing about some strange blonde woman hanging out in one of the upstairs windows. She only showed up there at sunset. Nobody knew her name or recognized her."

"Maybe it was just a mannequin." Like one of the many fakes I've seen in upstairs windows in both Deadwood and Lead. Plastic or not, those empty looks and flaxen faces gave me the creeps.

With a shrug, Jeff said, "Maybe. I figured the owner was just messing with people. Having fun."

Jeff was like me, a non-believer in the wispy population—

although, I was moonlighting in the believer camp more and more these days.

"So, hot breath and steamy mirrors then," I said. "Anything else happ—"

The muffled sound of my cell phone stopped me. I patted my pockets and came up empty. Where had I put it?

"Here," Harvey said, and pulled it out of his pants pocket and held it out to me. "You left it on the tailgate when you raced for the commode."

Oh, right. I grimaced at just the memory of drinking that liquid lava. It was a wonder I hadn't singed Harvey's beard when I'd coughed and gasped all over him.

I grabbed the phone. It was Mona. "Hello?"

"Violet, where are you?" Something in her voice made my heart pick up speed.

What was wrong? Where were my kids—oh, yeah, in the backyard. Whew!

"I'm at Jeff Wymonds prepping for the open house tomorrow. Why? What's up?"

"Have you talked to your newest buyer today?"

Damn! She'd heard about Cornelius and the broken mirror. That meant Jane had, too. And Ray, who would undoubtedly be gloating the next time we faced off for a duel.

"Not yet. I was going to call him here shortly. I was giving him 24 hours to make a decision."

"You'd better call him now."

"If this is about the broken windows and mirror—" I started.

"It's not," she interrupted. "It's about Ray."

"What about Ray?" I looked up to find Harvey frowning at me.

What did Ray have to do with Cornelius? Mona was the one helping me with the paperwork and necessary steps for this commercial sale.

"He's lined up another buyer. He's on the phone with Tiffany Sugarbell right now."

Doc's ex? My stomach kicked again, my lower esophagus burning. "What do you mean? I don't understand."

"Ray's trying to steal the hotel sale out from under you."

"That fucking rat bastard!" He was going straight for my throat.

Harvey and Jeff exchanged raised brows.

"You need to talk to your client right away," Mona ordered. "See if he's willing to buy the place or not. We don't have time for wooing anyone here."

"Okay, I'll call Cornelius as soon as I hang up."

"No, don't do this over the phone." I could hear her fingernails clacking through the line. How could she be typing during a blow like this? "It's too easy for a client to say 'No, thanks,' when he doesn't have to look you in the eyes. Face-to-face is better."

"All right."

"Do you want me to come with you to talk to him?"

No way! Mona would see how much of a freakshow Cornelius really was, and then she'd look at me in that way of hers that made me feel like I'd piddled on the rug. Besides, Cornelius had come looking for me and me alone.

"Thanks, Mona, but I want to fly solo on this."

"Okay. Call me if you need me. I'll talk to you in a bit." She hung up.

I tossed my phone on the counter and covered my face with my hands. "I'm so screwed."

"What's going on?" Jeff asked, rubbing my lower back, an intimate act that would have earned him a shove or shooing smack if my hands weren't busy trying to hide me away from the world.

"Let me guess," Harvey said. "Ray is tryin' to put a spoke in your wheel."

"If that means he's trying to screw me over again and get me fired, then yes."

"You want me to introduce him to Bessie?"

Yes, I did, and I wanted Harvey to aim low. "It's probably

not a good idea. I'm going to need you around to take care of Aunt Zoe and the kids after I suffocate Ray with his own dirty underwear."

"I could break his kneecaps," Jeff jumped on Harvey's bandwagon and squeezed me in an awkward side-hug.

I lowered my hands and pulled away from Jeff without trying to make it obvious how much his touch was *not* comforting me.

Enough wallowing in my kiddy pool of self-pity. I scooped up my phone and searched the room. "Where'd I put my purse?"

"By the front door," Jeff said.

"Where are you going?" Harvey asked as I raced out of the room.

"To see Cornelius." I grabbed my purse. "Addy! Layne! We need to go!"

"I'll take them home," Harvey offered. "You just skedaddle and take care of ol' Ray."

"Thanks," I said, and then turned to Jeff. "Keep painting and move the furniture around in your bedroom like we talked about." At his nod, I continued. "I'll be by early tomorrow to help with the final prep."

Harvey walked me out to the Picklemobile. The dark clouds had passed to the south, taking the rain with them. Turned out the northern hills wouldn't be watered today after all.

"Sure you don't want some help?"

"Positive." I crawled inside the cab. "Harvey, promise me you won't tell Aunt Zoe or the kids about any of this shit with Ray."

"Yeah, yeah, yeah." He frowned through the open window at me. "You sure you're okay? Your eyes are all buggy and rolling around in your head right now. Are you feelin' any hit from the firewater?"

I'd thrown it all up too soon for it to hit my bloodstream. "I'm fine and dandy. Happy as a dung beetle in a cow pie." I used one of his own lines on him.

"It's 'cow patty.'" His eyes narrowed. "You're not going to go off and do anything cuckoo, right?"

Maybe. Probably. Mostly likely. Define cuckoo. "No. Not at all."

* * *

I called Cornelius while sitting at a red light at the opposite end of Main Street from his hotel. In front of me, a dark green 1938 Dodge, just like Bogart's car in *The Big Sleep*, my all-time favorite Bogart film, idled in a low growl.

I rolled up the window.

"Hello?" Cornelius answered, sounding like a Vincent Price impressionist.

I ground my molars, wanting to tell him to knock off the act. "Mr. Curion, it's Violet Parker."

He breathed into the phone.

"Your Realtor."

"I know who you are, Violet. I came looking for you, remember?"

Right. "I'm calling to see if you have made a decision regarding the hotel."

"Yes, I have."

It was my turn to just sit there and breathe into the phone. Only he didn't continue. "What's your decision?"

My heart pounded so hard that my big toe throbbed.

"I've decided that I need you to see something first."

Like I hadn't heard that line before, but I hadn't expected it from Cornelius. "Excuse me?"

"I want you to come to my hotel room tomorrow night."

I sat there, my jaw resting on the steering wheel. Damned Tiffany for making my boobs look bigger in that dress yesterday.

Someone honked behind me. The light was green.

I hit the gas. "Why?"

"Just trust me," he said.

Surely Cornelius wasn't thinking I'd exchange sex for a sale. I mean, I was desperate and all, but not that desperate. I'd sooner use Addy's bike to deliver newspapers for a living than have sex with Abe Lincoln. My butt could use the exercise, anyway.

"Can't you just give me an answer now? On the phone? Then I can bring some paperwork over tonight for you to sign."

He chuckled. "You're going to be a fun nut to crack."

Between his feet dragging and Ray's property stealing, I was going to start having my own fun cracking nuts.

"Mr. Curion, if you could just let me know if you're still interested in the property, I could bring the appropriate documents over in the morning for your signature and we could get this rolling."

"What's the rush? This property has been for sale for over a year."

Cornelius had done his homework. As much as I wanted to tell him that someone else may snatch it out from under him, I didn't. Until I found out if Ray had a definite offer, I had to be careful. If I used another buyer to push Cornelius into making an offer, and then it turned out there was no other offer, I'd look like I lied to get him to speed up the sale.

"I just thought you were really interested and might be ready to put an offer on the place."

"Oh, I'm definitely interested. But I want you to come see something in my room first."

Images of his long, bony, pale, skinny, naked body flitted through my mind, making me wince. Nope, not gonna happen. "Why don't you just meet me at the office?"

I slowed to let a group of tourists cross the street in front of me.

"I don't like the voices in your office."

My arm's prickled. What did he mean? What voices? Doc didn't like the smell in Calamity Jane's, either. Most of the time he wouldn't even cross the threshold.

"I heard you had an accident over there," I said, switching subjects, tiptoeing around the truth. "Something about a window accidentally getting broken."

He laughed. "You should have seen it, Violet."

"What?"

"I'll show you tomorrow night. Come over around sundown."

"Mr. Curion, I really can—"

"Bring the paperwork with you and we'll talk."

Paperwork? I blew out a breath. "Fine. Okay." But I'd be wearing a snowmobile suit this time. There'd be no touching, no ogling, just signatures and smiles.

"Sundown," he reiterated.

"Got it."

"See you then." He hung up as I drove past the front of his hotel and just kept on rolling.

On the way back to my office, a plan sparked and caught flame in my head. I weaved my way to my parking spot behind Calamity Jane Realty and cut the engine, waiting with one eye closed until the backfire boomed.

Ray's SUV was MIA. Damn, I'd have to wait until next time to bust the dickhead in the chops.

Doc's Camaro was missing, too. Double damn. He was an essential part of my new plan. My idea of seducing him in person into playing along went up in smoke.

Oh, well, I was getting good at whispering sweet nothings to him via the phone. It was time to see how good. I pulled up his number on my cell phone.

He answered the phone on the first ring. "Hey, Trouble. Did Harvey tell you about your client?"

"Yep." I wanted to ask what else Tiffany shared with Doc in his office, but I clubbed my green-eyed ogre into submission and stuck to the plan.

I cleared my throat and slipped into my sex-kitten voice, "Doc, I've been thinking about you. A lot."

"Are you okay? You sound like you're catching a cold."

I cleared my throat and stuck with my usual tone. "I'm fine. But I need a favor."

"You need to borrow my car again?"

"Nope. Bigger."

He was quiet for a couple of seconds. "What do you need, Violet?"

The list went on and on, but I started at the top. "You."

"I like the sound of that."

"And your nose."

"That, not so much."

"I swear, it will only take a few minutes."

Just enough time for Doc to catch a good whiff of the hotel and for Cornelius to meet Doc—aka my boyfriend—in case he was thinking I'd trade sex for a sale. Although how I'd make it clear that Doc and I were an item while at the same time not being too obvious about our item-hood might take some clever smoke-and-mirrors work to pull off.

"Violet, you don't believe in ghosts, remember?"

I remembered that I couldn't make up my mind these days about the dead. Or were ghosts considered undead? No, that was vampires. "That's merely a technicality at this point."

"I'll be the judge of that."

"Does that mean you're in?"

"That depends on the details of the favor."

Wincing in anticipation, I whispered, "I need you to come with me to the Old Prospector Hotel."

Silence.

A late-60s black Mustang Fastback rumbled past my back bumper, Three Dog Night's version of *The Lion Sleeps Tonight* a-weema weh'd through the open windows.

Still, silence from Doc's end of the line.

Maybe he hadn't heard me. I cleared my throat again.

"Why?" Doc asked, finally.

"It's supposed to be haunted."

"I know. What do you want from *me*?"

Boy, was that a loaded question. What did I want? More sex—but that was a given. Some help setting up college funds for the kids would be wonderful. A guarantee that he wouldn't kick me to the curb and break my heart someday would make it much easier to come clean with Nat about stealing the man she thought she loved.

I clarified before answering, "We're still talking about the hotel, right?"

He chuckled. "Yeah, let's keep it simple for now."

What did that mean? Keep this relationship-thing we were doing simple? I shook my head. I hated this uncertainty crap when it came to having the man I wanted in my life.

"Maybe you can tell me if the rumors are true," I said.

"Are you saying that if I go to the hotel and tell you there are ghosts there, you'll believe me?"

"I'd certainly give a lot of thought to your answer."

"Well, if you don't believe me, then it's a waste of my time."

"I want to believe you, Doc, but try to look at this from my perspective. I can't see ghosts. I can't smell them, feel them, taste them, nothing. I'm a total dud. Yet I'm supposed to believe ghosts exist and you can interact with them."

I paused to give him a chance to refute what I'd said.

He didn't, so I continued. "You have to admit that's one hell of a big pill to swallow. You're going to need to give me more time."

And more proof.

He sighed. "I have an appointment with a client tomorrow evening. How long will this take?"

What client? A certain curvy redhead?

Oh, for crissake, get a grip, you big jealous dufus!

"Long enough for you to tell me if Cornelius is for real." I tugged the keys from the ignition and frowned at the smiley face keychain. "Or if he's just full of shit."

Chapter Ten

Sunday, August 19th

As open houses go, my first one started out slow, and then ended with a bang—as in an explosion.

In one big *kaboom*, Jeff's garage lost half of its roof, and my hopes of making a quick sale shattered along with several of the building's windows. At least the house and all of its accoutrements were still intact.

I wondered if I could get away with describing the garage as an "open-air" building on the listing sheet now. Or an inverse carport. I'd have to see how much of the roof was left after Captain Reid and his volunteer fire crew finished making sure all of the cinders were fully doused.

Speaking of the devil in yellow, flame-retardant pants …

Reid sidled up next to me as I stood at the end of the drive watching my career smolder. He smelled good and smoky. Several feet to my right, a crowd of Jeff's neighbors milled, murmuring among themselves, suddenly interested in our open house proceedings.

Marketing lesson of the day—to stage a successful open house and draw a lot of traffic, blow something up. The bigger the explosion, the bigger the crowd.

"You okay, Sparky?" Reid asked, his baritone voice rippling with undercurrents of laughter.

The back of my throat burned from holding in my fuming frustration and kept trying to leak out through my eyes in the form of tears. "Do I look okay?"

"You look slightly singed, especially your eyebrows."

"They aren't singed. They're still growing in from the

Hessler fire," I said, referring to the house fire where I first met Captain Reid and his merry crew of firefighters after almost being barbecued to a crisp.

"Well, in that case, they're growing back in nicely." He grinned. "The boys down at the station have come up with a new name for you."

Oh, this couldn't be good. I braced myself. "What's that?"

"Four-Alarm Parker."

I groaned. "Splendid."

"You're lucky they like you. I've heard worse."

"Right, lucky me."

Reid patted me on the back. "Cheer up, Sparky. Wymonds says this was probably his fault. At least you won't have Coop breathing down your neck about this one."

"Do you know what started it yet?"

"Maybe. I need to wait until it's safe to go in there and see for certain. I'll write up the report this afternoon so Wymonds can get his insurance company involved ASAP."

"So, it definitely wasn't arson?"

Initially, as the flames had raged, I had wondered if Ray had found another way to knock my knees out from under me. Blowing up Jeff's garage was an excellent idea. Now we'd have to reduce the price on the place for tomorrow's Hot Sheet listing. *Hot Sheet*—oh, how Lady Irony loved to toy with me.

Jane wasn't going to be happy about the loss of income, and while I had nothing to do with this fire, the soot mark would go on my not-so-spotless track record.

Maybe Jane should add a column on her Sales Pending white board for Fire Sales. At least I'd finally get some Xs on the board.

"Arson?" Reid nailed me with a narrow-eyed squint. "Have you pissed off someone this week? Someone besides Coop?"

There was Ray, of course. Possibly George Mudder, if Ray had told him about my snooping. And Tiffany, if she'd found out about Doc and me. Plus my sister was in the area—who knew how competitive for attention she was feeling these days. Who else?

I shrugged. "No. I was just throwing that out."

Reid squeezed my shoulder. "I'm thinking more along the line of an accident. But I've learned not to speculate until I get a chance to sift through the ashes."

An accident. I gulped. That's exactly what had the back of my knees sweating. Layne had a track record of blowing up dog houses. Sure, they were innocent chemistry experiments, but he'd been in Jeff's backyard unsupervised part of the time yesterday as we prepped for the open house. What if Layne had been playing Dr. Oppenheimer with some of the chemicals in Jeff's garage, coming up with his own version of the atomic bomb? He'd made it clear verbally how much he disliked Addy's not-so-brilliant idea of having Jeff as their new stepdaddy; maybe this was his way of acting out his feelings.

If Layne was at fault, how did I tell my client that my kid may have kind of sort of accidentally blown up his garage? How did I convince my boss that she shouldn't fire me over this?

"I'll get hold of you later and tell you more," Reid said and nodded at one of his crew members who was waving him over. "I gotta go."

"Thanks, Reid."

"You're welcome, Sparky. Do me a favor, would ya?"

I could guess where this was going, something about me not playing with lighters or taking out more fire insurance. "What's that?"

"Hide your Aunt's shotgun shells." He winked, flashed me another one of his charming grins, and walked away.

I stared after him, wondering what that meant for Aunt Zoe. She'd obviously been hurt in the past by Reid. It didn't take a doctorate in psychology to figure that out based on her urge to fill him full of holes. I hated to see Aunt Zoe hurt again, but Reid was a hot catch, and it had nothing to do with all of the time he spent around flames.

What if Aunt Zoe and he patched things up? Would he want to move in? Where did that leave me and my kids?

Shaking off worries about "what ifs" that Aunt Zoe would tell me were "never happens," I headed into the house to wrap up this disaster before returning to the office with my tail between my legs.

An hour later, when I pulled into the parking lot behind Calamity Jane Realty, Jane's SUV was nowhere to be seen. Mona and Ray were there, though. The Picklemobile announced my arrival with its usual calling card *BOOM*.

I slammed the pickup door closed, taking a calming breath before I faced the ridicule sure to be dished out in large helpings by a certain dickhead I loved to hate.

The pungent odor of burned garage still coated the back of my throat. I breathed in the pine-scented air, focusing on the warm afternoon breeze and how good it felt on my skin. A glass of cold, refreshing water would taste like nectar from heaven.

A flurry of movement by Calamity Jane's back door snared my attention. The site of George Mudder gesturing wildly as he talked to Ray made me forget about Mother Nature's pacifiers.

What was going on? What had George so animated?

There was only one way to find out. I weaved through a row of highly-polished classic Detroit muscle and steel of all types, trying to hear what George was saying above the V-8 engines rumbling in the parking lot and out on the street.

Ray shushed him as I approached. I heard that clear as day. Could he be any more suspicious? Hadn't he ever heard of changing the subject?

"Hi, George," I said, breaking the silence. I smiled wide, well as wide as I could after the day I'd had. Even my teeth felt scorched, singed, and brittle. "What brings you to Calamity Jane's?"

There. No need to dance around an unasked question

now.

His little yellow teeth greeted me, his eyes crinkled at the edges without even the tiniest bit of malice. It appeared that George was still clueless about me nosing into his secrets. Excellent. There was another viewing that I planned to drag Natalie to tomorrow night.

"I was talking to Ray about—"

"Never mind, Violet," Ray cut in, his eyes as sharp as his tone. "George, I'll stop by later with more details."

Details about their next shipment? About the guys who had followed him last time?

"It was nice seeing you, Violet." George held the door for me. "Give Natalie my love."

I slipped by him and cursed under my breath as the door shut firmly behind me. As tempting as it was to put my ear to the back door, I passed and headed to the front room.

Mona's jasmine perfume mixed with the residuals of smoke still in my sinuses, making for a sweet, smoky smell. She stopped clacking on her keyboard as soon as I dropped my bag on my desk.

"Did you hear?" I asked.

"I did. You okay?"

"I've been better." I walked over to the water cooler and poured myself a cup of nectar. "Does Jane know?"

"Not yet, but she'll hear about it. What happened?"

"We're not sure yet, but it looks like it was an accident."

"Anybody get hurt?"

"No, thank God." I downed the cupful of cold water, sighed in relief, and then pointed my thumb toward the back door. "What was George Mudder doing here?"

"I don't know. He dropped off some keys to Ray, and then the two of them went out the back."

"That's kind of weird, don't you think?" I was testing Mona, seeing if it was just my general loathing for Ray that had me full of suspicions about George's visit.

"A little odd, I guess."

Good. So, I wasn't totally nuts. I walked back to my desk. "Did you hear anything more about Ray's client putting an offer on the hotel?"

"No. Nothing. You're meeting with Cornelius tonight, right?"

I nodded. Back to Ray—I wasn't done yet. "Has Ray named his mysterious client?"

"Nope. He and Jane had some kind of pow-wow behind closed doors this morning, but she headed out for an appointment with her lawyer before I had a chance to drill her." Mona pointed at my desk. "She left a note for you."

I pushed my bag aside and picked up the Post-it note, my heart thudding in my throat. But it was just a list of two more buildings in Lead she wanted me to research.

Jane was interested in purchasing more real estate. For a couple of weeks now, she'd had me finding out past ownership and liens on several buildings along Lead's main drag.

This time she specified I go to the library in Lead. I usually hung out in Deadwood Library's South Dakota room, where I often found Doc researching, too. Only his subjects weren't usually so pleasant—death registers, cemetery plot details, and more.

"Jane wants me to go to the Lead library," I told Mona.

"You know where that is, right? Next to the old Opera House."

I nodded. "I was up there with the kids weeks ago. While they picked out a few books, I peeked through the Opera House's front doors. They've really fixed that place up."

Almost a century ago, the late, much-loved Thomas Grier, Homestake Mining Company's superintendent, worked with the wife of ba-zillionaire, George Hearst, to build the Homestake Opera House and Recreation Center for the mine's employees and their families.

I'd learned all about Mr. and Mrs. Hearst, along with Grier, Wild Bill, and Calamity Jane in history class back in high school. The black and white pictures of the glory days of old had often fascinated me, making me wish I could see it all in color.

Hearst had been one of the early owners of the Homestake Gold Mine, the largest and deepest gold mine in the Western Hemisphere until it closed its doors at the beginning of the new millennium. While the uber-wealthy tycoon had been focused mainly on digging riches out of the ground until his death in the early 1890s, his young wife had been more concerned about the citizens of Lead. Grier and she had each played philanthropic roles in making Lead a bustling, vibrant, cosmopolitan city in the early twentieth century, with Cornish, Italian, German, and other ethnic cultural sectors. The Historic Homestake Opera House was an example.

But then the mine had shut its doors for good, and the miles and miles of underground shafts, drifts, and stopes were allowed to fill with water. Those golden, glory days of old had been washed down the sluice into oblivion, along with the big company store stocked with everything under the sun and the well-paid mining jobs that had kept the northern Black Hills prosperous for over a century. The Opera House had limped along until a fire destroyed the roof and much of the inside.

But the old place was being restored by a group of volunteers. The whole process reminded me of the mythical phoenix, from ashes to rebirth. I couldn't wait to see the old building regain its reputation as the "Jewel of the Black Hills."

I dropped into my chair, leaning back. "I've been wanting to go see a play in there since we moved up here. I'm curious what the auditorium looks like now."

Mona pushed her glasses further up on her nose. "When I was a kid, they used to show movies in there. I'm so glad they're fixing it back up."

Wait a second. I sat up straight in my seat. Did the Opera House's restoration have anything to do with the reason Jane was so hot to get property in Lead lately? Did she have some insider tip from someone in the Lead City Council about a lucrative venture for the town on the horizon?

"They say the old place is haunted," Mona said.

"Why does that *not* surprise me?" These days, I'd actually be more surprised to find a century-old building in the Black Hills that was free of ghost-filled rumors.

"Back in the early days," Mona continued, "the Opera House was used as a hospital for a while. The Episcopal Church also used it for church services while it was being moved to its current location, and probably funerals, too. The building is certainly no stranger to death."

In other words, I wouldn't be attending any plays with Doc anytime soon, or Cornelius.

I read Jane's note again. While I wanted to wad it up and file it in my trash can, I stuffed it in my purse instead. Jane's wishes were my commands, as her unofficial gopher. Until I made enough money in sales to start carrying some weight around here, I had to keep my gopher tail firmly strapped on.

The sound of the back door closing drew both Mona's and my gazes. Ray sauntered in, his grin a mix of sneer and triumph.

Oh, how I wished I had a pie to throw.

I held eye contact, ready for whatever shit he planned to fling my way.

"Something smells like smoke," he said.

And so it began.

"Shut up, Ray." Mona beat me to the punch.

"What's burning? Oh, right, Blondie's future in realty."

"Think of that one all on your own, Skeeter?"

He sat in his chair and kicked his Tony Lamas up onto his desktop. "Did you hear my good news?"

"You finally found a penis enlarger that actually works?"

"Come over tonight and see for yourself. I'll show you what it's like to be with a real man and put that boyfriend of yours to shame."

"What boyfriend?" Mona asked.

Alarms whooped in my head. I needed to steer Mona and him off course. "What's new with the Mudder brothers, Ray?"

His eyes narrowed.

"You have another shipment to run tonight?"

"You don't learn very well, do you, Blondie?"

"I learn just fine. I'm learning more about you every day."

"Well, school's about over," he said.

"What's that supposed to mean?"

"I have a buyer for the Old Prospector Hotel. I told Jane about it this morning."

"I'll start sweating when I see an offer," I bluffed. "Until then, you're just blowing hot air, wasting my time."

"Who's your buyer, Ray?" Mona asked.

"You'll find out soon enough, Red." He smirked at me. "Blondie, you should probably bring in a box tomorrow and start packing your shit."

I rolled my eyes. "If I had a spoonful of dirt for every empty threat you gave me, I could fill up the Open Cut mine in Lead."

"Oh, this one's not empty. As soon as I sell the hotel, you'll lose your job."

I'd heard that before, too. However, while I kept my demeanor carefree on the outside, my armpits and back were coated in a dew of anxiety-inspired sweat. "How many times are you going to throw that at me, Ray?"

"Until it sticks. And this time, it will. Jane agreed to stand by her word. When I close the deal on the hotel, you're fired."

* * *

An hour before sundown, I stood outside the back door to Doc's office, chewing on my lip. The warm afternoon breeze had cooled off. It played with my loose curls, tickling my nose and ensnaring my eyelashes with wisps of hair.

Deadwood smelled like barbecued meat tonight, but my stomach was too filled with anxiety to fit in anything else. I'd escaped the office shortly after Ray finished with his threats, claiming the need to wash the smoke off of me, and raced home to pace my bedroom floor. An hour of worrying later, my job still dangled by a thread, so I went downstairs and hung out in the backyard with Addy and Layne, seeking comfort in their carefree laughter.

Now, I stared at Doc's back door. Should I go inside or not?

His car sat in the parking lot, but I was a good half hour earlier than we'd discussed. While I'd come up with several logical reasons for why I was showing up ahead of schedule, the truth of the matter was I hoped to catch a glimpse of the person he had an appointment with this evening.

Okay, that still wasn't quite true.

The ugly, jealous truth was that I wanted to see if he was with Tiffany. Plain and simple.

My self-loathing had reached a new high. My crappy-ass luck with the houses I was trying to sell catching on fire wasn't helping my cause any, either.

Glancing around to see if anyone was witnessing my public display of silliness, I tucked some curls behind my ear and noticed my hand was trembling.

Come on, Violet. Doc likes you. You like him. You're supposed to be a mature adult. Stop acting like you're giggling through your first crush.

I grabbed the door handle.

Wait! Should I go in the back door or the front?

Even though Tiffany's jeep was nowhere to be seen, she could be inside with Doc reviewing her financial portfolio, discussing some IRA options, showing off her new crotch-less panties.

Really, Violet? Come on!

I groaned. I needed a new brain. One with the jealousy button super-glued in the Off position.

So what if Tiffany was in there? She was his client and he was my client. As far as she was concerned, Doc and I were just pals. And if her tongue was in his mouth when I walked in, I'd grab her from behind, turn her upside-down, and pile-drive her sorry ass into Doc's hardwood floor. Or her sorry head, in this case.

I puffed my cheeks and blew out a breath. Screw it.

I twisted the knob and slipped inside the back door, pulling it closed behind me with a soft click. Pausing, I listened for the sound of voices. The hallway seemed stuffy. It must have been ten degrees warmer than outside.

Silence issued from the front, but the sound of running water came from the bathroom door just ahead on my left.

I inched down the warm hall lit by the last of the sun's light pouring through the front windows. I sniffed, checking for the scent of perfume, picking up hints of Doc's cologne mixed with something different but familiar, a little spicy, kind of manly.

"Hello?" I called.

Nobody answered.

The water turned off.

I was two steps from the bathroom door when the light seeping from under the door went dark. The knob turned and the door opened.

Smiling, I said, "I'm a little earl—"

Detective Cooper stepped out.

I yipped in surprise.

He jerked, his hands coming up in some Bruce-Lee-like karate block.

My eye twitched at just the sight of his chiseled face. "What are you doing back here?"

"Using the head." His gaze measured me, his hands lowering. "What are *you* doing back here?"

Busted! I tried to think fast on my feet. "I have a question for Doc."

Brilliant, Einstein. *Shut up!*

One of his eyebrows lifted. "At this time of night?"

"Night?" I pointed toward the end of the hall at the front

windows beyond. "The sun is still up."

"Barely." He crossed his arms and took a wide-legged stance, his usual drill-the-suspect posture. "Do you always come through the back door when you have a question for Mr. Nyce?"

I held his stare, determined not to let him ruffle my feathers. "Sure. He's a friend." That sounded lame, so I added. "And my client."

"I thought he'd already bought a house." Cooper's steely eyes probed.

Trying not to squirm or fidget, I said, "He did." A drip of sweat rolled down my spine. "He's considering picking up a rental for some extra income."

Smooth lie! I gave myself a mental thumbs-up and smiled again, determined to hide all of my dark secrets behind white teeth.

Coop just stared back. "Do you always adopt this kind of a casual relationship with your clients?"

"No, of course not." I realized he could call me on that lie when it came to his uncle. "Except for Harvey, of course."

"And Wolfgang Hessler," he added, his gaze challenging me to deny it.

"That was a unique situation." He was the only serial killer I'd dated ... so far.

His head cocked to the side a little, as if he had his doubts. I resisted the urge to plead my case.

"I heard Wymonds talking about you the other night at the Golden Sluice," Cooper said.

Jeff was talking about me in a bar? That couldn't be good. Hold up. I thought Jeff had stopped drinking after his soon-to-be-ex moved out.

I shrugged. "It's a free country. Jeff can say whatever he wants. It doesn't mean it's true."

"What about your new client? Mr. Top Hat from Vegas?"

How did Cooper know about Cornelius? Had the cops been called during the ruckus two nights ago?

"What about him?"

"Do you use his back door, too?"

I crossed my arms so that I wouldn't clobber him. "I don't see how this is any of your business, Detective Cooper. Being friendly with my clients isn't breaking any laws, nor does it incriminate me with regard to the headless corpse over at Mudder Brothers. So, what's your point?"

"I'm just trying to figure you out, Ms. Parker."

His smirk reminded me of Ray's earlier this afternoon and made me want to stomp on his toe. I leaned toward him, lowering my voice. "Really, Cooper? Or is it that you just get off on harassing smart blondes who can solve the cases you can't?"

His eyes frosted over.

Oops. I might have gone too far there. I glanced at the back door, wondering if I should retreat before he handcuffed me to a runaway stagecoach.

A muscle in his jaw ticked. "That was pretty low, Violet."

Yes, it was. "Well, you really piss me off sometimes."

"Only sometimes?"

Squeezing away the tension he'd caused in the back of my neck, I dropped my focus to his chest. His black tie was covered with little police crests.

"Why do you have to always be so bristly and probing?" I asked.

"It's my job."

My eyes returned to his face. "It's your job to be an asshole to me?"

"I tried to be nice to you yesterday in my office."

"True." I'd give him that.

"Then you puked on my favorite tie."

My cheeks flamed.

I heard the jingle of bells—someone had opened the front door. I'd been saved.

We both looked down the hall as Doc came into view wearing a white button up shirt with the sleeves rolled up and dark blue jeans that hugged his long legs. In his hand, he clutched a batch of mail.

He stopped at the sight of us standing there, and looked from Cooper to me, his focus dipping for a split-second to my dress before climbing back to my mouth and then eyes.

His eyebrows lifted slightly. "What's going on?"

I stepped back against the wall, putting some much needed space between the detective and me. "I stopped in to say, 'Hi,' and ran into Cooper. Silly me, I didn't realize the Deadwood police had moved their interrogation chamber to your bathroom."

Doc's lips twitched, but he kept a straight face. "Did you manage to convince the detective of your innocence?"

"No. He still thinks I did it in the conservatory with the lead pipe."

Cooper didn't even crack a grin. He really should try to remove that corncob from his anal cavity.

"Don't you have a question for Mr. Nyce, Violet?" Cooper asked.

Did I? "What question?"

"The one you had to stop in to ask him this late in the evening while dressed in your Sunday best rather than just giving him a call."

I glanced down at my blue paisley wrap-around dress. "This isn't my Sunday best."

"I can vouch for that," Doc said.

I fought the urge to shoot Doc a warning glare.

Cooper raised one brow, but said nothing. He waited for that question of mine.

Crap!

I looked to Doc for help, but he just grinned back, letting me flounder, damn him. Double crap!

"Right. My question." *Think, think, think.* "I was ah … wondering if you would … um … take a look at some papers my bank sent to me."

Jeesh. A ninety-five year old with cataracts could see

through that lie.

"Papers, huh?" Cooper squinted at me a couple more seconds, and then turned to Doc. "If you and I are finished here, I'll let myself out the back so Violet can show you her *papers*."

"We're done," Doc said, chuckling. "I'll call you in a couple of days."

Why? Was Doc handling Cooper's finances? Or was this about me? About the headless body? The fire earlier today? My snooping?

I took a calming breath, reminding the vain, hysterical broad in my head that not everything was about her.

Before he left, Cooper shot me a parting glare. "Stay away from Mudder Brothers. I meant what I said there the other night."

I waited until he'd closed the door behind him to flip him off. "God, that man drives me nuts."

"What did he mean?"

"About what?"

Doc leaned his shoulder against the wall. "That Mudder Brothers comment."

"Who knows what Cooper means most of the time? He speaks in some kind of cop lingo."

"He sounded pretty clear to me. What happened at Mudder Brothers the other night?"

Crud. This was not how I'd planned to let Doc in on my theory about Ray and George Mudder. Not the time or place. Some things are better shared when naked. Things like sneaking around in funeral homes looking for clues about a body-part-stealing crime ring.

"Violet," Doc's voice had grown serious, that lilt of mirth long gone. "Spit it out."

"I'm not sure where to start."

"How about the truth? Why you were at Mudder Brothers again?"

"For a viewing." That was the truth.

"Keep talking."

"Elsa Haskell died, and Harvey and I went to give our condolences to the family. Cooper showed up later and being the suspicious toad that he is, he decided I was up to no good and threatened me with a restraining order."

Doc's eyes took on a feral squint. "Why do I have the feeling that you just skipped from the introduction to the final chapter in that story?"

I shrugged, hugging my arms. "Okay, so maybe I skipped the part about using Harvey as a decoy during the viewing so that I could sneak into George Mudder's back room and look for clues for a body-part-stealing crime that I think Ray is involved in." I paused after spewing that bit. I needed a breath.

"What?"

Now that I had my tongue rolling, I figured I might as well let it all out.

"And maybe I omitted the part about Cooper showing up while Natalie was with me in the room behind the glass trying to help me see what George had locked up tight in one of his big crates. And maybe Cooper then busted Natalie and me after we'd escaped to the parking lot, and when she tried to show him the tattoo on her butt to prove our innocence, he threatened her with a public nudity charge and mentioned taking me down to the station. But come on, really, I think he's going a little too far with the restraining order warning. Don't you?"

Doc stared back at me, his jaw unhinged. "You're kidding, right?"

"Did I mention that the crate was so heavy that Natalie and I could barely budge it? Or that Harvey was wearing strawberry-scented love gel that he and his widowed lover-girl had gotten on the God-awful yellow plaid suit he borrowed from her dead husband's closet?"

"Holy shit." He scrubbed his hand down his face, leaving a furrowed brow behind.

"I know. Kind of crazy, right?"

"Just 'kind of?'" He crossed his arms.

His rigid body language kept me rooted in my spot by the bathroom door. He obviously wasn't thrilled with my Nancy Drew initiative. No surprise there. But then again, he didn't have Ray crawling up his ass day in and day out. Maybe if Doc walked a mile in my boots, he'd have a little more understanding.

"When were you going to tell me about this?"

I shrugged. "Eventually. I was building up to it."

"Violet, we made a deal, remember? No more secrets."

He was one to talk. Late meetings with Cooper and sneaky phone calls to his ex-lover aside, Doc still tended to change the subject during our nightly chats when I asked about his past or his ghost-sniffing ability.

My cell phone rang, saving us from a verbal tug-o-war regarding who was the bigger secret keeper.

I pulled it from my purse and looked at the number. Cornelius. "Oh, fudge," I'd forgotten why I'd come to Doc's office in the first place. I shoved my phone back in my purse without answering it. "We gotta go."

Sundown was fast approaching while Doc and I stood here in his stuffy back hallway not touching.

"You ready?" I hoped he wouldn't hold my secret-keeping against me and decide to skip tonight. I really needed his help.

"Who's driving?" he asked.

"I was thinking we should probably play it safe and drive separately." With Natalie out there spying on him from her truck, I didn't want to take any chances.

"No," he said flat out.

"No?"

Shoving off the wall, he shook his head. "If you want me at that hotel, you're driving me there. I want to talk to you about something on the way over."

"You do?"

"Just give me a minute to lock up."

I slipped out the back door and waited, keeping an eye out for Natalie's truck until Doc joined me and ushered me to lead the way.

Still, no touching. Not even his usual flirting brushes. I slowed, hoping he'd bump into me by accident, but he matched my pace. Damn him. After the crappy-ass day I'd had, I could really use some touching from Doc, a stolen kiss or two, some well-placed rubs, even.

"You were early this evening," he said when we reached the pickup.

Right. I learned my lesson on that one, too, thanks to Cooper. Doc held the door for me as I climbed behind the wheel, but managed to keep his distance.

"I got antsy."

He walked around the back of the pickup and crawled inside the cab next to me. "I heard about Wymonds' garage. You okay?"

"Yeah. Nobody got hurt."

"Good. Cooper most likely knows about us now, you realize. You should probably practice your lying on the fly a bit more if we're going to keep this up."

What did he mean "if"? I winced. I didn't like the sound of that.

"I doubt he'll mention it to anyone, though," Doc added.

"I hope not." I frowned over at him. "I don't mean that the way it sounded."

"Just drive, Violet." He stayed on his side of the cab with no attempt to reach out to me.

I started up the pickup and backed out of my spot. While I'd never been the touchy-feely kind of girlfriend, Doc's withdrawal stung. I searched for something to break the silence building between us.

"What did you want to talk to me about? Is it about that demon cult book?"

I pulled out onto the street, looking around for Natalie's truck. All clear.

"No. It's about the Old Prospector Hotel. I spent some time digging around in the library yesterday, then online at home."

"Sorry I could only text you last night." I'd missed the soothing sound of his voice way too much, which had kept me awake with frustration long after Natalie's sleep talking had stopped. The girl really needed a muzzle some nights.

"You had a sick kid, Violet. I understand. How is Addy?"

"Good. I think she learned her lesson about sneaking a half-pound of M&Ms into her room and eating them all in one sitting."

He chuckled, a deep, raspy rumbling sound.

A flame of hope rose in my chest. Maybe everything would be all right if I just allowed the ashes from today's explosions to settle.

I glanced at him, admiring, remembering the feel of his skin under my fingers. I corralled the strong primal need to reach across the bench seat and touch his thigh, his arm, any part of him.

Instead, I gripped the steering wheel, focused on allowing that flame of hope some space and time to breathe and grow, and asked him, "So, what did you learn about the hotel?"

"It was the site of a multiple suicide."

My flame of hope extinguished.

Chapter Eleven

Once upon a time there was a Realtor who drove an old green pickup off the edge of the Open Cut mine and screamed obscenities all of the way to the bottom.

The End.

In my peripheral vision, I could see Doc watching me. After dropping his bomb about the "multiple-suicide" tragedy at the Old Prospector Hotel, he probably was wondering if my head would go supernova right in front of him.

I eased the Picklemobile to a stop at a red light, pumping the gas pedal a little to ease it through a case of the sputters. The old beast seemed to be channeling my emotions.

I kept my eyes glued to the round tail lights of a blue, early-sixties Thunderbird in front of us. The rich fumes from its dual exhaust pipes seeped in through the vents, feeding the headache building behind my eyes.

"Define 'multiple suicide,'" I said, cranking my window down and sucking in some fresh air.

Doc followed my lead and lowered his window. "Four women found in one of the upstairs rooms."

"Only women?"

"Prostitutes."

Of course, painted ladies. My eyes watered from the stink of exhaust, not so much the sad loss of lives. Death was too often a casualty of their rough-and-rowdy careers.

"How long ago did this happen?" I asked.

According to Jeff and Harvey, the last cat house had closed in the eighties. A multiple suicide didn't bode well for business, I guessed, which would explain the hotel's history of decline as noted in the figures Tiffany shared with Cornelius and me.

"Back in late 1800s, after the Black Hills Gold Rush."

That long ago? Maybe I wouldn't drive off the rim of the Open Cut after all.

Doc continued. "The only other instance I found of a death on the premises was from a stray bullet during a gunfight in the street in front of the place."

I squeezed the bridge of my nose, trying to squish my headache. "So, if this hotel really is haunted," and heaven help us all if Cornelius was legit, "it's probably one of those four prostitutes?"

"Most likely."

Finally, the light turned green and the Thunderbird left us in a cloud of smoke. Nice. I hit the gas. "Are ghosts always tied to the place where they die?"

"No."

I waited for more of an explanation and, as usual, I received nothing but dead air. I shot Doc a frowning look. "Care to expand on that."

"It gets complicated."

So had our relationship, and in such a short time, too. Go figure. "Try me."

He seemed to hesitate.

I thought I knew why. "Before you bring up me not buying into this supernatural business, let's just pretend for a moment that I believe in ghosts, and that you believe I believe in ghosts." I turned right onto Main Street. The hotel was at the other end. "Okay?"

"If you say so."

"Could the ghost rumored to haunt the Old Prospector have actually died somewhere else?"

If memory served me right, Cornelius had claimed to see possibly three ghosts during our first visit to the place, and then hear two more in the wall upstairs. So, either the four prostitutes had been having a slumber party, or they were playing musical walls with Cornelius.

"Yes," Doc said. "Some of the ghosts I've encountered died elsewhere."

I pondered that for a moment. "So, you're saying these dead prostitutes may not be hanging around the joint still. The ghost could be some lonesome, lovesick dead miner who'd come looking for his favorite prostitute. Only when he arrived, she'd already moved on to the next town, so he stayed at the hotel, pining for her ever since."

"Sure. I guess." Doc chuckled. "Those are nice rose-colored glasses you're wearing tonight."

I shrugged. "I'm a romantic at heart."

"I'll keep that in mind the next time I'm trying to woo you."

As if he even had to try. One flirting glance from him most days and I swooned like an Elvis groupie.

"Well, if ghosts can roam," I said, "that changes things."

"For whom?"

"You."

"What do you mean?"

"You don't know what you're going to walk into at the hotel. It could be one of those prostitutes," or more than just one, "or someone else entirely."

"Right. What's your point?"

"How can you prepare for what you're about to experience?"

And for that matter, how could I? I had figured on Doc being ready mentally for whatever hit him so he wouldn't have a repeat, keeling-over performance like what had happened weeks ago in the Carhart house, when he'd crumpled and been knocked out cold for a good five minutes. But now I wasn't so sure this was a good idea. My two-inch heels weren't appropriate attire for catching a six-foot-plus male in my arms.

I needed to have a game plan. If Doc passed out on me in the middle of the casino, I couldn't just sweep him under the rug and move on. People would notice the big lump in the carpet, the EMS might be called in, Reid could show up,

Natalie would catch word of it all and Tiffany, too. Crap! My lower back started to sweat.

This could blow up in my face—and Doc's. He didn't need folks thinking something was wrong with him, not when he handled other people's money for a living.

"That's the catch, huh?" Doc said. "If I walk in and get hit hard, I'm going to have to leave."

If he could walk out on his own, that was.

I pulled into the parking lot behind the hotel. We both were silent while I found a spot to park the Picklemobile. The backfire sounded ten times louder in clear, early evening air, and surprised a yelp out of an older couple passing by.

Doc grinned at me in the semidarkness. "There's no sneaking around in this thing is there?"

"Harvey likes to arrive with a bang."

We stared at each other for several heartbeats, while the air thickened with a tension that had nothing to do with ghosts and haunted hotels.

So many pheromones, so little time. Damn.

He reached across the seat and tugged one of my many wayward curls. "You ready, Boots?"

The heat in his eyes warmed away my chills, but my hands stayed locked on the steering wheel, my anxiety churning in my chest. "Maybe this isn't such a great idea."

"Chickening out?" His grin teased.

"Yeah, I think I am."

His left eyebrow rose slightly. "You have no problem sneaking around in a funeral home with a dead body in the next room over, but a hotel rumored to be haunted gives you pause."

"It's not the hotel that has me concerned."

"Is this about being seen with me in public? Will it help if I promise not to touch you?"

While his smile still teased, his gaze had an intensity that spoke of something more serious. I ignored the reference to the Natalie mess. "I'm worried about what I'm dragging you

into."

"I think I can handle a few ghosts."

"Are you sure?"

"Let's go see." He shoved open his door.

We walked single file across the parking lot with me in the lead. I hesitated outside the hotel's main entrance in front of a couple of benches divided by an ashtray. The smell of smoke hung heavy in the warm evening air. Doc stepped around me and pulled one of the glass doors open, holding it wide enough for me to enter without touching him.

The hotel greeted us with a whoosh of cool air, the jingling of slot machines, and Johnny Cash singing about a boy named Sue.

I heard Doc sniff and looked up into his face, searching for any of the typical signs I'd witnessed when he was about to be slammed with a ghost—pale skin, shallow breaths, dilated pupils. His usual grin was gone, his tension visible in the lines on his forehead.

Leading the way, I walked through the lobby, past the rows of slot machines lined with patrons. By the time we reached Socrates, we'd traversed several invisible walls of flowery perfume, making my headache a dull roar. I paused and pretended to read the placard about the old mule.

Doc's hand brushed mine as he joined me. "Socrates could use a nose job."

A peek at Doc showed no signs of trouble. "You okay?" I asked, anyway.

"No problem."

"Does that mean the rumors are false?"

"Not necessarily. It just means the only beings down here still have blood pumping through their veins."

I peered around the room, looking for any familiar faces—Natalie's and Tiffany's, in particular. Spotting only strangers, I grabbed Doc's hand, squeezing it.

He lifted both brows. "You're taking a chance."

Everything about Doc was a gamble for me. "I know."

I tugged him toward the elevator. He didn't pull free.

The elevator doors opened as soon as I hit the button, as if they were waiting for us to arrive. Squeezing Doc's hand tighter, I drew him inside behind me and pushed the third floor button as the doors shut.

Closing the distance between us, I wrapped my arms around his neck. "Still feeling good?"

He stood stiff as a tree as I pressed against him. "What are you doing, Violet?"

Throwing myself at him, as usual. "In most cultures, this is considered a pre-mating ritual."

The corner of his mouth twitched. "There's a camera in the corner watching us."

"I don't care."

"You should. This is a small town. People talk. A lot."

Pushing aside all of the angst about my screwed-up life, I leaned my forehead against his chest and just breathed. The scent of his skin mixed with his fabric softener and woodsy cologne eased some of the tension pounding behind my eyes.

The second floor bell dinged; we kept rising.

"Thank you for helping me tonight, Doc."

"I haven't done anything."

"You're here."

"I'm curious."

"Maybe so," I smiled up at him, "but you're here with me."

His dark eyes searched mine, then his easy grin surfaced. "Yeah, well, I have a weakness for smart blondes with sexy curves."

I nuzzled his neck. "What are you doing later?"

The third floor bell dinged.

His hands skimmed down my ribs and over my hips. "Peeling that dress off of you."

I pulled away from Doc as the doors opened, loving the fire in his eyes as they drifted down the front of my dress.

"Ready?" I asked.

"For you, Boots, on cue."

I stepped out of the elevator into the third floor hallway. Halfway to Cornelius' suite, I realized Doc wasn't following me.

A glance behind me found him leaning against the wall, bent part-way over. His eyes were closed, each ragged breath visible in his bent back.

I rushed back to him. "Doc?"

"It's here."

"Is the smell as strong as Prudence's was?" I said referring to the presence he claimed was in the Carhart house.

"I told you before, Violet; it's not just a smell."

"Humor me."

"It's stronger. Something is wrong."

"Maybe we should leave." I glanced back toward the elevator.

"No. Just give me a minute."

He inhaled deeply several times, his Adam's apple bobbing with each gulp. I stood by and kneaded my hands. The third floor seemed unnaturally quiet, thank God. The sight of Doc all pasty-gray and wheezing would draw attention.

"Okay, let's go." Doc pushed off the wall, and led the way. "Which room is it?"

"Just up ahead on the left." I followed Doc, close enough to try to catch him if he dropped.

When we reached Cornelius' room, Doc leaned against the jamb.

I frowned up at him. "You sure you want to do this?"

He knocked on the door.

The sound of footfalls came from the other side. As the door clicked open, I stood up straight and pasted on my happy-Realtor smile.

"Hi, Corn—" I started.

Only it wasn't Cornelius. It was Safari Skipper from behind the hotel's reception desk.

She smiled back. "You must be Violet. Master Curion awaits you."

I must be Violet? She said that as if we hadn't already met at the reception desk.

She held open the door, ushering us inside the shadowed entryway, and then led the way into the chilled suite. Cornelius must have the windows open, or the air conditioner cranked on high.

I hesitated, leaning back to whisper to Doc, "Did she say 'Master'?"

He nodded, sweat beading his upper lip. His eyes looked like black marbles against his too-pale skin, his pupils were dilated.

"Doc, you should—"

"Just go." He nudged me forward.

I took several steps across the plush carpet and came to an abrupt stop just inside the darkened, in-suite living room. "Holy crap."

Every available surface was covered in computer screens, video cameras, and black boxes with blinking green and red lights. In the midst of the digital wonderland, Cornelius sat at a round table with three people I'd never seen in my life. Each sat in front of an open laptop, the screens lighting their faces in an eerie glow—the only light in the room. The tang of heated plastic and electronic bits mixed with a sweet vanilla aroma, undoubtedly from the dinner-plate-sized white candle flickering in the center of the table. The scene alone gave me goosebumps, the blast of cool air from a fan to my right increased my chills.

Where had Safari Skipper run off to? Who were the others at the table? And why in the hell was Cornelius wearing a Viking-like hat with only one horn?

Cornelius glanced up from the screen, looking absurd with the horn sticking out the side of his head as he stroked his goatee. "Violet, you came, just as promised."

I didn't remember promising him anything. It was more

like an ultimatum.

Cornelius' cornflower blue eyes glanced behind me, his smile appearing, making his cheekbones look even more gaunt. "And you brought a friend—excellent. Seven will help us make a stronger circle of power."

"Circle of power?" What was this? A casting call for *The World's Greatest Super Friends* cartoon?

"Is your friend a believer?" Cornelius continued in spite of my slack jaw. "Skeptics might skew our results tonight."

"A believer in what?" I asked. A stupid question, but I had a short history of misunderstanding Cornelius, and I wanted to make sure we were on the exact same page tonight.

Cornelius laughed. It sounded like a horse whinnying. My headache clenched my brain. "Ghosts, of course. I told you we were having a séance tonight."

No. He had not told me *that*.

I would have remembered if he had, and I would've worn something much more black and ninja-ish, like everyone else—if I'd actually decided to show up.

And I would never have asked Doc to join me.

Oh, shit. Doc. Wincing, I slowly turned to look up at Doc and ran headlong into his very dark, very pinched glare. A muscle ticked in his jaw.

"You should have told me, Violet," he said. He might have been compressing pieces of the Earth's mantle into diamonds between his back molars.

I opened my mouth, but hesitated, not sure where to start in my please-forgive-me speech, especially with Cornelius listening.

"Don't waste your breath," Doc said in a low, disgust-thickened tone.

After shooting a wary glare behind me, he turned and stalked out the door, leaving me alone with the ghost whisperer and his crew of ghost-seeking ninjas.

* * *

After Doc left, Cornelius spent time explaining to me the purpose of all of his meters and gadgets and cameras, and what each of us were supposed to do throughout the séance.

Safari Skipper and her leather-covered-biker-boyfriend were in charge of the video cameras. They were to make sure all fifteen, spread throughout the suite, stayed running while the ghosts came calling. According to Cornelius, ghosts were often shy and had a funny habit of turning off electronics.

The other two ninjas were fellow hotel guests who had overheard Skipper telling her boyfriend about the excitement several nights ago at the last séance. They looked to be in their early twenties. Both were tall, skinny, and a bit gangly, like they'd been stretched on a taffy pulling machine. I couldn't tell if they were siblings or a match made in heaven, since they sat close to each other at the table, but never touched. They told me their names, which I promptly forgot and decided to go with Thing 1 and Thing 2, in the spirit of Dr. Seuss.

Cornelius made an excellent Cat-in-the-Hat, with the way he flitted around the room in his kooky, one-horned Viking hat. I hadn't found the guts yet to ask what the purpose of the hat was, but the night was young.

During the séance, Thing 1 and Thing 2 would have the job of keeping an eye on all ten of the Electro-Magnetic Field meters set throughout the room, which Cornelius explained were supposed to measure the fluctuations emitted from entities. These EMF fluxes supposedly occurred when entities tried to communicate or interact with someone in our "human realm." The greater the flux, the stronger the entity, according to Cornelius.

My role during the party would be just to sit still and listen. When I asked "to what?" Cornelius laughed at me like I was joking, and then gave me a small, palm-sized digital recorder to monitor—as in push the Record button when he instructed, and then make sure it continued recording no matter what happened.

I'd rather have been in charge of watching cameras. At least then I could move around a little and try to walk off my worries about whether Doc would ever talk to me again after today's multiple disasters.

Finally, Cornelius announced it was time to start the séance. Much to my surprise, he didn't want us to sit around the table and hold hands.

"Hollywood's idea of a séance is pure fiction," he told us and sat down alone at the table.

I still had trouble understanding which part of a séance wasn't fiction. But, since he'd reminded us multiple times that skepticism would draw negative energy, and then reinforced his warning with a menacing frown, I kept my big, skeptical mouth shut.

"Violet, have a seat on the ottoman and close your eyes. I need you to channel your energy with mine."

Okay. No problem. I dropped onto the ottoman and squeezed my eyelids closed—that part I could handle. But the only kind of channeling I knew how to do involved a remote control and a television.

It's too bad Harvey wasn't here with me. He would have made this whole scene much more palatable.

I sat quietly in the dark as Cornelius began to chant in a low-pitched voice. What he was chanting I had no idea, but I was pretty sure it wasn't English.

For the umpteenth time, I asked myself why I hadn't followed Doc's lead, chased him down, and apologized all over myself.

Money. Oh, right. The green stuff that kept my kids fed and clothed.

I stifled a yawn.

I so needed this sale. My gut churned at the "what ifs" that kept creeping up on me in the darkness.

What if Cornelius decided not to buy the hotel?

What if I lost my job and had to start over … again?

What if Doc had just walked away for good?

Another yawn surfaced. I remembered where I was and swallowed it. My shoulders relaxed as Cornelius's chants became rhythmic, mesmerizing, hypnotic.

What was I thinking about? Oh, right. What-if crap.

What if Ray really was stealing body parts?

What if I stumbled upon the whole mess in the Mudder brothers' garage?

What if Natalie found out about me and … .

A kaleidoscope of colors whirled around me, then blackness chased it all away.

… I jerked awake at the sound of the suite's door slamming open.

Blinking through my sleep-hazed vision, I whirled around to see if Doc had returned to join the séance.

But it wasn't Doc.

Instead, Wolfgang Hessler stood in the doorway in all of his breath-taking, handsome glory.

I sprang to my feet, my heart battering my ribs, almost bruising.

What was *he* doing here? He was dead. I'd seen him dead, even confirmed his identity to Cooper as Wolfgang's corpse laid on a stretcher.

Time seemed to slow to a crawl, my vision tunneling.

I gaped at the killer who'd tried to torch me in his mother's house last month. His handsome face began to shrivel and darken, like he was smoldering from the inside out. Wavy blond locks fell from his head in clumps, until only scorched patches of flesh and bone were left on his blackened skull.

His silk shirt and dark trousers smoldered, small fires breaking out here and there on his body. He stood there in that doorway, staring at me with cobalt blue eyes that seemed to bulge from their sockets as his skin blackened and crinkled around them.

Heat rolled over me in waves as he burned. Small pops sounded from the flames. The sweet, but acrid smell of burning flesh surrounded me, filling my lungs, making me retch. I tried to step back, but couldn't. My knees had locked up tight.

Wolfgang lurched forward. The sudden movement caused his nose to fall off his face.

I watched with hysterical, horror-filled laughter tumbling from my throat as it bounced across the carpet and rolled out of sight into the bathroom. Tears ran down my cheeks.

He staggered toward me, his body stiff-legged like rigor mortis had begun to set in.

"Violet, darling," he said through rusty sounding vocal chords. Smoke seeped out from his swollen, split lips as he spoke.

I opened my mouth, but could only manage to whimper back at him. My feet refused to budge, no matter how hard I willed them to get the hell out of Dodge. Shudders started in my shoulders and moved south. An icy layer of terror coated my muscles, freezing me in place.

The last vestiges of what was Wolfgang disappeared in a lick of flames, except for his eyes. Those blue-blue eyes I'd stared into so many times as I'd daydreamed of what could be. Now, framed in a blackened skull, they promised nightmares.

Several more lurches and it stood before me, reeking of cooked flesh and bone and smoke. I tried to scream, but only air escaped, no sound.

"Violet," it rasped again, then clawed at its face, ripping away strips of charred flesh. It opened its jaws wide enough to grab what was left of the sides of its mouth with each gnarled fist. Then it tore its face in half right in front of me.

I screamed. Every cell inside of me screamed.

Wolfgang's skull cracked like an eggshell, and from its center a pair of horns pushed out, followed by a misshapen slick, black head covered in pustules with two orange eyes that glowed like embers. It sneered at me, showing off its sharp, sword-like incisors.

My scream died, all of my breath feeling like it'd been sucked from my lungs.

"Violet Parker." Its voice was smooth and deep; its accent sounded strange, like a blend of a Southern drawl with a hint of some Slavic tongue.

"What do you want?" I whispered, my vocal chords tight with dread.

It leaned in close enough for me to smell its foul, rancid breath. Tendrils of wispy steam leaked out through its snout. "GET OUT!" It screamed, spraying bloody spittle in my face.

I shrieked and stumbled backwards, my body free suddenly from its frozen state. Tripping over the ottoman, I tumbled ass-over-teakettle onto the floor behind me. When I scrambled back to my feet, the thing was gone. The pieces of flesh, the smoke, the smoldering carpet, everything. Even the stench was gone, replaced by the vanilla scent of the lone candle still flickering on the table.

In the monster's place, Cornelius and his group of ghost hunters all stood around me, slack-jawed, their eyes wide.

"Holy fucking shit!" Safari Skipper's biker boyfriend broke the silence.

My gaze bounced from one to the next. "Did you see that?"

"What?" Thing 1 asked.

"Was it a ghost?" Thing 2 asked.

"It was a ..." I paused, stumbling for words. What was it?

Cornelius stepped forward and grabbed me by the shoulders. "Violet, what did you see? Was it hazy, kind of white? Floating?"

Not at all. Wolfgang had been crystal clear, in full color, lurching and stinking. I blinked, trying to make sense of what had just happened.

"Did it talk to you?" Cornelius continued. "Did it mention me?"

Him? Why would Wolfgang mention Cornelius? A weariness settled into my limbs, making them heavy. I dropped onto the ottoman. "Tell me what happened?"

"No, *you* tell us," Skipper said. "One minute you were over here snoozing away, even drooling a little, and the next thing we knew, you jumped up and started screaming your head off."

Snoozing away. The séance. The chanting. The yawning. Oh, Christ. I'd fallen asleep. I covered my face with my hands and spoke through my palms. "I've been having trouble sleeping lately. I must have had a nightmare."

"That was some messed up dream, lady," biker guy said. "You have one hell of a set of lungs on you."

I lowered my hands and pushed to my feet. "I'm sorry I messed up the séance, you guys. I should probably go."

Cornelius put his arm around my shoulders and walked me to the door. "I want to talk to you more about this," he said for my ears only. "But your eyes are all red-rimmed and you look like you've been up for a week straight. You need some rest."

"Gee, thanks," I tried to laugh, but a noise came out that sounded like someone sat on a chicken.

I tensed as he opened the door, afraid I'd see Wolfgang

standing on the other side and it would start all over again.

The hall was empty.

"We should do this again, Violet. You are an excellent conduit." Cornelius shut the door behind us. "Come see me in the morning."

"Cornelius, I'm not really in the mood to sit through another séance anytime soon."

"No, silly," he lightly punched my shoulder with his fist, like I was quite a kidder.

I wasn't laughing.

"Come and see me about the hotel."

"What do you mean?" My brain was still choking on smoke and adrenaline.

"I want to put an offer on it."

I blinked. Twice. "You do?"

"Of course. This place is a ghost gold mine."

"Did something happen while I was sleeping in there?"

"Hell, yes. The EMF meters redlined."

"Which ones?"

"All of them." He leaned forward and pinched my cheek. His weird half-smile almost three-quarters full. "Violet, this place is going to give the Winchester Mystery House a run for its ghost-touring money."

"Great." I tried to sound enthusiastic, but after having the piss scared out of me, all I could muster was another blink. "I'll see you in the morning."

He practically danced back into the room.

I, on the other hand, shuffled to the elevator like I was ninety, using the walls every now and then when my legs wobbled and threatened to give out. I made it out the front doors without seeing anyone I knew, thank God. I sat behind the wheel of the Picklemobile for a few minutes, just breathing in and out. Then, I eased out of the parking lot and cruised back up Main Street under the streetlights.

The idea of going home and to bed practically gave me the hives. I needed to let the ashes of Wolfgang's freakshow settle first. I needed something comforting to soften the vivid smells and dull the scenes of the nightmare.

I needed Doc. But he seemed to have disappeared into thin air. His office and house were dark, his car missing. I checked the library parking lot, even though it was closed. He wasn't there, either.

Cruising through several back streets, I cursed all of the Camaro SS muscle cars parked around town for repeatedly making my pulse speed up again and again by mistake. Damned Deadwood and its Kool Nites.

I parked next to the Rec Center and pulled out my cell phone. He didn't answer. I didn't leave a message.

I started to put the phone away, and then changed my mind and dialed Natalie.

She answered on the second ring. "Wonderland. This is Alice."

I smiled, the sound of her voice taking some of the edge off of my night. "Hey, girl, I need to talk to you."

"Can it wait a bit? I'm kind of busy."

"You on a date?" I could only hope she'd finally moved on to a new man.

"Sort of."

"Define 'sort of.'"

"I'm with Doc."

My gut clenched, but my brain knew better. "Define 'with Doc.'"

"Well, I'm watching him."

"Define 'watching him.'"

"Geez, what do you think I am? Webster's talking dictionary?"

"Natalie, where are you?"

"Parked down the street from the Golden Sluice."

"I take it Doc is in the bar."

"Yep," she said, whispering as if he could hear her from her pickup. "And he's not alone."

Chapter Twelve

Monday, August 20th

V iolet, wake up." The soft sound of Aunt Zoe's voice
dragged me out of my dead-to-the-world state. She stared
down at me, her brow wrinkled. "You're gonna be late for
work."

Frickity-frack! I threw off the quilt that had shielded me
from the morning's cool finger-jabs and stumbled to my feet.
A lack of blood flow to my gray matter made me swoon, sort
of like my reaction whenever Doc worked his magic on me.
Damn him and his cold shoulder.

Aunt Zoe grabbed my arm, steadying me. She smelled of
fresh coffee and baked apples, and I wanted to drool all over
her. I blinked until the spinning world stood still.

"Why were you sleeping on the back porch?"

I glanced around Aunt Zoe's screened in porch and the
lawn chair I'd used for a bed, trying to remember how I'd
gotten down here.

Then yesterday's train of events backed up and chugga-
chugged over me again—Cornelius in that stupid one-horned
hat, Wolfgang on fire, Natalie and her obsession with my
kind-of-boyfriend.

I held my head and groaned.

Thank God, Doc's companion at the Golden Sluice had
been Harvey and not a certain red-haired sexpot. I'd almost
reached through the phone and thumped Natalie upside the
head for scaring the crap out of me with her comment about
Doc not being alone. After how angry he was from the
surprise séance party, it didn't take much spurring for my

inner-jealous-ogre to believe the worst and twist my guts like a tie-dyed shirt.

I was going to have to do something about Doc. But not now. "I'll explain later," I told Aunt Zoe. "I need to shower and get to work."

I had a hotel offer to prepare and turn in. With any luck, I could beat Ray to the punch.

Aunt Zoe followed me upstairs. "You took sleeping pills last night."

It wasn't a question. Crap, I must have forgotten to put the bottle away.

"I was tired." More like zombie-fied after that stupid nightmare at the séance.

"You've been dead-tired for a month."

Had it only been a month since I'd hopped on this runaway mine cart that was now my life? It felt more like years.

Last night, I'd finally fallen asleep just after midnight, only to jerk awake, escaping from Wolfgang's reach yet again. This time, the scene hadn't been nearly as vivid, but between it and Natalie's sleep mumbling in our shared boudoir, I'd decided to see if the pills would keep me from dreaming. Hell, things couldn't get much worse for me in slumber-ville than they already were.

In the darkness of Aunt Zoe's kitchen, my hands had trembled so much that I'd dropped the bottle of pills—twice. The lawn chair was supposed to just be a sit-for-a-minute place, somewhere to pause and decide what to do about Doc, Cornelius, Ray, Cooper, and any other man who was trying to disturb my calm. But those pills coldcocked me right into coma-city.

"Why the pills? Why last night?" Aunt Zoe followed me into the bathroom, shutting the door behind her. Bloodhounds could take lessons from her on doggedness.

I looked down at the toilet, and then back at her. "I have to pee."

She crossed her arms, closing her eyes. "Tell me why you took the pills, Violet."

An underlying level of steel in her tone made it clear there was no slinking out of this. But I tried, anyway. "Natalie keeps talking in her sleep."

"That explains why you slept on the back porch, but not the pills, which you have fought me on taking for weeks."

Criminy! "I had another nightmare." I opted out of telling her it was during a séance, because that would lead to a bunch more questions undoubtedly followed by disappointment-filled frowns and head shakes. "I took the pills to forget it."

"How was this nightmare different from all of the others?"

Good question. I thought on that for a moment. "It was real."

I flushed the toilet and yanked back the shower curtain, turning on the faucet.

Aunt Zoe closed her eyes again as I undressed. "What do you mean 'real'?"

"I don't know." I remembered feeling the beast's spittle pelt my face right before I screamed and woke up. "The sound, the smell, the feel. It was all so realistic. Like I was standing there—all flesh, blood, and bones—while it … I mean Wolfgang came at me."

I didn't want to tell her about the monster-like thing. Wolfgang was bad enough. If I told her about his skull splitting open, she'd know for sure what a head-case I'd become and put the straight-jacket on me herself.

"Interesting," she said.

More like terrifying.

"What color were his eyes?"

Her question surprised the truth out of me. "Orange," I said, thinking of the glowing embers I saw in the demon's eyes.

"Did he say anything to you?"

I couldn't tell by looking at her if she was genuinely

curious or just playing therapist and letting me "talk it out."

"Yes," I continued with my honesty. "He told me to 'Get out.'" Or rather roared it in my face.

"Then what happened?"

"I woke up." Omitting the part about screaming and falling ass over teakettle in front of a group of ghost hunters seemed like the smart thing to do.

I checked the water, turned it a little hotter, and then stepped under the shower's spray.

"Did something spur this?" Aunt Zoe called over the noise of the shower. "Something at work, like Jeff Wymonds' garage exploding?"

"Maybe." I closed my eyes and let the hot water cascade over my head for a couple of seconds, then reached for the shampoo. Or maybe it was the whole mess with Ray and the Mudder brothers. Or the stress of fighting with Doc or dealing with Cooper's squinty eyes. "How did you hear about the explosion?"

"News travels fast in Deadwood."

Especially if it was personally delivered, and I had a sneaky suspicion this had been. "A certain fire captain didn't happen to give you a call yesterday, did he?"

"No."

Oh. Then again, I was becoming known for my misconceptions about people. Shampoo washed down the drain.

"He stopped by," she added.

I pulled the shower curtain back enough to peek out at Aunt Zoe, who was leaning against the counter. Her dark blue eyes met mine.

"Did you shoot him?" I asked.

She scoffed as if she hadn't been as crazed and vicious as a cornered porcupine the last time he'd been over. "Of course not."

"Did you let him inside?"

She lifted her chin. "His voice came through the screen

door just fine."

"What did he say?" My heart pounded a bit faster than normal. Please, please, *please* don't let Layne have had anything to do with the explosion. Could I buy a new garage on lay-away?

"He officially ruled it as an accident."

"Did he say how it started?"

"He said Jeff Wymonds had left an open can of gas in the narrow side room and closed the door overnight. Add heat and a spark from the old fuse box when the compressor kicked on, and *ka-boom*."

Compressor? Oh, right, Jeff had been pumping up Kelly's bike tires so the kids could go for a bike ride and be out from underfoot during the open house.

"Good." All of my saggy parts sagged even more in relief. I smiled at Aunt Zoe. "Did you give Reid a kiss goodbye?"

"Hell, no!"

"Not even a peck on the cheek?"

"Shut your mouth, Violet Lynn."

"You ready to tell me about what happened between you two?"

"Not yet." She stepped forward and yanked the curtain closed.

I grabbed the conditioner. "Talking about it might make you less apt to want to fill his butt with lead."

"I doubt that. But what I would like to talk about is your *friend*, Doc."

"Shhh."

"Natalie already left for work."

The subject was still *shhh*, as far as I was concerned.

"What's going on with Doc and you?"

That was the question of the month. I stuck my head under the hot water, trying to wash away my Doc-laden insecurities. It didn't work.

I shut off the water and grabbed the towel Aunt Zoe handed me through the crack in the curtain. "Nothing is going on with us." No lie there at the moment.

Wrapping the towel around me, I stepped out of the shower.

"Right. Then how do you explain that love bite on your neck?"

"What?" When did that happen? I tried to look in the mirror, but it was fogged over.

"Gotcha," Aunt Zoe said and winked. "How do you feel about me paying him a visit?"

I froze. "Why?"

"Willis tells me Doc is a whiz with money."

Willis? Oh, she meant Old Man Harvey. I always forgot he had a first name. "I wouldn't know. I haven't had much money to invest since meeting Doc." Or any money at all.

"I am thinking about diversifying my portfolio a bit more."

"Sounds like a good idea." I grabbed my robe.

"I also plan to invite him to dinner."

Cinching the belt around me, I shook my head. "Bad idea. Very bad."

"Violet, I want to get to know the man who is going to help me invest my money. I'd invite him to dinner whether he was your boyfriend or not. This has nothing to do with you."

"I don't have a boyfriend," I said loud and clear while miming a lip-zip to Aunt Zoe.

"I told you, Natalie's at work."

"I'm worried about the two sets of smaller ears living in this house." I spritzed some leave-in conditioner on my curls, and then opened the bathroom door, waving for her to follow me to my bedroom. "Why don't you just meet him somewhere for dinner?"

"I don't want to talk about my financial business in front of strangers."

"You've lived here most of your life." I closed my bedroom door behind us. "You know everyone in town."

"All the more reason to have him here in my own home

without eavesdroppers." She smiled—all sweet and loving and Betty Crocker-like. I wasn't eating the cookies she was serving.

"No." I twirled my finger for her to turn around while I slipped into my skivvies and bra.

She obliged. "I'd also like to see how he treats you."

"You said this had nothing to do with me."

"I may have fibbed a little."

"Fine." I could tell by the set tone of her voice that she had already made up her mind. I yanked my dark purple pleated v-neck dress from the closet and slid it over my head.

"If you want to invite Doc over for a family dinner, I can't stop you. It's your house." I looked in the mirror and winced at my appearance and fluffed my wet curls a little. It didn't help. "However, I'm going to invite a friend to keep me company while you talk finances with Doc."

Aunt Zoe turned around and met my eyes in the mirror. "Okay, but I don't think it's a good idea to have Natalie here."

"I'm not talking about Natalie." Curious about how Aunt Zoe was going to get rid of Natalie when Doc was going to be on the premises, I slathered a coat of purplish, grape-flavored gloss on my lips.

"Oh. You mean Willis."

Since when did Aunt Zoe call Harvey "Willis" on a regular basis? What had changed between them?

"Nope." I smacked my lips and scooped up my makeup bag. I'd have to put the rest of my face on at my desk. "Not Harvey."

"Who then?"

I smiled at Aunt Zoe's reflection. "The chief of the Deadwood Fire Department."

* * *

Ray's SUV sat alone in Calamity Jane's reserved parking area when I arrived. I took a few minutes to apply my war paint in the Picklemobile's rearview mirror before going inside to face the horse's ass.

The sinus-burning scent of Ray's cologne slapped me as soon as I closed the back door. Why must he wear so much freaking cologne? Squaring my shoulders, I reminded myself that killing a coworker was a felony and I didn't need another visit from Detective Cooper anytime soon.

All I had to do was type an offer letter, print it, and I'd be out of here. Surely, I could play nice alone with Ray for an hour.

I took a deep breath and strode down the hall past Jane's dark office and then stopped. Backing up to take a second longer look inside, I frowned. Her door stood open, which meant that she'd been in already this morning and undoubtedly noticed my tardiness. But that wasn't what had made me put on the brakes. My focus bounced from her messy desktop to the scattered folders on the floor by her file cabinet to the half-empty bottle of Jack Daniels Whiskey on her wall bookshelf.

I tiptoed inside and sniffed the half-empty coffee cup sitting on her desk. My nose wrinkled at the smell of old coffee. No hint of whiskey in there that I could tell.

Jane was in the middle of a nasty divorce from her third husband, a rotten two-timing cowboy she'd found lassoed and hogtied in her own bed while another woman polished his saddle horn. From the sight of her office, Jane's well-ordered life had been shattered along with her heart.

Men like Jane's soon-to-be ex scared me single every time I started liking a guy a little too much. Doc was the first man I'd let get inside my safe little fortress in years and look how well that was working for me.

I tip-toed out of Jane's office and headed for my desk.

Ray had his desk phone to his ear. "Sure. You want me to bring it over tonight when you get back in town?"

He looked my way as I approached.

I met his sneer head-on with a glare of my own.

"Hold on," he covered the mouthpiece. "Ever heard of an alarm clock, Blondie? You should try one some time."

"Who died and made you Hall Monitor?" I tucked my purse in my drawer and turned on my computer.

"Punctuality is the key to success—not that you have a clue what success is outside of your client's bedroom." He uncovered the mouthpiece. "Sorry about that," he told his listener, his tone matching his smirk. "I needed to scold someone. You know how it is with hired help these days. You get what you pay for. Now what were you saying?"

With visions of nooses dancing in my head, I did my best to block out Ray and focus on the task at hand. The sooner I finished, the sooner I could get the hell away from the dickhead.

Ten minutes of "uh-huhing" later, Ray hung up.

I kept typing, my gaze locked on my screen.

"What are you doing over there, Blondie?"

"Working."

"On what? Your résumé?"

I didn't reply to his taunt.

"Does Jane have you working on another one of her gopher-girl tasks?"

"No."

"I'll tell you what. To show you what a nice guy I am, how about I give you the day off to go have your nails painted."

Kiss my ass. I pressed my lips together and kept my gaze on my screen.

"Maybe you could have that hot little brunette over at the Saddle-Up Salon teach you how to do something sexy with that mop of yours. The wet poodle look isn't going to win you any beauty pageants."

I didn't bite. I wanted to, starting with his head, praying-mantis style, but I gritted my teeth and kept to task.

"Tiffany Sugarbell could teach you a thing or two about dressing for success," Ray said, striking a little too close to the mark. "Want me to send her your way after we finish the deal on the Old Prospector Hotel?"

I opened an Internet search window and typed *human castration methods*. Results with mentions of elastrator and emasculator tools made me smile as I returned to Cornelius's offer document.

"You know all of this realty business is just a waste of your time, sweetheart," Ray continued his taunts. "I don't know why you keep coming in here every morning. You're like a bird with a broken wing. You keep trying to fly when there is no hope."

I rolled my eyes and scrolled through the document, scanning to make sure I hadn't missed anything.

Kicking his Tony Lamas up on his desk, he leaned back in his chair and locked his fingers behind his head. "I'm going to have that hotel in my pocket by nightfall, you know."

Not if I beat you to it.

I shot him what I hoped was a look of disbelief. "Right. Isn't there road kill somewhere waiting for you to dine on it?"

"You don't believe me? I have the offer right here on my desk."

"Sure you do." As much as I wanted to see for myself, I kept my gaze locked on the computer screen.

His chair creaked. His boots hit the floor with a thud. "See for yourself, Blondie." He strolled over and held the offer in front of my face.

With a key-click, I hid Cornelius's offer behind my email inbox so Ray wouldn't see it.

Focusing on the paper shoved in my face, I noticed that the offer price was for several thousand dollars more than the asking price. I also noticed there was no signature on it.

Then I saw the name of buyer: George Mudder.

What?!

I read it again.

Why would George want a hotel? Did he plan on moving the funeral parlor to Main Street? There was no way the town would approve that, would it?

Maybe he was planning on getting out of the funeral business. Where had he gotten that kind of money? From selling body parts? Drugs? Something worse?

What could be worse than selling drugs and body parts?

Ray's desk phone rang. He returned to his desk, taking George's offer with him. "Ray Underhill," he said into the receiver.

I stared at my screen, my fingers paused on the keys as my brain churned on the fact that George Mudder was Ray's buyer and what that meant in the theft scheme I had imagined for the Mudder brothers.

"Sure, I'd be happy to take the mayor of Deadwood's call," Ray said extra loud, obviously for my benefit.

Looking away from his big, stupid I-win-you-lose grin, I stared at my screen without really seeing it. What was I doing before I found out about George and the hotel? Oh, yeah—Cornelius.

I returned to my own offer letter and clacked away as fast as my fingers would go. Until Ray had a signature on that offer, I still had a chance on taking the lead in this race.

Twenty minutes later, Ray had finished his schmoozing, grabbed today's paper from outside the front door, and headed for the bathroom. As soon as he closed the door, I printed out the offer paperwork.

I knocked twice on the bathroom door on my way out, yelling, "Tell Jane I'll be back after lunch," and then raced out the back door.

I called Cornelius on my way over. "I'll be there in five minutes with the offer for the hotel."

"Yes." He sounded all deep and creepy, giving the "s" an extra-long hiss at the end.

Yes? I didn't realize I'd asked a question.

"Who is this?" he asked.

I laughed. Then realized he was serious. "Cornelius, it's Violet. Your Realtor."

"Oh, good. For a moment I thought you could be one of

the ghosts we reached out to last night."

"A ghost? Calling your cell phone?" *Seriously?* Must I be a human beacon for the nearly deranged?

"I did mention that I am a ghost whisperer, didn't I?"

I pulled the phone away from my ear and shook it. Then after a deep breath, I said into it, "You mentioned it in passing."

"Excellent. I'm going to need you to bring me a protein shake."

"Right now?"

"I can't focus without protein."

Maybe that explained why this train of conversation had jumped off the tracks. But where was I going to find a protein shake in Deadwood?

"I prefer vanilla-flavored," Cornelius said, "but strawberry will work, too. Don't you just love the smell of strawberries? It reminds me of my investigation of the Strawberry Hill Mansion Museum in Kansas City and the Lady in Red apparition there who is quite chatty with guests, especially those of us who can converse on her plane of existence. Although, she seems very depressed about being dead."

"Uhhh, okay then. I'll find a shake and bring it with me."

I'd have agreed to bring him a chunk of the moon if it meant I'd get to cram a *signed* offer down Ray's throat before the day was out.

I hung up. Now where was I going to find a vanilla protein drink?

Doc.

I knew from hands-on experience that he was in tip-top muscle shape. He'd surely have some protein drink.

When I called him, he didn't answer. Damn, that would have been a great excuse to break the ice between us.

Who else would have protein drink mix? Cooper? Or did he drink eggs like Rocky Balboa for protein? No, he probably just ate a live hen full of un-hatched eggs every morning.

I gave up, did a u-turn, and headed up to the Piggly

Wiggly in Lead.

An hour later, I knocked on Cornelius's hotel room door, vanilla protein shake in hand.

Safari Skipper opened the door. Déjà vu.

"Hi, Miss Parker," she held the door wide as I slipped by, and then followed on my heels. "Did you have any more wicked nightmares last night?"

"No," I lied.

"That's a bummer."

How nice that someone appreciated my terror-filled dreams.

Cornelius sat at the round table, the vanilla-scented candle snuffed out. A pair of over-the-head earphones took the place of his one-horned Viking helmet today; dark sunglasses hid his eyes.

I dropped into the chair next to him and put the protein shake and offer paperwork on the table.

He looked at me and lowered his sunglasses. "Hi, Violet!" he yelled.

I jerked back.

Slipping off the earphones, he said, "Sorry about that. I forgot I had them on."

"Were you listening to the recording from last night?"

"No. I like to start my day with polka music."

"Polka?"

"Yes, the beat really revs me up and opens my psychic ears. It's a trick I learned from my grandmother, who was the famous ghost whisperer from New Orleans."

I just smiled, because laughing hysterically in his face might have seemed rude. "I've brought the offer paperwork. We just need to come up with an amount and have you sign this, then I'll take it back to the office and send it to Tiffany to show to her client."

"Perfect. How much should I offer?"

More than George Mudder.

"Do I come in with a full price offer," he continued, "or

should I lowball it?"

Neither would be enough.

I hesitated, chewing on my lip.

Ethically, I was at a fork in the road. Because I knew what Ray's client was going to offer, I needed Cornelius to come in higher in order to be considered. However, telling Cornelius a certain amount that would guarantee we'd win over Ray and George was kind of like cheating, even though Ray had showed the offer letter to me of his own free will.

If Jane found out that I knew Ray's offer price ahead of time, would she figure out that I purposely had pushed Cornelius to place a higher offer? Would that be grounds to consider replacing me with someone more honest? More moral? Less apt to get involved personally with clients?

But, if I didn't push Cornelius higher, George would end up buying the hotel and I'd most likely end up out on my ass.

Either way, my job was at risk.

I cleared my throat. "Well, I'm not supposed to give you advice, but I'm under the suspicion that there might be another party interested in this property. So, I think we need to make your offer as strong as it can be." *Hint, hint, hint.*

His eyebrows flat-lined under the weight of his frown. "Why didn't you tell me someone else wants this place before now?"

"I just recently learned about it."

He stroked his pointy goatee. "What if I come at ten thousand over? You think that's enough?"

Yes! "Most likely."

I grabbed a pen from my purse, wrote his offer amount down and handed him the pen. "You just need to sign here and then initial here and here."

Taking the pen, he stared down at the document for a bit too long.

"What's wrong?" I asked, my heart picking up speed. "Did I spell your name wrong?"

"My name is correct." He removed his sunglasses and set

them on the table. "Tell me something, Violet. Last night during the séance, you said you saw an entity in your nightmare?"

I leaned back, crossing my arms over my chest, not sure where this was going, but not liking it, anyway. "Well, I don't know that it was what you'd call an entity."

That thing, whatever it was, was not some ghost. Not that it was real or anything. It was just another one of my nightmares, only in IMAX 3-D format.

Cornelius raised one black eyebrow. "Was this entity once a man who went by the name of Wolfgang?"

Chapter Thirteen

I choked on my own spit—and Cornelius's question about Wolfgang.

After a minute of coughing, and then a couple of slurps of stale black coffee from a mug offered by Safari Skipper, I found enough breath to answer him.

"No, there was no man named Wolfgang," I lied straight-faced, eye-to-eye.

There was no way I was going to feed Cornelius's idiosyncrasy. Plus, admitting I saw Wolfgang would only make him start poking and prodding me more, distracting him from the task at hand, which was buying this damned hotel and helping me keep my job.

"Hmm, that's odd," was all Cornelius said. "When I listened to the recording of the séance, you mentioned his name."

Then he signed the offer letter, and I did my best not to skip out of there like I was off to see the Wonderful Wizard of Oz.

Ray's SUV wasn't in the parking lot behind Calamity Jane's. Whew! The tightness in my chest eased, making me realize that as much as I looked forward to beating him at this game, avoiding confrontation was fine and dandy with me this afternoon.

Jane sat behind her desk, cursing into her phone as I walked by. I dropped my purse onto my desk and grabbed Mona, whose smile widened to match mine when I showed her the offer. The two of us hovered outside of Jane's open doorway until she ended her call with a slam of her phone.

She stood and grabbed the bottle of Jack Daniel's that was

on her filing cabinet, then noticed us standing there. Her focus bounced to the bottle in her hand, and then back to us.

She shrugged and put the Jack back on the cabinet. "It's either drink heavily or kill the bastard, and my skin tone is too fair to pull off an orange jumpsuit."

Unsure of whether to open that can of worms further and let her vent or change the subject to something less drink-inducing, I opted for the positive and held up the signed letter.

She waved us inside her office, where I noticed the underlying smell of alcohol not fully masked by her flowery perfume. She hadn't been joking about the drinking. The dark circles under her eyes reinforced my suspicion. I kept the smile on my lips to hide my concern.

Her eyes narrowed as she tried to see what the paper said. "Is that what I think it is?"

I looked at Mona, and she nudged me. "It's your party, Violet; you get to do the crowing."

"Cornelius Curion has made an offer on the Old Prospector Hotel." I placed the paper on the desk in front of her.

The corners of her lips creased slightly—her attempt at a smile, I guessed. "This is wonderful, Violet. Are you confident in his financial abilities to follow through on this?"

Absolutely not. "Definitely."

"Have you contacted the seller's Realtor?"

Tiffany. Ugh. Why couldn't Doc's ex-girlfriend have gray skin and scales and reside on another planet? "Not yet, but I will as soon as I fax this over to her."

"Have Mona take one last look through the offer first to make sure you have all of your 'i's' crossed and 't's' dotted."

Did she just say … ? I glanced at Mona, who shook her head slightly.

"Then fax it," Jane continued, "and go out to lunch on me."

"You should join us," Mona said.

"Not today. I'm not very good company. I wouldn't want to bring you down."

We turned toward the door.

"Oh, and Violet?" When I turned, she added, "I need you to fill in for me this afternoon down in Rapid."

"What do you mean?"

"I signed up for a workshop given by the South Dakota Real Estate Commission about proposed rule changes for brokers, but I need to run out to Gillette."

"Wyoming?"

She nodded and handed me a Post-it note with an address and time. "Just go listen and take notes for me."

Damn it. I had planned to attend another viewing tonight to try sneaking a peek into the windows of the Mudder brothers' garage-crematorium. This day job was seriously cramping my funeral parlor spying efforts.

Mona and I returned to our desks. She looked over the offer letter, nodded, and smiled at me like a proud parent.

I faxed off the offer and gave Tiffany a call. She answered with her annoyingly sexy-smoky voice and promised to get back with me within forty-eight hours with a "Yes" or "No" from her client.

Jane's Rapid City workshop crimped the celebration lunch plans for Mona and me. After waiting for a table, I had to scarf down everything the waitress placed on the table before me, and then run out the door leaving Mona to take care of the bill with the company credit card.

I sped home, calling my mom on the way to see if it was okay if I dropped the kids off to go swimming for a bit.

"Sure, your sister just finished skimming the pool."

Crap. I momentarily had forgotten Satan's concubine was holing up in the spare bedroom. "Maybe this isn't such a good idea."

"Violet Lynn, you're being silly. I'm here. I'll keep my eye on them just as I always have."

In spite of my sister's presence on the property, I agreed

to drop them off. It wasn't my mother's fault that her youngest offspring craved the life of a soap opera villainess. Besides, Aunt Zoe could really use the afternoon off.

How much corruption could my sister brainwash the kids with in one afternoon? I didn't like the answer my brain came back with and decided to stick with consulting the Magic 8 Ball rather than the other voices in my head.

The kids didn't waste time getting ready to leave when they heard they were going swimming at Grammy and Grandpa's place.

The ride down to Rapid was loud and windy, thanks to the Picklemobile's loose muffler and open windows. Layne had "called" the window seat, so I let Addy run the radio, which picked up only AM stations.

"Mom?" Layne yelled above the whistling wind and crackle-filled version of Johnny Horton's twangy *Battle of New Orleans*. I turned the volume down just as Johnny powdered the gators' behinds.

"What?"

"Have you considered homeschooling us?"

I glanced over at him, unsure where this was leading. He stared down at the book in his lap: *Ghostly Tailings. A Snapshot of the Past.*

"Is that the book my friend Doc helped you find at the library a couple of weeks ago?" I asked, delaying my abrupt "No" to his other question.

He nodded.

"I thought you were done reading it."

"I wanted to go through it again."

If I hadn't been fully awake and pushing when Addy and then Layne entered this world, I'd believe the doctor switched out my real son with the baby of a NASA engineer. Then again, his sperm donor of a father had been going to college to be a scientist.

I focused on the road and returned to his question. "No, I haven't considered homeschooling you. Why do you ask?"

"He's scared to go to school next week," Addy butted in.

"Shut up!" I saw Layne elbow his sister out of the corner of my eye, almost hitting her cast. "I am not."

"Layne, stop hitting your sister. Addy, zip your lips and let your brother speak for himself."

"I'm just trying to help," Addy said.

I shot her a *yeah-right* look. "Layne, is Addy right? Are you nervous about going to your new school next week?"

He shrugged. "Maybe."

"Why? Is this about meeting new kids, because you're really good at making friends."

That wasn't entirely true, since he tended to keep his nose buried in books more than engaging the children around him, but I was his mom. Sugarcoating the truth was in my job description.

He shrugged again and looked out the open window. The wind ruffled his hair, making him look even younger than his almost ten years. I resisted the urge to reach out and brush my fingers over his still-boyish cheek.

Instead, I asked, "Are you concerned about training a new teacher on your homework style?"

Layne preferred to give long, detailed, elaborate answers on all of his homework, including his art projects and basic math problems. Each year, we went through a few weeks of teachers' notes repeatedly telling him to cut back on his long-winded responses until they gave up and just let him do his thing.

Addy, on the other hand, preferred to keep everything short and sweet, if she answered at all. As Doc said, she hadn't fallen far from the tree.

"Maybe." He sighed, the weight of his young world rising and dropping with his broadening shoulders. "Mostly I'm worried about you."

I blinked. "Me? What are you talking about?"

"This is a pivotal year for us."

Pivotal? The kid must be reading the dictionary in the

bathroom again. I swallowed a chuckle. "Why is fifth grade *pivotal*?"

"Before you know it, we'll be looking into colleges."

Addy blew a huge pink bubble and popped it with her own fingers, and then giggled.

He might be thinking about college. His sister, on the other hand, had a few years of being a "kid" yet to stumble through.

"You'll be wondering what you are going to do for the rest of your older years," Layne continued.

My older years? Nice. As forty crept nearer, I preferred to think that old meant ninety and I wasn't even halfway there. Layne was jumping the gun about half a decade with this little prophecy of his, and I had a feeling there was something more to it than homeschooling and me getting more wrinkled.

"Don't worry, Momma," Addy said. "I'm going to live with you until you're a little old woman." She wrapped her gum around her finger, and then twirled the other end of it like a lasso.

I knew my daughter meant well and loved her dearly, but that offered me no comfort at all. "Addy, put the gum in your mouth."

I hit my blinker and made a right into my parents' neighborhood. "Layne, what does homeschooling have to do with me getting old and lonely?"

"If you homeschool me, I would be home with you more."

"Have you forgotten that I work all day?"

"I could make sure to take care of the house while you're gone, do things like mow the lawn and take out the garbage."

"You already do those things."

"Yeah, but I'd do it for free—no allowance required. It'd be one of my regular jobs."

Oh, now I got it. "You mean you could act more like the man of the house."

"Sure, I guess."

I wasn't buying his feigned innocence in that response. "Do you think that if you're at school every day, I'll find another man to take on that role?"

He looked down at his book again. "Maybe."

I pulled to a stop in my parents' drive. Addy scrambled over her brother, shoving her way out the door.

"Hold on, Layne." I waited until Addy was climbing Mom's front steps and well out of earshot. "Look at me."

He did, his forehead pinched. "What?"

"I'll never replace you. Understand? You're always going to be my favorite boy of all time in here." I patted the left side of my chest. "If I were ever to fall in love with someone and want to get married," *and pigs started manning space shuttle flights to the moon*, "you will still be my favorite boy of all time."

His frown didn't waver. "You've never mentioned getting married before in that speech."

I hadn't? "Oh, well, it just kind of popped in there as a possibility."

"That's what concerns me, Mom." He leaned over and kissed my cheek, and then jumped to the ground and followed his sister into the house.

My mother looked out the door and waved at me, then closed it. Guess I wasn't invited in for cookies and milk.

Shaking off Layne's worries, I backed out of the drive and headed for the address on Jane's Post-it note.

Twenty minutes later, I parked in front of a boring, rectangular brick building, where I ended up spending the longest four hours of my life doodling in between taking notes for Jane. Three times I'd almost nodded off, and one time my forehead actually touched the tabletop. Turned out I'd found a non-chemical solution for insomnia.

It was after dinnertime when I escaped to the Picklemobile. I growled at the setting sun, knowing the viewing at Mudder Brothers was going on as I stood there, a good hour away when figuring in the amount of time to go home and change into a funeral ensemble.

Since there was no way I could make the viewing, I sat behind the steering wheel and checked my messages. The first was my mom telling me she was taking the kids to a movie and keeping them for the night; she'd drop them off at Aunt Zoe's tomorrow.

I thought of my sister and debated on insisting on bringing them home with me, but it was Monday night and Aunt Zoe was working at the gallery. If Mom kept the kids, I could sneak down to Mudder Brothers and maybe peek into their garage-turned-crematorium windows without worrying about finding a sitter for my kids.

Decision made.

The second message was from Harvey. He was in Deadwood and wondering what I was up to, hoping it was no good.

The old bugger knew me too well.

I thought about calling Harvey back and having him join me at Mudder Brothers, but then Cooper's face popped into my thoughts. After Harvey's and my last adventure at Mudder Brothers, the detective might be keeping tabs on his uncle as a means to watch me. Maybe that was just paranoia talking, but Harvey was a risk and I couldn't take a chance on Cooper catching me. Like Jane, bright orange jumpsuits clashed with my skin tone and hair color.

Instead, I called Natalie.

"Hey, Sleeping Beauty," she said. "How was the porch last night?"

"I don't remember. I slept like the dead." Well, the dead that didn't come back and haunt Deadwood.

"Was I snoring that loud?"

Not snoring, just mumbling. "I couldn't sleep. I didn't want to toss and turn and wake you."

"I could've bored you back to sleep with stories about my childhood."

"I've heard them all before and lived most of them with you."

"Well, you are the center of my universe. So, what's up, my queen?"

"Are you busy tonight?"

"It's Bingo night at the VFW."

"Crap, I forgot." I could have used her to keep me from being too lily-livered.

"Want to come and fondle some hard little balls with me? We can stick them in our bras and ask folks if they think it's cold."

I grinned. "As tempting as that sounds, I'm going to have to pass."

"I'll be home around eleven, after I drive my parents home. We could do something then. Hang out at the Purple Door Saloon? Go up to the Golden Sluice and stare at the other bored locals? Maybe Cooper will show up."

Cooper? Why would I care about … oh, yeah. "Nat, I told you that I'm not interested in Detective Cooper."

"Your mouth says one thing, but your eyes tell a different story."

"Then my eyes are full of shit."

Natalie scoffed. "Says Cleopatra, the Queen of de-Nile."

"Is that your sad attempt at a pun?"

"Shut up. So, you want to head out when I get back from my parents' or not?"

"No, that's too late. I'll see you later."

"Don't have too much fun without me."

I hung up and started the Picklemobile.

By the time I rolled into Deadwood, the streetlights had kicked on. I cruised by Mudder Brothers on my way home. The parking lot was still a third full, but a handful of people were walking out to their cars.

If I hurried, maybe I could change my clothes and get back there while the family of the deceased was still inside to distract George.

It took me ten minutes to get home and change into my spy-wear—black leggings and a purple Elvis t-shirt. I couldn't find my tennis shoes anywhere, including under my bed or in the shoe bin by the front door. After ransacking my closet one more time, I grabbed my purple boots and Aunt Zoe's dark gray hoodie, slipped them on, and then raced out the door.

I parked the Picklemobile behind Calamity Jane's, where the old beast coughed, sputtered, and then died with its usual final gunshot "bang." If Cooper came looking for me, I planned to use work as my alibi.

I stepped inside the office, turned on the overhead lights, and dropped my tote on my desk in plain view of the large plate-glass windows. Then I turned on the bathroom light and fan and shut the door.

There. All bases were covered if Cooper came snooping.

After grabbing the emergency flashlight from the cupboard under the coffee maker, I zipped up the jacket and pulled the hood over my head. Finally, all of those years of watching Charlie's Angels reruns were paying off. Dad would be so proud.

I slipped out the back door and snuck through the parking lot, keeping an eye out for a cop car or Cooper's unmarked sedan parked among the shiny classic cars.

The coast appeared to be clear. I hesitated, gripping the flashlight tight in my palm. Without Harvey or Natalie by my side, sneaking around a building where corpses were incinerated wasn't nearly as fun as it had seemed in the light of day.

Slinking around the back of the Rec Center, I paused on the other side and peeked out at the street, and then at Mudder Brothers. As I watched, one of "Deadwood's finest" cruisers turned in the funeral parlor parking lot, pulled into a spot, then reversed and rolled back out onto the street. I didn't put it past Cooper to have one of his patrol cars watching the funeral parlor for the Picklemobile or Natalie's pickup. Word on the street said the detective was as thorough as a blind proctologist.

My phone vibrated in my pocket. I pulled it out and

frowned at the number. It was local. I let it go to voice mail.

Before I had it jammed back in my pocket, it started vibrating again. I pulled it back out. The same number filled the screen. I forced it to voicemail and dared it to ring again.

It did.

Dang it! I hit the answer button and whispered, "What?"

"I knew you were there," old man Harvey said. "What are you doing?"

"Knitting a quilt in front of the TV."

"You're such a lousy liar. You don't 'knit' quilts. Besides, I'm looking out your neighbor's front window right now, and your Aunt's place is dark."

He must be using Miss Geary's home phone. That explained the strange phone number.

"How is Miss Geary tonight?" I tried to distract him.

"Horny. I think her estrogen pills need some adjustin'. Twice during Jeopardy is enough. I sent her off to microwave some popcorn so I could hear the final question."

There were times when being around Harvey made me wish I could scrub my memory cells on a washboard with some lye soap. "Then why are you calling me?"

"Doc's looking for you."

My heart sat up and wagged its tail. It was sad, truly.

Why didn't Doc call me? Why go through Harvey? The dirty bird wasn't my personal secretary.

"He is?" I tried not to sound like I just found out the boy of my dreams had a crush on me.

"Well, he didn't say as much."

Ahh. Damn Harvey for baiting me, and double-damn me for biting his hook.

"But something was buggin' the boy last night when we were at the Golden Sluice. He finally caved when I leaned hard enough."

"And?" I was still dangling from that stupid hook.

"He said he needed to talk to you."

Oh, hell. What did that mean? "Did he mean to talk to me

about the weather or something else?" Like never wanting to kiss me again.

"I don't know. I didn't ask. There is some stuff men just don't talk about."

"Bullshit. You tell me all about your women."

"Yeah, but you're a girl. You like to hear about all of that emotional mumbo jumbo."

Not really. "You talk about sex, too."

"That's just for the fun of watching your cheeks turn pink."

I growled in my throat. "Remind me of the purpose of this phone call."

"I need to know where you are."

"Why?" Was Doc wondering?

"I'm your bodyguard, remember?"

"Right."

"There was a viewing at Mudder Brothers tonight. We missed out on another chance to sneak around the place."

No *we* hadn't. "Maybe next time."

The Adams Museum's clock chimed, announcing the hour. In the still of the evening air, the ringing sounded much closer than the two blocks separating me from the old building.

"Hold up!" Harvey said. "I know those chimes. You're at Mudder Brothers right now, aren't you?"

I hesitated, not wanting to tell him the truth and risk him joining me. But if I tried to lie, he'd think I was up to no good and be correct, and then he'd race down here, anyway.

"I am, but you can't come down here."

"Why not? You need me."

"You need to catch that final Jeopardy question, remember?"

"I already missed it."

"Harvey, all I'm doing is looking in the garage windows, and then I'm coming right home."

"Is Natalie with you?"

"No."

"I don't like this at all."

"There's nothing to worry about. Like I said, I'm just peeking, I swear, nothing else. I'll be home before you know it, and then you can come over and tell me more sex stories that make my cheeks turn pink." Or not.

"Okay, but hurry your ass up. The lady of the house just waved at me from the kitchen. She has that look in her eye again, and I don't think my fishin' tackle can take much more cranking."

I winced. "Goodbye, Harvey."

I hung up and took another look over at Mudder Brothers to make sure the coast was still clear.

With my hand partially covering the flashlight's beam, I zig-zagged up along the base of the tree-lined hillside that led clear up to Mount Moriah cemetery, snapping twigs and breaking branches along the way. This route allowed me to approach the funeral parlor from the backside. At the edge of the trees, I tripped over a small stump and landed nose-down in the tall, scraggly weeds.

Cheese and crackers! A gaggle of brain-starved zombies would have been quieter. I sat up, brushing myself off, swallowing some Black Hills dust. Luckily, I'd ended up with just a few stinging scratches on my palms for all of my klutziness.

I squat-ran to the pine tree closest to the steel back doors, squinting in the darkness at the light fixture above the back door. Was it a motion sensor light? I couldn't remember noticing that detail last week when Natalie and I had been watching Ray and George back here.

I picked up a pinecone the size of a Bingo ball and tossed it in the general direction of the light.

The light stayed off.

Maybe that wasn't big enough.

I picked up an egg-sized rock and threw it. But my aim went askew. The rock clunked against one of the two steel back doors, about two feet below the light.

Shit!

I squatted behind the tree, my breath held.

Nobody came to see who was knocking. Thank God!

Should I try a bigger rock?

Should I go back home and wait until I had Natalie by my side? *Scaredy cat!*

The garage was just twenty yards away. I could sprint across the drive, and if the light came on, just keep on running all of the way back to the Picklemobile.

Sure. No problem. I could handle this.

Wait! Did something just move in the shadows behind the garage?

I wrangled a grip on my imagination.

Before I could talk myself out of it, I ran across the asphalt, trying to keep my boot heels from clomping.

Darkness shrouded me the whole way.

Leaning against the side of the garage, I peeked around the corner at the light. It wasn't on a motion sensor. Excellent. Now what?

I scooted over to the garage window, stood on my tiptoes, and peered into the darkness on the other side of the glass. I couldn't see a single thing. It would have been considerate of the Mudder boys to leave a night light on for peeps like me.

After another glance around me to make sure I was still alone, I held the flashlight against the glass. A counter covered with boxes big and small ran half the length of the far wall. I tried to read the labels, but I was too far away with bad lighting.

At the other end of the counter, a couple of wheeled-gurneys sat parallel to each other like taxis waiting for their turn to rush to the next death.

I shined the light the other way. Floor-to-ceiling shelving held a bunch of shiny stainless steel trays, buckets and funnels of various sizes, and shallow baskets full of long skinny instruments. Next to the big shelf was a cupboard about the same size, the doors padlocked shut.

On the floor in front of the locked cabinet was a thick steel basket that looked rusted. I could see several odd shaped black pins sticking out of the top. Some of the pins were pointed; some had metal balls instead at the ends. The pins appeared to be several inches long, the balls a little bit smaller than the bingo balls Natalie was probably pulling from a cage at that very moment.

Mixed with the pins in the basket were several rusty-looking small steel rectangles with rounded corners. They look like tea party plates.

Plates … like something a surgeon would screw into a skull to hold it together. My focus returned to the pins with the balls on the end. Could those be from the remains of— e*wwww! Yuck!*

The sound of the funeral parlor's steel door thumping shut almost made me pee my pants right there on the spot. I switched off the light and pinned my back against the side of the building, listening while taking shallow breaths.

Footfalls hitting the asphalt came closer.

Shit, shit, shit! I did my best impression of paint, plastering myself to the wall in the darkness. My heart played the bongo drums in my throat.

I heard several beeps, then the creaking of hinges and another thump of a door shutting.

Someone had gone inside the garage.

Light blared suddenly from the window next to me.

My feet tingled in my boots, ready to run as far and fast as necessary to save my ass. I stayed still, resisting the urge to give them free rein.

With just a step and a lean, I could get a well-lighted glimpse inside the room.

My cell phone vibrated in my pocket.

God damn it, Harvey! I knew from experience he wouldn't give up. I needed to shut the damned thing off.

I plucked it from my pocket. A glance at the screen turned into a double-take.

It wasn't Harvey calling. It was Doc!

Something crashed on the other side of the wall.

The phone vibrated again.

Damn it. I really wanted to talk to Doc. But I had this whole spying thing I was a little busy with at the moment.

Another crash reverberated through the wall.

Who was in there and what were they doing? Throwing bodies around?

The phone buzzed again.

I caved, sliding along the wall away from the window.

"Hello?" I whispered.

"Violet?" Doc's voice sounded hesitant.

"Yes?"

"Why are you whispering?"

I didn't want to lie to him, but I didn't exactly want to announce that I was sneaking around in the dark outside the Mudder brothers' garage at that very moment.

"I'm not in a cell phone friendly zone." No lie there.

"You want me to hang up?"

"No!" I said a little too loud. I glanced around in the shadows, and then dropped my voice again. "No, I want to talk to you about the other night."

"Before you go any further," Doc interrupted me, "I need to say something first."

I didn't like the sound of that. "Okay."

The light coming from the window went dark. I covered the earpiece of the phone, muting Doc's voice just to be safe. I couldn't hear anything from the other side of the wall.

Whoever had been in the room was either gone, or had heard me and was standing in the dark listening. I waited another couple of seconds, and then held the phone back up to my ear.

"… leaving you alone," Doc was saying.

Leaving me alone? Was he really breaking up with me over the phone? Right now? In the middle of my attempt to sneak a glimpse of a crematorium?

"Wait! No."

"What?" Doc asked.

"I swear, I had no idea he was going to have us there to talk to ghosts."

"Are we even sharing the same conversation, Violet?"

"Yes. No." I covered my other ear as a loud, rattling and clattering sound passed by on the street in front of the funeral parlor. Someone was losing a muffler. When the vehicle moved on, I said, "I don't know. What were you saying again?"

Silence came through the line.

"Doc?" I whispered. "Are you still there?"

"Yes," he said, but he didn't sound thrilled about it.

The door to the garage thumped shut again. The sound of shoes hitting asphalt rang clear in the night.

I peeped around the corner of the building, catching sight of Eddie Mudder's silhouette walking toward his new pickup.

Something crashed in the trees behind me.

What was that?

I couldn't see anything in the darkness.

"Violet," Doc's voice reminded me that I was still pressing the phone against my ear. "Where are you right now?"

I checked in on Eddie—he was looking my way.

Jerking back, I flattened myself against the back wall again. Crap!

"I can hear you breathing, Violet," Doc said.

Double-crap! I didn't dare say a word.

"Fine," Doc said. But his tone sounded anything but dandy. "When you're ready to stop playing games, Violet, come and see me."

He hung up on me.

Fuck!

The growly sound of Eddie's truck cranking to life made me wilt in relief. I could hear his stereo cranking out some organ-heavy riff through the closed windows.

When I looked around the corner, Eddie's red taillights were coming right toward me. Pulling back, I waited as he shifted into gear and rolled off. I counted to ten and checked to make sure the coast was clear. Much more of this sneaking around and I'd have to add adult diapers to my spy kit.

As my breathing slowed, I realized how dark and quiet it seemed behind the garage.

Extra dark.

Unusually quiet.

I reached for my flashlight, covering the face of it, and clicked it on.

A twig snapped close behind me.

Spinning around, I raised the light, spotlighting a grizzled face.

I sucked in a breath.

"Gotcha!"

Chapter Fourteen

God damn it, Harvey," I growled under my breath and snapped the old bugger's suspenders. "You scared the bejeezus out of me."

His two gold teeth gleamed in the flashlight's beam. "Anyone ever tell you that you're lousy at sneakin' around in the dark?"

"I was doing just fine before you crept up on me."

He snatched my flashlight away and shut it off. "If you were good at this, you would've heard me comin'."

I had heard something crash earlier, but I hadn't wanted to let my imagination wander while tip-toeing around alone in the dark outside a funeral parlor.

"And I suppose you're a real pro at it." I whispered.

"Damned straight."

I grabbed my flashlight back, catching a whiff of something sweet with a hint of lemon. I sniffed in his direction. "What's that smell?"

"I got carried away with the lemon meringue."

My stomach gurgled, reminding me that I hadn't eaten anything since lunch with Mona. "I love Miss Geary's pies."

"I'm not talking about pie. This was some of that homemade love gel."

Before he could explain in greater detail, I told him, "No. Don't tell me." I didn't want him to ruin all future lemon meringue pies for me. "Let's get out of here."

"We're not done yet."

"Yes, we are." I glanced around the corner of the garage again, feeling sweatier and more paranoid with Harvey standing next to me. The last thing I needed was to be caught creeping around in the dark behind Mudder Brothers with Detective Cooper's uncle.

"Did you take a look-see inside this place yet?" He knocked on the wall of the garage.

"Shhhh." I grabbed Harvey's hand mid-knock. "Mostly. The only thing suspicious is a basket full of scorched surgical parts."

"I always wondered what George did with all of the stuff that didn't burn."

"Now you know." I tugged on his hand. "Let's get out of here before someone hears us and tattles to your nephew."

He didn't budge. "Nobody is out here sneaking around but us, and Cooper's too busy right now to care."

Knowing Cooper's squinty-eye glare as well as I did, I doubted Harvey. "What do you mean he's too busy?"

"He's in the middle of a poker game with that lousy, good-for-nothing sheriff."

"The one who stole the love of your life and married her?"

"She wasn't the love of my life."

"Then what's with this big grudge of yours?"

I heard more than saw him scratch his whiskers. "A man needs to have something to hang on to and growl about all of his life."

"Death and taxes aren't enough for you?"

"You can't pick fights with either of those things."

"But you can with the county sheriff?" I preferred to run from the law, not throw punches at it.

"You betcha. Just the sound of his name gets me all riled up—huffin' and puffin', jabbin', dodgin'." His clothes rustled in the shadows as he showed me his version of Mohammed Ali.

I crossed my arms over my chest, chuckling when he did a spin move that had him stumbling into the back of the garage. "Huffing and jabbing and dodging, huh?" I couldn't resist and added, "Sounds similar to what you do with Miss Geary during Jeopardy."

Harvey snickered. "Not quite. For one thing, when I'm riled up about the sheriff, I'm wearing my skivvies, so my boys aren't swinging along with me, keepin' time with each poke."

Bleck! What had I been thinking encouraging him? "Stop right there," I whispered.

"You started it."

"And now I'm ending it." I headed for the hills … or rather the hill behind Mudder Brothers that led up to Mount Moriah.

"Hold up there, girl." Harvey grabbed my arm, pulling me back. "I told you, we're not done yet."

"We were finished with that subject last week as far as I'm concerned."

"I mean we're not done *here*." He tugged the flashlight from my grip and flicked it on, directing the beam at the base of the garage. "There is something you need to see."

"I told you I already looked inside. The place is full of autopsy goodies and cremation leftovers." Yuck. That came out wrong. I shouldn't mix death and food.

"Did you look in the other window?"

"There is no other window." At least I hadn't seen one earlier when I was checking the place out from the trees.

"I'm not talking about the garage." Harvey tugged me around the other side of the building, pausing at the front corner. He leaned out. "You see anybody?"

I pulled my arm free and took a step back into the safety of deeper shadows. "The only thing I see is an ornery old man who is going to land my butt in jail."

"Quit being such a girl," he whispered. "You really need to grow a pair of balls if you're gonna to do this sneakin' around stuff more often."

Again with the testicle talk. "I'm not being a 'girl,' I'm being a responsible parent."

"You're being a big weenie," he said in a slightly louder

voice.

"Fine. When they start selling ball sac seedlings down at the hardware store, let me know. I'll be the first in line."

He chuckled low and quiet. "I don't think Doc would have as much fun fondling those as he does your—"

"Leave Doc out of this." *And my you-know-whats.*

He grunted. "Seems to me that's what keeps gettin' you into trouble with the boy. You two need to work on your communication skills and stop building these walls between you."

I stared at him in the dark for a handful of seconds. "Have you been reading Miss Geary's copies of *Woman's World* again?"

"It has some really good recipes, and I need something to look at when I'm lollygaggin' in the john."

Shaking my head, I leaned back against the garage. "Trust me, romance therapy is not your forte. You should stick to reading the backs of shampoo bottles."

"Quit trying to change the subject. You know I'm right. Doc should be the one standing here with you right now, not me."

"Doc would never have come."

"You don't know that. You didn't even ask him."

"Of course not. He would've tried to talk me out of coming."

"See, that right there is the problem with your relationship. A lack of communication, starting with you."

"We don't even have a relationship yet." It was sex mixed with a few steamy phone calls.

"Are you sure?"

"Harvey, I don't even know where the man is from."

"Have you asked him?"

"Kind of."

"How do you kind of ask someone something? You do or you don't."

"Doc is a closed book."

"And you're all open arms and secret-sharing?"

He couldn't see my eyes roll. "Are we really going to stand here in the dark outside a crematorium and discuss my love life, Dr. Ruth?" Or lack of it, as it was lately.

"She's a sex therapist, not a love doctor."

"Whatever."

"Don't 'whatever' me," he scolded under his breath. "Think about it. If you're not in a relationship, why has he hustled to save your bacon time and again? Doesn't that tell you anything?"

"Doc has saved my bacon once, thank you very much." An old lady with a shotgun saved it the other time. Well, mostly.

"That's because you won't give him a chance to come to your rescue, like I did tonight. Men like to play the Lone Ranger, ridin' in with guns drawn."

"Come to my … like you did, my ass." I jammed my hands on my hips.

"Like I said, think about it." He turned and walked away from me then, stealing across the drive toward the house.

"There's nothing to think about," I murmured and rushed to catch up with Harvey as he reached the back corner of the funeral parlor. Thinking too much about my fears revolving around Doc meant opening dusty old trunks in my brain that were better left shut and locked.

"You know, I was doing just fine here before you snuck up on me."

He harrumphed me and whispered, "You call finding nothing but a bunch of stainless steel bedpans 'just fine'?"

"They aren't bedpans. They are autopsy pans."

"Piss or blood—what's the difference? Both get sticky when they dry."

I frowned at his back as he slipped into the deep shadows along the side of the big house. *Sticky?* I mouthed. What had he been drinking?

I caught up with him as he bent over with a grunt next to

a basement window surrounded by a half-circle of corrugated tin that kept the earth at bay.

"Here." Harvey handed me the light, then leaned over and spoke low in my ear. "Crawl down in there and take a look. Tell me if you see what I think I saw earlier."

"What do you mean 'earlier'? How long have you been here tonight?"

"I came down right after you hung up. Just in time to see you trying to play Cy Young with that rock. You throw like a girl, too."

"I am a girl, and I can throw just fine, big mouth."

"Not from what I saw." He nudged me forward. "Get down there and take a gander before somebody sees us."

Now he was worried about that? I hopped down in the hole and squatted in front of the window. When I flicked on the flashlight, my breath whooshed out.

"Holy shit!" That came out as more of a hiss after I'd filled my lungs again. Staring at the strange, barbaric-looking tools nailed to the walls, lining shelves, hanging from the ceiling, I whispered, "What is all of this stuff?"

It looked like a scene from the house in *Texas Chainsaw Massacre*.

"Antiques," Harvey said.

"From a butcher shop?"

"No. Those are mortician's tools. See that black box over on the floor under those big ol' shears? The open one?"

I nodded, pointing the flashlight at it.

"That's an amputation kit from the Civil War era."

I leaned in closer to the glass, shining my light at other similar-looking open boxes. Rows of long, razor-sharp looking knives lined up like little soldiers in the gold and scarlet velvet-lined cases. I grimaced at the scenes of filleted cadavers that popped into my head. Pointy-ended pinchers snuggled up alongside the knives. An array of uncomfortably long dental-like drills and scrapers were placed perpendicular to the blades. My grimace became a series of winces as I studied each frightening tool, my imagination running wild, screaming like a banshee. In three of the cases, I noticed some specialized kind of handsaws secured to the lid. I'd seen too many gory movies to spend any alone time in this room in the dark.

"How do you know it's from the Civil War era?"

"Don't you ever watch the History Channel?"

"I'm a little busy raising kids and working my ass off."

"Yet you have time to sit on the couch eating peanut butter fudge ice cream and watching old Bogart whenever you feel like it."

"Leave Humphrey out of this," I said with a low growl.

"Or those Elvis—"

"Zip it with the blasphemy." I directed the flashlight's beam up the wall, stopping on a pair of glistening blades. "What are those?"

"I already told you—big ol' shears."

"They're very shiny."

"I'm betting they're nice and sharp, too. Good for amputating."

"Are those from the Civil War, too?"

"Nope, not with that tooling. Those babies look pre-Civil War to me."

I glanced up at Harvey. "I don't think I've ever seen shears that big. How do you know they aren't just old-fashioned garden loppers?"

"Because they're hanging in a room with a collection of death tools."

"Maybe that's because the garage is full of autopsy equipment," I said, rising to my feet.

"I don't think those belong in the garden shed. I think they're used to cut off something big."

"What do you mean? Like a leg?" I asked.

"Or a head."

"Or a head." I shivered as the words sank in.

Funny thing, there was a headless corpse with a very cleanly sliced neck chilling somewhere on this very property. I stared up at Harvey. "Are you thinking what I'm thinking?"

He shrugged, looking toward the front of the funeral parlor. "That depends."

"On what?"

"On whether you can see that police cruiser inching by out front with the really bright spotlight heading our way."

"What?!"

"You better duck, girl," he said and jogged off toward the back of the building, leaving me there alone in the hole.

Shit! I scrambled out onto the grass, pushing to my feet, and chased after him, slipping around the back of the building as the spotlight swept past.

"That was close," I said, huffing as much from fear as the sprint. I socked Harvey in the arm. "I can't believe you just left me back there. Some bodyguard you are."

"What?" He rubbed where my punch had landed. "I warned you, didn't I?"

I glanced around the corner, the cruiser was gone. "What are we going to do about those shears?"

"Nothing."

With a frown, I turned on him. "Well, that seems a bit anti-climactic after dragging me to that window and filling my head with stories of amputation and decapitation."

"Haven't you learned anything about jumping to conclusions yet, girl? You can't just go running around playing town crier without hard evidence to support your crazy notions."

"So, what do we do? Wait until someone else loses their head and shows up on your ranch clutching another one of my business cards?"

"No." He caught my wrist and dragged me toward the trees. "But I have an idea that just might work."

* * *

Tuesday, August 21st (just after midnight)

Once again Mr. Sand Man was refusing to pay me a visit. After lying in bed for an hour, listening to Natalie call out Bingo ball numbers in her sleep, I gave up and escaped to Aunt Zoe's kitchen.

Alone in the darkness, I dropped into a chair and stared at the bottle of sleeping pills on the table in front of me.

Speculating.

Worrying.

Twitching.

Scratching—but that had more to do with the mosquitoes that had been sneaking around Mudder Brothers along with me.

All of the "what ifs" from my snooping field trip had my brain churning, keeping the sandman away like a nocturnal restraining order. I'd played Bo-Peep counting my stupid dang sheep for an hour, but the images of all of those horrible antique tools the Mudder brothers had collected kept distracting me.

And what in the hell were they transporting in those crates?

I wanted to talk to someone about it all, someone more rational than a trigger-happy old man who was just looking for a reason to drag his favorite shotgun, Bessie, down to Deadwood for a night on the town.

The mantel clock in the living room rang out two short chimes, announcing it was half past the witching hour.

I picked up the pill bottle and turned it upside-down. The pills rattled against the inside of the cap.

Harvey's idea wasn't going to work.

For one thing, it involved Bessie. For another, it required the two of us taking risks that could land both of our asses in jail. While Cooper would undoubtedly take great pleasure in locking me up, when he found out I'd gotten his uncle involved, I had no doubt the detective would throw the key down the nearest mine shaft.

There were just some risks I wasn't willing to take to rid my life of Ray's bullshit.

So, that left me back at square one—Ray and the Mudder brothers were up to no good, but I had no way of proving it. Maybe this wall between me and the truth was a sign—all neon bright and flickering—that I should just focus on beating Ray at the real estate game and be happy with that.

The overhead light flicked on.

"Hey," I said and shielded my eyes.

"Oh!" Aunt Zoe's voice was higher than usual. "Violet Lynn, you scared the hell out of me."

I lowered my hand, my pupils adjusting to the light.

"What are you doing down here, child?" Her eyes locked onto the bottle of pills in my hand, a frown settling between her brows.

"Nothing." I dropped the pill bottle on the table, pulling back like it had cooties, and tried to hide my anxieties behind a smile.

With her long, wavy salt-and-pepper hair hanging loose around her shoulders, she looked ten years younger. Her red satin robe and favorite yellow slippers—the ones with a smiling sun on the tops—added a measure of sauciness to her, and not the ketchup and mustard kind. Reid would be a great match for her.

"What are you doing up?" I tried to distract her.

"Getting something to drink." She pulled out a chair and joined me at the table. The smell of her lavender soap reminded me of how I used to sit in her lap when I was a little kid and tell her all of my problems. Now I'd probably break her legs.

She stared me down, like an old West poker player looking for a bluff.

"The sink is over there," I said, looking away first.

She ignored my finger. "Did you have another nightmare?"

I shook my head. "I just can't sleep tonight."

The decision not to tell her about the whole decapitation shears thing that was weighing on my mind was a no-brainer. I also opted out of mentioning my radical theory that Ray had decapitated a man with them, planted my business card on the corpse, and left the body behind on one of my properties in order to get me in trouble with the law and force Jane to fire me. Some things are just better left unsaid.

"Did you take another pill?" she asked.

"No. Not yet."

Her blue eyes narrowed. "Why not?"

"I'm not sure I want to go to sleep yet." Or that I want to get hooked on sleeping pills.

"Does this have anything to do with Jeff Wymonds' big mouth?"

Huh? "I don't think so." I tried to remember if Jeff had said anything lately that should have me troubled. I didn't remember saying "Yes" to any indecent propositions or marriage proposals. "Are you referring to him mentioning my name up at the Golden Sluice?"

"No. I'm referring to his quote in today's issue of the *Black Hills Trailblazer.*"

"Why would he have a quote in the newspaper?"

"It was an article about his garage fire."

"Oh, yeah." I'd forgotten about that mess in lieu of my much bigger messes. My stomach tightened. "What did Jeff say?"

"He told the reporter that you two were 'busy in his bedroom' when the garage blew its top."

No. Fucking. Way. I looked at her for several blinks. "He said it just like that?"

She nodded, her lips pressed tight.

I groaned and lowered my forehead to the table's edge with a thwump. I was going to need a good-sized shovel to dig two graves—I wasn't going down alone this time. I was taking Jeff with me.

"Is any of that true?" Aunt Zoe asked.

"We were in his bedroom," I admitted while looking at my bare feet. "We were busy cleaning up the red Kool-Aid Kelly spilled on the carpet, not 'getting busy' in there."

Aunt Zoe snorted. "Well, that's not the way the reporter told it."

I just sighed. I had nothing else left to give at this point. "Splendid. My boss is going to nail my hide to the wall for this and Ray is going to have me tarred and feathered by the realty world. Then there's Doc."

"What about Doc?"

It was too early to come up with half-truths about my lack of love-life. "He's not talking to me right now." Well, he was for a moment there on the phone while I was hiding behind the Mudder brothers' garage, but then he hung up on me.

"It's not because of this article is it? He knows you better than that by now, I would think."

"No, it's not. But this thing with Jeff isn't going to help matters."

"Is that why you were sitting down here in the dark? Because of a fight with your boyfriend?"

"He's not my boyfriend."

"Fine. Your loverboy."

"That sounds worse yet."

"Quit being so nit-picky about names." She smiled, taking the sting out of her words, and squeezed my wrist. "Maybe you should go talk to Doc."

"It's late."

"Not that late. The bars aren't even closed yet."

"Natalie might wake up and notice I'm gone."

"She sleeps like the dead and you know it. She won't stir until morning. What's your next excuse?"

Zap. She got me there. "He's mad at me."

"So? Are you going to give up that easy? "

"Maybe this is proof that we're not meant to be together."

"Now you're just looking for a reason to run."

"There's nothing wrong with running. You're running from Reid." I threw back at her.

Her eyes narrowed. "That's not true. My situation is different."

"Different how? What happened between you two?"

Aunt Zoe took a big breath and then said, "I'll tell you that tale some other time."

"What's wrong with right now? You have a hot date you're late for?"

"No. But you do."

"I do?"

She pushed to her feet and pulled out my chair, hauling me up by my upper arm. "Yes, you do. Go."

"Where?"

"To Doc."

"Aunt Zoe, you've lost your mind. It's too late." And maybe too late in more ways than one.

"No, it's not. Go." She nudged me toward the back door.

"I'm not dressed for it."

She smiled down at my T-shirt and old boxer shorts. "I don't think he'll care about your clothes." She opened the door and pushed me out.

"If Natalie wakes—" I started.

"If she wakes up, I'll handle her." She shucked her satin robe and handed it to me, along with her yellow slippers. "You just go."

Out of excuses, I just stared at her, my mouth catching mosquitoes.

"Violet, go!" She shut the door in my face. The lock clicked. With a little wave, she turned and left me standing there on the back porch.

Crickets chirped around me.

I looked around, my gaze landing on the lawn chair I'd slept in last night. I could bed down there again tonight, but without that old quilt, I'd freeze my ass off.

A knock on the window over the sink made me jump. Aunt Zoe stood behind the glass, scolding me with her index finger. Then she pointed in the general direction of Doc's house and mouthed *Go!*

Fine. Okay. I'd go. Sheesh. But I stuck my tongue out at her before I left. She grinned back, then walked away. The kitchen went dark.

I took a deep breath and looked out over the shadow-filled backyard. It was now or never.

Clutching Aunt Zoe's red satin robe around me, I jogged through the backyard in her sunny slippers, squeezed through the gate to the front, and then scuffed down the sidewalk.

Five minutes later, Doc's house loomed in front of me. I tiptoed up the front porch steps, turned around and scuttled back down them, then stopped at the end of the walk and marched right back up and knocked on his screen door.

A dog barked several houses down.

A count of twenty later, nothing else had happened. No footfalls on the other side, no curtains moving, nothing.

I opened the screen door and knocked on the wood.

The dog barked again.

Hell, if Doc didn't answer, I could go down and hang with the mutt. At least he seemed interested in my company.

I counted to thirty this time. Still nothing.

Wincing in advance, I rang the bell. That would wake him for sure.

The dog didn't reply.

Neither did Doc.

Maybe he wasn't home. *Where was he then?*

I walked down the porch steps and paused, wondering if I should call it a night or go peer in his garage windows.

The garage won the coin toss. I snuck around back and for the second time in twenty-four hours, I found myself peeking into a garage window. Unfortunately, I was short a flashlight this time, but the moon cast enough light through the opposite window to show an outline of Doc's Camaro SS.

He was definitely home, just not answering his door. I hoped it wasn't because he knew I was the one on the other side of it.

Since I was halfway around the house, I decided to hop into his backyard and see if his bedroom light was on.

There was no squeaky gate to go through. I paused next to the birdbath sitting in the center of his backyard—a leftover from the previous owner.

Dim light spilled from his bedroom window. The window was closed, the screen missing. He must have it shut to keep out the mosquitoes.

Ah, ha! *What light through yonder window breaks?*

I called out, "Doc?"

I got no response. Nobody flew to the windows like a flash, tore open the shutters, and threw up the sash.

Great. Now I was mixing Santa with Shakespeare. Maybe it was best Doc didn't answer. I should just go home and get some sleep. I could try again in the daylight when my sanity had regained a foothold.

The light coming from the upstairs window went out.

Wait! He was in there, and probably still awake.

"Doc," I called a little louder.

The dog down the street answered with more barking.

"Oh, shut up!" I said and grabbed a pebble from the stone path leading to the bird bath.

I tossed the pebble toward the window. It hit the glass, clinking as it bounced off.

"Harvey, eat your heart out. You, too, Ty Cobb."

I waited for Doc to open the window.

He didn't.

Dang it.

I picked up another stone, twice as big as the last, and threw it at the window. As soon as it left my hand, I realized what I'd done.

The crash of breaking glass sent the neighbor's dog into a tizzy.

"Oh, shit," I whispered and stood there frozen on the lawn wondering if I should run or hide.

The light came on.

"Shit, shit, shit." I looked around for something to hide behind. The birdbath!

I scrambled behind it, squatting low.

The window slid open and Doc's head and bare shoulders filled the square.

"Who's there?" he said in a growly voice and flicked on a halogen flashlight as bright as a lighthouse beam.

The light landed on me. I stayed frozen.

He cursed. "Violet, I can see you behind that birdbath."

Damn. This was not how I had envisioned this going at all. Maybe I could woo him with my words.

I stood and shielded my eyes from the light. "O Romeo, Romeo, wherefore art thou Romeo?"

"You've got to be kidding me," he said and killed the flashlight. His torso disappeared from the window.

"Doc?" I called out, hesitant.

The dog barked back.

Chapter Fifteen

My knees wobbled a little while I stood there in the dark next to Doc's birdbath for what seemed like an eternity. Would he shut off his bedroom light and go back to bed or open his French doors and give me a chance to plead my case?

A mosquito buzzed my ear. I swatted in its general direction and cinched the belt of Aunt Zoe's satin robe tighter. Maybe I should just head home, write Doc a check for the broken window, slip it through his mail slot at work in the morning, and call everything "Done"—including our half-assed relationship.

Yeah, right.

And then I could just sit back and spend every minute of each day wondering what Doc was doing, agonizing about who he was touching, and struggling to forget about what it felt like to kiss him.

Please, please, please open the door.

I looked to the stars, thinking of a certain chicken I'd be happy to offer as a sacrifice to the gods.

The creak of a door hinge breached the shadow-filled stillness. Doc's dark silhouette filled the door frame.

I breathed a quiet sigh of relief. *Thank you, Aphrodite!*

"Violet," Doc said, leaning against the doorjamb, arms folded. "What are you doing?"

Following the stone path leading to his back porch, I hesitated at the base of the steps. "I need to talk to you."

"So you broke my window?" He sounded pissed about it, too.

"I rang your doorbell." That came out more defensive

than I meant it to, so I toned it down. "But you didn't answer."

"I was listening to music."

An awkward silence threatened to slip between us. I grabbed for something to say, wishing he'd stop barring the door and let me in.

"I'll pay for the window," I spit out. "I can drop off a check tomorrow, if you're going to be at work. If not, I can just mail it to you."

He stared down at me, his dark eyes hidden in the shadows, but said nothing.

I bumbled onward. "If you'd rather have cash, I can drop that off instead. Just let me know how much—"

"Violet." He cut me off with a curt slice.

"What?"

"I don't give a damn about the window right now."

"Oh."

"Why did you come here?"

"I told you, I want to talk to you."

"Why?"

He wasn't making this easy for me, dang it. I searched for the magic words that would get me past the bouncer blocking the door and settled on the truth. "Because I need you."

Again, a hooded stare and nothing more.

Maybe that had been too strong. If only I could see his face better so I could try to read his expression. "I mean I need your help."

"Are you wearing slippers?"

I looked down at the little suns smiling up at me from each foot. I could use a little of their optimism right about now. "Yeah."

"Do you want to come inside?" he offered an olive branch.

Yes! I looked back up at him and tossed the ball back in his court. "If you want me to."

I needed something from him that assured me tonight's

visit was worth wading through all of my insecurities and anxieties to stand here in front of him and make a fool of myself … well, a bigger-than-normal fool.

He stepped back and held open the door for me.

My hands trembled as I climbed the steps. I went out of my way not to touch him as I slipped past. Inside, I waited. It was his turn to lead in this dance of ours.

The house smelled like a mixture of furniture polish and cinnamon—none of the odd stinky odors I was used to coming home to in a house containing a chicken, a cat, a gerbil, two kids, and a microwave. I hadn't been inside this place since handing the keys off to Doc a couple of weeks ago—the same day we'd last had sex. Only his house had been an empty shell then, his bedroom window unbroken.

That was also the same day I'd gotten the phone call from Harvey about the decapitated body his dog had dug up from that old cemetery behind his barn. Thinking about my partner in crime reminded me of why I was standing here under Doc's roof.

Wringing my hands together, I turned to Doc as he closed the French door and locked it. "I think I know who the killer is."

He strode past me, his eyes averted, and headed into his kitchen.

I followed, noticing the clean, sparse marble countertops shining under the over-the-sink can-light. No opened boxes of cereal, no sticky pools of spilled juice, no half-empty glasses or dirty plates.

Doc pulled open the refrigerator door and grabbed a beer and a soda pop. He held both out toward me. The light from inside the fridge backlit his bare shoulders and the cargo shorts hanging low on his waist. I dragged my eyes away from all of his exposed skin and focused my attention on the offerings in his hands. The beer was a local brand, the pop was diet. I opted for beer, needing some liquid courage.

"I may have found the weapon used to kill the guy, too," I

told him as he twisted off the bottle cap and handed me the cold beer.

I waited for a response, for questions, doubts, anything.

He grabbed a bottle of the same beer from the fridge and twisted off the top, taking a swig before he set it on the counter and stared at me.

Swirling the beer around in my mouth, I tried to figure out what to say to break down the wall between us.

I held up the bottle. "This is really good. Kind of sweet. Isn't it from a brewery down in Rap—"

"What are you doing here, Violet?"

Sheesh. How many times did I have to say it? "I told you I need to talk to you."

"It's almost one in the morning."

"I know it's a little late, but I had a free moment." Oh, crap. That didn't come out right.

His eyelids narrowed. "A free moment?"

"I didn't mean that the way it sounded."

He took another swig, setting the bottle down a little harder than before.

"What I meant," I continued, my cheeks warming as I floundered under his gunslinger glare, "is that I was able to sneak away from Aunt Zoe's for a bit to come see you."

"Why?"

"What do you mean *why*?"

"Why me?"

I was getting tired of this twenty-questions game. I set my bottle on the counter, crossing my arms over my chest. "What's with all of the questions, Doc? Just tell me what you want me to say."

"I want you to tell me why tonight you were willing to push aside all of the reasons that you normally can't come to see me."

"Reasons I can't see you? You mean Natalie?"

"Natalie, Addy, Layne, your boss, Detective Cooper, half the town of Deadwood, and most of Lead."

I took a step back, winded a little by the underlying anger simmering in his voice. "You're mad at me."

"I'm not mad, Violet. I'm just tired of being kept at arm's length until you can find a 'free moment' to fit me in."

"That's not true."

"Hell, Wymonds gets to spend more time alone with you than I do."

I could strangle Jeff for opening his big, stupid mouth. "If this is about Jeff and that comment of his in the paper—"

Doc waved that off. "I don't think you're screwing around with Wymonds, no matter how much he wants to play 'house' with you."

"What then? You want to go on dates? I told you that as soon as Natalie stops staying with me, I can—"

"You can what?" he scoffed. "Sneak over here more often for a romp or two and then slink home again?"

Yes. "No."

"Don't fuck with me, Violet."

"I'm not. Jesus, Doc, what do you want from me? I'm doing the best I can with what I've been dealt."

"No, you're not." His tone challenged.

I lifted my chin. "What do you want from me?"

He opened his mouth to speak, hesitated, frowning, and then shook his head and gulped more beer.

"What, Doc?" My stomach clenched with the fear that he was going to tell me he wanted me to walk out his door and leave him alone for good. "Say it."

"I want you to make a choice."

Or that he'd ask me to make a choice.

"Between you and Natalie," I finished for him.

I'd dreaded this moment for weeks, but never fully believed he'd actually make me choose between him and my best friend.

"No, not that." He raked his fingers through his hair. "God, this is so—never mind. Forget it. Tell me who you think the murderer is." He swallowed more beer.

I almost let him sidetrack me, but he'd lowered his shield there for a moment, and I wasn't going to let him put it back up quite yet.

"How many women have you been with, Doc?"

His frown deepened, adding vertical creases between his eyebrows. "I'd rather talk about a decapitated corpse."

"How many?"

He shrugged. "Enough."

I nodded, absorbing that tidbit of his history. "How many have you been serious about?"

"What do you mean by *serious*?"

"How many of these women have been about more than just sex for you?"

"I don't know. A couple."

Tiffany? I didn't let my jealousy distract me. "Only two?"

"No. Just one."

"What happened to her?" I tried to prepare mentally for a tragic story about a long-lost love and the man who turned me inside out.

"Nothing."

Well, that wasn't very romantic. "You mean you just split up for no reason?"

"We haven't split up, but she did break my window."

I blinked as the meaning behind his words sank into my sleep-deprived brain. A wave of heat rippled outward from my core, melting my uncertainties about Doc, me, and our immediate future. "Oh."

He raised one eyebrow. "What was your point, Violet?"

"I can't remember." His answer had left me spinning. I leaned against the counter, needing something stable to support me for a moment.

Grabbing my hand, he tugged me toward him. "The choice I want you to make is to trust me."

Why did my jealousy have to flash loud and bright like a Las Vegas billboard? "I'm trying, Doc, I really am. But did you have to pick such a good-looking ex-girlfriend? How am I supposed to compete with her red hair?" Not to mention her complete lack of sag. It was abnormal, really. I suspected an alien invasion.

"Boots, there's no competition. Only you." He settled me between his legs. "But I'm not talking about other women."

"You're not?" I said, everything tingling in anticipation.

He reached down and untied my robe. "No. I want you to trust me with your secrets. Stop shutting me out."

"Okay." Right about then, I'd have agreed to shave my head and hand out flowers at the airport if it meant him following through with what his eyes were promising.

His focus drifted down to my open robe. "Is that Elvis?"

"Yes."

"What are you wearing under him?"

"What's it look like?"

"It's hard to see through his black leather jacket. I'm hoping for a velvet belly dancer top covered with sequins. Maybe you should show me so I can be certain."

"Where's the fun in that?"

He pulled me closer, his mouth hovering over mine, but holding back. "I want you, Boots."

"Yeah." I nestled against him, almost touching his lips. "I noticed."

He groaned, holding me still.

"Doc?" I ran my nails over his bare shoulders, down his chest.

"What?"

"I was at the Mudder brothers tonight with Harvey, looking in their garage and basement windows."

He toyed with the hem of my T-shirt, the back of his fingers brushing my stomach. "Why are you telling me this now?"

"I'm telling you my secrets."

"Oh, right."

His breath caught a little as I leaned forward and nuzzled his throat, licking the hollow at the base of it. He tasted like a mix of salt and sin—a sure-fire, high blood pressure cocktail.

His hands drifted lower, spanning then cupping. "You said something about figuring out the killer's weapon of choice."

My fingers scrubbed down his ribs, one at a time, nails scratching. "Scissors."

"I thought you said the neck was sliced, not stabbed."

"I did. Big scissors."

"Like loppers?"

"Yeah," I trailed my lips along the ridge of his shoulder toward his neck. "But with shiny slightly curved blades."

"Did you tell Detective Cooper about them?"

"No. I can't." I sucked softly on the skin where his shoulder met his neck. "He'll have me arrested for just breathing in the vicinity of Mudder Brothers."

"You really believe that?"

"Mostly." I breathed in his ear. "The man scares me."

Doc chuckled. "He's not that bad."

"You should try being on the receiving end of one of his glares."

I nipped his earlobe, then sucked on it.

Doc's grip on me tightened, his own hips starting a slow grind. "So, you think one of the Mudder brothers had something to do with the murder?"

"Or Ray. I'm pretty sure he's mixed up in it, too—if not directly responsible for the decapitation."

"Why are you so obsessed with Ray?" he asked, his chest rising and falling faster under my fingertips.

I really didn't want to talk about that jerk right at this moment, so I kept it short and sweet. "He's a dickhead."

"Besides the obvious."

Pulling back, I met his gaze head on, wanting him to understand. "I'm tired of him threatening me."

His jaw tensed. "He threatens you?"

Sometimes. "Mostly my job, which endangers my kids and pisses me off. I want to take him down a notch."

His eyes narrowed. "Accusing him of murder is a little more than just a 'notch.'"

"He's the one who got himself mixed up in this mess. I just keep stumbling into clues."

"Stumbling?" He laughed outright. "You've hidden inside a crate at Mudder Brothers. Seems more like you're looking with a magnifying glass to me."

Maybe so, but it was time to change tactics. I let my fingers drift to the waistline of his shorts. "I need your help."

He glanced down at my hands, then met my attempt at a flirty gaze with a crooked grin. "So you said earlier."

"Will you help me?"

"I don't know." He took my hand and moved it lower. "I think I'm going to need to be seduced into agreeing."

It was my turn to grin. I squeezed, then rubbed, spurring a deep guttural sound from his chest.

"I'll tell you everything I know about Ray and the Mudder brothers later," I whispered.

His brow wrinkled. Grabbing my hand and holding it still, he asked, "How much is 'everything'? How long have you been working on this?"

That was enough sharing about Ray and the Mudder boys for the time being. I pulled free of his hold and unbuttoned his shorts. "A little less conversation, Doc," I said with a purr.

In one fluid move that I probably wouldn't be able to repeat even if I practiced, I swept my T-shirt over my head and tossed it aside. "A little more action, please."

Doc's eyes darkened as he ogled my bare chest. "Damn, Boots." He licked his bottom lip. "I can't believe you used an Elvis line on me."

"Did it work?"

He lifted me and spun me onto the counter. His lips and tongue answered my question.

"Want to know what I have on under my boxers?"

"Later," he said against my bared skin. "I'm busy right now."

I leaned my head back against the cupboard doors, my fingernails digging into his shoulder muscles. Two little kicks and my slippers dropped to the floor. I wrapped my legs around his back, his skin burned hot against my cool calves.

His mouth climbed to mine, his lips soft, teasing. His tongue tasted, then sought mine, the kiss deepening, growing more forceful. When he came up for air, he leaned his forehead against mine. "Stay with me."

My heart did an awkward flip-pitter-patter-flop, like it had fallen off the back of a speed boat and tumbled across the water. "You mean like long-term?"

His eyes crinkled in the corners. "How about we start with just tonight and see how things go?"

I closed my eyelids, feeling like a big dope. "I didn't mean to sound like I'm hinting for commitment. I just wanted to make sure I understood—"

"Shut up and kiss me, Boots."

If I did, I wouldn't be stopping at just his lips, and we both knew it. He wanted me to stay. The kiss meant I would, risking Natalie waking and finding me gone.

My libido won the tug-o-war with my guilt.

"Okay," I nudged him out of the way and hopped off the counter. "But not here."

"Where?"

Grabbing his hand, I tugged him to the narrow back stairwell that led from his kitchen up to his bedroom. His broad shoulders practically rubbed the walls in the cramped space.

"Shut the door," I told him.

He did, shrouding us in darkness. He moved forward to climb the stairs, but I blocked his path. We stumbled, his hands catching me before I fell onto the steps.

"Doc," I whispered in the black silence, drawing him against me.

"What?" his quiet tone matched mine.

"Here. Where you first kissed me. I want to finish what

we started."

"It's a little cramped."

"We'll manage."

"I have a new bed, you know," his breath fanned my forehead.

"I know."

"Horizontal sex would be a nice change."

I climbed one step to be more level with him. "Humor me."

He pressed me up against the wall, just like he had a month ago. "You're missing your boots."

"I'm missing my shirt, too."

His hands double-checked, his thumbs circling, flicking, lighting me up.

"Violet." His lips brushed mine.

"What?" I writhed under his touch, lifting my knee to rub my inner thigh up and down his leg.

"What do you have on under your boxers?"

"See for yourself."

"It's too dark."

I led his hand. "Feel your way."

He did, his fingers skimming, strumming, exploring. I swayed against him, the tightness inside of me swirling faster and faster. The heel of his palm rubbed against the front of my pelvic bone, adding a dizzying pressure.

I gasped.

He cradled the back of my head with his free hand, kissing me hard and deep. The taste of beer and Doc made me push my hips into his touch, wanting more, needing more.

"Is this what you wanted, Boots?" he asked between breaths.

I didn't have it in me to speak, only moan. The tightness spread up through my abdomen.

He increased the pace and friction.

"I want to feel you let loose, Violet." He whispered in my ear, his deep voice deliciously seductive, making me shiver.

I panted, writhed, and pressed his hand harder against me. "Don't stop."

He didn't.

"And when you're done," he said. "I want to taste you."

Yesssssssssss!

"Oh, my—Doc!" I cried out. The tremors started deep inside and rippled outward, sapping me. I clung to his shoulders to keep from sliding to a heap on the steps.

He held me up, leaning into me, pushing me against the wall. "You're so damned sexy, Boots," he said and found my mouth, this time with a gentler touch.

I moaned, missing him when he pulled his hand away from me.

His mouth hovered over mine. "I need to be inside of you now."

I shimmied out of my boxers and reached for his shorts. He caught my hand. "I'll do it."

"I'll be gentle," I said.

He let go. "You need to be fast."

His shorts hit the floor, then his briefs. I snuck in one touch before he hauled my leg up again and eased in.

"God, I missed you," he said in a growly voice.

"Show me."

He did, slamming me against the wall.

"Is that all you got?" I taunted, shifting my hips to take more of him.

"Vixen!" Then his lips shut me up as his body wooed mine with a captivating rhythm that raced faster and faster.

This time, he beat me to the finish line, stilling for a couple of heartbeats as his groans echoed in the narrow stairwell.

I rocked my hips against him, luring more from him.

"Holy shit, Violet," he shuddered against me. "What are you doing to me?" He growled low in his throat and shoved deeper into me.

"I'm so close," I whispered, hovering on the edge of

pleasure.

He lifted me fully off the step. "Wrap your legs around me."

I obeyed and he shifted, lighting my fuse in a few strokes. I gasped his name again, clinging to his damp skin. He kept going until I stopped pulsing around him and lowered my feet to the floor. Then he buried his fingers in my hair, tipping my head back.

Butterfly kisses brushed over my face in the dark, melting my heart even more.

"Doc," I breathed in the delicious scent of him and sex, hungry for more.

"Hmmm?"

"Take me to bed."

"I thought you'd never ask." He led me up the steps and into his bedroom, leaving the overhead light off.

His room smelled fresh, the cool air coming in through the broken window filled the room with a clean, pine scent.

"Wait," he said, and picked me up, carrying me around the field of broken glass.

"Wasn't there a screen on that window when you moved in?" All of his other windows had screens; I knew that for a fact as his Realtor.

"It was slain by a rail during the bed delivery." He set me down on the bed.

I bounced a little, testing its softness, and smiled at him in the shadows as he slid onto the bed next to me and leaned on his elbow.

"You have magic hands and fingers," I said.

The objects of discussion trailed over my breasts and down to my bellybutton. "You have unbelievably soft skin."

"It's the peanut butter fudge ice cream I lather in every night."

"That reminds me of something I can't stop fantasizing about. How long can you stay?"

"Until dawn."

"Then you turn into a pumpkin?"

"Or a mouse, take your pick."

He rolled onto his back and pulled me with him. I straddled him, sitting upright. He tucked his hands behind his head. "I like this view."

I rocked against him and he stopped me. "Not yet. Tell me what happened the other night when I left you at Cornelius's hotel room."

I hesitated, unsure how much to admit. Now that I'd had a full twenty-four hours to think about the whole Wolfgang thing, my anxieties seemed silly. It was just another nightmare, probably made more intense due to not being home and in my own bed.

"Violet, tell me."

Diving in, I said, "Well, Cornelius gave each of us a task. Mine was to run the recorder to pick up any random ghost chatter. He turned the lights down, started doing this weird chanting, and then ..." I hesitated.

"Then what?"

"Then I fell asleep."

Doc chuckled. "I'm sorry I missed that."

When I didn't smile in return, his face sobered. "What? Did something happen?"

I shrugged. "Sort of."

He waited, his eyebrows raised.

"I had another nightmare."

"During the séance?"

"Yeah. Only it was different." I hesitated again, anxious about how he'd react to my dream.

He nudged me with a slight thrust of his hips. "Keep going."

"Wolfgang was there, which isn't really anything new. He's often in my nightmares. But this time he caught on fire and melted right in front of me."

"Oh, Christ." Doc sat up and gathered me close, tucking my head under his chin. "I should've stayed with you."

"It gets worse."

He eased me back, watching and waiting.

Taking a deep breath, I told him what I hadn't told Aunt Zoe. "Wolfgang opened his mouth and grabbed it like this." I showed him. "And then he tore his face open and his skull cracked and this black demon-looking thing came out." I shivered just thinking about it. "It had bumpy skin with pustules all over it and these twisty little horns, long sharp teeth and a little snout."

"Damn."

"Then it called me by my name, and when I answered, it screamed at me, covering my face with bloody spit."

He drew a breath between clenched teeth. "Gross. What did it say?"

"It told me to get out." I blinked away the memory and looked at him, trying to read his thoughts from the creases lining his mouth, his forehead. "Doc, do you think I'm going crazy?"

He tipped my chin up and kissed me—no lust, just slow and simple.

"No, I don't." A slight smile curved his lips. "But you should probably try to avoid taking naps during séances in the future."

"I'm sorry about that whole Cornelius mess I dragged you into. I swear I didn't know he was—"

Doc's hand over my mouth shushed me. "I shouldn't have left you there. I was just messed up from what I was picking up in the hotel, and when I realized what I was walking into, I got pissed, which was stupid. And then I took it out on you, which was even worse."

We stared at each other for several seconds in silence.

Shit. I was going to have to break my best friend's heart.

I grabbed Doc by the sides of his head and crushed his lips with mine. As my tongue explored his mouth, I rubbed against him, dragging more groans and growls from him.

He clutched my hips, but instead of helping with my

rhythm, he held me still and pulled slightly away. His gaze was dark with lust, but focused. "Violet?"

"What?" I tried to kiss him again, but he shook his head.

"Hold on. Tell me something. What color were the demon's eyes?"

I'd much rather have talked about the color of Doc's eyes, but I answered, hoping we could get back to the good stuff. "Orange. Glowing."

Doc rolled me off of him, leaving me in a heap on the bed.

"Hey!" I said, sitting up. "Where are you going?"

Muffled thumps came from his closet. Then he came back to bed, turning on the light on the bedside table before crawling in next to me.

I stared at the book he held in his hand—Lila's freaky book that I'd found at the Carhart house weeks ago. "If that's your idea of erotic reading material to spice up our sex life, I'd prefer something with happier cartoons in it."

"We don't need any spice, Boots. All I have to do is think about you naked." He flipped through several pages, then stopped, his lips flat-lining. "Those twisty little horns you mentioned reminded me of something. What you said about its eyes cinched it."

"What?"

"This." He held the book out to me, showing me a drawing on one of the pages. "It's called Kyrkozz. The description matches yours."

Kyrkozz? Why did that sound familiar?

I took the book from him, my breath catching.

"Is that your demon?" he asked.

"Yes," I whispered, staring down at my nightmare.

Chapter Sixteen

*K*yrkozz.

The leading star of my nightmare had a previous billing in Lila's story. Now the question was why had my brain given him a role in the newest Violet Parker scream-queen blockbuster?

An icy finger of dread scratched down my spine, trailing goosebumps. What if it was real? What if it wasn't just a nightmare? What if Cornelius had opened some door that had allowed Kyrkozz to come through? What if—*stop!*

I took a deep breath, blocking out the hysterical voice in my brain.

No, I must have seen this picture of the demon before when I'd flipped through the pages of the book. This was just one of those cases where I had plucked bits and pieces of my waking life and cast them into my dream world.

Yes, that had to be the deal. Otherwise … well, otherwise the worry-etched lines around Doc's eyes and mouth meant his concern was for more than my mental well-being. Something to do with his own guarded world, his own demons.

Scrubbing my hand down my face, I fell back onto Doc's bed. If I could just slow this slide into insanity until I got the kids through high school, they could avoid the "my-mother-lost-her-marbles" leg of the talk-show circuit.

"Violet?" Doc took the book back and tossed it on the bedside table. "It may be a coincidence."

He didn't sound entirely convinced, though.

The bed shifted. He drew me against his warmth, his lips brushing my temple.

"You're exhausted, more than a little stressed, frustrated with your job, and trying to support a family." He traced the contours of my face. "Cut yourself some slack."

Doc was right. He had to be. But he was scrambling my brains even more with his gentle touches and soothing words, making me wonder what it would be like to share more of my life with him than just stolen moments like these.

"I should probably go home," I said, hiding behind closed eyelids. It was safer there.

His fingers kept tracing, lulling me.

"I'm sorry about your window," I said just above whisper level several minutes later.

"Shhh." His hand moved to my hair.

My eyes stayed closed, my muscles softening, my body melting into the mattress.

"This is a very nice new bed." I yawned. "I can't remember where my shorts are."

He trailed his fingers down to my arm, lightly grazing my skin. I snuggled deeper into his body heat.

"Maybe I'll just take a little …"

Sleep sucked me under its black waves.

The next thing I knew, the crows were making their usual morning ruckus.

I pushed upright with a gasp and looked around.

Doc's bed.

Sunlight shining through the broken window.

The sound of a shower coming through the open door of the attached bathroom.

"Oh, no," I whispered, tumbled from the tangle of sheets onto the floor, and wobbled onto my feet.

The shower shut off.

Where was my shirt? Flashes from last night's activities before I'd blacked out into oblivion replayed in my head.

"Nice," Doc said from the bathroom doorway, his towel cinched at his hips, his hair wet and spiky, his jaw shadowed with whiskers.

Wincing at the not-so-sexy picture I must be, I grabbed a pillow and hid behind it.

He leaned on the doorjamb. "It's too late for that. I got an eyeful while you were sleeping."

Dear God, naked and ass-up in broad daylight. I'd probably drooled in my sleep, too. Gah! My whole body burned in mortification. "I have to go."

"Your clothes are on the end of the bed, under the sheet."

I lunged for them. Doc watched me scramble into my T-shirt, his focus south of my chin.

"You want me to drive you home?"

"No!" I pulled my boxers up. "I mean, no thanks."

"The neighbors are going to see you."

"I'll jog. They'll think I'm exercising."

"In a red satin robe and slippers?"

"This is Deadwood, remember? They won't even look twice."

"I would."

"Yeah, but you're biased. I'll call you later."

He grabbed me as I beelined for the back stairwell, pulling me back for a quick peck on the mouth. "Thanks, Boots."

He smelled clean, his mouth all fresh from toothpaste. I smiled in spite of the shit-storm undoubtedly waiting for me at home. "For throwing a stone through your window?"

"Yeah, for starters."

I pulled away before I shucked sensibility and yanked off his towel. "You'll be in your office later?"

He nodded.

"So will I. I'll see you then."

"Watch the glass," he reminded me. "Your slippers are by the French doors."

On my way down the stairwell, I patted the wall where Doc had rocked my world.

My slippers were lined up and waiting for me to run on home, which I did, only I went barefoot on the sidewalk for speed's sake. Everything on me bounced with each step. I clutched my chest and bobbled onward.

Only two people noticed me. One honked and leered—asshole. The other finished shaking out her rug and went back inside.

Five minutes later, I snagged the paper off the front porch and huffed around through Aunt Zoe's side gate. The grass was damp with dew, the bugs still flying low to the ground. I climbed the porch steps, dropping the slippers next to the lawn chair that had been my bed the night before last.

The smell of freshly brewed coffee seeped out through the open window over the kitchen sink. Lowering into the lawn chair, I scrambled to come up with a plan.

I had to tell Natalie the truth about Doc. It was time. I was tired of the game, sick of hiding from her. Last night had clinched it. I wanted to see where this thing with Doc led, even if it meant me curled up in my closet nursing a bottle of tequila and a broken heart in the end.

It's not like Doc and Natalie had ever had anything going. It was always fiction of her making. I should have stepped in sooner, squashing it before she'd daydreamed up her own happily-ever-after with him. But like Elvis—Addy's chicken, not the King of Rock and Roll—I was too often covered in feathers and clucking when called to task.

I heard the clanking pipes of the kitchen faucet through the wall next to me. Taking a deep breath, I stood and looked in the window.

Natalie jerked in surprise, then laughed.

She shut off the water and grabbed a towel. The back door opened.

"There you are." Natalie stepped out and closed the door behind her. She glanced down at the newspaper in my hand. "I didn't hear you go out."

Here went nothing. My heart throbbed in my throat, aching. "Natalie, I have something to tell you."

"Wait, let me go first."

I slammed on the brakes, words clogging and jumbling at

the back of my tongue.

"I wanted to tell you this when I got home last night, but you were sleeping. I didn't want to wake you."

Not sleeping, just lying there with my eyes closed not wanting to talk.

"When I left the Bingo hall last night, I stopped at the minimart up in Lead to get gas. Guess who was inside buying beer?"

I had no idea—Shaggy and Scooby Doo?

"Your buddy, Detective Cooper."

She said the word *buddy* with an exaggerated wink.

"And guess what the first thing was he said to me?"

"Bingo?"

She snorted. "No, smartass. He asked where you were."

Contrary to her big-toothed grin, his question didn't bode well for me. My stomach tightened for a whole new reason that had to do with Cooper and handcuffs, and not in a sexy way at all.

"When I asked why he was looking for you," she continued, "he said that he needed to see you again."

Uh oh.

"Did you hear that, he 'needed' to see you. You know what that means?"

That I was going to jail? "Not a clue."

"He wants you," she said with a nod of her head, like it was all said and done and the engagement announcement would appear in the newspaper next week.

"Possibly, but not like you're thinking."

"Trust me, I'm right. You didn't see him. His eyes were a bit bloodshot, his face covered with stubble, his hair all finger-raked. He had on some old torn Levi's and this T-shirt that I swear had bullet holes in it."

I knew that T-shirt. They were bullet holes. He'd worn the shirt the first time I'd stopped over to assess his house and have him sign a sales contract.

"He was the picture of a pining lover, standing there in a

minimart late at night, buying a twelve-pack of beer so he could go home and drink until he forgot you."

Or just drink with his buddies and keep playing poker. "Natalie, this is Deadwood, not Casablanca. I'm not Ilsa, and Cooper certainly isn't Rick."

"I stand by my observations. That man wants you. He wants you bad."

He wanted me all right—behind bars. Sweat dotted my upper lip. Had someone seen Harvey and me last night sneaking around Mudder Brothers and called Coop? Maybe that cop trolling with the portable lighthouse beam had caught a glimpse of my hair. I knew I should have worn a ski mask, but it was August for crissake.

I just wasn't cut out for this sleuthing business.

"Coop told me to have you call him today on his cell phone. When did he give you his private number?"

"When he hired me as his Realtor."

"Oh, yeah, I forgot you were selling his place."

I did, too, sometimes. Like when I was hiding from the law—aka Cooper.

"Wouldn't it be romantic if you two got together because he hired you to be his real estate agent?"

Been there, done that. Oh, the irony. Which dragged me back to why I was standing out here barefoot with the scent of Doc still on my skin.

Blowing out a sigh, I tightened the belt of my robe. "Natalie, I need to tell you something."

"What?"

I paused, gathering up my courage like the long train of a fancy-schmancy wedding dress.

"Please don't tell me you slept with Wymonds," she said. "I saw the article."

"No, I didn't screw around with Jeff."

"Thank God. I know you don't have the best record with men, but trust me, underneath that prickly façade, Cooper's a good guy. He could be *the one* for you."

Jeez, I'd had enough of this Cooper fantasy of hers. At least the truth about Doc would end this before she started Phase Two of her matchmaking game—coincidental double dates.

"Natalie, I have been—"

"Violet!" Aunt Zoe hollered through the window screen over the sink.

I jumped at the sound of my name. When I looked over, Aunt Zoe had the phone held up for me to see.

"Mona's on the phone."

"I'll call her back in a bit." *After I finish breaking Natalie's heart.*

Aunt Zoe spoke in the phone, "Can she call you back, Mona?"

"Anyway," I continued, taking a deep breath, avoiding Natalie's eyes. "I have—"

"Violet," Aunt Zoe called outside again. "You need to take this."

Argh!

"Hold on," I told Natalie and met Aunt Zoe at the back door.

Her focus flicked to Natalie, her brows raised.

I shook my head, taking the phone. "What's going on, Mona?"

"Ray."

"What about him?" *Had he been busted last night transporting body parts? Is that why Cooper wanted to talk to me?*

"He just faxed a second offer over to Tiffany for the hotel."

That hit me like a right uppercut to the chin.

"A s-s-second offer?" I stammered, reeling.

"Yes. For fifteen thousand more than our offer."

That vile, loincloth-chomping jackass!

"And that's not all," she added, her tone weary. "You need to get in here."

"I'll be right there."

My tell-all, soap opera moment with Natalie would have to wait until I figured out how to keep Ray from getting his grubby mitts on that hotel—well, his and George Mudder's.

I handed Natalie the newspaper. "I'll catch you later."

"Hey, you had something to tell me."

"I'll tell you later. I gotta go."

"Don't forget to call Cooper," she called after me.

Aunt Zoe raised her brows at Natalie's mention of the detective.

"Cooper can't live without me," I told her and raced up to the shower.

A half-hour later, sporting an ankle-length black and purple paisley dress, my curls still damp, and just enough makeup to look human, I parked next to Ray's SUV. As much as I wanted to door-ding the hell out of it, I resisted, taking the higher road … for now.

I smelled the rat-faced fink as soon as I walked through Calamity Jane's back door. Did he really expect to ever get laid wearing that much cologne? Or was he covering up some odor like the rank smell of something dead? Of many dead "somethings" being hauled around in a big crate? Maybe I should steal his keys and sniff around in his SUV.

But first, coffee.

Jane's office was dark and in shambles, like someone had rifled through her shelves and file cabinet. I tiptoed inside, which wasn't easy in my purple cowboy boots, and took a longer look, noticing the dried coffee covering the front corner of her desktop. The empty cup lay on the floor, half under the desk. I sniffed the dried stain, picking up a hint of something strong under the coffee. Baileys Irish Cream? Kahlua? Southern Comfort?

I picked up the cup and tossed it in her trash. Had Mona seen this? Ray? How long should they let this go on before intervening?

Backing out of Jane's office, I closed the door partway,

shielding the signs of a potential nervous breakdown from view.

Mona wasn't at her desk when I stepped into the front room, but her laptop was there, the screensaver activated. The bathroom had been empty and dark, so she must have stepped out for a moment.

I didn't acknowledge *Señor Burro Grande* at all and made a pit stop at the coffee pot.

"Well, well, well." Unfortunately, Ray had picked up my scent and started his braying right off. "Look who crawled out of one of her client's beds and decided to grace us with her presence."

Doc wasn't officially a client, anymore. "Shut up, Ray."

I really didn't feel like sparring this morning. I had a job to do that involved Cornelius, an increased offer, and another fax to Tiffany. If Ray wanted to add "kick a jerkoff in the teeth" to my to-do list, I'd be happy to tack it on at the end.

"Ah, is little Blondie upset because I took away her lollipop?"

"You might want to hold off on the celebration fireworks, Ray." I mirrored his sneer and carried my coffee cup to my desk. "It's only fifteen thousand. I can top that."

"You sound pretty confident for a girl whose client spent the better part of last night in a jail cell."

What!? I spilled hot coffee on my fingers. My eyes watered from the sting.

Why was Cornelius in jail last night? What in the hell had happened in that hotel room? Was that why Cooper wanted to talk to me?

I grabbed some tissues from my drawer, buying time to school my expression. I couldn't let him see how much his announcement had knocked me on my ass. "It's not what you think."

"Oh, really? So, it's not that your client is wanted for a murder that occurred near New Orleans?"

There was no shielding the shock that left me slack-jawed.

"What?"

Ray grinned like he'd eaten the Cheshire cat, tail and all. "You really should take some time to do a little research on your clients before signing a contract."

"You're full of shit."

"Am I?"

I honestly didn't know. "You're just trying to rattle me."

"Where do you think Mona has run off to?"

I shrugged, dabbing at the drops of coffee that had landed on my desk. "To the post office."

"More like to make bail."

Fuckity fuck! Fuck! Fuck!

"It doesn't matter." I glared at him, done with trying to hide behind a pleasant veneer. "You're not going to get the hotel sale commission."

"Who's going to stop me? You and what client? Jeff Wymonds?" His laughter grated on my calm.

"Jeff could wipe the floor with you."

"Wiping floors is about the only thing he's capable of after drinking away any hopes of making something of his pathetic life. The idiot's wife left him for another woman. I repeat, a *woman*. The man is a disgrace to his sex—pun intended."

I set down my coffee cup before I dumped it over Ray's bloated head. Jeff might be a big dope at times, but he didn't deserve this battering. He was a hard worker and a good father. It wasn't his fault his wife traded teams.

"I'm going to stop you on my own, Ray. Just me."

"Right. What do you have in the bank now? A hundred dollars?" He laughed again.

I fantasized about tearing off his boots and cramming them down his throat.

"Oh, wait, I forgot, Blondie. You screwed Doc Nyce in exchange for him buying Mona's listing. Make that a thousand bucks in the bank and an old piece-of-shit pickup."

God, he was such a ginormous turd.

"What happened, Ray? Did your mommy ignore you when you wanted to be picked up? Who made you hate women so much?"

"I like women just fine, Blondie, especially those who know their place in life."

Where would that place be in Ray's world? On their knees?

"So, it's just me that turns you into a foul-mouthed cretin?" I asked.

"Yep. You're special, Blondie." He winked at me.

Lucky me.

I leaned back in my chair, crossing my arms over my chest. "I know what's in the crates, Ray," I said, bluffing.

His eyes narrowed.

"I followed you the other night," I added for good measure.

"You lie."

Yes, I did. More often than I probably should, too. But the way his eyes searched mine, he wasn't so sure of it.

"I know all about the tools," I continued, reaching, using his reactions to guide me.

Ray's cheeks darkened.

"And the money." This was pure guesswork, but George had to be getting funding from somewhere if he could top Cornelius's offer. Death couldn't be paying that well, could it? "I know what you did and how you're using Mudder Brothers to cover it all up."

Ray's nostrils flared. "You lie," he said again, but he lacked his earlier conviction.

"You shouldn't have come after my job, Ray. Big mistake. When I'm done with you, Mona will be over at the police station bailing your ass out of jail."

He shoved to his feet, the force of his abrupt rise slamming his chair backward into the wall. "You'll end up dead, you stupid cunt."

Ohhh, he'd thrown out the C-word. I'd nailed a nerve,

which meant I was on course with my suspicions.

I rocked in my chair, feigning nonchalance. Inside, adrenaline spread, making my legs and arms tingle, preparing me for fight or flight.

"Is that a threat, Ray?"

He rushed me, his eyes rimmed with rage. "Consider it a warning, Blondie."

Months of built-up anger exploded. I shot to my feet, ready to clash horns with him head on.

"Remember this, dickhead—Detective Cooper is one of my so-called *clients*. Sweet nothings aren't the only things I whisper in his ear."

Ray stepped closer, bending so we were almost nose-to-nose. His cologne clawed at the back of my throat, but I held my ground, standing tall.

"Trust me, Blondie," he whispered, his breath reeking of stale coffee and onions. "If you don't back the fuck off, Cooper won't be able to save you."

The bells over the front door jingled.

"What's going on here?" Mona asked, striding over, her cheeks matching her pink silk blouse. She pushed us apart. "Ray, Detective Cooper wants to talk to you over at the police station."

Cooper was being awfully chatty these days. A regular talk show host.

When Ray didn't budge, Mona grabbed him by the ear and yanked. "Damn it, Ray, knock it off."

"Owch! Jesus, Red, that hurts."

"Good." Her green eyes flashed. "Now, get out of here before I rip it off your head!"

Ray paused long enough to grab his phone and shoot me one last wrinkled-lip sneer.

I saluted him with my middle finger.

Mona waited for the door to close behind him before asking, "What was that about?"

I clasped my trembling hands behind my back. "He was

just being his usual loving self."

Worry lined her cheeks. "You okay?"

Not really. Confrontation usually left me wanting to lock myself in the bathroom and pay tribute to the porcelain goddess. "I'm fine."

"Good, because you need to call Cornelius."

"Is he out of jail?"

Mona rolled her eyes. "He was never in jail."

"What? Ray was lying?"

"Yes and no. Yesterday, the police got a tip about Cornelius being involved with a murder down in New Orleans earlier this year, so they brought him in last night."

"They put him in a jail cell based on a tip?"

"No, he asked to be put in the cell."

I blinked. "I'm confused."

Her forehead wrinkled. "Why didn't you tell me Cornelius claims to be able to talk to ghosts?"

Because that made him sound a teensy bit insane. "I hadn't gotten around to it yet."

"It turns out that while the police were questioning Cornelius, he claimed to hear some whispers coming from the cell area. When he mentioned his ghostly occupation, one of the rookies told him about a prisoner who'd hung himself in one of the cells a couple of decades ago."

"Is that a true story?" Could Cornelius really hear ghosts?

She nodded. "Cornelius convinced the police to lock him up in the same cell as the dead prisoner for the night so he could try to make contact with the ghost."

"Oh, jeez." I sat down on the edge of my desk. "So, did Cornelius make 'contact' during the night?"

"No, but he asked to come back another time with his equipment." Mona hesitated, then added, "And he mentioned you."

Of course he did. Great. Just what I needed over at the cop shop—to be linked with a person-of-interest in another murder case.

"You mean regarding me being his Realtor?"

"Yes," Mona said. "He also told them you can channel ghosts."

I looked to the ceiling, waiting for it to crash down on my head. "Mona, please tell me you're kidding."

"I wish I was." She squeezed my shoulder. "You have a new nickname: Spooky Parker."

That wasn't new. Ray called me that, too. He probably planted it there. "Maybe I should add that to my business cards." Along with the fire department's new favorite, Four-Alarm Parker.

"Is Cornelius still there?" I asked.

"No, he left when I first got there, saying something about hunting down a protein shake."

Good luck with that. "And the murder in New Orleans?"

"He has a solid alibi. The police will just keep an eye on him for a bit."

"That's a relief." Although, Cornelius wouldn't be my first client who'd committed murder. It seems I'd found a new niche in the realty market.

"I know. But you need to go see Cornelius about the hotel, pronto. We have forty-eight hours to up our offer."

I grabbed my keys and purse. "I'm on it."

"Call me on my cell after you talk to him," Mona said, dropping into her chair. "I have an appointment in Spearfish for lunch."

"Will do." I paused next to Jane's partially closed door. "Mona? Have you seen Jane today?"

"She was leaving the parking lot when I got here this morning. Said she'd be back tonight."

"Good." I closed Jane's office door with a quiet click, hiding the mess inside. "I'll talk to you later."

I looked for Doc's Camaro on my way through the parking lot, but didn't see it anywhere. In my haste to race home this morning, I hadn't thought to ask him what time he'd be in the office.

Shaking thoughts of Doc from my head, I crawled inside the Picklemobile and called Cornelius's cell phone. He didn't answer, so I tried to reach him in his room via the hotel switchboard.

He answered on the first ring. "I thought I told you not to call me, anymore."

I held the phone away for a second and frowned at it. Why couldn't I find normal clients?

"Cornelius, this is Violet Parker," I said into the mouthpiece.

"Oh, Violet, I'm sorry. I thought you were someone else."

Who? A ghostly jailbird, maybe?

"We need to talk," I told him and decided to lay it all out right then and there. "The other party interested in the hotel submitted a second, higher offer."

"Persistence is an admirable quality."

He sounded like a fortune cookie. I leaned back in the seat, tapping my thumb on the steering wheel. "Does that mean you are willing to up your offer?"

"That depends."

"On what?"

"You."

My thumb stopped. "On me?"

"Yes."

"Is this about me getting you another protein shake?"

He laughed so loudly that I held the phone away from my ear until he quieted. "No. It's about you and this hotel."

My shoulders tightened. "I don't understand."

"It's simple my dear. If I can get positive proof that this hotel is haunted, I don't care what it costs us, you will get it for me."

"Proof? What about that broken mirror from your first séance or the meters redlining the other night?"

"I want something more definite."

More definite? We were talking about goddamned ghosts. "No problem," I said with false bravado. I could find the book Doc spoke of that talked about the multiple suicides. Get the ladies' names for him to call through the walls. If it came down to it, hire some actors to do something ghost-like, maybe drag chains around in the middle of the night.

"Great. You'll be here at dusk then, I assume?"

"You mean to sign the revised offer papers?"

"I mean to act as a channel for me, like you did before."

I glared at the phone. No. Absolutely not. No way in hell. Channeling was something I only did with a television or radio.

"Violet?" I heard him say. "Are you still there?"

I needed a new job.

Holding the phone to my ear again, I jammed the key in the ignition. "What do you want me to bring?"

Chapter Seventeen

Since Cornelius wouldn't sign off on a second offer until I pulled a ghost out of my ass, that left me the remaining hours of daylight to come up with a game plan.

I started the Picklemobile, holding down the gas pedal as she cleared her throat. Puffs of black smoke billowed past the rearview mirror.

Being that Cornelius dabbled regularly in the haunted realm, I couldn't just wing it this time, not with my job on the line. I'd have to put on the performance of a lifetime, even if it took a theatrical show big enough to bring Elvis back from the other side. David Copperfield could hide a plane, right? Surely, I could fake channeling a ghost.

There was just one teeny weeny problem—I had no clue what I was doing. I needed help, and I knew just the person to school me in the ectoplasmic world: Doc.

I called his cell phone and got his voicemail.

Strike one.

Shifting into reverse, I rumbled over to his house and repeated last night's performance—first a knock, then the doorbell, then a look in the garage. His Camaro wasn't there.

Strike two.

The library! Knowing Doc, he was probably there searching for more information on good ol' Kyrkozz. I swallowed the anxiety that fluttered in my throat at just the thought of the demon.

When I pulled into the parking lot, his car wasn't there, either. I checked inside the South Dakota room just to be sure and found it empty. Damn.

Strike three.

Now what? I was out of strikes.

I climbed back into the Picklemobile and shut the door. Maybe I'd cruise up to Lead and look for his car. Or call Natalie and see if she knew where he was since she kept tailing him. Or not.

My cell phone rang.

Doc!

I pulled it out of my purse. The sight of Cooper's name made my eye twitch.

Crud.

As much as I wanted to let Cooper's call go to voicemail, I knew he'd hunt me down sooner or later. Deadwood wasn't big enough for the two of us.

"Hello, Detective Cooper."

"Ms. Parker," his tone was brusque, all business and metal shavings. "I need you to come to the police station."

After Cornelius's stunt last night and my not-so-new nickname with Deadwood's finest, I'd sooner prance down Main Street butt-naked. "No."

Cricket chirps came from his end of the line. Then, "What do you mean 'No'?"

"I mean, I'd rather not, thank you."

"Violet, I'm not asking you out on a date here."

My cheeks warmed, Natalie's suspicions churning in my mind. "Of course you're not. Why would you?"

"I'm calling you as a detective with the Deadwood Police Department."

"Am I under arrest?" I asked.

"No."

"Well, then I'm not coming in there."

"But I need to talk to you."

"I'm listening right now."

He sighed. "Why are you always so difficult?"

"Is that what you need to talk with me about, Detective? My disposition?"

"No."

"Is it about the corpse?"

"Yes, and some other stuff."

I said nothing. I wasn't going in there, damn it.

"Violet, don't make me come and find you. You won't like me when I do."

I wasn't sure I liked him right now. "Does that mean you won't be your usual warm and fuzzy self?"

He growled through the line. "Tell me where you are or I'll put out an APB on you."

"Fine." I started the Picklemobile. "Meet me at Bighorn Billy's."

"When?"

"In ten minutes."

He hung up on me, abrupt as always. I stuck my tongue out at the phone and dropped it in my purse.

Four extra-long red stoplights later, I pulled into the parking lot at Bighorn Billy's diner. Besides the white 1950s-era Thunderbird convertible, the rest of the cars in the lot were modern vehicles. Kool Deadwood Nites and the rumbling of classic Detroit steel that came with it had come and gone, sucked back down into the sands of time. Now the town could return to everyday life—hard work, school, and gambling.

Cooper's unmarked sedan glinted under the afternoon sunshine, the engine still ticking as I skirted it.

I stepped inside Bighorn Billy's, my stomach growling at the delectable *eau de* fried beef. Garth Brooks played through the speakers in the upper corners of the room, singing about blaming it on his roots and showing up in boots. As entrances go, I couldn't ask for better theme music.

Across the room, Cooper held down a corner booth, his barbed stare poking holes in me like I was a Voodoo doll. Nothing new there. Why couldn't he be more like Barney Fife?

I might as well get this over with. Straightening my shoulders, I weaved through the tables, nodding at a few familiar faces and trying to remember where I'd seen them before—probably Mudder Brothers Funeral Parlor, my new hangout.

"Hello, Detective," I said and slid onto the bench seat across from him.

"You're late," he said as a greeting, storm clouds roiling over his brow. He'd left the top button of his dark blue shirt undone under his silver tie and had missed a narrow strip of whiskers on his jaw. Hmmm. Had it been a rough night or a rushed morning?

"It's a woman's prerogative to be slightly tardy," I told him.

"Yeah? Well, I took the liberty of ordering for you."

"What? Why?" I wasn't *that* late.

He shrugged. "It's a man's prerogative to be slightly impatient, especially when a stack of papers is waiting for him back on his desk."

My neck heated, guilt at making him come to me spurring the truth from me. "Sorry, but after Cornelius's antics last night—"

"And this morning."

I sighed. "And this morning, I'm not comfortable with stepping inside the police station."

"Policemen don't bite, Ms. Parker." His eyes crinkled at the corners. Was that his version of a smile? If so, it had skipped right over his lips. "But I can't speak for our ghostly pal in Cell B."

The waiter interrupted my glare. I waited for him to set down the two full coffee cups he'd brought and leave. "Why the sudden interest in Cornelius? From what Mona told me, the murder in New Orleans was half a year ago."

"A tip came in."

"What tip? From whom?" *Ray?* No, he wouldn't go that far, would he? I remembered his smirk this morning, the smugness plastered all over his face.

Of course! It all made sense. He knew that if he could

waylay Cornelius by siccing the cops on him, I wouldn't be able to get a second offer in before the final deadline.

I white-knuckled my coffee mug, a burning knot tightening behind my sternum. The asshole was hedging his bet. He must have searched online, sniffing for Cornelius's dirty laundry.

Cooper watched me with his steely gray eyes, his rugged face giving nothing away. "It doesn't matter who gave us the tip."

Was Cooper protecting Ray? Why?

"How long have you known Mr. Curion?" he asked.

"Interrogation over coffee, how lovely." I grabbed a creamer and poured it into my cup.

Cooper probably asked blunt, uncomfortable questions during sex, too. I could hear him now … *How long have your breasts been slightly lopsided, Ms. Parker? When was the last time you had a thorough pelvic exam? Did you use one or two prophylactics the last time you had sexual intercourse?*

"Just answer the question, Ms. Parker."

I stirred my drink while trying to look innocent of some crime I hadn't committed. The way Cooper could make me feel guilty with just his eyes made me grind my molars. "About a week."

"How did you meet him?"

"He walked into my office, asked for me, and said he wanted to buy a hotel."

"He actually asked for you in particular?"

"Yes."

"How did he know your name?"

"I don't know." I dumped some sugar in my coffee to offset Cooper's lack of sweetness.

"You didn't wonder about that?"

Yes, but Cooper's hint of scorn tickled my ornery bone. "No, not really."

"Did he have one of your business cards?"

I tried to remember. "I don't think so."

"Has it never occurred to you to ask why he chose you to represent him?"

"Nope." Hell, yes, but more in a *dear-Lord-why-me* sort of way, not for the reason the detective was asking.

"You do a background check on your buyers, don't you?"

"If you're referring to their credit history, then my answer is sometimes."

He scoffed. "A complete stranger walks into your office and asks for you by name. Shouldn't this have been one of those times, especially considering your record for attracting the criminally insane?"

He had a point, and I didn't like him poking me with it. "I didn't dig into his background because he showed me the money."

"Is that Realtor jargon for something in particular?"

"Yes. It means he took a wad of cash from his pocket and showed me that he had money."

"Christ! And you trusted him on that alone?"

I leaned forward. "Not all of us interrogate every person we meet. Some of us just like to take people at their word."

One of his dark blond eyebrows shot upward. "And how's that been working out for you so far?"

"Oh, bite me."

His grin showed all of his white choppers. "Where should I start?"

"I thought you said policemen don't bite."

"I lied. I do."

Being that Cooper was made up of sharp angles and stainless steel, I wasn't sure if that was supposed to be a joke, an attempt at flirting, or a threat. I decided to ignore it and ask for an answer that would play a role in making or breaking my career. "Are you going to arrest Cornelius for murder?"

"No. He's just a person of interest at this time. More so now that we know what he does for a living."

"Talking to ghosts doesn't make you a killer."

"It could if you wanted to extricate a spirit from a young

girl who claimed to be possessed and things didn't quite go as planned."

I sighed and took a sip from my coffee. It tasted old and weak, mirroring how I felt right then. "Why couldn't I just have a plain, boring client who doesn't believe he sees dead people?"

"You do."

"I guess Jeff Wymonds is pretty vanilla." And he didn't believe in Casper and his pals.

"I was talking about me."

Setting down my coffee cup, I chuckled. "You're not boring, Detective."

He sat back in his seat. "You don't think so?"

"No. Your T-shirts come with bullet holes in them."

"That comes with the job."

"Right. In real estate, we just get business cards."

He laughed. I stared at him in shock, wondering if I'd really heard it come from inside of him or if I'd just imagined the sound.

"That reminds me," he said. "What are you doing Friday evening?"

I could feel my eyes widen. Was he asking me for a date? No, surely not. Damned Natalie for even putting these uncertainties in my head.

Cooper didn't like me. Period. I'd bet my pathetic savings that if given the green light by his superiors, he'd be happy to shove me in the back of his sedan, drop me off at the state line, and tell me to keep heading west until I ran out of land.

I shrugged. "I'm not sure yet, why?"

"I was wondering if you'd be interested in coming over after I get off of work."

I just looked at him with my tongue imitating a bump on a log.

"Is that a 'Yes' or 'No' in your world, Violet?"

We were back on a first name basis now that the interrogation lights had dimmed.

"Why do you need me to come over?"

"I don't *need* you to come over, but I thought you'd like to do a final walk-through before you put my place on the market."

Oh, we were back to me being his Realtor. "Of course I can come by."

"You're sure you don't have any funeral viewings to attend that evening?" His tone held a note of suspicion that made my ears perk up.

"I'm not going to dignify that with an answer," I said all cool and collected. The Fonz would have given me two thumbs up.

The waiter stopped by just then to drop off our lunch: chef's salads with dressing on the side. This was what Cooper ordered for me?

"I noticed you are watching your weight," he explained when I sent him a questioning glance.

"You 'noticed' it, huh?"

"Paying attention to what people say and do is my job."

I chewed my lip. What else had he noticed about me?

He dug into his salad. "Speaking of Mudder Brothers," he started.

We hadn't been. *We* were trying to avoid that subject completely.

"A call came into the station last night about a possible prowler sighted over by the funeral parlor. The caller said the person in question had a slight limp and looked a little bowlegged." Cooper squinted at me. "You wouldn't know anything about that, would you?"

Harvey! Damn it, he'd been seen. That must have been why the cruiser came by with that spotlight.

I maintained steady eye contact with Cooper, knowing he was scrutinizing my every blink. "I didn't make any phone calls," I said, playing obtuse.

He took another bite, chewed slowly, and then swallowed, his gaze unwavering. "Where were you last night around seven thirty, Ms. Parker?"

"Working late." I popped a cherry tomato in my mouth and smiled around its sweet burst. "Where were you, Detective Cooper?"

"Playing poker."

"Natalie said she saw you buying beer after the Bingo hall let out. How long do your poker games usually last?"

"Long enough to run out of beer. Did you happen to see my uncle at some point after you left work?"

"No. I went home and spent the rest of my evening with Elvis. Did you need to talk to your uncle about something?"

"Yes, but he was not answering my phone calls. Who's Elvis?"

"My daughter's chicken. Maybe Harvey was a little busy with one of his old flames and didn't hear the phone ring. Some people enjoy after-supper activities other than cleaning guns and getting shot at."

He nodded, stabbing another bite of salad. "Maybe, but those are two of my uncle's favorite hobbies, outside of pursuing the opposite sex. Are you sure he didn't pay you a visit last night?"

"Positive." In an effort to remove Harvey from our conversation, I switched subjects. "Have you found out anything more about that foot and hand left hanging in the trees?"

A month ago, Layne had found a human foot dangling from a tree limb with a sprig of mistletoe stapled to the big toe. A couple of weeks later, a hiker up on Mount Roosevelt had found a hand in similar style—hung from a tree and stapled with mistletoe. Cooper had sent both parts to a mysterious CSI lab somewhere far, far away where it took weeks to hear results. Real-life crime scene evidence deciphering didn't move nearly as fast as it did on television.

"Nothing yet," he said over the brim of his coffee cup.

"What about the ear caught in that trap behind Harvey's barn? Has anyone missing an ear showed up in your system yet?"

Last month, something started killing the wildlife around Harvey's ranch. So, being made up of fifty percent piss and the same amount of vinegar, Harvey had set an illegal trap instead of calling the Sheriff, whom he liked to curse about.

Between the ear and the decapitated guy, the possibility of a sale of Harvey's place didn't look promising. Short of selling it as a haunted house, which Harvey also claimed it to be, I had yet to come up with an idea on how to spin these events and secure a sale ... or even a single lookie-loo.

"The ear is still at the lab."

Of course it was. I was beginning to think that was police code for mind-your-own-business.

"But," he paused, "I do want to talk to you about the corpse."

I lowered my fork. Sharing salad over a decapitation just seemed crass. "What?"

"We've figured out the name of the individual who owns the phone." When I just looked at him, he added, "The phone the text came from that named you and your aunt."

Oh, right. The subject of our conversation days ago right before I'd thrown up on Cooper's tie. "Who owns it?" My grip on my fork tightened, the metal pressing into my skin.

He took another drink of coffee before replying. "Rex Conner."

No.

It couldn't be.

No. No.

My heart jackhammered in my ears muting the outside world. I could see Cooper's lips moving, but could only hear two words over and over.

Rex Conner.

Rex Conner.

Rex Conner.

What in the hell did that lousy, good-for-nothing bastard want?

Cooper's lips stopped moving. He reached across the table and pinched my forearm.

"Ouch!" I rubbed my arm and glared at him. "Stop using Harvey's tricks on me."

"How do you know that name? And don't even try to tell me you don't know it after what I just saw in your eyes."

I hesitated. If I told Cooper the truth, that would lead to another truth, and then another. There were things in my life that needed to remain buried, that's why I'd dug the holes so deep in the first place.

But if I didn't fess up and Cooper figured it all out, he really would bite me. Or shoot me. I wasn't sure which was worse.

Either way, I was screwed six ways to Sunday. Wait, double that.

"Okay," I said, clenching my icy hands under the table.

When I didn't cough it out immediately, he leaned across the table. "Tell me, Violet. I need to know for this investigation."

"Rex Conner is the father of my children."

Chapter Eighteen

In spite of the rage that kept clawing up my throat and a twitchy eye, which Cooper so kindly pointed out—three times—I made it through the rest of lunch without a hitch.

Cooper wrote down the scant bit of information I could give him on the kids' father, and then changed the subject back to selling his house. Smart man.

Rex Conner. His name alone made me snarl and paw at the ground like a mother bear.

After I left Cooper and Bighorn Billy's, I drove up Strawberry Hill, noticing the storm clouds stacking up to the west. Mother Nature and I both needed to let off some steam. If only I had lightning bolts at my disposal.

About a mile up the hill, I turned left onto a dirt road leading away from humanity. Four bends in from the highway, I hit the brakes, shifted into park, and shoved open the door. I hefted a thick branch I found in the ditch; it felt just about right to use as a club. I looked around at the surrounding trees. Any good-sized pine would do.

A flash of memory from the last time I'd laid eyes on Rex Conner was all it took to let the fury fly.

"You God damned—"

I whacked a big pine, the branch reverberating in my hands.

"—self-worshiping—"

A piece of the branch splintered off.

"—whore-mongering—"

A chunk of bark broke off.

"—crap-weaseling, punk-ass—"

The top half of the branch splintered.

"—prick!"

The end of the branch broke off and went flying into the underbrush.

"And stay the fuck away from *my* kids!" I yelled after it.

Huffing, I strode back to where the Picklemobile sat idling, waiting for me to regain my senses. I brushed my hands off on an old rag Harvey kept in the glove box and shifted into reverse, whipping the old pickup around in a cloud of dust.

My cell phone rang as soon as the front tires hit pavement again.

I didn't even look at the screen. "Yes?"

"What are you doing for lunch?" Doc asked.

His deep voice smoothed some of my neck bristles. "Already did it."

"I figured. What are you doing now?"

"Just some relaxation therapy."

He was quiet for a moment. "Something piss you off this morning?"

Not something, but rather someone. Make that several someones. First there was Ray, then Cornelius, then Ray again, then Cooper, and finally the grand finale—a piece of shit from my past whom I'd released from any paternal or financial obligations almost a decade ago with my lawyer's help.

I kept it simple, though, since I was driving down a steep hill and had no branches within reach. Plus, if I didn't talk to anyone besides Cooper about Rex Conner, maybe the jerk would fade back into my past.

"Ray turned in a higher offer today for the hotel," I told Doc. "His client outbid mine by fifteen thousand."

"That's not much," he said. "Surely your client can come back with more than that. Didn't you say he's paying in cash?"

"Yep, cash. And you're right, he can. But the problem isn't where he'll get the money, rather what I have to do in order to get him to agree to use it."

"What you'll have to do? He's not expecting you to sleep with him is he?"

"No. Not that." I laughed. It came out harsh and cold sounding, like a frigid wind. "God, I wish it was just that."

"Oh, really?"

"Well, no, not really, but at least sleeping with a client is something I know how to do."

"And you do it quite well, I must say," Doc said. I could hear the grin in his tone. "What does Mr. Planet of the Apes want you to do?"

"Prove the hotel is haunted."

"And how are you of all people going to manage that?"

"I'm going to channel a ghost for him."

His silence stretched on for long enough that I thought I'd lost him. "You still there?"

"What aren't you telling me, Violet?"

Oh, boy, the list was long and the day still young. "A lot," I admitted. "Will you just fill me in quick on what a channeler person does and I'll tell you everything else later?"

"No."

"What? Last night you said you'd help me."

"Ah, so that's why you came over and had sex with me."

"No, of course not." As if I needed a reason. "Last night had nothing to do with Cornelius and everything to do with you and the smoldering looks you were giving me."

"I don't smolder."

"You definitely do, but in a sexy way, not like you're mad—well, sometimes you are mad at me, but ..." I trailed off before I ended up cramming any more of my boot in my mouth. "Anyway, it's a huge turn on."

I pulled into the parking lot behind Calamity Jane's. "Doc, will you please just give me a couple of parlor tricks I can do tonight?"

"What's tonight?"

"Another séance."

I thought I heard a growl come through the line. Maybe it

was just thunder. "Where are you right now?"

"Pulling into the parking lot behind your office."

"Good. Cruise by my back door. I'll be right out."

I did as he said. "Where are we going?" I asked.

"To the Old Prospector Hotel."

"Why?"

The back door to his office opened. Doc climbed into the passenger side, slamming the door behind him. He looked damned fine in his dark maroon shirt and khakis, but I preferred him in a towel. Or sans towel.

I tucked my phone in my purse. "Why are we going to the hotel?"

"To find out what's in that place before you subject yourself to another nightmare." His focus dipped to my dress and slipped clear down to my boots, his eyes darkening.

"See, now you're smoldering at me again."

"This isn't a smolder," he said, pointing at his face. "It's straight-up lust. What are you wearing under that dress?"

"I've never had a man so curious about my underwear."

"I'm sure you have, he just wasn't asking out loud."

I turned back out onto Sherman Street and headed for the hotel, passing him a quick frown. "Doc, I don't want you to do this."

I wasn't dressed to catch him if he keeled over onto me again. Although, the boots were an improvement over my mule sandals.

"You said you wanted my help."

"I do." But I didn't want him to suffer psychologically because of me. "I just want you to teach me a little about how to channel. I mean, should I just pretend to talk to some ghost, or should I scrawl out freaky words, like that woman in *The Changeling*?"

When I glanced over at him, he was staring out the front window. "How much do you want this sale?"

"Enough to pretend I can talk to dead people."

"Before I can help you, I need to find out what's in that

hotel."

"Does that mean you think Cornelius is legit?"

"No, although that is a possibility."

"Then why do you have to find out about any ghosts?"

"Because I think *you* might be legit."

I scoffed in good humor. "Legitimately insane, sure."

"Violet, do you know what you are?"

Was he serious? "A single mother who has a hankering for peanut butter fudge ice cream, John Wayne movies, and …" *you*, "soft couches."

He didn't smile back. "That's you on the outside, but what about who you really are and what you're doing here?"

"I think I'm going to need some tequila in me to continue with this conversation."

"Fine." Pointing at the hotel looming in front of us, he said, "But for now, we need to know what we're dealing with in there."

"Can't we just make something up? I'm great at playing charades."

He shook his head. "I'm not risking you running into Wolfgang again."

"You mean Kyrkozz."

"Especially Kyrkozz." He sounded serious, which made my upper lip sweat.

I swung into the parking lot and shut down the Picklemobile. The backfire scared off a bunch of crows hanging out on the hotel's roof. Good—the scene was creepy enough this afternoon with the storm clouds that now darkened Deadwood's doorstep. The black birds acting as the hosts for the haunted hotel were overkill.

Doc reached for the door handle. I caught his arm before he shoved open the door.

"Doc."

He looked at me, waiting.

"Why don't we just go to the library and look up some dead people?"

Creases formed at the corners of his eyes. "As much fun as that sounds, I'd rather just run into them here."

I still held his arm, not wanting to let go just yet. "But what if there is more than one?"

"You say that as if you believe in ghosts now." One dark eyebrow lifted. "Do you?"

I sputtered and stuttered, which pretty much summed up my answer.

"Well," he said, grinning, "it appears that I'm making progress on that front."

"I don't know what to believe when it comes to you."

"Are we talking only about ghosts here?"

No. "Mostly."

He took my hand and laced his fingers through mine. "Here's how this is going to go. We'll head inside, take the stairs up to the third floor, and see if whatever I noticed the other day is still hanging around. If not, we'll drive over to the library and figure out how you can convince Cornelius the place is worth more money without turning you into a morally corrupt sideshow freak."

It sounded like a solid game plan, but I did have the hair for the freak job, if needed. One question bobbed to the surface. "And if something is on that third floor?"

"Then the channeling performance you put on tonight will be based on truth, and the only thing at risk will be your reputation."

"And my job."

"Right. That, too." He winked at me, a smile curling the corners of his mouth. "I could start paying you for sex."

"Wow. So romantic. Be still my beating heart."

He laughed and kissed the back of my hand. "I'd quote a sonnet, but after last night, I fear I'd fall short of your wonderful Shakespearean monologue."

"Oh, God, don't remind me." Every time I tried to play Don Juan-*ita*, I ended up chasing windmills like Don Quixote. "That reminds me, I need to reimburse you for that window."

"No you don't." He let go of my hand, which stuck to his a little. He sniffed his palm. "Violet, why do you have pine sap on your hand?"

Because of Rex 'the bastard' Conner, but now was not the time to talk about him—if ever. "I don't know. I must have picked it up somewhere this morning."

Without further ado, I exited stage left. Or was that stage right?

Anyway, Doc met me at the tailgate. We crossed the lot to the hotel's double glass doors. He pulled open one of them for me to lead the way, but before I could, Tiffany came striding out.

I stumbled backwards into Doc, shocked to see his ex-girlfriend up-close and personal all of a sudden. He caught me, and I righted myself before Tiffany could sniff out anything funny going on between us. This close to the sale, with Ray playing his games, I needed her on my side, not pissed because I was frequenting Doc's bed.

If Tiffany was surprised to see us, she hid it like a pro behind her starlet sunglasses and red lipstick.

"Doc!" She nudged me aside to plaster herself against him in what some might call a hug. To me it looked more like she was trying to become another layer of skin.

Then the bitch kissed him on the cheek.

Then I tackled her and cut off all of her long, stupid red hair with a pair of blunt kindergartner scissors … .

In reality, I just clasped my hands together and looked up Main Street with a big, undoubtedly ridiculous-looking smile tacked onto my mouth.

"What are you doing here?" I heard her ask him, her voice all smoky sexy. I wondered what she'd sound like trying to talk around my socks.

"Violet is showing me the hotel."

I looked around then, fake smile still stuck in place. "Hello, Tiffany."

Tiffany assessed me from head to toe, her gaze lingering

on my hair. "Violet, yes, there you are. It's always nice to see you."

She could at least try to mean it. And here I thought we'd bonded the last time we'd talked and would be swapping cookie recipes by Halloween.

She leaned in closer to me and whispered loud enough for Doc to hear, "The hair looks good, but you could stand a little shorter dress for this client. Doc is a leg man."

My eyes jolted to his, an image of Tiffany's bare legs wrapped around him burning into my brain. Fury combined with humiliation, lighting me up like a Molotov cocktail, the flames singeing my neck and cheeks.

"Oh, really?"

Doc shook his head. His lips looked like they were struggling to hold down a smile.

The bastard seemed to actually be enjoying this public display of torture.

Tiffany stepped back from me, her gaze fawning on Doc again. "She's showing you the hotel, huh? You're not actually thinking of buying it, are you?"

"It's a possibility."

Her laughter tinkled, like a dog pissing on my leg. "Not much of a possibility, anymore, right, Violet?"

"He knows about my other client," I told her.

"So does Ray." Her lipstick-outlined smile lost some of its luster. "He's sure sunk his teeth into this one. I haven't seen him so motivated to make a sale in years."

"I bet."

"He even offered to take me to dinner at The Wild Pasque if I'd move the deadline on your window to make a second offer to twenty-four hours instead of forty-eight."

"He's pretty excited." The rat bastard!

The Wild Pasque was Deadwood's fanciest joint. The cloth napkins alone probably cost more than any of the dresses I had in my closet to wear there. Ray wasn't screwing around, anymore. He wanted me gone, gone, gone, and then some.

"How does that work in your office?" Tiffany asked. "If Ray gets the sale, what do you get?"

Fired. "The opportunity to sell something else to my client."

"Right, Mr. Curion. That man is such an interesting character." She shook her head, her expression amused as if she were enjoying a private joke. "You should be able to find something else suitable, I'd think. I have several listings in Sturgis and Spearfish if this falls through."

"Thank you." I think I meant that, too.

Thunder boomed loud enough that I felt it in my chest.

"Well, I should get going before we get drenched," she said and patted me on the arm like I'd already lost the game. Then she moved toward Doc, but before she could clutch him in her arms again, he sidestepped and reached for the door.

"See you later, Tiffany," he said and motioned for me to step inside. "After you, Violet."

Feeling slightly battered after that encounter, I avoided looking at Doc when I strode through the open door. I didn't stop and wait for him, just aimed for the elevator and took swings at my inner doubt demons along the way.

I pushed the button for the elevator, but Doc grabbed me by the elbow and led me along beside him to the stairwell door.

Oh, yeah. I'd forgotten how the game plan went for a moment thanks to Tiffany's interruption.

Doc closed the door behind us and sniffed.

"You pick up anything?" I asked.

"Just a hint. Let's go."

I looked up the narrow stairwell—three flights straight up with landings offering resting spots. The wooden-step stairway must run along the side of the building. But why did they have to paint the walls baby-blue? And by the smell in the corridor, they'd done it recently, too. It must have been in preparation for selling.

The weak light from sconces at each floor did little more than deepen the shadows. I started up the stairwell, glancing back at Doc. "Why not take the elevator this time?"

"It's not as scenic."

"Seriously?"

"I don't want to take a chance on being trapped in there with a ghost."

Pausing on the second floor landing, I waited for him to join me. "That's happened to you before?"

"Twice, but not here. Yet."

Nodding, I frowned up at him. "Why does Tiffany think you're a leg man?"

He eyed the next flight of stairs. "Do you really want to go there right now?"

"No." I climbed a few steps and stopped, turning around. "Yes, I do."

He still stood on the landing, sniffing. "I don't have a thing for legs."

"Then why did she—"

"Tiffany is insecure."

"What? No way."

"Trust me. She makes up for it by being aggressive and competitive."

"Competitive? You mean besides her job?"

"I mean physically."

"She could be a model."

"That's definitely one way she competes."

"What's the other?"

He hesitated, sweat glistening on his upper lip.

"Let me guess, during sex."

He nodded just once. "Can we go up now?"

"Okay." Two steps later, I stopped again. He was coming up on my tail.

"So, was she all athletic, doing backbends and splits like the U.S. Women's Gymnastics team?"

His lips twitched. "No. I mean she competed constantly—without stopping."

"You mean when it came to how long—"

"Yes!" He cut me off. Were his cheeks a little pale or was that just the weird lighting in here?

"Is her competitiveness why you stopped seeing her?"

"It was one reason."

"Was there another?"

"Yeah." When I refused to budge, he continued, "She wanted to get married."

"Oh." That made me take a step up in surprise. "Okay then." I'd have to remember to never say the M word to Doc. It would probably be best not even to think of that word in the same train of thought as him. "I'll just ... uh ... keep going up." I practically ran up the rest of the steps to the third floor landing.

When Doc caught up to me, he was breathing hard. Sweat trickled down from his temple.

It wasn't *that* hot and stuffy in here, and Doc was in much better shape than me. "Are you okay?"

"Yeah." He leaned against the wall, resting the back of his head on it. "But I need to tell you something," he said in between breaths, "about Tiffany."

As much as I didn't want to hear any more about Jessica Rabbit, I kept my mouth closed. My gut churned as I waited to hear what he had to say.

He sniffed a couple of times and squinted at me in the crappy lighting. "You look different."

He didn't say it as if *different* meant *good*. "Of course I look different. She and I are about as different as women get." And if he asked me to dye my hair red, I would string him up by his testicles.

"No, I mean you look different right now." He reached toward my face. "As if your face is—"

His hand jerked back all of the sudden, his eyes widening. "It's here," he whispered.

"You mean a ghost?" I looked behind me, circling like a dog chasing its tail. "Where?"

He flattened himself against the wall, his face pallid. The moon had more color to it. "Right here."

The hairs on the back of my neck prickled. "Like right behind me?"

He shook his head. "I mean inside of you."

"You think I'm possessed?" Funny, I always thought I'd notice if something else was controlling the mother ship.

"No, I don't mean it's possessing you. It's just hiding behind your face, wearing you like it would a mask."

Whether or not I believed in ghosts, that freaked me out. I stumbled back across the landing, swiping at my cheeks and hair as if ghosts were made of cobwebs.

"Oh, shit." Doc's Adam's apple bobbed. His face tightened, his shoulders scrunching inward.

"What?"

"Here it comes."

"Doc." I reached for him. "What can I do?"

His gaze locked onto mine. "Stay back."

Chapter Nineteen

S tay back?

I did just that for a few seconds, but there was no way I could just stand there and watch while Doc shuddered, his eyes, his face—everything—crumpling in pain.

I had to do something.

Rushing forward, I caught him as he started to teeter toward the stairs. I grabbed him by the shoulders, shoving him back against the wall with enough oomph that his head snapped back with a thud.

"Sorry, Doc."

He didn't seem to hear me.

Under my palms, his muscles were rock hard, tense. Tremors tore through him with enough force to make my arms shake, too. I leaned against him hard, praying his knees didn't buckle. Or mine.

He groaned. Sweat streaked down from his temples. Heat radiated through his shirt—way too much heat. He was burning up under his clothes. I could feel the slickness of his skin through the thin cotton, smell his cologne or deodorant as if he'd just put it on.

"Doc," I said, making my voice strong, hard. "Look at me."

At first, I didn't think he heard me. Then his eyes opened slowly. His pupils were fully dilated. He was looking at me all right, but I doubted he was seeing me.

"Can you hear me, Doc?"

"Yes." It came out mixed with another groan.

"Who am I?"

"Vi—" A huge tremor rocked through him. His breath

caught.

"Doc," I said "Stay with me."

His eyes started to roll back. I was losing him.

"Oh, no you don't." I used Harvey's trick and pinched Doc on the bicep—really hard.

His focus snapped back, his eyes still dilated, but no longer lost.

"Doc, who am I?" I asked again.

"Violet." His voice sounded raspy, as if he hadn't used it in days. His tremors slackened, reduced to just quivering now.

"Good." I still held him against the wall, waiting to make sure he was fully back among the living before I stepped away.

"Damn." He gulped breaths, reminding me of the last time I'd chased the ice cream truck for a few blocks. "That hurt like hell."

I nodded. "I bet. You were shaking like crazy."

"I'm talking about your pinch."

"Oh."

He rubbed his arm where I'd worked my Harvey-inspired magic. "Did you have to do it so hard?"

"I was saving you."

"Who taught you that life-saving technique? Nurse Ratched?"

Nurse Ratched! I stepped back, my jaw gaping. "Of all of the ungrateful ..." I almost pinched him again. "I was trying to keep you from keeling over so you didn't break your neck falling down the damned stairs, thank you very much."

"Violet," he started, but I wasn't finished.

"Next time, buddy boy," I said, poking him in the chest with my index finger, simmering with leftover adrenaline to burn off. A wiser man wouldn't have lit my flame. "I'm going to—"

He caught my finger and tugged me against him, holding me tight. "I'm sorry," he said over my head.

"You should be." I grumbled a few more choice words into his shirt before his calming touch doused my anger. From the ashes came the truth. "When you do that ghost-thing, it scares the shit out of me."

"Me, too."

"Still?"

"It's not really something I ever get used to. I've been trying to do more preparation before going into it, practicing some mental defenses and techniques someone told me about a long time ago. But when it's an entity that's new to me, like this one, I can only do so much to prime my mind. Mostly, I just have to stand here and wait for the maelstrom to hit. Although today, you were able to snap me out of it early, pulling me back to present day. That was a first ..." he trailed off, as if lost in his thoughts.

I leaned my forehead against the open neck of his shirt, struggling to listen through the clamor of logic and reason. If only I could see something of these entities of his, even a shimmer, or experience a cold chill when they came near. Any kind of sign that would make it all more tangible and easier to believe would be spiffy.

Hell, today the thing had somehow hidden inside of my skin before working over Doc. He'd nearly passed out from the experience, and I hadn't even felt a single goosebump. Not even a hint of sensation that someone had just walked over my grave, nothing, nada. I was a total dud.

The nightmare with Wolfgang and his demon pal had to have been just that—a bad dream. Most likely, it was the result of not enough sleep and an overdose of stress.

Crud. I was so tired of thinking about all of this paranormal shit.

I changed the direction of my thoughts to something tangible. "It was Harvey," I told Doc while staring down at our shoes.

"What was Harvey?"

"He taught me that wicked pinch move."

His chuckle rumbled in his chest. "How many times has he used it on you?"

"Too many times to count. Now he has his nephew pinching me, too."

I felt Doc tighten under his shirt. He pushed me back, his eyes narrowed, questioning. "Why did Detective Cooper pinch you?"

Rex Conner.

Crappity crap. I should have thought before mentioning Cooper.

"Because he suspects I was sneaking around at Mudder Brothers with Harvey the other night." That was kind of true, at least about Cooper thinking I was up to no good. I was sure he would've loved to pinch me just out of suspicion alone.

"But you *were* sneaking around Mudder Brothers."

"I know that, but I'm not going to fess up to Cooper about it."

Doc snorted. "I should have started a bail bonds company." He turned me toward the stairs. "Let's get out of here. I have plenty to think about now. I'm not anxious for her to return."

Her? I led the way down, glancing back up at him as I stepped. "So, you a ... saw something while you were experiencing those shudders up there?"

"Yes," he answered when we reached the first floor. He pushed open the stairwell door for me.

I waited until we stood out under the front awning, rain pouring down hard enough to bounce off the pavement all around us, before asking, "What did you see? Was it the four ladies who ..." I mimicked slitting my wrists.

"No. It was something akin to Prudence's experience."

"You mean Prudence-Prudence? The ghost from the Carhart house in Lead was up there?"

He glanced around us, nudging his head at a smoker standing further down under the awning, and shushed me with a mimicked zip of his lips.

Oops, I spoke soundlessly.

He grabbed my hand, tugging me out from under the

awning's protection. We dashed through the cool, clothes-penetrating rain and scrambled into the Picklemobile.

I slammed my door shut, shivering in my damp dress. I checked my mascara in the rearview mirror—no raccoon eyes yet, but my lip gloss was long gone. The fragrance of my peach-scented shampoo masked the odor of old grease that usually filled the cab.

Doc caught my hands and rubbed them between his, warming them. "You smell good enough to eat." He tugged on my hands and leaned toward me like he was going to take a bite.

I leaned away from him. "Quit trying to distract me. Do you mean to tell me you saw Prudence up there?"

"No, not Prudence." He returned to warming my hands. "It was some girl—a prostitute."

"How could you tell? Did she have a certain smell?"

"I told you before, it's not a smell. It's more like some kind of imprint left behind that I can sense. The scent isn't real."

"And I told you that until you come up with a better word, I'm using the word *smell*. Now, how could you tell it was a prostitute?"

"Her lingerie and stockings." His hands stilled, but kept ahold of mine. "And the paraphernalia in her room while they were doing it. Stuff I've seen repeatedly in historic photos of brothels."

"They? You mean she was murdered by one of her customers while she was working?"

How many prostitutes died at the hands of the men they were servicing back then? I imagined most murders were just shrugged off by the local authorities due to the line of work and lack of the prostitute's family around to raise a fuss.

"No, she wasn't working at the time," Doc clarified. "I meant there were two men who were on the scene during her murder."

I winced, not liking the sound of this already. "What did

they do?"

"You don't want to know the details, trust me. Most people don't treat prostitutes kindly in life. When it comes to death, it's even worse."

"So, what does Prudence have to do with any of this?"

Had she been nearby when the prostitute was killed? That seemed like a pretty far-fetched coincidence, since no upstanding lady dared to step foot in Deadwood's Badlands and risk her reputation. Yet, unfortunate coincidences happened every day. Take our run-in with Tiffany, earlier. Very unfortunate. But now I knew all about Doc and his reaction to marriage, which left me with a problem I didn't feel like facing while sitting next to him in the Picklemobile.

"I said it was akin to Prudence's experience."

I pulled my focus back to the present—or rather the past. "What does that mean?"

"They were the same men who murdered Prudence."

"How can you know that for sure?"

"Both had the same masks as Prudence's killers.

"The potato sacks with the eyes cut out." I remembered this detail from when Doc had told me the story of Prudence's horrific death, which he'd relived from her point-of-view during a vision—or whatever it was he experienced.

"Yes, those masks."

I shook my head. I couldn't imagine the terror Prudence or the prostitute must have felt. "Why did they kill the girl upstairs?" I asked.

"I'm not sure yet. I need to replay it in my head a few more times."

I nodded. I knew from before that this was how Doc worked, letting things soak in, picking up more details as he peeled back the layers.

"But there is another thing that ties her killers to Prudence besides the masks," he said.

"What?"

"They pulled the girl's canine teeth out with a pair of

pliers."

Again with the teeth. Had her teeth been in the collection from the Carhart attic that I'd handed off to Cooper? "That is so creepy weird. Why would they take her teeth?"

"I don't know, but she wasn't dead yet when the bastards yanked them out."

"Jesus," I whispered staring back at him. Was experiencing that part of the vision what had made him stop breathing for a moment back in the stairwell?

My cell phone rang, startling a gasp from me. I checked my phone, seeing my mom's name.

"I have to take this," I told Doc and answered the call. "Hi, Mom. You want me to come get the kids?"

"No need, dear. They're at Zoe's right now. Your sister drove them home."

"She's in Deadwood?" My jaw tightened at the thought of my kids riding in a car with *her*. "Well, that explains the doom and gloom that's settled over the town this afternoon."

"Cute, Violet, but I've heard enough out of you about your sister." She sniffed, as if that was the final word on the subject.

But it wasn't. Not by a long shot.

"I need to talk to you about something serious," Mom told me.

"What?"

"Adelynn told me about your new boyfriend."

My heart picked up speed. How did *she* know?

I looked over at Doc, who was leaning against the headrest with his eyes closed. His hair still damp from the rain. "My new boyfriend?"

He opened one eyelid, his head turning my way.

"And while I know it's none of my business," my mom continued, "I am concerned about Layne's reaction to this announcement."

"What did Layne say?"

"He denied it rather vehemently. And when Addy refused

to take back her words on the subject, he hit her."

"Where and how hard?"

"On the mouth. He made her lip bleed."

"Oh, shit."

Both of Doc's eyes were now focused on me.

"Have you talked to Layne about his feelings on a new man in your life?"

"Sort of." Just yesterday we'd touched on the subject.

"I think you're going to have to talk to him some more if you're going to keep seeing this Jeff Wymonds guy."

Jeff Wymonds? Addy was at her matchmaking game again. It turned out both kids were going to need a talking to in order to straighten everything out. I pinched the bridge of my nose.

"I don't have a new boyfriend named Jeff Wymonds, Mom." And that was the honest truth.

Doc reached over and brushed his fingers over the back of my neck, his hand lingering there, massaging.

"Addy seemed pretty definite about it," my mom said. "When I suggested that it wasn't nice to tell tall tales, she swore she'd seen you kissing this Jeff guy."

"She did see us kissing, only it was him kissing me, and it wasn't at all what she thought." It was more like Jeff trying to get into the *Guinness Book of World Records* for how far he could stick his tongue down an esophagus—my esophagus. "I have told her that multiple times. She's just not listening."

"Sounds like another hard-headed girl I know."

"I'll take that as a compliment, *Mother.*"

Mom chuckled. "All right. I just wanted to let you know why Addy has a split lip."

"Thanks. I'm sorry you had to deal with that."

"They're my grandchildren, Violet. I expect life to be messy when they're around. It's all part of the fun."

"I appreciate you keeping them overnight." Even if the Wicked Witch of the West had been under the same roof as them. I'd needed the time alone with Doc, whose hands were currently working magic, turning my neck and shoulders into finger Jello.

"Any time, dear."

"I'll call you in a couple of days after the kids get settled into school."

"Okay. Oh, and Violet," Mom caught me before I hung up. "It's okay if you do have a boyfriend. I'd like to see you happy again someday."

"I am happy," I insisted.

I was actually very happy at the moment, on the verge of being positively tingly thanks to Doc's massage. As long as I didn't think too much about anything outside of this pickup cab, my life was charmed—all moons, stars, green clovers, and purple horseshoes.

"If you say so. Just be careful. You don't have the best track record with men."

"Thank you for that loving reminder, Mommy Dearest."

I hung up before she decided to go into detail on my spotty past when it came to the opposite sex. I didn't have that many minutes left on my cell phone plan this month to cover it all.

"Wymonds deserves solid marks for trying," Doc said, "don't you think?"

"Beh!" I answered and started the Picklemobile.

Pulling up behind Doc's office, I let the pickup sputter, otherwise referred to as idling. "I need to go home and see my kids." And then whip them with wet noodles.

He nodded. "You want me to pick you up for the séance?"

"You still want to go after what happened today?"

"Of course. Now you have an actual ghost to channel."

That was still up for debate in my book.

"I'll go dig around in the library," he continued, "and see if I can come up with a name to go with the murder scene."

"Don't you need to rest or something after what happened?"

"I'm fine."

The lines around his eyes told another story, but I didn't argue.

He caught my hand. "You pulled me out of that before it sucked me totally under"

"What's that mean?"

"She wasn't dead yet when you pinched me."

"Have you ever had that happen before? Been pulled out early?"

"Yes, but not for a long time." He lifted my hand to his lips and kissed my knuckles. "How about you just pick me up here tonight."

I nodded, still feeling the warmth of his lips on my skin. I'd rather go back to his house and let him make me forget all about the séance.

He stepped down from the Picklemobile, shooting me a wink before disappearing into his office.

Five minutes later, I parked in Aunt Zoe's drive next to her truck. Both kids were playing in the front yard. Elvis the chicken watched from her regal roost in the shade on the porch.

There was no sign of my sister to be found—no bubbling cauldrons, no flying monkeys, no unhappy little people—well, not counting Layne and his worried frown when he caught sight of me. Heck, even the dark, ominous thunderheads had floated away. Oz was happy again, and the Good Witch Glinda was home to lecture the munchkins and threaten them with a life of slavery if the fighting didn't stop, pronto. If only I had one of those cool star wands and a field of poppies to roll around in.

Addy was at the Picklemobile's door before the old truck stopped burping and belching and booming.

"Hi, Mom!" She said around a thick wad of gum. "Look what Layne did to me. I sure hope you're gonna tan his hide to teach him a lesson about hitting girls."

Wow, she didn't even let my boots touch the dirt before lobbying for a beating.

I slammed the pickup door and tipped Addy's chin up for a closer inspection. Layne had done a bang up job on her mouth.

"It really hurts," she said and blew a pink, fruity-smelling bubble in my face.

I popped her bubble. "Yeah, I can see how miserable you are."

When I glanced over at Layne, he was busy poking a stick in the flowerbed all of the sudden. I sighed, my heart panging a little. The poor kid was battling his own demons.

Damned Rex Conner for running off and leaving me to raise a son without a father. For the first time in years, guilt burned in my chest. Writing Rex off for good had been the right thing to do, I reminded myself. A sperm donor did not a good father make.

"Okay, everybody inside right now. We need to have a family meeting at the kitchen table."

"Oh, man," Layne moaned and trudged inside.

"But I didn't do anything wrong," Addy whined.

I turned her around and nudged her toward the front door. "Go, Adelynn Renee. Now."

Complaining the whole way, she followed her brother inside and stomped all of the way into the kitchen.

Aunt Zoe was leaning against the counter cutting up lemons when the three of us plopped down in our usual dinnertime places. Home sweet home—the land of fresh lemonade and a molting chicken.

"You must have seen Addy's lip," Aunt Zoe said to me.

Nodding, I looked specifically at Layne. "Let's hear your side of the story."

"I asked her to stop saying you were marrying Kelly's dad," he said, his big hazel eyes pleading his case. "But she wouldn't be quiet."

"You didn't ask," Addy swooped in with her rebuttal. "You yelled at me to shut my big fat mouth, and then hauled off and hit me."

"Did not!" he bellowed

"Did, too!" she bellowed back.

"Both of you knock it off," I snapped, nailing each of them with a silencing glare in turn. "The three of us need to get something straight here and now. Jeff Wymonds is *not* my boyfriend."

Addy frowned. "But you kissed—"

"There is no 'but,' Adelynn. He is not my boyfriend, understand?

"Maybe someday you'll—" she tried again.

"Nor will he ever be my boyfriend." When she opened her mouth, I repeated, "Ever."

"How can you be so sure?" Layne asked.

I pondered my answer for a moment. I thought about all of the philosophical ways of explaining the concept of everlasting love, the essential ingredient that was supposed to go with marriage, at least in my world.

While I was busy pondering, Layne flipped his eyelids inside out and grinned at his sister. Addy giggled and tried to do the same back.

At that point, I realized I was putting way too much thought into my response and answered, "I'm sure because when Jeff kissed me it grossed me out."

Addy leaned closer, her forearms resting on the table. "Did he French you?"

My face warmed. Addy must have picked that up from the TV or one of her friends.

"What does 'French you' mean?" Layne asked.

I left that answer to Addy, curious to hear how much she really knew.

Aunt Zoe walked over, joining us while she dried her hands.

"It's when a boy licks your lips," Addy said with a confident nod.

"Ewww," both Layne and Aunt Zoe replied.

In that case, "No, he didn't French me, Adelynn."

Addy lowered her chin onto her arms. "That blows, Mom. I wanted Kelly as a sister."

"I know, sweetie." I ruffled her hair. "But you'll have to settle for having her as a really good friend for the rest of your life."

"Like you and Natalie?" Addy asked.

"Yes, like me and Nat."

Until Natalie found out about me and Doc.

She wanted to get married. I heard Doc's voice repeat his earlier comment about Tiffany in my thoughts.

Change that answer to IF Natalie ever found out about us.

After learning that Tiffany had wanted to get married and Doc had left without looking back, I was back to where I'd started when it came to Doc and me—torn, unsure, wanting to hide under my bed.

Two pairs of eyes watching me reminded me that I still had an audience. It was time to adjourn this family meeting.

I turned to Layne. "I don't like it when you hit your sister like that. It's rude, mean, and unacceptable. If I catch either of you hitting each other like this again, I won't let you watch television for two weeks."

"Two weeks!" Addy moaned.

"I'll just read in my room," Layne told me with a hint of stubbornness.

I leaned closer to him, squinting in emphasis. "Not if I ban you from books."

"You wouldn't dare," Layne whispered.

"How's that going to work with school starting, Mom?" Addy asked. "Does that mean we won't have to do any homework?"

"Don't push it, child." I reached over and squeezed both of their shoulders. "Now give me a kiss, and then go outside and play. I need to talk to Aunt Zoe alone."

"Is it about a new man?" Addy whispered.

"Let it go, Adelynn."

They each kissed me on the cheek, and then scrambled

out the back door.

Aunt Zoe joined me at the table as the dust settled. "When are you going to tell them about Doc?" she asked.

"I don't know."

She wanted to get married.

"How did it go with him last night?"

In-freaking-credible. "Good."

"You didn't come home."

"I fell asleep there."

"Any nightmares?"

"No. I slept like the dead." Doc's bed or sleeping pills—both remedies for my insomnia came with worrisome side-effects.

"So, things are all patched up between you two?" she asked.

"Yes, we're fine."

She wanted to get married.

Aunt Zoe took a drink of lemonade, watching me over the rim with those damned all-seeing eyes of hers. I looked down at my hands, fidgeting with the Picklemobile's smiley-face key chain.

She lowered her empty glass to the table. "What's going on?"

"Nothing."

"Violet Lynn, cough it up."

I sighed and rested my forehead on the table. "I found out that Doc isn't into marriage."

"Who told you that?"

"He did."

"What? What preceded him saying that?"

I sat upright. "Well, he didn't actually come right out and say he'd never marry, but it was inferred."

Her gaze narrowed. "Why don't you just tell me what happened and let me determine what may have been inferred."

Fine. "I asked him why he broke up with his ex-girlfriend,

and he told me it was because she wanted to get married."

I skipped the part about Tiffany and her competitive sex streak. I wished I could go back in time and skip it myself. The sooner I could purge that notion from any association with Doc, the better.

"That doesn't mean Doc won't want to marry you someday."

"Aunt Zoe, if he didn't want to marry a gorgeous redhead with a killer rack, no stretch marks, a successful career, and no kids hanging off her skirt, why would he ever want me?"

"Because you're you."

Right. That explained everything so clearly. Of course he would be head-over-heels for me because I was me—the one and only Violet Parker, bumbling clown extraordinaire.

I patted Aunt Zoe's hand. "You're biased, dear. Not everyone finds me as charming and loveable as you do."

"And you're blind to your own beauty, but that's a good thing. It's probably one of the main things that makes you irresistible to men."

"Irresistible, sure." If I were irresistible, I wouldn't get Doc's voicemail all of the damned time. "You should sell snake oil for a living."

She waved me off. "Violet, how much do you like this guy?"

That was a question I asked myself hourly some days.

"I don't know." I drew invisible hearts on the table. "Sometimes he's all I can think about. Other times, I feel like moving forward with a relationship with him is only going to hurt everyone around me. And if he leaves town someday ..." I didn't want to finish that thought, so I stopped.

"He just bought a house, remember? That's not a sign of a wandering man."

"A house is not a ball and chain." Like my kids and I would be. "I'm so confused when it comes to him."

She watched my finger trace the hearts. "Do *you* want to marry him?"

I sputtered for a moment before saying, "No, of course not." Then I added, "Not right now, I mean."

Aunt Zoe watched me with raised brows.

"Well, probably not, anyway."

Her lips twitched.

"Maybe someday, though," I admitted to myself as well as her. "Or not. But I'd like to know that the option might be there in the future."

Aunt Zoe grabbed my hand, stopping me at half a heart. "Besides the fear of hurting Natalie's feelings and Doc someday leaving you, what's holding you back?"

I looked at the back door. "I have two kids out there who each could really use a father figure in their lives."

Rex Conner.

Absolutely not!

"If I start bringing a man around, I'm basically telling them that he is potential father material. If there's no future with Doc, my heart isn't the only one at risk here."

"True," Aunt Zoe said, "but I don't know that you're correct in assuming Doc isn't willing to put a ring on your finger someday just because he wouldn't put one on his ex's finger. You're comparing apples to oranges here."

I hoped she was right. I really, really did. But until I had something more concrete than wishes and daydreams, I wasn't going to admit to my kids that Doc and I were anything other than just friends.

And the same went for admitting anything to Natalie. I knew she was in my life for the long haul, she'd proven that to me time and again.

Was Doc?

Chapter Twenty

Rather than spend the rest of the afternoon mutilating daisies while asking the universe if Doc would ever love me or love me not, I decided to take a bath. A tub full of bubbles would help me escape from my troubles. At least that's what it said on the bottle.

I grabbed the dog-eared book Natalie had left sitting on her side of the bed along with my cell phone, just in case Cornelius changed his mind and called to free me from my channeling duties. The book turned out to be a quirky romance narrated by the hero's mule. While the coconut-scented bubbles tickled my nose, I tried to sink into the story and not think about ghosts and demons, or a certain dark-eyed tormentor, or any Abe Lincoln look-a-likes. But the narrating mule reminded me of the stuffed, bald-nosed beast of burden down at the Old Prospector Hotel.

By the time I'd gotten my skin good and wrinkly, I was plenty wound up about all of the things that could go wrong at the séance, including the possible appearance of Fire Captain Reid and Detective Cooper. Another creepy demon paled in comparison to the two of them.

I trailed drops of water into my bedroom. From the window, I watched Layne digging in the yard near the back fence. A shovel and hard soil would make for a wonderful physical release where the bubbles failed, even if I had to shower afterward. I pulled on an old pair of jeans and a T-shirt and headed outside to join him.

Two hours later, my arms and back ached. I leaned on my shovel. In my digging frenzy, I'd unearthed a football-sized rock mixed with rose-quartz, an old tin can and spoon, two rusted railroad spikes, and the jaw bone of some small animal. Aunt Zoe's house must have been built on top of an old trash dump.

Addy joined us, admiring our dig findings. She disappeared into the house, intent on locating Layne's book on animal bones so we could try to decipher the owner of the jaw bone.

At the sound of the back door banging shut, I looked up expecting to see Addy lugging the book. Instead, Aunt Zoe waltzed our way, carrying a tray loaded with three glasses of lemonade and my cell phone.

"You have a phone call," she said. When I took the phone, she mouthed Harvey's name.

"Hey, Harvey."

"We have a slight problem," he said, his voice hesitant.

"What's up?" I took a drink of lemonade, the tart sweetness making me pucker after an afternoon diet of Black Hills dust and dirt.

"We may know who the corpse is."

We? Had Harvey cloned himself? "Who is it?"

"Well, I'm not sure, but it looks a little like one of the local yokels from Slagton who takes care of the cemetery back there—well, he used to."

I walked a few steps away from Layne. "How did you figure that out? Was it the single testicle?" Just thinking about my close encounter of the testicular kind made me cringe all over again.

"Nope," he said.

Through the phone, I heard another voice in the background say my name.

My heart picked up speed. "Harvey, where are you?"

"At home."

"Is someone there with you?"

"Yep, Coop's here. And some of his boys."

Cooper? I realized then that when Harvey used the word "we" earlier, he'd been referring to "we," as in Cooper and his merry men in blue.

If the cops were milling about, the *slight* problem Harvey had mentioned must be a little more significant. My gut tightened. "Are they there to take you to jail?"

He snorted. "Of course not. Why would they?"

"Because of the corpse. Because it was found on your land. Because you know who it is and you didn't tell Cooper the first three times he asked."

"Whoa, girlie-girl. You'll break your neck if you keep gallopin' at that speed. I didn't tell Coop at first because I didn't have a clue who it was before."

"What's changed?" I asked, sipping more lemonade.

"Old Red found the head."

What?! "Was it in your cemetery?"

"Nah, that's the funny thing. He found it in the old shitter."

"You mean your bathroom?"

"No, I mean in the old outhouse behind the barn."

"What was it doing there?"

"Bein' eaten on by the pack rats—well, the soft parts, anyway."

"Oh, errggg." I gagged a little in the back of my throat. "That's just nasty. How did it get—"

"Coop says I gotta go now."

Of course, Detective Cooper would interrupt during the exciting, need-to-know part. "Give him my love."

I heard Harvey say, "Coop, Violet sends her love."

"I was kidding." My cheeks warmed.

Cooper mumbled something in the background that made Harvey chuckle. "He gave you some love back."

I bet he did.

"I'll fill you in later," Harvey told me.

"No, you won't," I heard Cooper say clear as a bell this time. "This is police business, not Realtor gossip."

The phone went dead.

I glared at the screen, wishing I had a doll that looked like Cooper and a cushion full of pins.

"What's going on?" Aunt Zoe joined me, her voice quiet so the kids couldn't hear.

I filled her in on what little I'd just learned about Harvey and the head. When I finished, her lips were pinched tight.

"Well, I'm glad Detective Cooper is out there with Willis. He'll get to the bottom of this mess."

"Right." No offense to Cooper, but I wasn't so confident in his or the Deadwood Police Department's ability to save the day.

It was nothing personal, in spite of Cooper's talent for being the world's biggest butthead. It was just that after facing off with Wolfgang and then Lila, I'd come to realize that the cops weren't superheroes. They simply were men and women with more training than the average Joe, who had sworn to try to keep the public safe. Most of the time, they were able to react to situations only in which shit had already hit the fan, like at the Carhart house, where I'd been present to witness the actual shit flying.

The screen door slammed shut, jarring me back to the sunny present day. Well, not so sunny, anymore. With dusk just a little over an hour away, shadows were growing. So was my apprehension. In spite of Doc's assurances earlier, my gut was of the opinion that tonight's ending wasn't going to include "they lived happily ever after."

"I found it, Layne," Addy said, lugging a thick book over to where Layne kneeled over the hole I'd dug.

"Are you going to head out to Willis's place?" Aunt Zoe asked.

"I can't. I need to sing and dance for my client until he's convinced that the Old Prospector Hotel is worth another twenty grand." I debated on telling the whole truth and nothing but the truth to Aunt Zoe, but I bit my tongue. Her tolerance for my crazy antics had limits, which I didn't feel like overstepping today.

"If you need to go into the gallery tonight, Miss Geary said she'd let the kids hang out at her place. They worship her tarts."

"So does Willis," Aunt Zoe said with a smirk. "Oh, wait, you said, 'tarts.' My mistake."

"Aunt Zoe!" I slapped her arm in fun, chuckling.

"Actually," she said, "The kids and I have plans to veg in front of the National Geographic channel tonight. There's a special about sharks on later. You know how much I love all of those teeth."

Her mention of teeth sobered me right up. What in the hell was the deal with taking people's teeth? To what end? One of these days I was going to brave asking Cooper what he did with that box of teeth. Was he having each tooth analyzed, or did he just tag the box and shove it onto a dusty shelf in the police property room?

"Thank you for being such a wonderful aunt." I gave her a quick squeeze.

I needed to go get ready for tonight's big show. What did one wear to a séance? The last one had been a surprise, so that didn't count. With Doc joining the party, I sort of wanted to wear something that would make him want to touch me.

But logic reminded me that we weren't there to flirt and fondle. This was about money, lies, and a dead prostitute. And to think I once worried that the real estate business might be too boring for my taste.

After I kissed the kids on their sun-warmed heads, I headed for the shower. Forty-five minutes later, I rolled into the parking lot behind Calamity Jane Realty. Jane's shiny black Mercedes was parked askew, taking up a spot and a half. Doc's Camaro was nowhere to be seen.

I pulled into a spot three down from Jane. Doc stepped out the back door of his office before I could kill the Picklemobile's engine—or at least maim it, since I doubted the green machine could be murdered with bare hands.

Whistling under my breath, I watched him cross the parking lot. His faded blue jeans crinkled and clung in all of the right places, his dark gray shirt boxed his shoulders, making them look even broader, sexier.

My pulse quickened—for real, just like some infatuated heroine in a romance novel. I touched my neck, feeling it flutter there like a moth caught in my palms. Holy cupid's balls, I was so in over my head with this man.

Doc opened the door and climbed inside, his eyes widening when he caught sight of my ensemble. His grin followed suit.

I slid down in the seat, feeling overly gothic in my black tunic, leggings, eyeliner, and platform boots. The only things missing were the black lipstick and nail polish. I'd settled for red instead on both counts.

"Morticia Addams, *cara mia*," he said, lifting my hand to his lips. "How are Wednesday and Pugsley this evening?"

There was nothing like some Addams family humor to put me in the mood for a séance. "I can't be Morticia. My hair isn't black and I only speak English. Well, except for *Oui* and *Mon cher*," and other phrases I'd learned from Pepé le Pew.

"Oh, Tish, that's French," he replied in a Gomez-like Spanish accent and kissed his way up to the soft skin on the inside of my elbow.

The brush of his lips tickled me clear down to my hips. The woodsy smell of his cologne made my bells and whistles clang and peal. My libido stood, stretched, and roared to life. I beat it back with a circus chair and a whip.

"Doc, uh ..." my voice had already downshifted into Lusty Lil mode. I cleared my throat and tried again. "You'd better stop."

He did. When he looked up at me, his grin faded. "I'm going to have trouble keeping my hands off of you tonight," he said, eyeing my mouth.

Success! My evil plan had worked. I raised one eyebrow. "You like your women to dress in Goth, huh?"

"No. Just you, Vixen." He brushed his lips over mine, his tongue skimming my lower lip. "You taste like cherries."

"It's flavored lip gloss." I pulled away from him, glancing around, looking for Natalie's pickup.

He sat back, his arm draped over the seat. "We could skip the séance. Go back to my place." He trailed his finger down my neck and kept heading south, following the horizon over hill and dale. "Let me see where else you taste like cherries."

Oh, wow! My heart bounced and shuddered like a runaway stagecoach. "I can't. I need this sale."

"Okay." He shifted so he faced forward, but his palm remained on my thigh. I'd have to check for scorch marks in the cotton later. "Let's go introduce your Abe Lincoln wanna-be to the stairwell's soiled dove and see if he really can talk to ghosts."

I shifted into drive and rumbled out onto Sherman Street. "Did you go to the library this afternoon?"

"Yes."

"So, what's the prostitute's name?"

"I don't know. There wasn't any record of her death in the usual books."

"Really?"

"Yeah, but that's somewhat normal for a prostitute back

then, especially in a town like Deadwood, full of outlaws, miners, and gunslingers. Most of the records from that era focus on mining news. Precious metals ruled."

I thought of the death record books I'd seen in Mudder Brother's closet-like room weeks ago. "Do you think the funeral parlor might have some mention of her? They keep track of deaths, too, don't they?"

"Maybe, if their books go back that far."

As the only funeral parlor in town, they might, especially if the Mudder boys had taken it over from a previous owner. Some of the book spines I'd glanced at had looked plenty old enough. I'd have to see if I could sneak a look the next time I was at a viewing.

"Don't even think about sneaking into Mudder Brothers, Violet." He squeezed my leg to emphasize his point. "There are legitimate ways of finding out what's in their records that don't end with you behind bars."

"Fine." I parked behind the hotel, climbing out before the Picklemobile stopped sputtering. "Stop reading my mind," I said and slammed the door shut.

His chuckles were drowned out by the Picklemobile's echoing *boom!*

He caught up with me, matching my stride.

"I need a name, Doc. I have to have something to call out during this channeling gig besides 'Hey, you, ghost prostitute chick.'"

Doc beat me to the door, holding it open. "Pick a name. Any will work. If we find out her real name eventually, you can just claim to have been using her alias."

Any name? That seemed so detached, so cold. She'd been a living, breathing girl with hopes and dreams, somebody's child.

I stalled mid-casino. The rings and dings from the slot machines faded into the background. Wait. That was assuming I believed she'd really existed. That *ghosts* really existed. Did I believe that? Doc hadn't found any proof of her to back up his claim. True, but he had with Prudence—a picture even. Right, but ... .

"What's wrong?" Doc said in my ear, his voice pulling me out of my spiral of doubts. The casino sounds flooded back in a rush of noise. "Did you forget something in the truck?"

Shaking my head, I made a beeline for the stairs, trying not to think too hard the whole way there. I beat Doc to the stairwell door and waited for him to close the door behind us.

Inside the stairwell, he sniffed, frowning up at the three levels of stairs.

I knew better than to sniff. It would smell only like a musty old stairwell.

"You sure you're ready for this?" I whispered.

"As ready as I can be. Why are you whispering?"

"I don't know," I still whispered.

"You whisper in my stairwell, too." His smile took a smoldering turn. "You also moan and cry out my name." He grabbed my arm, tugging me toward him. His eyes held devilish promises.

Temptation beckoned like a house made of candy in a dark forest. I resisted, pulling free. "Doc, not here."

"I warned you, Boots. You do things to me."

"Even now? Here?"

He nodded. "Most of the time, especially at night."

That had to be something to hope for future-wise, right? Or was I grasping at straws? I turned and led the way up the stairs before I gave in to Doc and agreed to spend the rest of my life peeling grapes for him and fanning him with palm fronds.

At the top he said, "Hold up a minute."

"What's wrong? Do you smell her again?"

"No." He caught my hand, staring down at me with a very serious expression. "Listen, Violet, no matter what happens in there, I need you not to worry about me out loud."

"Meaning what?"

"Don't ask me if I smell anything, don't check to see if

I'm feeling okay, don't draw any attention to me no matter how pale or shaky I get."

"What if you pass out?"

"I won't."

"You have before."

"True, but the whole reason we came by earlier was so that I could prepare for tonight. Now that I know what I'm dealing with, I can keep her at bay." He squeezed my hand. "Are you ready?"

I could have used a shot of tequila first, but, "As ready as I can get."

We made it to Cornelius's room without a hitch—or a ghost. A glance up at Doc as I knocked on the door gave me a breath of hope. His skin looked tan as usual, his eyes were bright and assessing, his face relaxed and unstrained.

Here we go.

The door opened and Safari Skipper beamed at me. She smelled like bubblegum. How appropriate. "Hi, Ms. Parker."

Her resemblance to the plastic doll still made me stare. It was a bit eerie, really.

She stood back to let us enter, smiling up at Doc. "Hi, Ms. Parker's friend."

Tonight, Skipper wore silver, from her sparkly heels to her hair band, she looked like a Christmas tree ornament. Her biker boyfriend kept with the leather and chains motif he'd used previously for spirit calling.

"Hey, babe," Skipper's boyfriend called out to me from the kitchen as she closed the door behind us.

Babe? Apparently I'd missed the moment at the last séance when I'd moved from being a stranger to one of his women. It must have happened while I was sleeping.

Doc's hand on my lower back nudged me further into the room.

Just as before, a single candle sat in the center of the table, the electronics hummed, and the host was one horn short. Thing 1 and Thing 2 were missing in action, though. The place was much darker, too. The candle was the only source of light besides the glow from the electronics.

Cornelius looked up from his laptop long enough to notice I brought company. "Violet, you brought your friend again."

"This is Doc Nyce." I made introductions this time since Doc planned on sticking around. "Doc, meet Cornelius."

Eye contact and nods took the place of a hand shake.

"Are you a believer in ghosts?" Cornelius asked Doc.

"I've had some brushes with the paranormal," Doc answered.

Brushes? I started to scoff and turned it into a cough. "S'cuse me."

Doc shot me a warning frown.

"Well, tonight, you're in for an amazing treat. Violet is a talented conduit." Cornelius advertised me like the sideshow freak I'd become.

"Her talents and treats often amaze me," Doc said with a wide grin, and then grunted when I elbowed him in the ribs.

"Where do you want us?" I asked. The ottoman I'd tripped over last time was missing. I hoped the same could be said of Wolfgang and Kyrkozz.

Doc sniffed behind me, twice.

I almost looked back at him, but remembered his pointed stairwell speech and kept my focus on Cornelius's stupid horn. I couldn't wait for tonight to be in my rearview mirror.

"We're all going to sit around the table," Skipper told us, playing hostess and pulling out chairs.

"Who's going to monitor the video equipment?" I asked.

"Nobody. Several more pieces of my equipment came in today. I could practically do this on my own now."

I wished he would.

Cornelius indicated for us to sit across from him.

Doc waited for me to sit, holding my chair, and then settled himself into the seat next to mine. He squeezed my thigh under the table, reassuring me with his touch.

Pushing a pad of drawing paper over to me and a black marker, Cornelius pointed at the pad. "Tonight, we're all going to watch as you channel another ghost, Violet."

"Groovy." Shit. Not only was I going to have to perform, I would be under a microscope at the same time. I really could use a shot of tequila to grease my channeling gears. I needed to think up a damned name, too.

Doc sniffed again.

I frowned down at the paper, wondering if anyone would be up for a game of hangman instead.

"Take your seats," Cornelius instructed Skipper and her biker dude. "It's time. I can hear the whispers in the walls growing louder."

I trembled, every muscle in my body anxious to jump up and race from the room.

Doc's grip tightened on my leg. "Relax," he said for my ears only.

Relax? Ha! I was starring in a fucking séance, for crissake. If I couldn't fake out Cornelius, I was going to lose my job. My breath turned to quick pants, my cheeks warm. Shit, shit, shit.

Doc's fingers crawled up the inside of my thigh, heading straight for the mother lode. What was he doing? I clamped my thighs together, blocking his spelunking attempt, and shot him an are-you-kidding-me glare.

The lack of lust in his eyes clued me. He was trying to pull me back from the edge before panic shoved me off the cliff.

Breathe, he mouthed, and then lifted his chin and breathed deeply, giving me an example.

I followed his lead, taking one breath after another until I felt sanity grab the reins again. I could do this. I picked up the marker and wrote a tiny note for Doc: *One ghost coming up.*

He took the marker from me, scribbled something, and then turned the paper back to me.

I leaned over, squinting in the candlelight at his scrawls.

She's already here.

Chapter Twenty-One

The thing about séances was that a belief in the supernatural sort of greased the wheels in rounding up some dead participants.

I peeked out from under my closed eyelids, checking to see if any of my cohorts were watching me. Surprise, surprise, they all were, including Doc. I growled in my throat. Damn it, faking this would be much easier if nobody was watching me.

I frowned at them in turn. "Aren't you all supposed to close your eyes and say "Ohhmmmm"?

"Like we do in my meditation class?" Skipper asked in her chipper voice.

My gaze narrowed on her. "Yeah, sure. That's how I roll when it comes to channeling. Now close your eyes." I looked around the table. "All of you, close them, now."

They listened, including Doc. Miracles did happen.

"Now say 'om.'" I ordered.

The room hummed with their voices.

That was more like it. I cleared my throat. Here went nothing. "If there is a ghost in this room, speak now or forever hold your peace."

Nice one, bonehead! Well, it worked for weddings, so why not séances?

Doc's "ommm" paused, his lips twitching, his chest shaking in silent laughter.

I reached under the table and pinched his hand, which still warmed my thigh.

"Do you hear anything yet, Cornelius?" I asked, willing him to say he did and put an end to my misery.

His one-horned helmet shook side-to-side. "Patience,

Violet. Just do what you did last time."

What? Fall asleep? Fat chance.

Wait! I remembered something from before. "Cornelius, you need to chant."

Without further prodding, he obeyed, his rhythmic words barely audible over the group's low humming.

I let him work his magic for a handful of seconds, then cleared my throat and said to the ceiling in what I hoped was a medium-like voice, "If you are here, please tell me your name."

"Butch," the biker dude answered.

"I was talking to the ghost," I said dryly.

"Sorry, babe."

Doc's laughter vibrations spread to his hand. I could see him struggling to keep his lips straight.

The chanting continued from Cornelius. Skipper was doing a bang-up job on the "oms," too.

After counting to ten, I tried again. "Would you like to tell us how you died?"

I really didn't want to hear that, not if it happened as Doc told me, but I doubted the prostitute felt like giving me her list for Santa.

"Is it a man or woman?" Skipper broke her meditation to ask.

If she'd been within flicking reach, I would have started with her perky little nose. "Are you a man or woman?" I asked the ceiling.

Cornelius' chanting cranked up a notch. He was really getting into it now, rocking with the beat.

"What did it say?" Skipper asked, her eyes still closed like an obedient séance groupie.

"It's a girl," I lied ... well, kind of. Doc did write that *she* was here.

"Make her tell us her name." Skipper pushed.

"Will you please tell us your name?" I figured it was nicer to ask than demand.

Skipper gave the ghost all of two heartbeats to answer. "What did she say?"

"Hold on," I told her. Sheesh, give the prostitute time to get back with me. Then I remembered I was making all of this crap up. Oh, right. I got back into character and picked up the marker. "She's going to speak through my hand," I decided.

Doc raised his brow, which I noticed was glistening, so was his upper lip. The heat coming from the vanilla-scented candle didn't warrant perspiration. Why was he sweating? Was his ghost-girl messing with him?

The rest of the group kept omming and chanting.

I scribbled gibberish on the papers, flipping through them like I'd seen mediums do in many movies. Then I lowered my head and pretended to be taken over by the presence in the room in case anyone was peeking.

I needed a name, damn it.

Think, think, think.

My brain flipped through the names of soiled doves I'd heard over the years in rolodex fashion. They were all so cliché. Finally, a name popped into my head. I wrote it down in a cursive scribble.

"What does it say?" Butch the biker dude whispered.

Skipper leaned over the table and read my writing upside-down. "It looks like *Big Lisp Sally.*"

"Big Lips Lolly," I corrected, watching for Cornelius's reaction. He paused for a couple of my racing heartbeats, then nodded as if agreeing with my name choice and returned to his chanting.

Doc, on the other hand, suffered from a tickled funny bone. He masked the laughter lining his face behind both of his hands, but his wheezes shook his whole body.

I kicked his foot with the side of my boot. He was going to blow this for me, and I didn't need any more help—I was doing a fine job of screwing it up on my own.

"How did she die?" Skipper asked as she sat back in her seat.

Who was running this show, anyway? I hit her with a flat stare since I didn't have a cast-iron skillet handy. "Your questions are causing a disturbance in the Force. I need your oms."

Doc coughed, apparently choking on his laughter.

"Oh, yeah, sorry." She returned to her closed-eye meditation routine.

When Doc sobered enough to stop hiding behind his hands, his hot palm returned to my thigh.

I glanced at him, and then did a double take, frowning as I watched a drip of sweat roll down from his temple. Oh, crap. His breaths were deep and rhythmic, as if he was busy with a little meditation of his own.

Leaning toward him, I murmured, "Doc?" in his ear. I remembered his earlier don't-ask instructions, but I couldn't help myself. I didn't like to see him suffering for my sake.

A gentle squeeze and brief nod from him encouraged me to continue.

With the marker back in my fingers, I asked the ceiling, "Will you tell us how you died?"

I scribbled for a moment, then wrote: *murdered*, and shoved the paper into the center of the table for others to read.

Skipper gasped. She was eating out of my hands now.

Hiding my small smile of triumph, I asked, "Do you know who your killer was?"

Scribble, scribble, then: *Two men.*

"Oh, how horrible," she whispered, gaping across the table at her boyfriend. Butch mirrored her expression.

Cornelius didn't even seem to know we were there, anymore. He appeared totally lost in his chant-a-thon.

I checked on Doc and my chest tightened. His face looked gaunt, his skin now coated with sweat, his Adam's apple bobbing like he was gulping down air as fast as he could.

Oh, hell. I knew those signs too well. He was one big

sinking ship, hull-ripping explosions and all. I needed to keep going, keep distracting, keep the band playing as he went under. I licked my lips. "Do you know why they killed you?" I asked the ghost.

Scribble.

Teeth.

God, that looked totally stupid on paper, even if it had an element of truth to it.

"She must have had gold teeth," Skipper surmised.

I stole a glance at Doc out of the corner of my eyes. The tendons in his neck were visible, his jaw clenched.

My jaw tightened, too, my angst mushrooming. What if he … ? *Keep on track!* "Where did they bury you?" I asked.

Good question. One I wanted to ask George Mudder to see if he had an answer for me.

Scribble. *Under the—*

I gasped as Doc's hand squeezed my thigh hard, bruising. I tore at his hand, which seemed to have a mind of its own. Prying one finger from my muscle at a time, I freed my leg. My thigh throbbed in complaint.

A glance at Doc turned into a gaping double-take. His eyes were squeezed tight, his body quaking and shuddering, locked in the midst of convulsion. The intensity of his reaction was unprecedented. My adrenaline cranked up in response, my breaths coming faster, matching his.

Fuck! What could I do? How could I help him? If I didn't do something, his struggle to maintain control would tear him apart.

My gaze darted around the table. Nobody had noticed him yet, but they would as soon as they opened their eyes. I had to cover for him and quick. Talking to the ghost wasn't going to cut it. Smoke and mirrors would have been handy. So would a big tarp to hide him under.

"Keep oming," I ordered to buy me some time.

I needed to pull Doc out of this, like I had earlier this afternoon in the stairwell. Wincing for his sake, I reached over and pinched him hard on the back of his arm.

His jerking grew more visible, more violent.

Yikes! I pinched his thigh, twisting a little to add more oomph.

He listed away from me.

No, no, no. I caught him before he slumped off his chair and tugged him back upright.

He groaned loudly.

Ack!!

I mimicked his groan to fool the others and poked him hard in the ribs.

Nothing, not a single reaction to me.

ARGHHH! It was a matter of seconds before Skipper opened her big blue eyes again; I just knew it.

He jerked hard, his knee slamming into the table leg, moving the whole table to the right.

"Was that the gh—" Skipper started.

Before she could finish, I did the only thing I could think to do. In one combined move, I clocked Doc with my elbow, nailing him in the cheek with enough force that his chair toppled backwards. Then I screamed and threw myself face-down across him.

He grunted as my knee jabbed into his thigh. My hip landed on his gut, pushing an "Oof" from his lips.

As falls go, it wouldn't go down as one of my most graceful cinematic moments. It could have been choreographed a little better with some rehearsal and a bit of participation from Doc, who lay there, crushed under my weight on the floor until Butch lifted me off of him.

"Are you okay?" Skipper asked, steadying me when I faked wooziness.

"Yeah, what happened?" I asked.

"You screamed and fell again," Butch said and leaned over Doc. "I think you knocked your friend out cold, babe."

Skipper giggled. "The next séance we do with you, I'm bringing a spare pair of underwear."

The next séance? Oh, hell no. I was cashing in my séance playing chips after tonight.

Cornelius stared at me, his expression a mixture of concern and astonishment. His gaze lowered to his laptop and his jaw fell open. "Sweet Mary Jane," he said, bending over his keyboard. A huge grin spread his mouth wide. It was the first time I'd seen him smile on both sides of his cheeks. "Would you look at this?" His finger raced over the keys.

What?

A groan from the floor interrupted my curiosity.

I squatted next to Doc, noticing the red welt right below his right eye where my elbow had connected. I grimaced. That was going to leave a mark. I grabbed his hand, squeezing.

His eyelids flickered open, his dark gaze bouncing around until it landed on me. "What happened?"

"I had another episode," I told him, squeezing his fingers again, imploring him to go along with me until I could get him out of there. "I accidently knocked you down when it hit me."

"It?" he asked, his eyes searching mine.

"The ghost girl," I said.

"Big Lips Lolly," Skipper clarified.

"It hit *you*?" Doc asked.

"Uh … yeah." Crap, had he forgotten that the whole reason we were here was for me to fake contact with a ghost in exchange for a sale? Come on, I hadn't elbowed him *that* hard.

He touched the mark on his cheek bone, wincing. "Then what hit me?"

"She did," Butch tattled, pointing at me.

I reached up and smacked his finger away. "It was an accident."

Doc's eyes narrowed for a fraction of a second. "An accident. Right."

Butch helped Doc into a chair.

Skipper turned on the lamp next to the couch. "That was so cool, Ms. Parker. You really can talk to ghosts, huh?"

I just smiled at the silly life-sized Christmas tree ornament. It was that, or kick something, knowing that my Realtor reputation had just hit an all-new low. Homestake Mining Company hadn't delved so deep.

"Violet," Cornelius said from behind his laptop, his voice breathless. He tugged on his goatee. "You need to see this. It's incredible. I haven't seen this many spikes in paranormal activity since we channeled in the Amityville house."

I looked at Doc, but he had his head in his hands. I didn't think he was laughing this time, not with the way his shoulders drooped. I reached out, noticing my own unsteady fingers, and touched the back of his neck. He was burning up.

"I need to go," I announced. I had to get Doc out of there before he had another major quake roll through.

"Already?" Cornelius asked, his expression sad like I was going home and taking my toy with me. "I thought maybe we could try again."

Ha! I'd sooner jump off the edge of the Open Cut mine.

Rubbing my stomach, I moaned. "I think I'm going to be sick. It happens every time I do one of these things."

"Talking to ghosts makes you sick?" he asked. "Interesting."

Not really. I nodded and groaned again for good measure. "Butch, will you help me get Doc into the elevator." No way were we trying those stairs with him in this condition.

"I'll call you later," I told Cornelius. When he frowned at me like I'd suggested flying to the moon via jetpack, I added, "To discuss the sale of the hotel."

The lights clicked on behind his eyes. "Oh, right. Yes, call me at eleven-thirty-two."

I opened my mouth to ask him why that particular exact time, and then thought better of it and led Butch and Doc into the hall.

Butch rode down in the elevator with us "just to make sure." I thanked him and turned down his offer to help us out to the Picklemobile.

By the time we left the casino, Doc's color was coming back, especially the red and now purplish-blue spots on his right cheek. The lines around his eyes seemed deeper, but his focus was strong, especially when it landed on me.

I smiled like a cheerleader at a pep-rally and bit my tongue all of the way to the pickup, not wanting anyone to hear the barrage of questions stacking up behind my closed lips.

When I moved to open the pickup door for Doc, he didn't object, just crawled inside. He settled onto the bench seat next to me with a sigh, his head resting against the back window, his eyelids closing.

I shut his door, breathing a sigh of relief. We'd made it, in and out, Doc's secret still intact. I needed a drink.

Climbing behind the wheel, I shut my door and just stared at him. The overhead parking lot light added an orange tint to his skin.

"What?" he asked, his eyes still closed.

"You okay?"

"I will be."

"What happened back there?"

"I'm not sure. I got slammed."

"I thought you said you could handle her." I grimaced at how accusing that sounded. To make up for it, I caught his hand and laced my fingers through his.

His lips curled. "I could, but not all of the others."

"Others? What do you mean?" Had Wolfgang been there? Had I really been able to channel something? Someone?

"At first, I sensed her there—just her," he explained. "The next thing I knew they were everywhere."

"They?"

"Yeah, Violet." He opened his eyes, holding me in his sights. "They."

I had the feeling he was looking for doubts from me. I didn't allow any to surface and just went with what he claimed. "How many are we talking here?"

"There were too many coming at me too fast to count. It

was like being engulfed in a wave of ... of ... Christ, I don't know." He closed his eyes again. "I have to sort it all out in my head."

"You were engulfed. Then what happened?"

He smirked. "Then I was waking up on the floor with you on top of me, everything throbbing, especially my cheek."

My face warmed. I rolled down the window.

"And not in the good way that you usually make me throb," Doc added.

"Yeah, that was something, huh?" I laughed. It sounded canned.

"It's my bad luck that you don't hit like a girl," he said.

I didn't pinch like a girl, either, but there was no need to bring that up now.

He rubbed his forehead. "I can't believe you hit me."

"I had to. You were convulsing right there in front of everyone. I had to cover for you."

"By punching me?"

"Technically, I elbowed you." When he just frowned back at me, I explained, "I needed a distraction. It was all I could think to do."

"You could have ... I don't know, flashed them maybe."

I had wanted to distract them, not psychologically damage them. After two kids, my fun bags had sagged into sad sacks.

"That would distract me plenty," Doc continued.

"But that wouldn't have helped *you*, though."

"As opposed to how much giving me a black eye was helping."

I scoffed. "I didn't give you a black eye."

But he was right. I had. The blue-purple bruise was spreading north, circling under his eye. Shiznit. I'd miscalculated my aim.

He grinned. "Morticia Addams gave me a black eye. How fitting. Gomez would be turned on by that."

No comment. I jammed the key in the ignition and revved the engine.

"What's next, Tish? Whips and chains? A vice clamp? Electrocution?"

"You should be so lucky." I backed out of the stall and turned onto the street. "Where to?"

"Home, please."

I nodded. "So, what do you think? Is Cornelius a ghost whisperer like he claims?"

Doc didn't answer. When I checked on him, he was frowning out the front window, rubbing the back of his arm—the one I'd pinched.

"A ghost whisperer," Doc repeated, as if rolling the title around on his tongue to see how it tasted. "He wasn't doing much whispering, just chanting."

True.

I made a right, heading toward Doc's place. "You know, that was all he did last time, too," I told him. "It's what put me to sleep."

More silence from Doc, his hand still rubbing his arm. I had the feeling his mind was still processing tonight's events, his hard drive chugging.

I turned left up into the Presidential District. A couple of minutes later, I pulled up in front of his house.

"But it was after his chanting began that I started feeling funky," he said as if there'd been no pause in the conversation.

"I thought the prostitute was already in the room by then."

"Make that funkier." He pushed his sleeve up and turned his arm, peering at his skin in the dim lights from the dashboard. "Violet, why do I have a big bruise on my arm?"

Yeah, about that ... "Maybe you hit something when you fell."

I could feel his eyes on me. "Where else am I going to find bruises?"

Opting for distraction by seduction this time, I reached over and ran my fingers up his inseam. "Who knows, but I could kiss them all better."

His hand stopped mine before I reached pay dirt. "Tempting, Boots. But you can't finish what you start."

Was that a challenge? "Oh, but I can."

"Not tonight you can't."

"Why not?" Did he know something I didn't?

"Your kids are waiting at home."

I knew that, but after ten years of always being there for them every night, a little separation time was good for all of us. At least that was what Aunt Zoe had informed me when I first moved in with her months ago and resisted her initial babysitting offers.

"Yeah," I said, "but we could be quick."

"I don't want quick, Violet. Not after the other night."

The night I stayed over? What was he saying? Had I been bad in the sack? No, I was pretty sure he enjoyed himself, too, even if our actual *sack-time* had been more like wall-time. So, what then? I was afraid to read too much into his words, especially after he'd left Tiffany for reading him all wrong.

"Okay. So, where do we go from here?" I asked, which was my brilliantly subtle way of asking him if he was falling for me as hard as I was for him without actually putting my heart on the line.

"Well, about that." He paused for a gut-wrenching couple of seconds. "I've been thinking, and—"

My goddamned, freaking cell phone rang.

"Ignore that." I grabbed it, saw Cooper's name, hissed at it, and hit the reject-call button. "You were saying?"

He raised one eyebrow. "Who was that?"

"Cooper."

The other eyebrow lifted. "Why would Detective Cooper be calling you at this time of night?"

There was no jealousy in his tone, at least none that I could detect. It sounded more like curiosity.

I thought about the last time I'd talked to Cooper, which had been with Harvey acting as mediator, and shrugged. "I don't know. It's probably about the head. What were you going to say?"

"The head? What head? The corpse's head?"

"Yeah. So, what were you thinking about regarding you and me?"

"The corpse's head?" He sat upright, frowning at me. "What about it?"

"They found it." Who cares about the head? I wanted to know what Doc was thinking about us.

"What? Why didn't you tell me they found the head?"

"I don't know. I guess I was distracted by the pending séance." Getting through the whole séance had been front and center in my thoughts since I heard the news, which wasn't much yet thanks to Cooper's unwillingness to let Harvey tell me more on the phone.

"Who else knows about the head?" Doc asked, his tone a little terse.

How should I know? "Harvey, Aunt Zoe, the Deadwood Police Department, maybe Reid," if Cooper shared information with him. "Oh, and Natalie." I'd texted her about it before I'd hopped in the shower to prepare for the séance.

Doc opened his mouth, acted as if he was going to say something, but didn't and pressed his lips together instead, shaking his head. Then he removed my hand from his thigh and pushed open his door. Before I could do more than gasp in surprise at his abrupt departure, he shut the door behind him.

I shoved open my door and poked my head out between the cab and window frame. "What are you doing?" I asked as he rounded the front of the pickup and walked toward his front porch.

He turned around, walking backward. "Go home, Violet." He sounded disappointed on top of tired.

"What did I do?"

"Nothing out of the ordinary. I'm just starting to get fed up with being the low man on your totem pole. Especially after tonight's fun and games."

Speechless, I watched him climb the porch steps, unlock his front door, and disappear inside without even a wave goodbye.

But, but, but ... He was not the low man on my pole.

"No fair," I said, my chest burning from the frustration. He'd sidetracked me with that comment about him thinking about us, and then he didn't even give me a chance to explain how little I knew about the whole head thing.

I sank back into the driver's seat.

"No fucking fair!" I yelled and beat the crap out of the steering wheel.

Chapter Twenty-Two

Wednesday, August 22nd

"Mom," Addy's voice echoed in my head. "Mom, wake up."

I opened my eyes and stared into her light brown eyes just inches from mine. Her head rested on my pillow, her smile as bright as the sunshine streaming in from the window behind her. She smelled like bubblegum ice cream, all sweet and innocent. A chicken feather was stuck in her hair, fluttering ever so slightly.

She reached out and traced my forehead. "Why are you in my bed, Momma?"

Her bed?

Then I remembered yesterday in a rapid-fire slideshow—me at Doc's place, Cornelius in jail, lunch with Cooper, news about the kids' father, the stairwell with Doc, the séance disaster, Doc and my totem pole, Natalie's sleep monologue, my insomnia, and finally Addy's bed—a soft-sheeted refuge guarded by teddy bears.

"Oh, crudmongers." I covered my eyes, groaning. My life was tangled up into such a big clusterfuck.

Addy snuggled into me, her cast digging into my ribs a little, her blonde hair making my nose itch. I blew the chicken feather free.

"Did you come in here because something scared you?" she asked.

I thought about Doc and the way my chest had ached last night after his rejection. "Yes."

"Were you afraid of being all alone in the dark?"

Of just being all alone, dark or light. "Definitely."

"Me, too, sometimes." She trailed her fingers down my arm, tickling me, and then looked up at me. "Me and Elvis will always be here to keep you company, Momma."

I watched her blink, soaking up her words. She was right—well, so long as I didn't manage to psychologically damage her until she hated my guts and wrote a screenplay titled, *Mommy Dearest II*. No matter what happened with Doc and Natalie, with my job, with anything, I'd always have Addy and Layne to kiss it better and make everything all right.

I squeezed her against me. "You promise, Adelynn?"

"Cross my heart," she mumbled into my old T-shirt.

"Good." I threw the sheets back and lowered my feet to the floor. "Let's go eat some breakfast."

I needed to catch Natalie before she left for work. Addy's promise prompted me to get busy on something I'd been putting off.

Then, I wanted to get into the office. On the phone with me last night at eleven thirty-two on the dot, Cornelius had agreed to add thirty thousand dollars to his previous offer, coming in at fifteen grand more than Ray and George. I planned to have our new offer in Tiffany's hand as soon as she entered her office this morning.

Downstairs, Aunt Zoe and Layne were at the breakfast table planning how to spend the kids' last day of summer vacation. I scooped up and pretty much inhaled a banana nut muffin from the dozen cooling on the counter, agreed to join them all for a picnic later out at Pactola Dam, and then headed up the stairs to catch Natalie. She was brushing her wavy brown tresses in the bathroom when I found her.

I leaned against the doorjamb and watched her in the mirror. It was kind of a déjà vu moment, replaying the same scene from many years throughout our past as we preened to go out to eat, drink, party, or just complain about life and men. Only today's version came with more of a melancholy feel due to what I needed to tell her. There was no way to go about this without hurting her feelings.

"Hey, you," she said, pointing the brush at me in the mirror. "You left me all alone again last night. Where did you end up?"

"Addy's bed."

"*Ay Chihuahua*. She kicks hard."

"Yeah, but Layne plays rugby in his sleep."

"Pick your bruiser, eh?" She exchanged her hair brush for her toothbrush.

Unsure where to begin, I just blurted out. "I think it's time for me to fly solo at night."

She paused in the midst of brushing her teeth and grinned at me in the mirror, looking like a rabid beauty queen. "If that's your way of saying you want time alone with a vibrator," she said through a mouth full of toothpaste, "don't let me get in your way. Go to town."

I chuckled in spite of my apprehension about my task.

"Although," she paused to spit in the sink, "I'm sure Detective Cooper would be happy to perform some *community service* on you if you'd just ask."

I rolled my eyes. "Nat, Cooper isn't into me."

"Not yet, but he could be after two shots of tequila to loosen you up and a ribbed-for-your-pleasure condom."

I winced at just the notion of sex with Cooper. I'd be scarred for life. I meant really, truly scarred. With all of the sharp points and rough edges on him, I'd show less wear after skinny dipping with a Great White.

"Let me rephrase that. I'm not into Cooper."

"You should at least try a taste before you make that decision."

Here it was suddenly in my face, a golden opportunity to tell her I'd already tried Doc and wanted to savor him and only him—if he'd still let me. I crossed my arms over my chest, squeezing tight in preparation for her to go all Medusa on me. "Natalie, there's something I need to tell you."

"I know, I know. Don't waste your breath."

My mouth fell open. "You do?"

"Yes. I'm not an idiot. I've been waiting for you to come to me for days and just say it."

She'd known for days? She wasn't bawling her eyes out and wanting to stab me with a fork? We must be talking about a different "something." To clarify, I asked, "Just say what in particular?"

"That you want me to move out."

"I do?" I mentally slapped my forehead, tires squealing as I whipped a U-turn and changed course again. "I mean, yes, I do."

"It's about my sleep talking, isn't it?"

"No, it's just time for me to figure out a different way of dealing with this insomnia. You've been a wonderful friend and I appreciate having you by my side, but the kids are starting school tomorrow and I want to start a new routine here—one with only them and me."

Okay, new game plan: first, get her out of the house, then tell her about Doc and me on neutral ground where she can't smother me with my own pillow.

She nodded. "That makes sense. Where does your aunt fit in?"

"She'll do whatever I ask when it comes to the kids." Which would be to just continue being herself at the moment—and keep the cookies and muffins coming.

"Alrighty, then." She shot me a smile that barely reached the corners of her mouth. "I'll be out tonight."

My heart panged a little at her hurt expression. "Natalie, you're not disappearing from our lives, you're just returning to yours."

"I know." She slipped past me through the doorframe, her booted leg thumping toward my bedroom. She added over her shoulder, "It's just going to be a little lonely at first."

I followed her into my room. "Just think, your own bathroom, your own bed. You'll have total privacy again. I'm going to be grinding my teeth with envy, you lucky duck."

"Ha! That reminds me of the 'it's not you, it's me' speech

the last jerk who broke up with me preached." She grabbed her work cowboy hat off the bedpost. "I'm the jealous one. You don't see where you're lucky."

"The grass is always greener," I admitted. I caught her forearm as she passed by me. "Stay for supper tonight?"

She squeezed my hand. "Sure. We can toast to our breakup, and then I'll head home with my broken heart in my hat." She tipped said hat at me. "I'll still be here whenever you need me, you know."

"I know. It's the sole reason why I put up with your sorry ass."

"You can kiss my sorry ass, you gomer. Let's go before you get all weepy about me leaving."

I followed her downstairs and into the kitchen, where Aunt Zoe stood at the window. Addy and Layne had moved their breakfast to the back porch, where they watched Elvis eat the seed they'd tossed out.

After stealing another banana nut muffin, I yelled "Goodbye" to the kids, dropped a kiss on Aunt Zoe's cheek, and flicked Natalie's ear in passing. Then, I hopped into the Picklemobile and putted into work.

Doc's car was missing from his usual spot. I purposely walked around the front of the building so I could peek into his office without being too obvious. Turned out peeking wasn't necessary—it was dark inside. I could press my nose against the plate-glass window and gape for all he cared.

I'd thought about calling him on the way into work, as well as every ten minutes since driving away from his house last night. But I wasn't sure what to say yet besides, "please don't be mad at me, anymore," which sounded like something a seventh grader would write in a folded note.

Inside Calamity Jane's, Mona staffed the front room, her fingernails clacking as usual. Some days, she clacked so much I swore she was re-writing Michener's *Hawaii*.

"Morning, Mona."

The familiar scent of her jasmine perfume added a spring

to my step. Natalie was right. I was lucky in many ways I hadn't thought about, like with Mona, who had made a point of helping me succeed from my first day on the job. She always offered a hand up when needed and periodically filled Ray's orange juice glass with Benefiber to give me a break from the asshole's needling.

"Hey, Vi. How did it go with Cornelius?"

"Quite spiffy. I'm about to type up a new offer for fifteen thousand more than George Mudder's."

She took off her rhinestone rimmed glasses and smiled wide. "I knew you'd be able to work your magic on him."

It wasn't really magic since I'd never gotten around to the smoke and mirrors bit, only parlor tricks.

"Thanks for your confidence." She had way more in me than I'd had. I grabbed some coffee and got busy typing. "I'm giving Ray twenty-four hours to come back with a higher offer. I hope Tiffany is on board with that timeline."

"It's pretty typical," Mona said. "I'll be surprised if Tiffany bucks."

I could ask Doc if she bucked or not. Blah! I had to squash that jealousy bug, damn it. Tiffany was Doc's past. I needed to grow up and get over her before my green-eyed tormenter chased Doc away from me—assuming Doc wasn't already done with my shenanigans.

As I sent off the new offer, I said, "I guess we'll see how much George Mudder wants the place now."

"And how far Ray is willing to go to see you fired," Mona said while clacking.

I felt pretty confident I had this sale after my phone call last night with Cornelius, who'd still been a machine gun of chatter about the paranormal activity he'd recorded during the séance.

But I knew better than to get too cocky. Lady Luck loved to poke me in the butt with a sharp stick more often than not. And the way Cornelius talked about my so-called channeling abilities gave me a nauseous feeling in the pit of my stomach.

If Ray and George leaned on us more, I feared another séance might be in my future, which would make Safari Skipper and me BFFs forever. Butch and I could get matching I-love-Skipper tattoos.

After I sent the offer to Tiffany and confirmed its receipt with a short and sweet phone call to the Jessica Rabbit twin, my day turned positively rosy. A Disney tune played in my head, and my lips couldn't stop smiling. Now to go have fun with my kids for a few hours and forget about the flyswatter that life kept using to slap me down.

I looked back at Jane's office, noticing the light was on, but the door was closed.

"How's Jane this morning?" I asked Mona. "I want to see if she'll mind me taking the day off to spend with the kids since it's their last day of summer vacation."

"She's been in there with the door closed since I came in this morning. Enter at your own risk."

"Where's Ray?"

Mona shrugged. "I haven't seen him since yesterday."

Tiptoeing down the hallway, I stood outside of Jane's office, listening for her voice on the other side of the door. Silence seeped through the crack at the bottom, nothing more.

Should I just leave without saying anything to Jane? We didn't really have set hours, but a day off in the middle of the week wasn't usual. Until I had the sale of the hotel under my belt, the last thing I wanted to do was piss off my boss.

Taking a deep breath, I rapped on Jane's door.

A moan came from the other side.

My stomach tightened with concern.

I turned the knob. It was unlocked.

"Jane?" I called out in a quiet voice and pushed open her door. A musky, stale smell of liquor wafted over me.

My boss sat slumped behind her desk, her cheek a paperweight, a bottle of Jack Daniel's in her grip.

I grimaced. She looked like I felt most mornings, but having two kids that needed me kept me from sliding inside a bottle of whiskey.

"Jane, are you okay?" I asked from the threshold, unsure if I should step into the room or just leave and close the door behind me.

"Smut a life," she mumbled.

"What?"

She raised her head an inch. "Shut-off-the-damned-light," she said as one grumbled word.

I flicked off the switch. A lamp in the opposite corner of the room filled the room with a soft glow. "Can I get you something?" I asked, stepping toward her desk.

With a grunt, she lifted herself from the desktop. That's when I realized she wasn't wearing a shirt, only a lacy cream-colored bra and a couple of reddish-blue bruises on her shoulder. Jeez, she was a poster model for the divorce-was-hell series.

I shut the door and looked around for her clothes. "Where's your shirt?"

She looked down at her chest and groaned. "Oh, my God, I thought it was just a nightmare."

"What do you mean? What happened?"

She shook her head, and then squeezed the bridge of her nose.

I found her silk blouse wadded up in the corner, one stocking was wound up in it. I shook out her blouse, trying to loosen the tight wrinkles.

"Here you go." I placed the shirt on her desk, laying the stocking next to it.

"Ugh, I've really messed things up now," she said in a voice thick with self-disgust. "What time is it?"

"Just after nine."

"It's Thursday, right?"

"No. Wednesday." I clasped my hands together, not sure if I should help her get dressed and on her feet, or just slowly slip back out the door. The mother in me won out. "Can I help you with your shirt, Jane?"

She gave me a smile. I'd seen expensive teacups that looked less fragile. "I could use a hit man. I have a soon-to-be ex-asshole of a husband just yearning to be run over by a truck."

"How about we start with some coffee? Mona brewed a fresh pot this morning."

Her face sobered. "Is Ray here?"

"No, not yet."

"Good." She shoved to her feet and stumbled into the cabinet behind her.

I rounded her desk and steadied her. She reeked of stale whiskey and something else. I sniffed as subtly as I could, almost recognizing the other scent. Then she reached out and grabbed my shoulder for support, and the smell slapped me like a pizza pan: Stetson cologne.

Ray!

The bottom of my stomach dropped out.

"Jane," I waded into her troubles on my very tippy-toes. "Did Ray do something to you?" I'd seen him furious many times. He spoke *Violence* as his second language. Had he taken out his frustrations with me on her?

She groaned and reached for her shirt. "You could say that."

"Do I need to contact the police?"

She shook her head, buttoning. "It's not like that."

"Did you get in an argument with him?"

"No, it's worse than that."

"Did he grab or hit you?" That would explain the bruises I saw.

"No."

"What happened?" I asked, my fists clenched. It was one thing for the asshole to come after me, but not Jane, not when she was taking such a beating from her ex-husband.

"Nothing," she mumbled, avoiding my stare.

"Jane, just tell me."

Her gaze met mine, the dullness from the whiskey gone,

replaced by her usual sharp stare. "Ray and I had sex last night."

I took a step back. "What?"

"You heard me."

I took another step. "Where? Why?"

"Right here in my office. I was drunk, feeling old and unattractive, and he said I looked beautiful and had a great body."

"Ray said those nice things?" That couldn't have been Ray. She must have been hallucinating.

"Yes, Ray. He can be very charming when he tries. How do you think he lands so many sales?" She ran a hand through her short gray-blonde locks. "He has flirted with me for years and I've never had a problem resisting. But last night …" she sighed and dropped the empty bottle of whiskey into her trash. "Last night, I needed to feel wanted. He gave me that and more."

I winced and cringed at the same time, clasping my hands again, wanting to go wash them. Maybe even sandblast them, and then bleach them.

She slipped on her shoes, and then tucked the lone stocking in her purse. I stood aside as she passed by me and reached for the door knob. "Now, I'm going to go home and try to forget this big mess."

"You want me to drive you?"

"No, I'm okay. I just look worse for wear." She looked back at her desk and shook her head. "Violet, promise me you'll keep quiet about this. I can't face the disappointment in Mona's face if she finds out—not yet."

"My lips are sealed." Although I'd like to take a two-by-four to Ray's knees for taking advantage of Jane when she was at her weakest. But that would mean breaking my promise, and Jane needed a friend right now, not a heroic big mouth.

Then I remembered why I'd braved her office in the first place. "Oh, Jane."

She raised her eyebrows, and then winced as if it hurt.

"I just sent off a new hotel offer that gives Ray's client twenty-four hours to counter. Would you mind if I took the afternoon off? My kids start back to school tomorrow. I'd like to spend the day with them."

Her eyes grew a little glassy. "Go, be with your little ones. Cherish them." She cleared her throat and blinked a couple of times, her face hardening again. "Let's get out of here and enjoy the sunshine."

I had a feeling she'd be hiding under her covers instead. If it was me, I'd be checking into having my vagina steam cleaned.

She shut her door after us, twisting the knob to check that it was locked. "Tell Mona I'll see her tomorrow," Jane whispered and snuck out through the back door.

I did just that, avoiding eye contact with Mona while informing her I could be reached on my cell phone. I wanted to know as soon as Ray checked in to see if I'd need to pull another ghost out of my hat to wrangle more money from Cornelius.

My cheeks warmed under Mona's steady gaze as if I were the one who'd had sex with Ray the snake. Ugh. I couldn't escape to the Picklemobile soon enough.

I spent the afternoon trying to forget about Jane and Ray doing the horizontal hokey pokey in her office. During the picnic with the kids and Aunt Zoe at Pactola Dam, I shucked what I could of my worries and let the sun wash over me while they all played in the water.

Over dinner later that evening, the anxieties returned in a flood. I played with my mashed potatoes while wondering if Ray having sex with Jane meant that he had a leg up when it came to my being replaced by his nephew, Benjamin.

Ben was more successful than I was in real estate sales and didn't let himself get entangled emotionally with each of his clients. He ended the business meetings at dinner. I, on the other hand, was just getting rolling by the time dessert arrived.

Several times throughout the meal I caught both Natalie

and Aunt Zoe watching me with furrowed brows. I tried to hide my fretting behind an overly bright smile, but neither of them seemed to be fooled by my billboard of faked happiness.

After dinner, I walked Natalie out to her pickup, enjoying the smell of freshly mowed grass and the feel of freedom in the air. Finally, no more hiding in the bathroom with the water running while on the phone with Doc, no more worrying if I cried his name out in my sleep.

She tossed her bag into her pickup. "What's up, Vi?"

"What do you mean?" My cheeks warmed. Thank God she couldn't read my mind.

"Something has you distracted tonight. Is it work? Or is it a man?"

Yes to both questions—it was work and Ray, but I'd made a promise. "I'm just a little nervous about this hotel sale not going through."

"I thought you said things were looking pretty good. That the oddball is extremely interested and motivated."

"He is. It's just you never know what can go wrong."

She squeezed my arm. "Have a little faith in yourself."

A screen door slammed across the street.

"Hey, you two!" Old man Harvey waddled down Miss Geary's drive towards us.

"Hey, yourself," Natalie said, her smile welcoming.

Harvey glanced around, as if checking to make sure the coast was clear. When he got up close, he poked a finger at me and whispered, "I've got something juicy for you, girl."

I grinned at Natalie. "Being that he just came from Ms. Geary's place, I'm not sure I want to think about him and anything juicy."

She snickered.

Harvey gave a fake laugh, and then wrapped his thumbs around his suspenders, rocking back on his heels. "I found out who the head belongs to."

"I know. You told me already. It was one of your weirdo neighbors from Slagton. The one who took care of the cemetery."

"I was wrong. The chew marks on his nose and cheeks threw me off."

"Eww!" I shivered in revulsion.

"You think that's bad, you should have seen what the critters did to the eyes and tongue."

"Ack! Stop. We just finished eating." I threatened to plug my ears.

"Anyway," Harvey knocked my hands back down, "Cooper had an artist produce a rough sketch of what the man looked like based off what was left of him."

Natalie and I both leaned in closer. "And?" I nudged.

"He was the owner of the funeral joint in Belle Fourche."

"The owner of the funeral joint ..." I whispered. "Just like George Mudder."

"Aye," Harvey said.

"Aye?" Natalie frowned at him. "What are you, Scottish now?"

"Beatrice likes it when I talk dirty to her with a Scottish brogue. I kind of get stuck in that mode."

Come on! There was too much sex going on in this little town, and not enough involving Doc and me.

"Do you think George has any connection to the corpse?" I asked Harvey.

"If he did," Natalie surmised, "Eddie could have gotten rid of the evidence during the autopsy."

"Aye, that was my thought, too."

I elbowed him. "Knock off the Scottish crap." It conjured images of him in a kilt and suspenders sans his boxers that had no business in my brain. "We need to get back into that funeral home."

Harvey nodded, combing his beard with his fingers.

"Why?" Natalie asked.

"To see what's in the crates," I told her. And to see the records room again—I hadn't forgotten about Doc's prostitute ghost. I had a dead girl to find on paper.

"There's another viewing tomorrow night." Harvey said. "I'll run decoy."

I shook my head. "If Cooper catches wind of you at Mudder Brothers, he'll arrest me on suspicion alone."

Harvey and I both turned to Natalie.

"No," she said. "I'm going to go home now and live my quiet life." She hoisted herself up into her pickup and slammed the door.

I leaned in through the open window. "Please, Nat."

"No. Definitely not."

"I'll let you borrow my black velvet bustier."

"Nope. My boobs don't look as good as yours in it."

"How about my purple cowboy boots?"

She chewed on her lower lip for a moment. "Can I wear them bull-riding at The Blue Outlaw down in Rapid?"

The Blue Outlaw bar was known for three things—rowdy crowds, unisex bathrooms, and the hanky panky that happened when the two were mingled and too much beer added to the mix. The idea of my boots touching the floor in those bathroom stalls made me grimace. The leather would need to be professionally cleaned and the bottoms resoled. Was Natalie's company at Mudder Brothers worth that price?

The flashback of those love bite bruises on Jane's shoulder sealed the deal. Ray was up to no good. It was time to put a stop to his bullshit.

At my nod, Natalie grinned. "Sweet! I get to keep them for a month, too," she decided. I nodded again. "Bring them with you tomorrow night."

Doc would be less than thrilled to hear his favorite boots were out on loan. Oh, well, for all I knew, it might take me a month to woo him into touching me again.

Natalie started her truck. "And this time, if Cooper threatens to take us to jail, you have to show him your cha-chas. My tattooed ass is on hiatus."

"Aye!" Harvey's gold teeth showed. "Now that'll give Coop's wee bits a fine heft."

Chapter Twenty-Three

Thursday, August 23rd

A fox had gotten into the chicken coop. At least that's what Aunt Zoe's kitchen looked like this first back-to-school morning. Feathers even floated in the air thanks to a very excited and agitated Elvis, who Addy wisely shooed outside before I turned the damned bird into a Kentucky Fried variety.

While I herded the kids through their bathroom routines, playing drill sergeant in order to get them into their clothes, Aunt Zoe packed lunches and prepared breakfast. With a few growls and whines, we all fell back into the roles we'd established during the last school year.

I dropped both kids off at school, watched them until they stepped through the doors, then made a beeline to the Tin Cup Café for a much-needed punch of caffeine. Only after I had caramel-flavored coffee flowing through my system did my pulse flutter into its usual chaotic rhythm.

I pulled into the parking lot behind Calamity Jane's and gaped at the empty parking spots. Where was everyone? No Mona or Ray, no Jane or Doc. I pulled out my cell to check the time. Was I that early? Not at all. I was actually ten minutes late.

The voicemail notification on my cell phone might explain what was going on. I checked the caller. It was Doc. He'd called this morning during the get-ready-for-school bedlam.

I shut off the Picklemobile. The tailpipe's goodbye salute scared a couple of crows from a nearby pine tree. I played Doc's message as I crossed the parking lot.

"Violet, call me when you have a moment." His tone was all business, no love.

Damn it. I glared at my phone. I hated it when he left that kind of message.

Well, Doc would just have to wait for me to get inside and sit down. If he planned to knock the wind out of me, I was not going to land on my ass.

The lights were on inside Calamity Jane's, but Jane's office was dark, the door still closed and locked. Someone had been in this morning—there was fresh coffee in the pot. I caught a hint of Mona's jasmine perfume, but that could just be permanently embedded in the walls. No smell of Ray's Stetson whatsoever, thankfully, since I was beginning to associate it with the urge to hit someone in the face with a cream pie, and that was such a waste of good cream.

I'd expected a call from Mona all day yesterday. I'd even called her late last night, waking her up, to ask if she'd heard if Ray and George had upped their offer. Between yawns, she'd said he hadn't come in all day, nor called in.

I'd figured this thing with Jane might be a little awkward, but Ray usually thrived on discomfort. Plus, this was an excellent power play over me. Waiting for the backlash from it had me chewing my knuckles.

When I pulled out my chair, I found a piece of paper sitting on my seat with a pink Post-it note stuck to it. Mona's handwriting on the pink note gave away the author.

Ray never showed up or submitted another offer. This came in from Tiffany this morning. Looks like we might have a hotel on the Sales Pending board soon! Back this afternoon—in Spearfish all morning. You can reach me on my cell.
Mona

I fell into my seat, holding the acceptance letter with the signature of Tiffany's client. Then I jumped back up and whooped with victory, spiking an imaginary football off Ray's empty desk. When the burst of glee ran its course and I stopped spinning and grinning, I sat down on top of his desk and frowned out the front window at the passing traffic.

Something was up. This win was way too easy. Ray must be playing some kind of dirty trick. Maybe sleeping with Jane was all part of his diabolical plan to get rid of me in spite of the hotel sale. Maybe he knew something about Cornelius that I didn't. Maybe ... .

My cell phone rang. I hopped off Ray's desk and grabbed the phone.

The screen showed Doc's name and number. Falling into my chair, I answered with a little bit of hesitation, still gun-shy after our last parting. "Hello?"

"I almost called you last night," Doc said without introduction.

Why? To say what? I took a calming breath, leaning back in my chair. I asked myself what the cool, leather-clad Olivia Newton-John version of Sandy would say to Danny Zuko while she took a hit off her cigarette. *Tell me about it, Stud.*

"What stopped you?" I asked in a voice I hoped sounded sultry.

"Cornelius."

I sat up in my chair and stubbed out my imaginary cigarette. "What? Why? Did you run into him yesterday?"

"No, I didn't, thank God. I'm not prepared for a second meeting yet."

What did that mean?

"I decided not to call you," Doc continued, "because I figured you'd want more of an explanation about what happened at the séance."

Silly man. I'd rather he'd called even if it was just to talk about the weather. I'd envisioned him at home drawing a mustache on my picture and throwing darts at it. Doubts and anxieties had made for dark clouds on my horizon during the picnic at Pactola Dam, which had me periodically cursing under my breath.

How could I have allowed him to burrow this deeply

under my skin so fast? One of us needed to be the adult in this relationship and fess up to some feelings soon.

I opened my mouth to take the first step and tell him I'd missed hearing his voice, but then my tongue got shy and stuck with the easy stuff. "What's your explanation?"

"Well, after trying to analyze what happened to me in that room, the things I was sensing and visualizing, I came up with three possibilities."

I waited, my eyes closed to give him my full attention.

"The first is that the Old Prospector Hotel is full of ghosts, and only one or two usually come out at a time, like with our adventure in the stairwell."

"That sounds like the setting to a kickass movie."

"Right. The second is that Cornelius's chanting really works, and he has the ability to communicate with ghosts. Although, from what I could tell, he seemed oblivious to them, just drawing them into the room, where they turned on me as soon as they realized I could sense them."

Cornelius was legit? The possibility seemed farfetched what with all of Cornelius's eccentric fanfare, but so did Doc meeting a prostitute in the stairwell, and yet I was willing to swallow that horse-pill of a concept. "What is the third possibility?"

"That you were the one channeling the ghosts."

I laughed out loud. "I highly doubt it was me. I'm a dud, remember?"

"I don't believe that entirely. That whole Kyrkozz event from the previous séance still has me scratching my head."

"You're forgetting about another possibility," I told him.

"Which is?"

"That you are responsible for channeling the ghosts."

"I thought about that, but I don't think so."

"Why not?"

"Because I've been playing this ghost detection game for years, and that was the first time I've ever experienced a rush of so many entities. The dead are usually loners."

He'd been dealing with the ghost visions for years? One of these days, I was going to make him tell me his whole story from the beginning.

I picked up a pencil and tapped it on my desk calendar. "When you say a 'rush' of entities, how many are we talking?"

He hesitated, the line quiet for several seconds. "You're not going to believe me."

"Give me a chance. I'm trying here."

"From what I can determine, I was rushed by thirteen different entities within a few seconds, including the prostitute I met in the stairwell earlier."

I stopped tapping. "Thirteen? How could you tell?"

"It took me most of yesterday to sort it all out, but I wrote down the different pieces of memories I experienced as the entities passed through me along with the unique essences that came with each. Then I sorted through flashes of images to distinguish individual beings. When I was finished, I had ended up with thirteen."

"You mean you relived thirteen different dying moments within seconds?"

"Yes."

Christ. That explained the total loss of control for him, including his badger-like grip on my thigh. "It's no wonder you passed out."

"Passed out? Yeah, about that, I have a strong suspicion I was knocked out before I could pass out. You should see my black-eye."

Wincing, I scratched at a spot of dried coffee on my desktop. "Sorry about that."

"Apology *not* accepted. I'm going to need you to kiss it better first."

I savored his peace offering, wishing he was close enough to touch. "I'm your Huckleberry."

"I also have two other big bruises that are going to need your attention. And after you finish with those …"

"I'll take care of the rest of you," I finished for him. "I'll bring my favorite flavored lip gloss."

"What flavor are we talking about here?"

"Cherry." I lowered my voice to a purr-level. "How about I show you the magic trick I can do with my mouth?"

I heard him suck in a breath. "Damn, Boots. You shouldn't say that kind of stuff to me while I'm standing around in public."

"Where's 'public.'"

"Rapid City, near the airport."

Airport? "You flying somewhere?"

"No, just going through a client's financials onsite today."

"Good. When can I see you again?"

"I'll call you tonight after I get home."

Taking a deep breath, I leaped. "Or you could come over and watch a movie with me."

Silence filled the line. I heard the rumble of a plane engine in the background.

I was about to ask if he was still there when he said, "What about Natalie?"

"She's no longer staying with us. It's just me and the family."

"Addy and Layne might get ideas about us."

I smiled at the idea that an *us* might exist.

"I'll explain that you're my friend and I want to hang out with you. We'll start there and see where this goes."

"Aren't you worried the kids might say something to Natalie?"

"No."

"Why not?"

"Because I'm going to tell Natalie the truth."

Another plane engine rumbled through the line, filling a second bout of silence.

"You sure you want to do that?"

"Yes." Not really, but I was sure I wanted more of Doc.

"When?"

I didn't know exactly, or even how I'd broach the subject,

but it would have to be soon if Doc took me up on my offer. I wasn't going to have my kids lie for me. "Soon. Very soon. But first I need her help tonight, and she's going to need a clear head."

"Help with what?"

"We're going to another viewing."

He groaned. "Why? Don't try to tell me it's because you want to pay your condolences, either. I'm not Cooper."

"Something is going on with Ray."

"Besides being an asshole at work?"

"Well, that's the thing. He hasn't been in to work for two days."

"Maybe he's taking a little vacation."

"He missed the deadline to counter Cornelius's latest offer. Tiffany sent me a fax this morning. We got the hotel if we don't hit any other snags."

"That's great, Violet. Congratulations."

"Yeah, thanks, but I'm not celebrating until I figure out what Ray is up to."

"Let me guess, you think Ray's not at work because he's coming up with a way to screw up your deal?"

"Pretty much, yes."

That and maybe he was feeling awkward about Jane. Then again, Jane had been gone all day yesterday and wasn't in yet today. Maybe they were somewhere together, locked up in a hotel room where Ray was securing his place in Jane's bed, from where he'd order my dismissal.

"That sounds a tad paranoid," Doc said.

"I like to think of it as envisioning all possible outcomes so that I can choose the proper course."

"Right," he said, dragging the word out. "What do you hope to accomplish at Mudder Brothers tonight?"

"You mean you're not going to try to stop me?"

"If I've learned anything about you over the last few weeks, Violet, it's that there is no stopping you once your mind is set."

My father called that being driven and smiled down at me with pride. Mom used labels such as borderline compulsive and obsessive and offered green tea every time I stopped by.

"I'm going to Mudder Brothers to pick George's brain—with Natalie's help. I want to find out if Ray was pushing him to buy the hotel just to screw with me. I also want to see if I can find out the name of the prostitute from his records, one way or another."

"One way or another, huh? Are you sure that's a good idea? Cooper is watching you like a hawk right now. If he hears you're even at the viewing, he'll be hell bent to track you down. I won't be home to bail you out of jail until later."

Every time Doc mentioned bailing me out of jail, I felt all warm and bubbly inside.

"Cooper isn't going to find out," I said, trying to ignore the bubbles. "Natalie and I will be in and out in a flash. Plus, we're having old man Harvey run interference. He's going to go hang out with Cooper until I give him the all-clear sign."

"Violet." He paused for several beats. "Be careful."

I had a feeling he'd edited out several comments before tossing out that short and sweet warning. "I will."

"Promise me you will not try to sneak into the side room to see what's in those crates."

"I promise," I said, but crossed my fingers just in case something came up that changed my plans. "My focus tonight is asking George about Ray and checking out his death records."

"Good. Because I really want to see you tonight." He paused, and then added, "Along with your cherry-flavored lip gloss."

I grinned. Lusty Lil strikes again. "See you later, Doc."

"You will."

For the next several heartbeats, I sat in my chair and daydreamed about rolling around naked with Doc on a bed of cash from the sale of the Old Prospector Hotel.

Then I remembered what Harvey told me last night about

the corpse's identity and I smacked my forehead. Dang it! I should have told Doc about that.

Or maybe not. After all, our little falling out had been over that damned head. It was probably better to broach that subject tonight in person, picking up right where we'd left off—with my hand on his thigh.

I glanced down at the acceptance letter Tiffany had faxed, and then frowned at Ray's empty desk. The snake was up to something. I'd lay odds it had to do with my job going up in smoke—poof!

Tonight, I was going to get some answers out of George Mudder so that the next time Ray attacked, I'd be ready and waiting.

* * *

Judging from the parking lot at Mudder Brothers Funeral Parlor, the majority of the viewing crowd had gone home to catch the last half of *Jeopardy*.

"Don't park here," I told Natalie, and directed her around behind the Recreation Center instead. "Cooper might be watching."

I looked at her as she killed the engine. "Remember, we're going to be legit this time. Nothing funny with George."

She pulled a bottle of perfume from her glove box and spritzed her wrists. A sultry fruity scent filled the cab, making me hungry for mango.

"Why are you so worried about Cooper all of a sudden?" she asked.

"Because I don't want to end up spending the night in the Deadwood cop shop." Plus Doc was coming over for the first time, and I didn't want to screw up our little date night by not showing up because I was too busy sitting in a jail cell.

She snorted. "You're obsessed with Coop."

Clinically, she was probably close to the mark. He was like my own personal Eye of Mordor these days, seemingly always watching, rarely blinking. I envisioned poking that big eye with a pencil eraser.

"He's only human, you know," she added, pulling her keys from the ignition and reaching for the door handle.

I thought of his gunshot riddled T-shirt. "I'm not so positive about that."

I stepped to the ground and brushed some tiny chicken feathers off of my black velvet slacks.

The sun had dropped below the hills to the west, but the air was still filled with warm thermals rising from the asphalt. I watched for cop cars as we snuck across the Mudder Brothers lot.

"Who are we paying our respects to tonight?" I asked Natalie as we neared the front porch.

"Victor Haskell."

"Haskell? Didn't we just go to a Haskell viewing last week?"

"Yeah, Victor's second cousin."

"How many Haskells are there around here?"

"Lots. They're old-school Catholics."

Mudder Brother's front porch area smelled like cigarette smoke, but there was no smoker to be found.

I held the door for Natalie, and then followed her into the foyer, passing several folks on their way out.

We found George in the main room. Only a handful of mourners filled the seats. George stood by the casket, consoling an older woman dressed in black from the tip of her veiled hat to her black patent leather spiked heels. Good thing I hadn't brought Harvey along. Saucy-looking widows were his kryptonite.

We sat in our usual seats at the back of the room and waited for George to greet us with his row of little corn-on-the-cob teeth.

"So," Natalie whispered, "am I going to ask him about Ray or are you?"

"I will." I whispered back.

"Remind me why I'm here again instead of down at the Blue Outlaw kicking it up in your purple boots?"

"Make that purple boot," I said, nodding at her injured leg. "You're here to help me grease the wheels on getting into the records room."

"Right, the dead prostitute." She grabbed a toothbrush from her pants pocket and shoved it down into her cast boot, grunting in satisfaction as she scratched. "Remind me again how you learned about this dead girl's ghost and why we care."

So many reminders—she could use some of that Ginkgo Biloba. "Cornelius claims she exists," I lied. "And I care because I'm curious if Cornelius is legit."

"Curious enough to bug George to see his records?" She watched me with a narrowed gaze. "Are you sure that's the only reason?"

She knew me too well. "The poor girl was supposedly murdered in the hotel my client is buying." I poured on some compassion. Not to mention that the murderers had taken her teeth, just as they had Prudence's, which had me curious. How many more people were murdered back then by these brutes and why? It had to do with something more than just a fetish for canine teeth.

"It sounds like you are actually beginning to believe in ghosts. What's up with that?"

I shrugged. "I'm not saying I do or don't at this point, but if there really is a ghost, she deserves a name." And I wanted an answer about that little box of teeth Cooper was sitting on. I wondered if Doc had had a chance to dig deeper into his vision of the murder scene.

"Fair enough. What about the headless guy? The other funeral home owner. Are we going to ask about him, too?"

I wanted to, but decided to focus on Ray for now. Too many questions might make George run away. "Let's hold off on that until another viewing. Unless the subject comes up."

She snickered. "Comes up? You mean like, 'Hi, George,

nice weather we're having, huh? Have any more headless corpses come in? If so, were they more of your cohorts? Oh, and by the way, did you happen to kill the last headless corpse-dude and destroy the evidence during the autopsy?'"

I wrinkled my nose at her. "You're lucky I'm not wearing socks or you'd be chewing on them."

She grinned wider, stifling a giggle.

Ten minutes later, George had just four of us left in the room. He made a point of coming over to hug Natalie and shake my hand, bestowing me with a closed-lip smile that barely tipped the corners of his lips. I wondered what bullshit Ray had been spreading about me to his client.

"Hello, ladies. Good to see you again. How is your Aunt Beatrix doing?" he asked Natalie.

"She's looking for love in all of the wrong places again. You know how she gets."

George nodded, his eyes darting to the one-way glass on our right. "That's good to hear."

Huh? I shared a narrow-eyed glance with Natalie and forced myself not to look at the one-way glass. I didn't want to let on to George that I knew about that viewing room. I had plans to come back another day and sneak in there to open one of his damned crates.

"George," I said, touching his arm to bring his attention back to us. "Have you seen Ray? I need to …" rub it in, "to talk to him about some real estate business, but he hasn't shown up at work in a couple of days."

His barely-there smile grew twitchy on the left side. "No, I haven't."

"You mean he didn't contact you in the last twenty-four hours to discuss increasing your offer for the Old Prospector Hotel?"

"No, I haven't heard from him at all. Maybe he's visiting his mother over in Brookings."

"Maybe," I said, but I wasn't buying the mom in Brookings theory. Ray was hatched from a reptile nest. Snakes didn't make loving sons.

Something was wrong with this picture. Ray sleeps with a very drunk Jane, and then he disappears without keeping tabs on the bidding war that could result in my dismissal from his precious real estate world?

George frowned at his reflection in the one-way glass, shaking his head so slightly that I wasn't sure if he was doing it on purpose or if it was just a tick. Then he made a cutting gesture across his throat, as if to silence someone who was watching.

"What are you doing?" Natalie asked him.

"The sound system has been giving us grief all evening. There is something wrong with the mics up front." He made the motion again to the one-way glass. "I'm sorry, girls, but I need to take care of this." He turned toward the front of the room, but Natalie's hand on his arm stalled him.

"George," she said, "we are looking for the name of a prostitute who was murdered in the late 1800s for one of Violet's curious clients. Can we take a quick look at your books?"

"My books?"

"Yes, it seems like Aunt Beatrix told me that you keep records on the deceased and that you have some historic volumes that came with the funeral parlor when you purchased it from the previous owner."

Relief etched lines on his face. "Oh, you mean my registers of the deceased. Yes, of course. You're welcome to them. Let me show you where they are, and then you can just let yourself out the front when you're finished."

"We'll be out of your hair before you know it," Natalie assured him with a shoulder squeeze.

I knew there was a reason I'd brought her along. I smiled at her with pride. Maybe if I got her really drunk, and then told her about Doc and me, she wouldn't want to kill me straight out. She was a happy drunk, which was when and why her men problems usually started.

She stuck her tongue out at me and followed behind George.

He led us to the little room off the foyer. Both Natalie and I faked surprise that it was more than just a coat closet.

With a quick smile, he left us outside the door to go say goodbye to the last of the deceased's family as they left the viewing parlor.

Natalie opened the door to the records room and ushered me in, "After you, Sherlock."

"Thank you, Watson."

We left the door open a crack so George wouldn't get suspicious about our true motives … which really were just to find out the prostitute's name. I wasn't used to being within legal limits when it came to Mudder Brothers.

The foyer grew quiet as Natalie and I began digging through the thick books of deaths gone by that were divided by decade. She took the 1880s and I took the 1890s. As we perused the tattered, ancient-looking volumes, the sounds of the funeral parlor quieted to dead silence.

I flipped another page, scanning down the Cause of Death column. Because Doc didn't know the exact year of the girl's death, I had to focus more on the how of it all, not the when. "George could use some classes on filing. I get the feeling these books were just thrown in here on the shelves and left to rot."

Natalie peeked out through the crack. "I think we're the only ones left. Let's go see if they have a crate next door."

"No," I said, giving her a warning squint. "I told you I didn't want to do that tonight. Besides, it's too dangerous. Did you see the way George kept looking at the glass? Someone must have been in that room."

"Fine, you big baby." She turned another page, her fingers trailing down the page. She appeared to be about a third of the way through the book. "We're looking for something about murder, right?"

"Yes."

Several minutes later, Natalie closed the book she had been checking out with a dust-inducing snap.

"I have to pee," she declared, stretching.

"Thanks for the news flash, Ace Reporter Natalie Beals."

She poked me in the ribs. "Try not to freak out while I'm gone, Chicken Little." Grinning at my one-fingered bird gesture, she hobbled out of the room, taking her crutch with her, and shut the door on me.

I picked up the volume she'd been reading through and opened to somewhere close to where she'd left off, a third of the way into it. I read through the list full of causes of death, finding things like: Murdered—Shot in the back, Natural Causes—TB, Natural Causes—Smallpox, Murdered—Mining dispute, Murdered—Scalped, and Murdered—Gun shot wound. The violence on the pages told stories of Deadwood and Lead's rough past, sucking me in with teasers, filling my imagination.

I found two possible candidates, both listing women with odd names that sounded like they could be prostitute pseudonyms, showing no next of kin, and the Cause of Death was Murdered—Knife wound. The first was Ruby Redbone, the second was named Iris DeFleur.

I pulled up the notepad feature on my phone and typed in the information on both women. When I'd finished, I took a picture of the pages on which the names were located and one picture of the book itself. I bent the tiniest bit of the corner on each page to mark it, in case I had the chance to come back and show Doc in person.

When I reached the last third of the volume, I looked up, blinking, and realized that Natalie hadn't come back. I pulled out my phone and frowned down at the time. I should have paid attention to when she left. She must have been gone for over twenty-five minutes already.

I sent her a text asking where in the hell she was. While I waited for her reply, I flipped through a few more pages, my gaze landing on an entry under Cause of Death that had:

Murder—Multiple knife wounds (and dental surgery).

"Dental surgery?" I whispered. Her date of death was close to the time Doc had mentioned. I looked at the name: Annabelle Devine. Kate Rogers was listed as her next of kin.

Devine? Wasn't that the last name of the prostitute who was murdered in that god-awful house with the striped wallpaper bedroom and the freaky basement that had set off Doc's radar?

I repeated my note and picture-taking routine with Annabelle's record.

There. Done. I had a few names and dates. Maybe these would give Doc what he needed to find out even more.

Now where in the hell was Natalie? She still hadn't replied to my text.

I opened the records room door and stepped out into the empty foyer, pausing to listen for sounds. The place was silent.

There was no sign of Natalie. Maybe she was still in the bathroom. Maybe she'd slipped and hurt her leg again, or worse yet, bunged up her other leg.

A quick check of the facilities resulted in washing the musty book smell from my hands, but no Natalie.

The French doors to the main viewing parlor were shut, the curtains closed. I eased one door open enough to check inside. The room was empty except for Mr. Haskell's casket up front. I could see his hands above the edge of the coffin, which made me shiver. Too creepy.

I closed the door and stepped back over to the records room to see if Natalie had returned while I was in the bathroom.

No such luck. The room was still empty. A hint of her sultry perfume lingering among the musty smells of the books, the only sign that she'd even been there.

Where in the hell had she gone?

I looked at the doorway leading into the hidden viewing room, the one with the crates. It was open a tiny bit, shadows leaking out through the crack. Hadn't that been closed when we went into the records room?

Natalie wouldn't have … I growled in my throat.

Oh, yes, she definitely would have, even though I'd asked her not to. I was going to skin her hide if I landed in jail tonight because of her. I had plans involving a good movie and a hot guy—a real flesh-and-blood male for once, not just a selection from my imagination.

I grabbed the door knob and eased the door open, squinting into the dimly lit room. "Natalie?" I whispered, inching inside.

Closing the door behind me, I glanced through the one-way glass. The parlor was still empty except for the dead guy. I could see his folded hands from this viewpoint, too. Eek.

There were two crates sitting end-to-end on the other side of the room. Curiosity lured me to them. When I got close enough to see the lids in the dim light cast through the one-way glass, I stopped short.

The lid on one of the crates was part-way open. I tiptoed forward and peered inside.

There was something in there.

Holy freaking moly! I had finally caught the Mudder brothers in the act. I fumbled for my cell phone. Pushing a button to light up the screen, I lowered it inside the crate. Pale white light reflected off black shiny bottles packed in straw.

I pulled one out, taking a closer look. There was no label, not even one stamped into the glass. The bottle was heavy, full of liquid, and sealed closed with a cork covered in wax.

Holding my cell against the side of the bottle, I tried to see the liquid through the glass, but it was too dark.

Setting my phone down, I hefted the bottle between my hands. What was in it? Was it beer? Wine? Poison? Some kind of Voodoo potion? Blood? I tried to wiggle the cork free with my fingers, then my teeth. The sucker wouldn't budge.

"What have you done?" George Mudder's voice came from behind me.

Chapter Twenty-Four

I gasped at the sound of George's voice and almost dropped the bottle.

My heart galloping headlong toward a heart attack, I swung around. The room was empty, except for me. What the hell? Was I hearing voices now?

My breathing was shallow, but too loud. I double-checked each and every shadow for movement, but found nobody.

Was it a ghost?

No, you spaz. It was George's voice, and he was still kicking. At least he was the last time I saw him.

"You've gone too far," George said again, sounding as if he stood right next to me.

I noticed movement out of the corner of my eye. On the other side of the one-way glass, George stood next to the casket, looking down at the corpse. He was talking to the dead guy, not me. The sound system he'd been telling Natalie and me about earlier must still be on.

It looked like Cornelius had some competition. No wonder George wanted the haunted hotel.

Relief flooded my limbs, but the feeling didn't last long. I needed to get out of here now, before George found me playing voyeur.

"Do you hear me?" George said.

His one-sided conversation with a corpse gave me goosebumps. What else did he do with corpses?

I hurried toward the door, hoping George would keep right on chatting while I made my escape.

Where in the heck was Natalie, dammit? Maybe she went out to her pickup for some reason and was back in the records room, waiting for me.

"Do not speak to me with that disrespectful tone, you insignificant little speck," another voice said, freezing me in my tracks.

The tone was deep and rich, but terse, with a hint of something foreign discernible underneath the English. Something Slavic maybe, like Count Dracula. It reminded me of Kyrkozz's voice in my nightmare, and that made my knees wobbly. In slow motion, I turned back to look through the one-way glass.

On the other side of the coffin from George stood one of the two tall albino smokers I'd seen weeks ago on Mudder Brothers front porch. I'd nicknamed the two men Huey and Dewey, Donald Duck's nephews in grizzled form. Both men were tall and thin with thick tufts of pure white hair and bulbous eyes. Suit them up in matching sailor outfits and the caricature was complete.

Even though they had reminded me of cartoon ducks, something in their pale-eyed stares had made my skin crawl. Tonight, this particular albino was dressed in a black suit and black tie. Add some black sunglasses and he could start hunting down aliens. Who was he and where had he come from? Slagton? No, not with that accent.

The urge to run far and fast hit so hard my toes tingled. The French doors leading out of the parlor were still closed, so maybe I could sneak out the front door with neither man the wiser. Please, please, please let Natalie be sitting in her pickup waiting for me with a shit-eating grin on her face when I got there.

As I reached for the viewing room door knob, I heard George say, "What have you done with her?"

Her?

I whipped back around.

"I've removed her," the albino said.

"You can't just take her."

Her who? My heart fluttered. Oh, Jesus. Don't let him be

talking about Nat.

The albino shrugged, his broad straight shoulders lifting up and down all at once like he had a yoke on under his black suit jacket. "She saw what was in the crate." He rounded the coffin, heading toward the door on the other side of the room. "She must be eliminated."

I glanced over at the opened crate. "Oh, no," I whispered, taking a step toward the one-way glass. *Natalie* ... What had she done?

George blocked the doorway, keeping the albino from leaving the parlor. "You will not lay a hand on her," he said, shoving against the much taller man's chest. "Do you understand me?"

The albino didn't budge. "Or what, little mouse? What will you do? Try to hurt me?" His laugh was low and menacing. The sound chilled me clear through. I covered my mouth with my trembling hand.

George held his ground. "I'll go to your boss and have him put you back on a leash—where your kind belongs."

His kind? What kind was that?

"Squeak all you like, little mouse." The albino leaned over, his nose almost touching George's. "But be careful I don't eat you for dinner."

The big guy brushed George aside as if the funeral director was just clothing stuffed with goose down.

"No! Stop!" George shouted, making the mics screech.

My ear drums ringing, I watched him race out the open doorway after the albino.

She must be eliminated ...

I had to do something to save her. I ran to the door that led to the parlor.

Wait! I stopped, my hand squeezing the doorknob.

I had to think this through. Before I ran headlong after George and the albino, I needed a plan. Something other than jumping on the albino's back and bashing his brains in with my cell phone.

My cell phone. That was it!

I pulled up my contact list, scrolling down to Doc's name, and hit the Call button.

Ring.

Ring.

Ring.

"Damn it, Doc," I whispered. "Answer the goddamned phone for once."

After the fourth ring, his voice mail kicked in. Waiting for the fricking beep took forever.

"Doc," I whispered, "I'm at Mudder Brothers and the albino has Natalie. He's going to do something to her and George can't stop him. I need your help."

I hit the button to end the call and stood there, my hands really shaking now. *Come on, Doc, call me back.*

Eons later, which may have been just thirty seconds in non-panic time, my cell still hadn't rung.

I glared down at Doc's name on my contact list. Where was he?

Now what? I needed a Plan B.

I looked through the one-way glass. Still no George. No Eddie. No tall albino. Just the dead guy. My vision narrowed, tunneling on the corpse's hands. Shooting stars darted at the edge in my peripheral vision.

Breathe, Violet. Breathe.

I listened to the sane voice in my head, which sounded more like Aunt Zoe than me. After taking several deep, slow breaths through my nose, the stars faded. The tunneling widened until the shadowed edges disappeared. My senses returned, picking up the stale dusty scent of the straw from the crate, the hum of the mics coming from the other room through the speakers, the waft of cool air brushing across my hot cheeks.

I checked my phone. Still no Doc. My eyes locked onto the name above Doc's—Detective Cooper.

Right. Plan B.

I selected Cooper's name and hit the Call button.

He answered on the second ring. "This better be good, Parker," he said. "The waiter just brought my steak."

"Is that Violet?" Harvey asked in the background, sounding like his mouth was full. "Let me talk to her."

No! I needed the cop. "Cooper, they have Natalie," I whispered. "They're gonna hurt her."

I heard a chair scrape across the floor. The background chatter quieted. "Repeat that, Violet."

"They have Natalie. I was going to go help her, but I don't have any weapons."

"Who has her? Where are you?"

"Mudder Brothers."

"God damn it! I told you to stay away from there."

"Save the lecture for when I'm safely tucked behind bars. I've got a big problem here and I need your help now."

"Who has Natalie? George?"

"No. A big albino. He took her somewhere downstairs, I think. He's going to do something to her if we don't stop him quick."

"The albino," he said. "He's six-foot-five with short white hair and a birthmark on his left cheek shaped like a horseshoe, right?"

I hadn't noticed the birthmark. When had Cooper seen the albino?

That didn't matter now. "Yes, that's him. He told George that Natalie needs to be eliminated. I need to help her, but I don't know what to do. He's too big for me to take down."

"Stay right where you are—wait, where exactly are you?"

"The hidden room behind the one-way glass."

"Of course you are. Don't move. I'm on my way."

"Okay."

"I mean it, Violet. Stay put. Don't do anything stupid."

"Thanks for that vote of confidence after I called *you* instead of going after her on my own."

"Just shut up." He hung up on me.

I pocketed my cell phone. *Hurry, Cooper!*

Twisting my hands together, I walked back over to the opened crate. One of the black bottles would make a good weapon, but I'd rather hide behind Cooper's badge and gun.

I picked up a bottle and pulled on the cork, putting my nervous energy to work. It wiggled slightly. I squeezed the bottle between my arm and rib cage and tugged on the cork.

The sound of a distant scream played through the speakers.

I gasped, my lungs frozen in fear. *Natalie!* The bottle almost slipped from my grip.

The scream played again—louder, longer. Definitely female.

"Stop!" I cried, staring through the glass at the dead man's hands as if he was the one responsible.

Tears welled in my eyes, fear clogging my throat. I couldn't sit here. I couldn't stand by while my best friend was murdered. Cooper was just going to have to be pissed at me.

Clutching the bottle, I rushed through the door and into the parlor. My muscles crackled with adrenaline, making me feel like Jackie Chan's sidekick, but I knew better than to leap from the frying pan into the fire. I approached the other doorway on my tiptoes.

My visit to Mudder Brothers last week to identify the headless corpse had taught me the layout of the building. I peeked around the doorframe. To the left, a hallway led to a much smaller viewing room, and then out to the bathrooms and foyer. Across the hall was an office George used to console the deceased's family members and plan the funeral. To my right, a doorway led to the basement stairwell that ran parallel to the back of the building.

I kicked off my mule heels and trod barefoot down the steps, ready to bound back up them if George or Eddie or the albino appeared below me. At the bottom of the stair, I paused and listened. I knew the stairwell emptied into the elbow of an L-shaped hall, but I couldn't hear any voices or sounds of movement.

After sneaking a quick look, I eased out from the stairwell door. Straight ahead were two doors on the left and one on the right. I was pretty sure the first left-side door opened to the room full of those Civil War amputation cases and the big nasty scissors. The second door led to George's office, where Cooper had been waiting for me on a morning that now seemed like years ago rather than days. The door on the right could be a gateway to the planet Jupiter for all I knew.

To my right, the long leg of the L-shaped hall dead-ended at two sets of closed steel doors on each side. The pair on the right led outside, where I'd seen Ray and George hanging out with a crate a couple of times now. Those on the left with small square windows opened to the Autopsy room.

Which way should I go? If only Natalie would let out another scream, I'd have a heading, not to mention that I'd know she was still alive and breathing.

One of the overhead florescent tube-lights flickered at the end of the shorter hall, drawing my gaze. I noticed George's office door was opened a crack with the light on inside. A check of the autopsy room doors at the other end of the other hall showed no light in the windows.

George's office won the coin toss.

I tiptoed forward, shifting the bottle from one hand to the other. My sweaty palms made the glass neck slippery. I hoped like hell the thing wouldn't fly right out of my hands if I had to enter swinging.

If George was alone with Natalie in his office, I might have a chance of taking him. If the huge albino was there, too, the most I could hope to do was delay the two men long enough for Cooper and the cavalry to arrive. There was no way I could take the albino down, not with the way he brushed George aside as if he were a speck of dust on his sleeve. For him, I'd need a shotgun.

George must know I was still in the building. He either wasn't looking for me on purpose, or was too distracted by what the albino was doing to Natalie to pay me any mind.

Outside the door, I stopped, listening, hearing nothing. My throat felt powder dry, fear coating the back of my tongue.

My fingers quaked as I reached out and pushed open the door. It creaked and swung inward. The room looked the same as it had the last time, only Cooper and his ever present frown were missing and so was any other breathing being, thank God.

I raced inside and glanced behind the door just to make sure there was no boogeyman hiding there. The faint scent of George's cologne hovered in the room, but the little man was nowhere to be seen, nor was the albino.

And no Natalie, damn it.

I inched back out into the hallway, my ears pinned back, my internal radar scanning. The coast appeared to be as clear as it was going to get.

Next up on my to-do list—the gateway-to-Jupiter door. It was unlocked. When I opened it, I smelled grease, like a mechanic's break room. Upon further inspection, I discovered a lift system sitting in the middle of the small room. The lift had a grated, steel-plate floor attached to a few pulleys via cables.

On the other side of the lift, was a set of closed, windowless steel doors. I guessed they led to the autopsy room, and this was how the Mudders got caskets and bodies up to the parlor. It also explained how they moved the big crates up and downstairs.

I slipped back into the hallway. The sound of a door thumping shut around the corner and heavy footfalls coming toward me spurred the return of the stars and tunnel-vision effect. Crap. I was going to pass out right there at the bad guys' feet.

With seconds to spare, I dashed inside the antiques-filled room. The window in there could serve as an escape hatch, if needed. I eased the door closed behind me and backed up against it, gripping the door knob. I wanted to lock it, but if I pushed the lock button, whoever was coming might hear the click.

Breath held, I waited for the knob to turn in my hand, for the door to push against my back.

The sound of footsteps stopped for a count of three, and then faded in the other direction.

After I'd gulped a couple of breaths and the haze of panic that had filled my head cleared, I realized I'd forgotten to shut the lift room door.

Is that why the footfalls had stopped? Had someone— namely George—noticed the open door and gone looking for me upstairs?

My gaze skimmed over the large rectangular cases and freaky-shaped shadows from the light seeping under the door past my feet. The musty odor of rotting leather and cardboard reminded me of the records room upstairs.

Why did Natalie have to poke her nose in that goddamned crate? I could be home primping for an evening with Doc right now instead of gearing up to arm-wrestle a huge albino.

I pulled out my cell phone and hit a button to shed more light on the scene. Oddly enough, being able to distinguish the amputation saws and plexi-glass cases full of old-fashioned scalpels, bone shavers, and other deathly paraphernalia did not ease my quivering soul. That musty smell sat heavy on the back of my tongue, making me swallow to keep from gagging.

The window beckoned. The primal need to scratch and claw my way toward the safety of the orange streetlights and fresh air gave me a push of courage to move away from the door, my stronghold.

I stepped over a small stack of cases. A gleam to my left caught my attention. Within an arm's reach, hanging on the wall, were the shiny big scissors. The long steel blades screamed *lethal!* Now that I'd seen them up close, I had no doubt the suckers could lop off human appendages, including a head.

I reached out to touch one of the sharp edges, but then

pulled back. My fingerprint on a possible murder weapon might not go over well with Cooper.

Speaking of the cop, where in the hell was he? Maybe that explained the footfalls. Cooper might be upstairs, distracting George at this very moment. That meant Natalie might be alone with the albino, who wouldn't dare do anything to make her scream while the cops were on the scene.

Unless he gagged her ... or silenced her permanently.

That instinct to flee for safety eased. I turned back to the door. It was time to stop messing around and find my best friend.

I shoved my phone into my pocket. In my other hand, I still clutched the bottle. While my conscious mind had paused to sniff the lilies, my subconscious remained prepared for attack. Thank God some part of me was able to stay focused.

Easing the door open, I checked both ways. The hall was empty. I pulled the door the rest of the way open. The small creak of the hinges made me wince, but it was too quiet to be heard beyond the bend in the hallway.

I stepped over the threshold and pulled the door closed behind me, turning toward the stairs.

Someone grabbed me around my waist from behind. My scream was stifled by a large, callused hand that covered my mouth and blocked my breath.

My attacker jerked me backwards. Our feet tangled and I stepped on the toe of his shoe. He stumbled, dragging me with him. Just as he tried to catch himself, I planted my right foot on the floor and shoved hard. We lurched through the doorway into George's office, his hand still covering my lips. Losing his balance, he fell, dragging me down on top of him.

As we landed, I whipped my head back, trying to free my mouth enough to bite his hand. My skull connected with something soft that crunched from the impact. After a grunt, the hand on my lips went limp.

I shoved his hand away and scrambled to my feet, whirling and raising the bottle at the same time just in case he was playing possum.

Then I gasped.

Detective Cooper laid spread eagle on the floor, blood seeping from his left nostril. Uh, oh. I didn't remember his nose being crooked before.

"Shit," I whispered and squatted over him, making sure he still had a pulse. He did, thankfully.

Rising to my feet, I grimaced at the unmoving detective. Now what in the hell was I going to do for backup? If Cooper didn't bring any of the other boys in blue with him, I was fucked.

Way to go, ninja princess.

If I lived through this mess tonight, Cooper was going to kill me when he woke up.

A muffled high-pitched scream laden with panic rang out from down the hall. My skin prickled at the sound of it.

I looked down at Cooper's handgun, riding in his shoulder holster. A cold layer of calm fell over me. I knew what I had to do.

"Enough of this shit," I whispered, putting the bottle down on the floor next to him and yanking his gun free.

I ran out the door and down the short section of the hall, Cooper's gun pointed at the floor just in case a cop jumped out in front of me. At the stairwell doorway, I banked left and hurried down the long hall. Slowing as I neared the autopsy double doors, I crouched below the windows.

Success here would depend on the element of surprise. I squeezed the door handle and pulled the steel slab open with my left hand, entering with the handgun raised in my right.

The sight stopped me just over the threshold.

No. Fucking. Way.

The closing door bumped me in the ass, nudging me into the room.

Ray lay on the autopsy table where the decapitated body had been last week, his wrists and ankles strapped down.

Unlike the other guy, Ray still had his head. The rag

stuffed in his mouth poked out from a strip of duct-tape.

Like the decapitated body, Ray, too, was naked.

I tried not to look in the general direction of his mid-section as I crossed toward him, but by then it was too late. The image had been burned into my brain the moment I'd stepped into the room, the knowledge of his lack of tan lines embedded in my memory until death did us part.

Ray's wide, panic-filled gaze held mine. He yelled something through the rag, but I couldn't understand him. I ripped the tape off with a little more glee than a rescuer probably should have and pulled the rag free. I set the cloth down on a metal tray on a table next to Ray's head, noticing the array of frightening-looking autopsy tools laid out on the stainless steel. What had they been planning for him? A live autopsy? I shuddered.

"Get me loose," Ray said, his voice raspy. "Hurry before he comes back."

He? Not *they*? Was he talking about Eddie?

I tucked the gun into the back of my waistband, hoping like hell I didn't end up with my ass shot yet again. The metal felt cool and empowering against my sweaty lower back. No wonder Cooper was so sure of himself.

Starting at Ray's left hand, I tugged on the straps, keeping my eyes averted from his naked nether regions. "What the hell is going on here, Ray?"

"What's it look like, Blondie?" he snapped, his usual sneer in place.

I stopped with his hand still strapped tight and glared at him. "Get yourself free, dickhead. I have a friend to save."

I turned to leave.

"Wait!" He cried at my back. "I'm sorry, Violet."

I couldn't remember the last time I'd heard him say my name. It was a nice change, but I kept walking toward the door. "Fuck you, Ray."

"Violet," my name came out as a sob this time. "Please don't leave me here like this. He's going to come back and cut me."

If we were talking castration, bring on the buttered popcorn and soda pop.

At the door, I hesitated. Damn it. Natalie needed me, possibly more than this asshole. But no matter how much the part of me that had taken Ray's shit for months wanted to walk away and not look back, I couldn't leave him tied to the autopsy table.

As I turned to free him, I heard voices on the other side of the door.

"Someone's coming," I mouthed and rushed to the tall pantry-like cupboards on the far wall where I'd seen Eddie hang his lab apron the last time I was here.

"Wait!" Ray whispered.

"Shhhh." I pulled the gun from my pants and showed it to him. "I won't let them hurt you."

That was big talk for someone who had trouble stepping on spiders.

I climbed into the cupboard, grimacing at the chemical odor coming from Eddie's coats, and pulled the door partly closed behind me. Better chemicals than something red and chunky, I told myself.

I heard the Autopsy room doors creak and swoosh shut. Through the cupboard opening, I watched the albino approach the table full of tools next to Ray, George followed, nipping at his heels.

Ray lay strapped down between them and me, his eyes darting back and forth between us. The idiot was going to get me caught if he didn't knock it off. I held the gun raised and ready. Sweat trickled down my spine.

"Tell me where you hid the girl or I'll kill this one," the albino said, his back to me now, blocking my line of sight to George.

"I told you there will be no killing tonight. We can clean this up without bloodshed."

"You're a fool if you believe that. This one has looked in

the crate one too many times. The woman should have left with her friend."

He must mean me. Goosebumps peppered my arms at the thought of him watching without my knowing it. George must have lied about me leaving to save me from joining Natalie.

"Both need to be disposed of," the albino continued, "before someone comes looking for them." He picked up the largest scalpel and leaned toward Ray's face.

Ray screamed like a woman.

I winced at the piercing level, blinking at the realization that all of this time I'd been hearing him screaming for help, not Natalie. Where was she then? Where had George tucked her away?

The albino stuffed the rag back in Ray's mouth, his bulging eyes narrowed. "Someone took off your muffle." He placed the scalpel tip at the upper corner of Ray's eye socket.

I gripped the gun harder, gearing up to leap out of the cupboard and start shooting. I prayed I didn't trip.

"Tell me who," he said to Ray, "or I'll remove your eyeball and feed it to you."

"No!" George shouted and shoved the autopsy table with Ray on it away from the albino and his scalpel.

The table skidded sideways, and I saw the wheels on it for the first time. One of the wheels stayed locked straight and caught on a floor drain, spilling the whole cart on its side with Ray still strapped on tight. His weight created enough momentum to pull the table upside down on top of him. With his cheek pressed against the cement floor, he stared at me, his eyes wide and brimmed with terror.

"Enough of you," the albino raged at George.

I looked up from Ray at the same time the tall man lunged at George. The albino's arms pulled back with what appeared to be long shiny blades in each hand, his huge body blocking most of George from my view.

There was a metallic clang, and then a thump.

Pushing the cupboard door open further, I leaned out to see what was happening. The albino moved sideways just then, giving me a full-on view of George's body as it crumpled to the floor, his neck sliced clean, his head no longer in place.

Covering my mouth, I gasped inwardly. *Oh, my God! Oh, my God! Oh, my God!*

"Stupid little mouse." The albino walked around the top of the overturned autopsy table, his swords no longer in his hands, and squatted in front of Ray with his back to me. "I've grown tired of your screaming."

I couldn't take my eyes off of where George had stood just seconds before, my brain replaying the scene again and again. Then, from somewhere deep within my core, a cold wave of clarity splashed over me.

I shoved open the cupboard door, Cooper's gun leveled out in front of me. "Freeze, asshole!" I said.

The albino's head turned slowly, like he'd been expecting me to pop out of the cupboard at any time. His sneer scrunched his whole face, making him look like a huge gargoyle squatting there, ready to pounce.

"What have we here?" he said in a calm, quiet voice.

"Get the fuck away from him," I said, the gun aimed at the center of the albino's head.

He stood with slow deliberation that oozed of confidence. He snorted at the gun in my hand. "What are you going to do?"

I stared down the barrel at him, wondering that myself.

He challenged me with a cock of his head. "Shoot me?"

"Maybe."

His laughter resonated so deep that it made my ears ache. How did he do that? He took a step toward me. "I've grown to like pain over time."

I eased toward the door. "Don't move."

"I like it a lot." Another step in my direction. His lips curled back from his teeth, which all seemed longer than normal, his gums almost gray.

I moved faster toward the exit. "One more step and I swear I'll shoot."

"I especially like delivering my kind of pain." He pulled out a long, shiny hook that looked like it was wrapped with barbed wire from his inner suit coat pocket.

That was enough inspiration for me. I aimed at his thigh and pulled the trigger.

The boom was deafening in the stainless steel-filled room. A searing hot casing bounced off my wrist and clinked onto the floor. The smell of gun smoke surrounded me.

His sinister laughter throbbed deep in my ears, making me cringe. With only a slight pause, he took another step toward me, his eyes gleaming so bright they seemed to glow.

I raised the gun, aiming at his gut and pulled the trigger again. Boom!

He jolted as if from the force of the blow, but kept

coming.

Was I shooting blanks?

My back was now against the door. "Stop or I'll aim for the heart."

He tipped his head back and roared at the ceiling, a guttural roar that made my knees shake.

I pulled the trigger, jerking at the last minute and grazing the top of his shoulder. Damn it! I adjusted, breathed through my nose like I'd been taught by my dad long ago, and shot again, twice, nailing him square in the chest. I was sure of it.

Stopping finally, he tugged his jacket aside and stuck his pinkie in a bullet hole just below the left side of his collarbone. When he pulled his finger out, blood smeared the tip. He raised his eyes to mine, his pupils morphing into snake-like slits.

What the fuck?

"That's enough playing, wench," he said, snarling. "Now it's my—"

I didn't give him time to finish that threat. I shoved out through the door behind me and sprinted for the stairs like the devil was grasping at my tail. Halfway there, I realized I should have headed straight out the back doors instead. Shit!

A crash thundered behind me. I glanced over my shoulder. The albino stalked after me, his face brimming with mad glee. Here came the big bad wolf.

I reached the doorway to the stair, looking back again as I skidded around the stairwell opening, and slammed into someone's chest, bouncing off. I stumbled.

"Violet," Doc said, catching me before I fell. His eyes widened at the sight of the gun in my hand. "Are you … ?" Then he must have heard the albino's footfalls. He glanced over his shoulder, his eyelids narrowing. "Give me the gun, Violet."

"Bullets don't work," I said, but I shoved the butt of it at him, anyway.

"Get out of here," he said, gripping Cooper's gun.

"No, Doc—"

"Go! You have kids." He shoved me away and faced the albino.

I couldn't get around him to the stair, so I ran toward the antique-filled room, thinking of that window.

Gunshots rang out, so many, so fast that I couldn't count them. I shoved into the room and leapt over a stack of plexiglass cases, the window in my sights.

A loud thump came from the other side of the wall, rattling the big scissors hanging there.

Doc? I stopped below the window, the bright orange glow beyond beckoning.

No.

I turned back toward the doorway. I'd seen what the albino could do with the swords hidden in his coat sleeves. George was dead. There was no way I was losing Doc to that pale-faced freaky-ass murderer.

Grabbing the big scissors off the wall, I raced back to the door in time to watch Doc fly past backward, crashing into the door across the hall.

Doc!

He slid to the floor, groaning, his eyes rolling back as his body followed suit.

I stepped back from view as the albino stalked past, his focus on Doc who lay on the floor out cold.

The albino bent over Doc. "Silly humans," I heard him mutter and he pulled his arms back, spreading them wide, like he had right before he decapitated George.

No!

I rushed at him, the scissors open and held out like dual swords in front of me. With a grunt, I buried the sharp blades into his back. My momentum rammed him forward into the doorjamb. I bounced off of him and spun away, crashing into the wall next to George's office door.

The albino bellowed, a deep grating, unearthly sound. I covered my ears, screaming, too.

Pushing to my feet, I edged toward the stairs. I knew that at any moment, he'd somehow yank those blades out and come for me.

He fell to his knees, frantically reaching for the blades. His body shook so hard that his bulbous features distorted, lengthening.

I thought I saw a snout, then a horn, then a beak, then a nose again. Everything on him blended and blurred. My breath locked in my lungs. I pressed back against the wall, unable to make sense of what I was seeing.

In a blink, he stilled and glared up at me with those snake-slit eyes. His upper lip curled. "*You* again."

Chapter Twenty-Five

M *e, again?*
What the hell did that mean?
Before I could do more than squeak like a cornered rat, the albino's skin caught on fire, just as Wolfgang's had in my nightmare.

No, no, no, no ... not again. A whiff of burning hair and skin made me cough and retch.

A bright flash of white light burst from his skin, blinding me, followed by a searing blast of heat. I cried out, shielding my face.

Then the fireworks show came to an abrupt end. In the silence, something clattered onto the floor.

When I dropped my arm, the albino was gone, a haze of smoke the only evidence of what I'd witnessed. Left alone with my panting breaths, I fell back against the doorjamb. My eyes burned like I'd stared into the sun for too long.

I looked at the floor, expecting to see ashes, burnt pieces of clothing, some trace of the fire. Instead, the huge pair of scissors I'd planted in the albino's back lay there, shiny and sharp, blood-free.

How? What? Where did he ... ?

A hand clamped down on my shoulder.

I shrieked. Tugging free of the grasp, I sprinted for the stairwell.

"Violet!" Cooper's voice stopped me at the foot of the stairs. He sounded nasally, like his nose was stuffed up.

I turned back. The detective stood next to where Doc lay.

"Come back here," he ordered.

I took a couple of steps toward him, obeying without

thinking, and then I noticed how beat up his face looked and hesitated. His nose was swollen now in addition to being crooked. Blood smeared his upper lip. His eyes were already turning black and blue.

Oh, man, I'd done a number on him. He was going to go all Terminator on my ass if I got too near him.

"Come closer," he said.

"I don't want to."

"Why not?"

"Because you're going to hurt me."

"As tempting as that might be right now, I won't. I promise."

I took a couple of steps closer, but stopped still out of reach.

"Where's my gun?" he asked.

I pointed at the floor next to Doc's hand.

Cooper picked it up, scowling. "It's missing the bullets."

"I needed to borrow a few."

His gunslinger glare made me pull back, glancing at the steps—my getaway route. "Do you happen to remember where you left them?"

That took a moment of thought. Things had gone a bit nutzo after Ray started with his girlie screams. Heck, I still wasn't even sure if the snake-eyed albino had disappeared for good, or if he'd used the old smoke and mirrors trick to hide somewhere and planned to grab me as I passed.

"Surely you remember firing my gun."

My glare mimicked his. "Of course I remember." I looked to my right, down the long hallway. "I used five in the Autopsy room." The casings were on the floor somewhere.

"What about the rest?"

"I think Doc used them."

"You think? Where were you when he was shooting them? In the bathroom standing on the seat again?"

I realized that Cooper probably had a not-so-nice headache thanks to the back of my skull, but his snarky comment dug into me like a pointy pair of spurs. I strode over to him. "I'm sorry I wasn't taking detailed notes, Detective, but I was a little busy running for my damned life. Where in the hell were you when your gun was being shot? Oh, that's right, passed out."

He jutted his chin "Knocked out."

"You shouldn't have scared the shit out of me like that."

"*You* should have stayed up in the viewing room like I told you to."

"I heard screaming. I thought it was Natalie."

"So, you ran into the middle of a possible murder scene without backup or a weapon."

"I had a bottle."

"Jesus, Violet. Who brings a bottle to a gun fight?"

"Someone whose best friend might get killed if she doesn't do something."

Cooper plowed his fingers through his hair. "One of these days …"

"What? You're going to throw me in jail?"

"If you live long enough, yeah, maybe I will, damn it."

I saw Doc's leg twitch in my peripheral vision.

Something inside of me crashed back to earth. Fear for Doc and Natalie whooshed back into my thoughts so fast my ears rang.

I rushed to Doc, kneeling next to him, squeezing his hand. "Doc?"

A groan rumbled up from his chest. His eyelids fluttered open, his dark eyes darting to and fro. When he focused on me, his eyebrows pinched together.

"Are you okay?" I asked

"I think so. Are you?"

I nodded. "How many of me do you see?"

"One."

"Good."

He grunted. "I know. One of you is all I can handle."

Cooper squatted on the other side of Doc. "Can you

move your arms and legs?"

"Yeah." Doc wiggled a little to make sure. Then his gaze shifted to Cooper and he grimaced. "Christ! What happened to you?"

"I tried to assist Violet. She didn't want my help."

"Ah," Doc gave a little nod. "She's tougher than she looks. Believe me, I know." He turned his head so Cooper could see his black eye and cheek bruise full on.

Cooper checked it out, and then glowered at me. "What is wrong with you?"

Doc tried to sit up.

"It wasn't my fault," I said, reaching for Doc. "Maybe you should lie still, Doc. It looked like you hit your head pretty hard."

"I'm okay. Just sore."

Cooper and I helped him sit up and lean back against the wall next to the doorjamb.

Doc rubbed the back of his head. "That last throw must have knocked me out."

"Throw? Who threw you?" Cooper asked, accusing me with his glare.

"What? You think I could actually pick Doc up and throw him?"

"Who knows what you're capable of when you're all jacked up on adrenaline."

I heard the scuff of a shoe behind me and jerked around, afraid the albino had returned for Round Two.

A pair of cops crouched in the stairwell entryway, guns drawn. They must have crept downstairs while Cooper had me distracted.

They looked at the three of us in turn, and then focused on Cooper. "What's the situation?"

Cooper turned to me, all straight-faced and business-only. "Spill."

"I don't know where Natalie is."

"When did you last see her?"

"Upstairs, about twenty minutes before I called you." I almost told him that the albino took her, but that would lead to a lot of questions about a man who'd turned into smoke and disappeared when we needed to be looking for Natalie. "I checked the Autopsy room, George's office, and in there." I pointed at the antique-filled room. "She could be upstairs, but I don't think so." *Because the albino and George came down here.*

"One of you check the rooms upstairs for Natalie Beals," Cooper instructed the officers, "the other search the garage. Stay alert. We don't know the location of George or Eddie Mudder or if they're armed."

"George Mudder's body is in the Autopsy room," I told them, shivering at the memory of his decapitated corpse folding to the floor. "Ray Underhill is in there, too. He's alive and tied to a table."

"Where's Eddie?" Cooper asked.

"I don't know. I haven't seen him all night."

Cooper stood, pulling a clip from a pocket inside his jacket, and reloaded his gun. "You two go look in the garage. I'll deal with the mess in the Autopsy room." He grabbed my arm after they headed toward the back door, his grip firm, almost bruising. "Don't go far, Ms. Parker. You and I need to have a little powwow."

"Am I going to the station?"

"Not yet, but the night is young and I need a statement."

He strode away and I focused back on Doc. "Are you sure you're okay?"

"Yeah, just beat up a bit. Where's the big albino?"

"You didn't see what happened to him?"

"No. I remember him choking me, and then going airborne—twice, first into the wall over there." I looked where he pointed and grimaced at the caved-in drywall. "Then here."

Damn, I could have used a witness to back up my story later when I explained everything to Cooper.

"You should probably go to the hospital, Doc."

"I'm fine. A couple of ibuprofen will do wonders." He frowned at the dented wall. "Violet, the bullets didn't even slow him down."

"I know."

He looked back at me. "So, where is he? Tell me what happened."

I checked over my shoulder to make sure Cooper or his men weren't there. "He disappeared." I felt silly saying it aloud.

"You mean he got out of here before Cooper woke up?"

"No. I mean he just disappeared in a flash of light and a little explosion like a magician. I had to shield my eyes when it happened, and when I looked back, he was gone. Totally gone."

Doc's brow furrowed. "You're skipping something."

I was pretty much skipping most of the evening's fun and games, figuring I'd save the gory details for later when Doc and Natalie and I were safe and sound somewhere other than here.

"He threw you," I told Doc, "then leaned over you like he was going to kill you—same as he did George. That's when I stabbed him in the back with those." I pointed at the big scissors on the floor. "Then he kind of short-circuited and caught on fire."

"Like Wolfgang at the séance?"

"Yes, only much faster. After the fire came the light show and explosion. All he left behind were the scissors and some smoke."

"So, bullets wouldn't stop him, but a pair of scissors in the back did. That doesn't make any sense."

What part of this whole Mudder-mess did? The secret shipments? The unmarked glass bottles? Naked Ray? The albino's snake-like eyes? Hysterical laughter bubbled up my throat. I squeezed my eyes shut and counted to five, fighting off the crazy giggles.

When I opened my eyes, Doc was watching me. "You

sure you're okay?" he asked.

"I'm fine."

"Because for just a moment there," he tucked a strand of hair behind my ear, "your expression kind of went all fierce and crazed, and your cheeks turned dark pink."

I grabbed his hand and held his palm against my cheek, leaning into it. I just wanted to stare into his eyes like a lovesick puppy until everything else went away—the cops, the dead bodies, the freaky shit, the fears for Natalie and my family.

"Did the big guy say anything that might hint at who he was or where he came from?" he asked, splashing cold water on our little moment.

I pulled away from his touch and told him about the fight with George that I'd witnessed first upstairs, and then in the Autopsy room. "When the albino leaned toward George, he pulled his arms back like this," I mimicked the pre-slicing action, "and these swords came out of his sleeves. Before I realized what was going on, he cut off George's head."

Doc sat forward. "And you saw it all happen?"

I nodded. Each time I replayed tonight's scenes, I kept expecting my throat to burn or my eyes to water, but nothing happened. I felt hardened, crusted over.

"Violet." Doc picked up my hand, rubbing his thumb over the back of it. "You're not okay. Witnessing that is going to mess you up."

"Most likely," I agreed. When the shock of it all had passed, I'd probably be comatose for days. This was going to add some new flavors to my nightmares. "But on the bright side, at least I didn't get tied to a damned chair this time."

Doc grinned and kissed my knuckles. "You saved my life tonight."

"You stepped between the albino and me, taking a beating in my place. I think that makes us even." I interlaced my fingers with his.

"Your call came when I was driving up through the

canyon from Sturgis," he explained. "I had no signal."

"Just my luck."

"Your message scared the hell out of me. I couldn't get here fast enough."

"I was trying to stay out of trouble tonight, I swear, but Natalie disappeared, and then all hell broke loose."

He looked back at the dented wall, his gaze narrowing. "The bullets didn't stop him," he said as if he was cross-examining every word, "but the scissors did."

"Maybe he had on a Kevlar vest."

"I hit him in the cheek with one. There should have been blood splatter, but the blood instantly coagulated in the hole. I saw it up close when he had me by the throat." Doc's frown deepened. "Did he say anything to you at all in the Autopsy room after he killed George?"

"He waxed on about his love of pain and torture. It was quite moving." As in moving me right out the door. Then I remembered something. "Right before he disappeared, he gave me this creepy stare." I didn't mention the snake eyes because it sounded completely delusional. "And he said, 'You again.' That was it."

"You again?"

I nodded.

"What does that mean?"

"I saw him once a few weeks ago when Natalie and I came for a viewing. He was out on the front porch smoking with a guy that looked like his twin. Maybe he remembered me."

"So, where's his twin?"

"Exactly. That's the million dollar question." I shivered, wondering if I now had a target on my back.

Doc tugged me closer. "You're going to have to tell Detective Cooper some of this, you know."

I wrinkled my nose. "The albino's magic trick is going to ruin any credibility I have with him."

"Better that than him tagging you with a 'suspect' label."

"You mean 'usual suspect.' My old standby." The thought of sitting through another interrogation with the detective sounded about as appealing as having all of my nose hairs plucked one by one. "God, I wish we were home on Aunt Zoe's couch watching the Duke ride across the western horizon right now." Natalie, too. *Where was she?* Chewing on my lower lip, I glanced down the hall.

"Natalie is alive, Violet." Doc seemed to read my thoughts.

"I hope to hell you're right. If anything happened to her …" I trailed off, not wanting to go any further with that thought.

"I am." Doc squeezed my hand. "If this is your idea of a date, I'm going to need to wear some protection next time. Body armor might cut it."

I smiled, liking the sound of a *next time*. "So, this thing between you and me …" I hesitated.

One of his eyebrows arched up. "What about it?"

"It's going to be about more than just sex, huh?"

"Yeah," he leaned toward me, his mouth closing in. "I think so."

"Are you ready for that?"

"Mostly." He angled his head to the side. "Are you?"

"I don't know," I whispered against his lips, my eyes closing. "I don't have the best track record."

"Playing the odds is what I do best, Boots." His lips brushed mine, soft and caressing. Then his hand cupped the back of my neck, pulling me into him.

I opened my mouth under his onslaught, trying to forget my worries and fears. I thought of him racing to help me, putting himself between me and the albino, and my heart tumbled over the edge into oblivion.

Someone gasped behind me. "No!"

Natalie!

I yanked away from Doc.

Natalie stood at the end of the hall, her face rigid,

stretched tight in pain. She clutched a gray blanket around her like a cloak on a frigid morning. Her eyes grew icy behind their watery rims as we stared at each other. "How long, Violet?" she asked, her voice trembling.

"Natalie, I've been try—"

"Don't! Just tell me how long this has been going on?"

"A month." Give or take a week.

She jerked as if I'd slapped her. "You, of all people. How could you?"

Nothing I could say would fix what I'd done to her. My eyes welled. "I'm so sorry, Nat."

She shook her head. "You two must have had some good laughs at my expense. No wonder you wanted me to move back home." Her jaw jutted. She turned to the man beside her. "Get me out of here."

Only then did I notice Cooper standing next to her. He ushered her toward the steps.

"Violet," Cooper pointed at me, his gaze warning. "I'll be right back."

As they clomped up the stairs, something inside of me cracked. Tears poured out, trailing down my cheeks.

"Come here, Trouble," Doc said, hugging me.

I did a bang-up job of soaking his shirt.

* * *

A couple of hours later, I sat alone in Cooper's office at the Deadwood Police Station—my new home away from home. Several of the officers I passed on the way in were on a first name basis with me now, as in "Hey! It's Violet again," and "Welcome back, Spooky Parker."

Detective Cooper sat behind his desk, his nose bandaged thanks to the EMTs who had arrived on scene at Mudder Brothers, along with a horde of cops, shortly after Natalie left. They were the same EMTs who'd insisted Doc go to the hospital after one had shined a light in Doc's eyes and stated that he'd suffered a mild concussion. Cooper's insistence that Doc get checked out was obeyed only with a promise that the detective wouldn't throw me in jail until Doc was available to bail me out.

Upstairs in the main viewing parlor, I'd recited my take of the evening's events to Cooper while Mr. Haskell rested there, listening. After the third time I'd stopped mid-story to frown at the dead guy's hand, Cooper closed the coffin lid.

When I finished, Cooper had one of his men walk with me across the street to the cop shop, where he'd joined me a short time later in his office. After he brought me some bitter, burnt coffee, I told my story yet again. With each telling, Cooper's frown lines deepened.

He leaned back in his seat, steepling his fingers together while squinting at me. "Now, let me get this straight."

"You put the lime in the coconut, you drank 'em both up," I sang, Harry Nilsson's tune popping into my head. I blamed post-traumatic stress disorder.

Cooper's eyes narrowed. "Funny, Ms. Parker. You're a real comedian. In lieu of your sad attempt at humor, let's go through the events that took place after you called me one more time."

I growled in frustration and sat back in his torture chair, the vinyl cushion squished flat. "I've told you exactly what happened from start to finish twice now. There's nothing more to it."

"I beg to differ. There are gaping holes in your story, which ends with a magical disappearing act."

"I'm telling the truth as I witnessed it."

"How do I know that you didn't use that big pair of shears to cut off George Mudder's head yourself, and then clean up all of the blood?"

I glared at him. "Why would I do that?"

"You tell me. There should have been a bloody mess in that room, yet there wasn't."

The lack of blood still had me scratching my head. At the

time, I had been too focused on the albino to think about it. Now, though, after hearing the EMT tell Cooper it appeared the wound had been cauterized instantly, I couldn't make sense of it. I'd seen the blades come from the albino's sleeves, I was sure of it. Could they have been superheated? Right, yet they didn't catch his sleeves on fire.

Shrugging, I said, "Why don't you just ask Ray about George's murder? He was in there with me when it happened."

"Ray claims not to have been able to see anything in relation to George's murder. He wasn't even sure George was dead until I unstrapped him from the gurney."

Great. My innocence now depended on Ray clearing me of George's death. I could only imagine how Ray would use this little kernel as leverage over me. "Did you ask him about the albino?"

"No, because I didn't know all of the details about 'the albino,'" he smirked as he said the name, "until Ray was removed from the scene of the crime. I'll touch base with him tomorrow."

It wasn't fair that Ray and Natalie got to go home while here I sat, fighting for my innocence. All I'd wanted to do tonight was research a freaking name.

There was something I wondered about while I'd been waiting for Cooper to join me in his office. "Why was Ray even there tonight? Have you asked yourself that question?"

"No."

"Why not?"

"Because I know why he was there."

That made me sit up straight. "You do?"

"Yes. He was running shipments for George. He got too nosey and opened a crate, even though I'd warned him not to yet."

"You warned him?" I glared at him. "You mean you knew about him working with the Mudder brothers this whole time?"

He nodded.

"Why didn't you tell me?"

Cooper cocked his head to the side. "Because I was unaware that you were hired by the Deadwood Police Department as an undercover detective. And here all along I thought you were just my Realtor."

He met my wrinkled upper lip head on. "So, Ray was working with you and with George Mudder, like a double agent."

"More like a snitch. This isn't a James Bond film."

I guffawed at Cooper, a beat up Daniel Craig clone. Oh, the irony. "So, why were you keeping tabs on George Mudder? Was it the crates?"

"Partly."

"Did Ray tell you what he found when he looked in the crates? Was it more glass bottles?" Or some other illegal contraband?

"I'm not at liberty to say at this time."

As usual, Cooper was keeping me at arm's length. I narrowed my eyes. "You know what this means, right?"

"No, enlighten me."

"You pull me in here and ask all kinds of questions to find out what I know about the whole deal because you don't have the answers. If you won't share anything in return, tell me why I should help you?"

"Trust me, Ms. Parker, you haven't helped. You've managed to screw up a six-month-long investigation on a possible drug and weapons trafficking operation in a single night."

"That's not true," I told him, tapping my index finger on his desktop with each word. "You said Ray peeked when he wasn't supposed to. It sounds to me like Ray screwed it up, and I saved him from being the victim of a live autopsy and you from having a dead snitch on your conscience."

Cooper's lips thinned and he sat back, visually corralling his inner pissed-off beast. "From what we can tell, the same type of weapon used to decapitate the body we found in Uncle Willis's cemetery was used on George Mudder. Now, you say this big magical albino had swords in his coat sleeves."

"Yes."

"You're willing to sign off on that in my report."

"Yes. I saw the swords twice. Once with George, and again when he was leaning over Doc."

"Right. And then the albino just disappeared in a puff of smoke. Hey, maybe he was part dragon."

I nodded, biting my lower lip. "I knew you were going to make fun of me if I told you the truth. I should have just lied."

"I'm not making fun of you, Ms. Parker. I'm just having trouble believing your rather tall tale."

Tall tale, huh? "Well, you would have seen it all for yourself, Detective Cooper, if you hadn't been snoozing on the floor of George's office."

"You mean if you hadn't knocked me out and stolen my gun."

"I didn't steal it. I borrowed it to go save my friend."

"I ordered you to stay upstairs, Violet. You shouldn't have been sneaking around in the basement, playing superhero."

"You shouldn't have taken so damned long to get there, and then snuck up behind me when you finally did."

He touched his bandaged nose. "Why can't you mind your own business and stick to selling real estate?"

In spite of my frustration with Cooper, I felt a twinge of guilt. "I'm sorry about your nose."

"Your apology is still not accepted." He sat back in his chair, crossing his arms over his chest.

What was it with men holding grudges about a black eye or two?

"What was in the other crates?" I pressed.

"That's police business."

Fine. If he was going to play that way, I wasn't going to tell him about the black glass bottle that I'd hidden under

Mudder Brothers front porch to grab later after the place had cleared out. One way or another, I was going to get some answers, because that albino had a twin. I had a feeling he wasn't going to be doing any happy dances about me having stabbed his brother in the back.

"Where did you find Natalie?" I asked, pushing aside the gut ache that came with thinking about my former best friend.

"In the garage. He'd locked her in the freezer."

"With the bodies?"

"Only the decapitated corpse. Mr. Haskell was in the parlor."

Only the corpse. Ick. "Did she say who locked her in there?"

"She doesn't know. Someone hit her from behind when she was in the room you were supposed to stay in until I arrived on scene."

Head injuries seemed to be contagious tonight. Then I thought of George's fate and sobered.

Wait, Natalie was hit on the back of the head? "So, she didn't actually see George hit her?"

"How could she if she was hit in the back of the—oh, you think your albino knocked her out."

"Yes." I knew so. With the way George had tried to protect her, he wouldn't have knocked her out, he'd have shooed her away with some excuse about the crate's contents. He'd probably locked her in the freezer to keep her safe. Poor George.

"Well, until we have any evidence that the albino guy was there with …"

"What about Ray?" I blurted.

"What about him?"

"He saw the albino." He'd almost been cut by him until George interfered.

"He didn't mention it tonight when we got him out of there, but he was in shock. Like I said, I'll pay him a visit tomorrow."

"Where was Eddie? Was he tied up somewhere, too?"

"He came home right before I joined you here. He'd been down in Rapid. George had told him to take the night off."

George must have known the albino was going to be there. Damn it. I kept hitting walls, which reminded me of something. "How do you explain Doc's concussion if there is no albino?"

"I'm not saying there wasn't another party present, Ms. Parker, or that a tall white-haired man isn't responsible for some of the carnage. I'm just struggling with your tale of how he disappeared."

Well, at least he wasn't pinning it all on me.

Cooper leaned forward, his elbows on his desk. "We need a suspect, Violet. Until then, you and I will be going over your story again and again, looking for clues that will lead me to the person responsible for George's death."

"So, I'm not under arrest?"

"No. You're a person of interest."

What was new? "Fine. Are we done here?"

"We never seem to be done, you and me. But for now, you can go home."

I walked toward the door.

"Just remember," Cooper's voice stalled me. "Don't be taking any long trips out of state."

"Or what?"

He sat back. "Trust me, Violet, you don't want me to come looking for you."

After the evening I'd had, his threat poked the grizzly snarling inside of me. "With your track record, Detective Cooper, I don't think you could find me even if I was wearing bells."

His face went all spaghetti western gunfighter on me. I half expected him to take out a cigar, bite the end off, and spit it out at my feet. "Don't forget about my open house on Sunday, Ms. Parker."

"I'll be there," I said with a smile. "With bells on."

Chapter Twenty-Six

Saturday, August 25th

Two days later, I woke up to the sound of my cell phone ringing. The clock said it was still the butt crack of dawn, and since it wasn't a school day, I refused to wake up and chatter about it with the birds. I rolled over, letting it go to voicemail. I had just started sinking back into sleep when it rang again.

"Damn it," I grumbled and grabbed the phone, looking at the number.

Cooper!

I hit the answer button. "Am I under arrest?"

"Why do you always think the worst of me?"

"Hmmm, I wonder."

"I talked to Ray yesterday," Cooper said.

I hadn't. I didn't go into work all day, just hung out at home with Aunt Zoe, letting her coddle me and convince me that everything was going to be okay. According to Mona, Ray hadn't shown up at work, either, or Jane for that matter. I wondered if Jane was nursing Ray back to health, not that he'd been injured according to Mona, just scared shitless.

Welcome to my world.

"Did you give him my love?" I asked, trying not to remember what Ray looked like naked. But that image had been burned into my brain, and I decided I was doomed to have it on file until I keeled over.

"He mentioned your albino."

I sat up. "He did?"

"He said your albino was the one who strapped him to the gurney and threatened to perform an autopsy on him while he was still alive."

That would make some great nightmare fodder. Ray and I should buy matching sleep masks.

"Ray also said you refused to free him after you found him."

"That's not true. I started to loosen the straps, but then …" *Ray was a jerkoff,* "George and the albino came."

"Hmmm. He's under the impression you enjoyed seeing him naked and wanted to prolong the viewing time." I could hear the laughter in Cooper's voice. "I believe he used the word, 'ogle,' to be exact."

That asshole! This was the thanks I got for saving his life? I should have let the albino cut off his dick with a scalpel.

Flopping back on the pillows, I asked, "Is this the only reason you called?"

"Yep."

"Why did you call so damned early?"

"Because my nose hurts, Ms. Parker."

"Goodbye, Cooper." I hung up and tried to go back to sleep, but I couldn't stop thinking about the albino's twin. Who was he? Where was he? Did he know what I'd done? Did I even know what I'd done?

I hadn't returned for the black bottle from the crate I'd stashed under Mudder Brothers front porch—not yet, anyway. I'd been too antsy with the cops crawling all over the place during daylight hours. Cooper would have my head on a pike if … *whoa!* I squeezed my eyes shut and rubbed them with my knuckles, trying to wipe away the horrific images of George and the other headless cadaver that had popped into my brain.

I flopped onto my back, watching dapples of reflected sunlight dance on the ceiling.

It wasn't just Cooper who had me watching the funeral parlor from afar. It was also the albino's twin. He might be waiting for me to return to the scene of the crime, especially alone in the dark.

After staring at the ceiling for another couple of minutes,

I decided to get up and head into work early. I needed to go see Jeff Wymonds today to plan another open house. I also wanted take a look at his garage and see if he'd found out whether his insurance would cover the cost of a roof repair and for how much.

I showered, gulped down some coffee, looked in on my sleeping kids, and then headed out to the Picklemobile. Miss Geary's screen door closed as I crawled into the cab. I looked in the rearview mirror and watched old man Harvey shuffle across the street toward me. The purple silk robe he wore showed off his hairy knees and skinny thighs.

He leaned on my open window, smelling fruity sweet.

"What's that smell?" I asked.

"My breakfast."

"Is it some kind of passion fruit?" If so, where did Miss Geary get it? It smelled marvelous.

"Oh, it's passion all right, but it ain't real fruit—well, she does have nice firm melons on her for an older gal and I'm eighty-seven percent sure they're real."

"Bleck!" I rolled my eyes. "What's on your mind, old man?"

"Did I see Doc's car in the drive last night?"

I nodded. He'd come over to have that date night with me. By the time he'd arrived, both kids had gone to bed, exhausted from their first couple of days back in school, so no questions had been asked. Well, except when I'd kissed Doc goodnight on Aunt Zoe's front porch and he'd asked what I was wearing under my dress.

Unfortunately, Mr. Stinkleskine had been playing voyeur again while taking his Chihuahua out for a late night potty walk. Doc had had to settle for a chaste kiss goodbye sans a peep show.

I had a feeling our lunch date today would take place in his back room with the door closed. I hoped so at least. I'd picked out my underwear this morning with him in mind.

"Coop said Natalie is pretty upset about you two being an

item," Harvey said.

"Yep." My chest ached when I even grazed the subject of Nat. I'd called her yesterday afternoon, leaving another apology on her voicemail. She hadn't called back, not that I'd figured she would.

Harvey's bushy brows wrinkled as he stared at me. "How are you doing?"

"I'm okay."

"You look like hell."

"You should see the other guy." He'd burned up and floated away.

"I have, Rocky. Cooper has two black eyes in addition to the broken nose."

"That was an accident."

He howled, scaring away a couple of crows. "First Doc and then Cooper. Damn, girl, you must be feisty as a she-devil in the sack. It's no wonder Doc can't keep his hands off you."

"That's it." I cranked up the window. "We're done here."

"Call me later," he said through the glass.

"Why?"

"Because you owe me my weekly dinner deal and I am cashing in on it tonight."

I left him standing there in a cloud of the Picklemobile's exhaust.

Calamity Jane's was empty when I arrived.

I started a pot of coffee and settled in at my desk, going through the local MLS listings to see what was new in the Black Hills world of real estate.

My phone rang.

"Calamity Jane Realty, Violet speaking."

"Hello, V," Cornelius said, sounding oddly chipper. He must have had his protein shake already.

Since when were we on first name letter basis? I must have missed that transition during one of his séances.

"So, do we have a hotel?" he asked.

Oh, crap! I'd forgotten to let Cornelius in on our victory over Ray. Although with George dead, winning the bid for the hotel had lost all of the fizz and sparkle.

"Congratulations, Cornelius. Your offer was accepted. We just need to wait for the paperwork to be finalized, and then you can start tearing down walls or whatever else you plan to do with the old place."

"Excellent. You're going to love what I have planned for this haunt, Violet. It's right up your alley."

What alley? I didn't really have any alleys. If he was talking about more séances, my alley was closed, barred, and blocked off until further notice.

"Well," I weighed my words carefully to be supportive, yet noncommittal. "I'm sure it will be an exciting venture."

"You'll see," he promised, which felt more like a threat. "Oh, I meant to tell you that I had a visit from a ghost last night."

"You saw one?" I thought he only whispered to them.

"It came to me in my dream. Did I ever tell you that my great grandmother was a renowned seer?"

"No, you didn't." Why did his disclosure not even make me blink?

"Anyway, the ghost last night was this little blonde girl who asked me to give you a message."

"Really?" I waited, playing along, strumming my fingers on my desk.

"She said she'd like to see you again."

Again? "She did?" That was creepy, but it was child's play compared to the albino's fun and games.

"Yes, but that's not it," Cornelius said. "She thinks you have pretty hair and wants you to have a tea party with her."

Wilda Hessler? I gasped, my fingers froze.

No. Surely he didn't mean Wolfgang's dead sister.

No. It couldn't be. That would mean Wolfgang hadn't been insane. Well, hadn't been entirely insane. Anybody who'd grown up in a house filled with so many garish clown decorations had to be warped.

Wait a second. This was Cornelius I was talking to, who took pride in shocking those around him with his eccentricities. This dream of his was just a weird coincidence. A lot of little girls were blonde, and tea parties with Addy had been standard practice for me until last year. I was making something out of nothing.

That had to be it.

Keeping in mind that he was a client with a lot of cash, I said, "The next time she pays you a visit, tell her thanks, but no thanks. I don't do tea parties." Not after the Hessler Haunt.

"Okay," Cornelius said, "but I don't think she's going to like that answer. I got the feeling she wasn't asking, if you know what I mean."

No, I didn't, nor did I want to. "I'll be in touch, Cornelius. Goodbye." I hung up the phone before our conversation digressed to stories of angry leprechauns and disgruntled trolls.

Returning to the MLS listings, I focused on real estate. Jeff would need a home soon, and so would Cooper ... and Harvey, if he'd stop digging up bodies on his ranch.

I clicked through pages of old and new listings. While the Mudder Brothers nightmare added a shadow to the bright spot on my horizon—the sale of the Old Prospector Hotel— the fact that everything looked like it was going to go through without a hiccup had me humming under my breath.

Death and Cooper's anger aside, everything was going to be all right—my kids, my love life, my job. I hoped that in time, Natalie would come to forgive me, but I wasn't holding my breath. Her ability to hold grudges rivaled Al Capone's.

Two cups of go-go juice and a breakfast bar later, I heard the back door creak open and then the sound of boot heels clunking down the hall. I smelled Ray's cologne before catching sight of him in my peripheral. His seat squeaked as he fell into it.

I glanced over at him and did a double-take at the sight of

his pale skin and wide glassy eyes. His jaw hung slack, and his breathing seemed heavier than usual, like he'd run to work this morning.

"What's wrong with you?" I asked. Was he still in shock from the Mudder mess?

"They found Jane." His voice sounded weak, sort of washed out.

"Oh, no. Don't tell me she went on a total bender."

What had her soon-to-be ex done now? Couldn't the guy cut her some slack? He'd gotten his cake in the form of a little blonde cupcake half his age, plus Jane's house. What else did he need? A golden fork to eat it with?

Ray blinked, but his gaze still seemed unfocused. "They found her up in Lead."

"Where? The Golden Sluice?" Under a barstool?

"No. The Open Cut."

"The Visitor Center? What was she doing there?" I imagined her passed out on the front steps.

"No. You don't get it, Violet." His use of my actual name gave me pause. "They found Jane at the bottom of the Open Cut mine."

"What?" I felt the blood drain out of my face. I clung to my desk. "You mean she's …" I couldn't say it.

Ray nodded. "Jane's dead."

THE END … for now

Five Fun Facts about Ann's Deadwood Series

Have you ever wondered if there is a story behind certain characters or events in my Deadwood Mystery series?

Purple has always been my favorite color, which explains Violet's name and her purple cowboy boots. I'm also a big fan of Elvis, Humphrey Bogart, John Wayne, and young Clint Eastwood; and I watch their films often.

* * *

I took a class on paranormal investigation and visited a renowned haunted house, taking recordings and notes. The class was excellent, the house was spooky, and the experience made great fodder for Cornelius in this book.

* * *

In the first two books, Violet drives an old red Bronco, which I based on a red blazer that my parents had for years. That old red blazer "went where no man dared to go" and resulted in many wonderful memories. Last year, it finally died, so I killed it off in the second book of the series. It was my epitaph to the old beast. My parents also had an old green truck that we called the Picklemobile.

* * *

Deadwood and Lead are real towns in the Black Hills full of hard-working, friendly people. While my books and the characters within them are fiction, some of the setting locations and history details are real.

* * *

I'm often asked, "Who would play the role of Violet? Doc? Harvey?" While I have actors in mind for many of my characters, I have yet to come up with the perfect actress to play Violet. However, I can't look at the actor Daniel Craig now without thinking *Hey, Cooper*.

About the Author

Ann Charles is an award-winning author who writes romantic mysteries that are splashed with humor and whatever else she feels like throwing into the mix. When she is not dabbling in fiction, arm-wrestling with her children, attempting to seduce her husband, or arguing with her sassy cat, she is daydreaming of lounging poolside at a fancy resort with a blended margarita in one hand and a great book in the other.

Connect with Me Online:

Facebook: http://www.facebook.com/ann.charles.author

Twitter: @DeadwoodViolet and @AnnWCharles

My Main Website: http://www.anncharles.com

My Deadwood Website:
http://www.anncharles.com/deadwood

CPSIA information can be obtained
at www.ICGtesting.com
Printed in the USA
LVHW111950011220
673137LV00002B/146

7